The Lost and Found Bookshop

ALSO BY SUSAN WIGGS

CONTEMPORARY NOVELS

The Oysterville Sewing Circle

Between You & Me

Map of the Heart

Family Tree

Home Before Dark

The Ocean Between Us

Summer by the Sea

Table for Five

Lakeside Cottage

Just Breathe

The Goodbye Quilt

THE BELLA VISTA CHRONICLES

The Apple Orchard

The Beekeeper's Ball

The Lost and Found Bookshop

A Novel

Susan Wiggs

HARPER LARGE PRINT

An Imprint of HarperCollinsPublishers

THE LOST AND FOUND BOOKSHOP. Copyright © 2020 by Susan Wiggs. All rights reserved. Printed in the United States of America. No part of this book may be used or reproduced in any manner whatsoever without written permission except in the case of brief quotations embodied in critical articles and reviews. For information, address HarperCollins Publishers, 195 Broadway, New York, NY 10007.

HarperCollins books may be purchased for educational, business, or sales promotional use. For information, please e-mail the Special Markets Department at SPsales@harpercollins.com.

FIRST HARPER LARGE PRINT EDITION

ISBN: 978-0-06-299989-4

Library of Congress Cataloging-in-Publication Data is available upon request.

20 21 22 23 24 LSC 10 9 8 7 6 5 4 3 2

For the booksellers, purveyors of dreams

The Lost and Found Bookshop

Prologue

The Flood Mansion
San Francisco

Standing before the gathering at her mother's memorial service, Natalie Harper glanced down at the podium. On the angled surface was a folder titled "Resources for the Grieving," along with her notes. The guide was a compendium of advice, but there was one thing it failed to explain: How was she supposed to go on after this?

Natalie had been carrying the pages around for days, hoping she'd somehow find an explanation for the inexplicable, or a way to express the inexpressible. But all the notes and resources in the world failed to penetrate the unfinished narrative of her mother's life, which seemed to dangle in the thin air of Natalie's grief, just out of reach. The words shimmered in a wet blur before her eyes.

She tried to remember what she meant to say—as if she could sum up Blythe Harper's life in a three-minute speech. What *did* you say at your mother's final farewell? That she had been with you every minute of your life from the second you took your first breath until a week ago, when she had left forever. That she was beautiful and inspiring. Brilliant, but often foolish. Quirky and infuriating. Complicated and beloved. That she was everything—a mother, a daughter, a friend, a bookseller, a purveyor of dreams.

And that, at the moment Natalie had needed her most, Blythe Harper had fallen from the sky.

PART ONE

Do not fear death, but rather the unlived
life. You don't have to live forever, you just
have to live.

—*TUCK EVERLASTING*

1

Archangel, Sonoma County, California
One week earlier

This was a big moment for Natalie. The biggest in her career so far, for sure. The whole company had gathered in the reception hall of Pinnacle Fine Wines to celebrate her promotion and the million-dollar deal she'd made for the firm. But her own mother was a no-show.

True to form.

To be fair, the drive from the city up to Archangel could be unpredictable in the afternoon. It was equally possible that Blythe Harper had completely forgotten that she'd promised to show up to celebrate her daughter's achievement.

Natalie pasted on a smile and smoothed her hands down the front of her blazer, a tailored, conservative piece she wore over the white silk pussy-bow blouse she'd splurged on for the occasion. Meanwhile, she tracked the company owner, Rupert Carnaby, as he made his way to the podium at the dais, pausing to greet colleagues along the way. Then she glanced at the door, half hoping her mom would come dashing through at the last minute.

The other half knew better.

Natalie reminded herself that she was a grown woman, not some kid who needed her mommy to show up for a school event. Not that Blythe had done that, either.

Although she didn't consciously keep score, Natalie knew her mother had missed many things in her life, from her Brownie investiture ceremony to the California Mathletics championship to her graduation from college. There was always a reason—she couldn't leave the shop, a sales rep was coming in, she couldn't find a car to borrow, she had an event with a VIP author— all good reasons, the kind Natalie would feel petty for disputing.

Whatever, Natalie thought, shifting from foot to foot in her fashionable but uncomfortable midheel pumps.

It's fine. Her mom would have an excuse and Natalie would be fine with it. That was the way it always worked. And to be fair, her mother—who had raised Natalie alone—rarely had a moment to spare away from the bookstore. She'd run it almost single-handedly for the past thirty-three years, often lacking the wherewithal for backup help.

Mandy McDowell, Natalie's coworker in logistics, milled past, a glass of wine in hand as she regaled a colleague with yet another story about her adorable but ill-behaved kids.

Too late, Natalie realized Mandy wasn't watching where she was going. Natalie failed to step away in time, and Mandy's glass of wine sloshed into her.

"Oh my God, Natalie," Mandy exclaimed, her eyes wide with distress. "I didn't see you there. Oh shoot, I am so, *so* sorry!"

Natalie plucked the white silk blouse away from her body. "Great," she muttered, grabbing a napkin and blotting at the splash of red wine.

"Club soda to the rescue." Mandy's friend Cheryl bustled forward with a napkin and a bottle. "Here, let me help."

While Natalie held her blouse away from her also-stained bra, Mandy and Cheryl dabbed at the large blot. "I'm such a horrible klutz," Mandy said. "Can you ever forgive me? God, you shouldn't. And today of all days, just as you're about to go up to the podium . . ."

"It was an accident," Natalie conceded, trying to keep her cool. Trying to minimize the situation.

"Promise you'll send me the cleaning bill," Mandy said. "And if the stain won't come out, I'm totally buying you a new blouse."

"Fair enough," Natalie murmured. She knew her coworker wouldn't make good on the promise. Mandy, a single mom, was perpetually broke. She always seemed to be scrambling to stay on top of her bills. Judging by her eyelash extensions and nail job, she didn't mind splurging on self-care. Yet she was always short on cash.

Don't judge, Natalie reminded herself. *People have their reasons.*

Mandy regarded her with dewy-eyed sympathy. "Oh hey, I thought your mom was coming up from the city today."

Natalie gritted her teeth, then forced her jaw to relax. "Yeah, not sure what happened. Traffic, maybe. Or could be something came up at the bookstore. She always has a hard time getting away."

"Are you sure you told her this whole party is in your honor?"

"She knows," Natalie murmured. Mandy was so very sincere, but her questions were not helping.

"And what about Rick? Wouldn't your boyfriend want to be here on your big day?"

"He had a test flight he couldn't get out of," Natalie said.

"Oh, that's too bad. Guess he's moving up the ranks at Aviation Innovations. When the two of us were dating, he never had a conflict if I had a big event on the calendar." Mandy and Rick had dated before Natalie had moved to Archangel. They were still friends, a point Mandy liked to make with annoying frequency. Now she whipped out her phone. "Here, I'll text him a picture so he'll see what he's missing."

Leaving no time for objections, Mandy snapped a picture of Natalie's unflattering, openmouthed expression, and she hit send before Natalie could stop her.

Thanks, she thought. And then: *It's not a big day. It's a job, is all.* She eyed her coworkers, snacking on amuse-bouches and refilling their wine goblets at the open bar. *Not one of life's peak experiences.*

Just then, the rapid clinking of a glass drew everyone's attention to the podium.

"Good afternoon, everyone," said Rupert, leaning toward the mic and surveying the gathering with his trademark boyish grin. "And by good, I mean great. And by afternoon, I mean happy hour."

A murmur of chuckles rippled through the crowd. "I wanted to take just a little time to celebrate today. Now, Natalie Harper needs no introduction because you all know her, but I'd like to say a few words. Natalie!" Rupert gestured. "Get your good self up here and join me."

She felt a blush coming on as she buttoned her blazer, knowing the wine stain would still be visible above the lapels. Her chest was clammy and damp, redolent of old-vine zin.

"A brief history, if you'll indulge me," Rupert began. One of his favorite things was to wax on about the background of the family wine distribution business. "When my grandmother Clothilde put me in charge of Pinnacle, she said, 'You have one job.'" He did a spot-on imitation of his grandmother's French accent. "'To bring wine to the world, and to be excellent.' And the way to do that is to work only with excellent colleagues." He stood aside and gestured for Natalie to step up. "My friends, Natalie Harper embodies that mandate. So today, I give you our new vice president of digital inventory."

A subdued smattering of applause accompanied her to the podium. Rupert beamed, his veneered teeth gleaming. In a small, petty corner of her mind, Natalie believed he knew she'd been keeping him afloat while he glad-handed with suppliers and accounts and played golf on company time. That was probably the real reason for this promotion.

"Thank you," she said awkwardly, unused to being in the limelight. Spoken aloud, the new job title sounded geeky, or perhaps even slightly made-up. That was the nature of the field she was in, she supposed. She had chosen this job for its stability and marketability. There would always be a place for someone who could manage information technology and logistics, because those were matters that 99 percent of people had zero interest in and couldn't stand doing.

Managing inventory was not like being a diplomat, a deep-sea diver, a winemaker, a bookseller—jobs people might actually enjoy. "I'm grateful for this opportunity," she continued, "and I'm looking forward to what we can accomplish."

Truth be told, she couldn't stand the job, either, but that was not the point. The point was to have a steady career that would never let her down.

"Another bit of history," Rupert said, winking at Natalie and taking the mic. "Once upon a time, this young lady came to me looking for a position here at the firm, and I, in my infinite wisdom, signed her up immediately." He paused. "Now look at her—she's got those puppy dog eyes, and the instincts of a barracuda, and probably more smarts than all of us combined. What she did with our inventory system was nothing short of a miracle. Thanks to Natalie taking the lead on this, we've had our biggest year ever here at Pinnacle." He laughed. "Okay, yeah, I can see I'm boring you. So I will wrap this up with one final announcement. Governor Clements's only daughter is getting married to the owner of Cast Iron." Cast Iron, a group of wildly popular luxury restaurants, had been founded by a wildly popular internet star. His creative food and wine pairings were taking the foodie world by storm. "As you can imagine, it's going to be the wedding of the year in our fair state." Another pause. "What's that got to do with us, you ask? Well, I'm going to have Natalie explain."

She caught a whiff of herself as she took the mic. Spilled wine and nervous sweat. How lovely. "I'll try to make a long story short. Pinnacle Wines now has an exclusive deal to supply the wine to Bitsy Clements's wedding. And afterward, we'll be the exclusive supplier to Cast Iron."

Her words didn't begin to convey the complicated

and tense negotiations she had gone through. Natalie had driven her team to their limits, putting together the perfect combination of products and discount rates. The multimillion-dollar deal was nearly complete.

There was one more deadline to meet—the procurement of a rare Alsatian white wine the groom insisted on. Once that was confirmed, the details would be finalized. "I'd like to thank my team—Mandy, Cheryl, Dave, and Lana—for helping with the project." That was a white lie, she privately conceded. The team had been an encumbrance every step of the way, requiring constant vigilance on her part.

"And with that, let's all have a drink," Rupert said, turning on the charm as he took over the mic again. He, too, had been challenging throughout the process. Though his intentions were good, he lacked the business and financial acumen needed to put together a complicated deal. He was happy enough to take credit, though, and decent enough to reward Natalie with a new position.

Glasses were raised. She gazed around the room at all the people talking and laughing, enjoying the view from the upper offices of the building.

With the promotion came a new office a good distance away from the cube farm where the inventory department resided. Now Natalie would have a corner space of her own. She had been eager to show it to her mother—a floor-to-ceiling window framing a forever view of the rolling Sonoma landscape, a refuge from the constant, unproductive chatter of her coworkers.

Rupert launched into more charming banter about the upcoming nuptials, which was already being compared, with hyperbolic enthusiasm, to a royal wedding. Natalie stepped down, took out her phone. Her daily affirmation flashed on the screen: I trust that I am on the right path.

She swiped it away and hit redial, but as expected, her mom's phone went to voice mail: *You've reached Blythe Harper of the Lost and Found Bookshop here in the heart of San Francisco's historic district. Leave me a message. Better yet, come see me at the bookstore!*

Natalie didn't leave a message. Her mother rarely checked voice mail. Natalie sent a text—You didn't miss much, just me getting red wine thrown on my shirt and being awkward at the mic.

Then she noticed a message awaiting her. She slipped out of the room, knowing no one would miss her. She had always been an under-the-radar type of person. She went down the hall, seeking the quiet of her new office. Most of her things were in boxes on the floor. She'd been hoping her mom would give her a hand organizing the place during her visit. Pausing at the window, she took a phone picture of the impressive view. Then she texted the photo to her mother. *Even better in person,* she wrote.

The voice mail was from Rick's number. She cringed ever so slightly as she listened. *Hey, babe, sorry to miss your big day,* he'd said in his deep, friendly voice. *Couldn't get out of this test flight today. Looking forward to the weekend. Love you.*

Did he? Did he love her? Did she love him?

A part of Natalie didn't want to contemplate the answer, but if she was being completely honest with herself, she would have to concede that the spark had gone out for them a while ago.

On the surface, she and Rick seemed like the ideal couple—an ambitious wine executive and a busy aviation engineer and pilot. He was good-looking and came from a nice family. Yet one thin layer below the surface, there was a flat line of predictability. Sometimes she worried that the two of them were together simply because it was comfortable. If *comfortable* meant an unimaginative, unchallenging relationship.

It was possible that each was waiting for the other to end it.

She was stirred from her thoughts by the doorbell ding of an incoming email. It was probably a work-related matter that could wait until Monday, but she couldn't *not* check her computer. And then she couldn't *not* see the boldface subject line that nearly stopped her heart: **Urgent: Licensing Deadline Missed.**

What the hell?

She plunked down bonelessly in her ergonomic rolling office chair, feeling the blood drain from her face. The message was from Governor Clements's executive social manager. Ms. Harper, I'm sorry to inform you that the licensing deadline from the Board of Equalization was missed and the agreement will be canceled pursuant to . . .

A silent scream built in Natalie's chest. Missing an important deadline put the entire agreement at risk. How could this have happened?

In her gut, she knew. Mandy had been in charge of the filing. Natalie had drummed into her again and again that the hard deadline was crucial. Mandy had drummed back that she had it handled. Natalie had double-checked with her.

But she hadn't triple-checked.

Holding in panic, she stabbed a number into the phone. This was the deal she had worked so hard to bring to fruition, competing fiercely with other suppliers for the wedding and franchise contracts.

If the deal fell through, Natalie would be faced with the decision about whether to protect Mandy from being fired. The woman made mistake after mistake, and typically, Natalie covered for her. Mandy was everyone's favorite. Everyone's pet. She was adorable, funny, charming, beloved.

Natalie practically strangled the phone in her hand as she contacted the state controller's office and the district manager. It was a good thing her mother and Rick had skipped out after all. It would not be fun for them—or anyone—to see her scrambling to undo her coworker's mistake.

A tense hour later, Natalie had rescued the situation. She was drenched in sweat and red wine and shaken to her core as she ducked into the bathroom. Somehow she had managed to save Mandy's ass—again. It had taken a great deal of groveling and an extra $10,000 in discounts—which Natalie knew would be taken out of her bonus.

In the stall, she didn't puke, but she had the dry heaves. She took off her blazer and blouse. Both likely ruined. She couldn't stand to wear the blouse another second, so she shoved it into the trash. Then she buttoned the blazer over her wine-spotted bra.

She was about to exit the stall when she heard the sound of a door swishing open.

". . . see her face when Rupert was droning on?"

The voice came from someone entering the bathroom. Mandy's voice.

Natalie froze. She stopped breathing.

"Yeah," said someone else. Mandy's friend Cheryl. "That's her resting bitch face. Thank God we don't have to look at that every day anymore."

"Right?" Mandy chuckled. "Her so-called promotion is the best thing that ever happened to us."

"You think?"

"That nice corner office? HR put her there so no one has to hear her constant nagging. She won't be in our faces anymore. So really, her only interactions will be with a spreadsheet. Perfect. I thanked Rupert personally for getting her out of the pit. Sweet freedom!"

Natalie heard a snicker and the sound of a high five. Two hands clapping.

"Cheers to that and cheers to no more toxic bosses."

One of them started humming "Ding-Dong! The Witch Is Dead" as they both entered the other stalls.

Now Natalie really felt like puking. Instead, she made no sound as she fled from the restroom, praying they didn't know she'd heard.

2

A shower and a change of clothes helped a little, but Natalie still felt devastated by what she'd overheard. Devastated, yet on some level unsurprised. She would never deny that she was precise. Orderly. Exacting of both herself and others.

Looking around her modest apartment, she admitted to a penchant for neatness.

But did that make her a horrible person?

Finger-combing her dark, curly hair, which was possibly the only unruly thing about her, she thought about her clean, paid-for hybrid car, her tidy home, her secure little life . . . and—the tiniest voice inside her whispered—the emptiness.

She didn't know what might fill it up. She had created the home she'd lacked as a child—predictable, simple, neat. The apartment, while pleasant enough, was missing some essential quality she couldn't quite pinpoint. It was in a pink stucco building as small and sweet as a cupcake, furnished with the things she liked to surround herself with—comfy chairs and shelves crammed with books, and a soft bed for curling up to read.

It should have been the right fit. It should have felt like home, like the place she belonged. Yet despite the idyllic Sonoma setting, surrounded by vineyards and apple orchards, the emptiness yawned. It never felt quite like home.

Certainly, the job wasn't helping, despite her hard work and dedication to Pinnacle. Most days, her career felt like a grind. Somewhere along the way, she'd grown to hate the work. That, combined with the depressing thought that she and Rick were coming to an end, rolled over her in a fresh swell of nausea.

Stop it, she lectured herself. The promotion had come with a hefty raise and equity in the company. If she stayed on this path, she'd be set for life. Growing up in the bookstore with her flighty mother at the helm, that sense of security, of equilibrium, had been lacking.

Most days, she reflected, trying to power through

the nausea, that was reason enough to stick with her job at Pinnacle.

She finished dressing in crop pants, a striped jersey top, and canvas sneakers. Trying to shrug off the unsettled feeling, she checked her phone. Her mom still hadn't answered the text. Rick was still apparently flying somewhere.

There was a message from her friend Tess, though, inviting her over. The one bright spot in an otherwise completely crappy day.

She jumped into her little hybrid hatchback and drove toward Tess's place. On the way, she stopped to grab a jar of honey from a roadside stand. Jamie Westfall, the owner, was a beekeeper who had moved to the area a few years back, alone and pregnant. She wasn't alone anymore, though. She now had a little boy named Ollie.

As Natalie selected a pint jar with its SAVE THE BEES label and stuck five dollars in the honor box, Ollie came outside. "Hiya, Miss Natalie," he said.

"Hi, yourself. What's up?"

Elaborate shrug. He was bashful in the most adorable way. "S'posed to be reading to my mom for homework."

"How's that going for you?"

Another shrug. His mother came out on the porch, a wisp of a girl in overalls and an embroidered peasant top. "He's a good reader, but he's super picky. He did love the last one you gave us—*One Family.*"

"Oh good, I'm glad you liked it. Wish that book had been around when I was your age, Ollie. Our family was just me and my mom and my grandpa, and it would have made me happy to read about all the different kinds of families. Not just families that had a mom, dad, kids, dog." She counted them off on her fingers.

He tugged at his lower lip. "I like reading about dogs."

"I'll bring you a new book next time. There's a good one called *Smells Like Dog.* Did I ever tell you my mom has a bookstore? I used to work there, and it gave me a superpower—picking out just the right book for just the right kid."

"How come you don't work there anymore?" asked Ollie.

"After the day I had, I'm asking myself that question," Natalie admitted. "I'm heading over to visit Tess for some tea and sympathy."

"I don't like tea," Ollie said. "What's sympathy taste like?"

Natalie laughed and ruffled his hair, then got back

in the car. "Like a melted marshmallow with chocolate sauce."

"Maybe we'll have that for dessert tonight," Jamie said. They stood together on the porch and waved goodbye.

As she regarded Jamie and her child, Natalie couldn't help but see how happy they were together. Every once in a while, she thought about kids and felt a tug of yearning. *All in good time*, she told herself.

She and Rick had once talked about kids. Correction: Rick had talked about kids. She'd listened. And doubted. They hadn't brought it up again.

En route to Tess's, other doubts crept in. *Was* Tess her friend, or had she taken Natalie in like a stray cat? After what she'd overheard at work, Natalie wasn't so sure anymore. She wasn't sure of anything.

Turning at the signs for Rossi Vineyards and Angel Creek Winery, she followed the long gravel lane. Like Natalie, Tess Delaney Rossi had been raised by a single mother and had been living in San Francisco before moving to Archangel. Yet unlike Natalie, Tess had settled in the small town to marry, following her heart, not a career.

Natalie parked in front of the rustic farmhouse where Tess lived with her husband, kids, stepkids, and two rescued dogs—an aging, pointy-nosed Italian greyhound and a hulking mutt that was part akita and part Wookiee, as far as anyone knew. The dogs were lolling deliberately in the middle of the walkway between the driveway and house.

Tess came out to greet her. She wore her red hair pulled back in a scarf and a grape-stained work apron tied over her clothes.

"Hey, Nat," she called. "Thought you'd like to join us for happy hour."

"Sounds heavenly. Thanks."

"Dominic and the kids are all out back. Big harvest day for our little vineyard." With a gesture, Tess led the way to a sunny spot beside a large shed. The harvest team unloaded the crates of just-picked grapes and dumped them on the long, stainless steel sorting table. At one end, the table vibrated, eliminating unripe or rotten grapes. At the opposite end, the grapes moved along a conveyor for destemming.

The family gathered around, sorting the grapes by hand, laughing and talking as the juice stained everything it touched.

She took in the sight of kids and dogs running around; Tess's whistling husband; the older children helping Dominic with practiced skill. It all seemed so normal, a family having fun just being together.

"Hey, everybody," she said.

"Hey, yourself," said Dominic. "Welcome to Friday night at Angel Creek."

Dominic Rossi was the type of husband who gave husbands a good name. The type of guy for whom the expression *tall, dark, and handsome* had been coined. The type of guy who exuded humor and heart along with a can-do attitude. He was the former president of the Bank of Archangel, but his passion was making wine.

And babies with his pretty wife, apparently. Natalie eyed Tess's apron. Viewed from the side, the bump was impossible to miss. "Are you pregnant again?" she asked in a low voice.

Tess answered with a redhead's classic blush and a grin of delight.

"She promised me a sister," said Trini. Dominic's daughter, now in high school, threw a glance at her brother Antonio, who had stepped away from the table to amuse Tess's two sons by chasing them around with his grape-colored hands. The little boys, known as Thing One and Thing Two, responded with squeals of glee.

"That's great," Natalie said. "Congrats, you guys."

The Rossis made the whole blended-family thing look easy. An illusion, Tess had assured her. Natalie knew it had been challenging to put together Dominic's kids by his first marriage and the two he and Tess had had together. But there was no denying that in moments like this, they looked happy and secure. It was impossible to miss the undercurrent of passion Dominic and Tess shared.

"People say the third time's the charm," Trini pointed out. "Why do they say that?"

"Good question," Natalie commented. "And does it imply the first two times are *not* charmed? Because when I look at those two little guys, I see something pretty special."

As she spoke, Thing One plopped a fistful of discarded grape pulp on his brother's head. The younger one howled with outrage.

Dominic's sister, Gina, wiped her hands. "I got this, Tess."

"Thanks." Tess settled herself on a stool and looked at Natalie. "So . . . Where's Rick tonight?"

"Not sure. He had a test flight late this afternoon."

"You look like you had a tough day," Tess observed.

Natalie didn't bother denying it. "So I got this giant promotion at work . . ."

"Hey, that's great," said Tess. Something must have flickered in Natalie's face, because she added, "Isn't it?"

"It all seemed like a fine thing. The company had a little party, even, because I put together a big deal for them. My mom was supposed to come up from the city, but she never showed. Which is probably a good thing, because it turns out the whole promotion was a ruse to isolate me so I don't have to work with anyone."

"What?" Tess's hands flew expertly through the grapes. "I don't get it."

Natalie sighed, staring at the ground. "I'm a toxic boss."

"No way. You're one of my favorite people."

"You don't have to work with me. Apparently I'm a nightmare. Micromanaging, control freak, see-you-next-Tuesday. According to the conversation I over-heard in the restroom, I've checked all the boxes."

"Oh, Natalie. That doesn't sound like you at all. For what it's worth, I'm guessing the trouble is with your coworkers, not with you. Someone who said what they said is objectively awful. I'm sorry you heard that, and I want you to know it's not true."

"Thanks," Natalie said. "You're probably right, but it was hard to hear. To tell you the truth, I'm kind of glad they moved me to a department where my only coworker is a flat-screen monitor." She sighed. "My coworkers can't stand me."

"Well, we love you here at Angel Creek Winery, so roll up your sleeves and help out." Tess tossed her a rubber apron.

"Putting me to work?"

"This time of year, everybody works."

"I'm toxic, remember?" She gamely tied on the apron.

"Say goodbye to your manicure," Tess warned. "The next one is on me."

Natalie always had a flawless manicure. It was something she considered necessary to look professional at work. For all the good that did her. She dove into the destemming with both hands, turning her fingers the deep rich color of old-vine zinfandel.

They worked side by side for a while. The repetitive task and the chatter of Tess's family helped a little. "What if they're right?" Natalie mused aloud. "My work peeps, I mean. What if they're right and I'm toxic, and no one can stand me?"

Tess didn't say anything right away, but Natalie felt her hard, studying gaze. "What?" she asked finally.

"You need a drink." Tess caught Dominic's eye. "We're taking a break," she said, gesturing Natalie over to a stationary tub with a hose.

"Slacker," said her husband with a grin.

Tess stuck out her tongue at him and turned away.

"I'm a toxic boss, too, sometimes. They just don't dare say anything."

After they washed up, Tess poured a glass of zinfandel from a cask labeled *Old Vine—Creek Slope*. For herself, she opened a frosty bottle of Topo Chico, and they sat down on the terrace adjacent to the house. Shaded by a pergola, the stone-paved area was littered with kids' toys and offered a commanding view of the vineyard. Beyond that lay the neighboring apple orchard, where Tess's sister lived and ran a wine-country cooking school.

"Listen," said Tess. "I used to be like you. I used to *be* you. I was a life-support system for a job, mad at the world without really knowing why."

"What?" Natalie frowned, then looked around at the house—which literally had a white picket fence—and the kids and dogs. "No way."

"Way. Do you know, I once ended up in the ER with a panic attack?"

"Seriously? Oh, Tess. I never knew that about you. I'm sorry."

"Thanks. Honestly, I was a hot mess. Thought I was having a heart attack." She was quiet for a few minutes. Then she said, "It seems like long ago—a different life, back when I was single and living in the city, before all this happened." She gestured to encompass the vineyards, the husband and family. "I was obsessed with my career. A career I was so, so good at."

She used to work as a provenance expert for a high-end antiquities auction house—that much Natalie knew. In fact, Tess had helped Natalie's mother in valuing some of the rare books at Lost and Found. "I'm pretty sure I drove people batty," Tess admitted. "I know for sure I drove myself batty."

"I can't even picture that."

"It happened. I survived. And I'm not trying to scare you. I'm not saying you're dealing with anything like anxiety, but for me, lying in the ER, convinced I was dying, was a wake-up call."

"I'm woke. Too woke, according to people at work." She told Tess about Mandy's habit of making mistakes, and her own constant vigilance and extra work to correct them.

"Let me get this straight," said Tess. "This woman screws up on a daily basis, and you cover up for her. Not that you owe her anything, but why would you help her out all the time?"

"Because I'm her supervisor. And because I can."

"Well, here's a question for you: What would happen if you stopped covering for Mandy and let her fail? What then?"

"I've asked myself that many times," Natalie admitted. "It would suck for the whole company. If I hadn't fixed things just this afternoon, we would have lost the account and the firm's reputation would suffer. So would mine, since I'm her supervisor. Eventually, she'd get fired. And she does need her job. She's single, raising a couple of young kids."

"And how is that your responsibility?" Tess asked.

"Because I—" Natalie paused. "It's not."

"So . . . ?"

Natalie swirled the wine in her glass. Wine was such a beautiful thing, complex and rich and delicious. The whole company she worked for had been founded solely on the basis of this fine substance, bringing comfort and joy to those who knew how to savor it.

Yet for Natalie, there was no joy. Just a job. A steady, lucrative job with benefits. A pension plan. Everything her mom had done without all her life. "Not bailing Mandy out when I know exactly how to do it seems manipulative. I don't want to be the agent of her downfall."

"I get that, and I get where you're coming from. We were both raised by single moms. Not a dad in sight. Did our moms fall down?"

Natalie thought about her mother, who had somehow managed to deal with financial struggles without collapsing utterly. Tess and her half sister, Isabel, had grown up without their father, who had gone missing before they were born.

Natalie, on the other hand, knew exactly where her father was. Though Blythe was fond of saying that life had given her everything she wanted, Natalie sometimes wondered if that was really true. Blythe was a bundle of contradictions. She would take any risk in business, but never with her heart.

"If you keep rescuing your coworker," Tess went on, "she'll never figure things out on her own. You'd be surprised by how much you can learn from failure."

"It's the gift that keeps on giving," Natalie remarked.

"See, my point is, you're not doing her any favors by constantly mopping up behind her. Saving a person takes away her power to learn and move forward."

"How'd you get so smart about these things?" Natalie asked. "Pregnancy hormones?"

"Right." Tess chuckled.

Natalie reminded herself to savor the deep, rich wine and the glorious colors of the gathering sunset. She had a good life. A good job. A good friend. "I have to say, you're better than therapy. It's been a crappy day. Not just work and my mom being a no-show." She sighed again. "I don't think Rick and I are going to make it."

"You and Rick? You seem so great together. What happened?" asked Tess.

"Well, that's part of the problem. Nothing really happened. Nothing at all. He's a perfectly nice guy and—outside of work, I suppose—I'm a perfectly nice person. We're compatible, but . . . I'm not sure compatible is enough. We've been together for almost a year, and things haven't really progressed."

"Oh, man. Do you want them to progress?"

Natalie gazed out at the sweeping landscape, vineyards and orchards, endless bounty. Rick sometimes took her flying to enjoy the scenery, and she loved it. She wanted to be able to say she loved *him*. "I want to be crazy about him. I *should* be crazy about him. He's great-looking. Successful. Good enough in bed. Has a nice family down in Petaluma."

"And yet . . ."

"Exactly. There's a *yet*." She studied the horizon, a gently undulating sine wave where the hills met the sky. "I wish there weren't. I wish I could feel all in." It was true. She craved some heady mixture of passion and certainty and excitement that didn't feel threatening or risky.

Maybe that was the point, though. Maybe the very nature of excitement was risk.

In that case, she could do without the excitement.

"Mom says I'm too closed off to intimacy," she confessed. "She would know, of course. She's been single all her life. And she claims she's happy. So why does she think *I* need someone? Can't I be happy too?"

"Of course you can. Your mom sounds like mine— a bundle of contradictions. Keeps things interesting. Ah, Nat. I'm sorry your mom couldn't be bothered to show up, and I'm sorry you and Rick are at a low point. But your promotion is awesome and well deserved." She paused. "You're my friend and I love you so this is coming from a place of love. Do you think maybe you're cranky because of the work?"

"Well, duh," Natalie replied. "The work is . . . ah, just work. But I'm excellent at it. Much as I wish I could find something both steady and inspiring, I don't think that exists for me."

"Somewhere along the way, you've convinced yourself that feeling excitement is risky."

"Growing up in a bookstore can do that to a person. I won't deny it was fun—surrounded by all those books, the customers coming and going, the shipments of new titles every month—that was the fun part. But at some point, I realized Mom was drowning in debt, month in and month out."

"And that scared you into going for a steady career with no surprises."

Natalie nodded. "I can't be fearless like my mom. Maybe she likes the roller coaster. She doesn't mind being behind on the bills, because she's always sure she'll have a better day."

The thought of living like that caused Natalie's stomach to knot. "The only time I've seen her rattled is when my grandfather fell and broke his hip. Now he's having something Mom calls 'cognitive issues.' I really wanted to see her tonight to hear more about that. Poor Grandy. Maybe that's why Mom couldn't come— something with Grandy." She hugged herself, picturing the lovely man who had been the father she'd lacked, the nanny looking after her, the homework mentor and tutor, the adored playmate of her childhood.

"I had that falling grandfather," said Tess.

"Old Magnus?" Natalie had met the elderly gentleman a time or two. Like Grandy, he was a fine old man. He had that soft-spoken affection that radiated from the best sort of grandfathers. "He had a fall?"

"Not recently. He fell off a ladder in the apple orchard years ago. It was a huge scare, but he got better."

"I hope I can say the same about Grandy. Ever since he broke his hip, he hasn't been the same. Maybe I'll head down to the city tomorrow and pay him a visit."

"I bet he'd love to see you."

Natalie got up and carried their glasses to the patio

bar. "And on that cheery note, I'll let you get back to your family. I need to head home and spend some time figuring out what to do about the people who hate me."

"Stop it."

"I'll try, Tess. I won't let it get to me."

As she drove back to town, Natalie repeated the words like a mantra. *Don't let it get to you.*

The mantra didn't work, so she switched on the car radio and sang along with Eddie Vedder while the sunset panorama of the countryside swished past. The song "Wishlist" had her compiling her own list of wishes. A different job. A different attitude. A different life.

"More on our breaking news story . . ." An announcer interrupted the next song.

Annoyed, she reached over to switch the station but stopped when she heard "Aviation Innovations." That was Rick's company.

"The FAA is investigating a crash of a small plane registered to Aviation Innovations in Lake Loma this afternoon," the announcer said. "Both the pilot and passenger were apparently killed on impact. The names of the deceased are being withheld pending notification of the families."

Natalie listened with gathering dread and a guilty sense of relief. It was Rick's company, but the victim could not have been Rick. He was flying solo today, a test flight. She pulled off to the shoulder of the road and called him. No answer. Then she sent a quick text message to him. I just heard about the crash. I'm sorry. Anyone you knew?

There was no reply, so she continued driving. It had to be someone he knew. It was a small company, after all. She might even know the victim. She and Rick had socialized with some of the other pilots, going on wine-tasting flights and scenic tours. She found herself wondering if life with Rick was really so bad. He was steady. Predictable. Reliable. Everything she valued.

On impulse, she turned off the main road and drove to the Aviation Innovations headquarters. The parking lot was jammed with official vehicles and people rushing around. She looked for Rick in the crowd—a squeaky clean–cut all-American guy with big shoulders, a clipped haircut, and a nice smile.

She didn't spot him amid the personnel swarming the main building and the hangars. Then she spied Miriam, his assistant, sitting on the front steps, talking on her phone.

Miriam looked up and saw Natalie. "I'll call you back," she said into her phone.

"Hey, I just heard," Natalie said. "I came to see if Rick got back yet."

Miriam took hold of the stair rail and drew herself up. "Natalie . . ." The woman's face was as white as the puffy clouds sailing over the Sonoma hills.

Natalie stopped in her tracks. Dread dawned in stages—confusion and disbelief, then flat-out denial. "It wasn't Rick," she said. Her voice sounded harsh, almost mean. Probably how she sounded at work, come to think of it.

"Oh, Natalie. It's terrible. Horrible. I'm so sorry. I can't even . . ." Miriam reached for her hand. "Come sit."

Natalie flinched and snatched her hand away. "I don't need to sit. I need . . . I . . . I . . ." She had no idea what she needed in this surreal, unbearable moment. She took a gulp of air. "He said he was going to be gone for the day. Yeah. Said he wouldn't make it to my party at work. He was on a test flight. Oh God, did he crash during the test? Did . . . did—"

"It . . . It wasn't a test flight."

"Then he's okay?" Natalie was desperate for that to be true.

Panic glinted in Miriam's eyes. She seemed to have trouble meeting Natalie's gaze. Then she took a deep breath. "He, um . . . He had a passenger."

"I heard that on the news, yes." Natalie's mind raced. Oh God. Rick.

His parents lived in Petaluma. He had a sister there, too. Natalie had met her just a few weeks back—Rita? No, Rhonda. "Should I go see his folks?" she asked Miriam. "Is someone with them now?" Her heart hammered furiously. Her hands were clammy, her lungs aching for air.

Rick was gone. How could he be gone? They had dinner plans tomorrow night at the French Laundry in Yountville. She'd been agonizing over the talk they needed to have about the fact that the relationship didn't seem to be working. She had been wondering which one of them would step up and end things.

How could he be gone?

"Natalie, I really need you to sit." Miriam put a hand on her shoulder and steered her to the blond limestone steps in front of the low, modern building. Her touch was firm, yet Natalie could feel her hands shaking.

"Yes, okay. I'm . . . I guess everybody's in shock . . ." She noticed a few others casting glances her way, whispering.

"He had a passenger," Miriam said again. "She died, too."

"Oh. Well, that's terrible." Her mind was racing. Running away from something too awful to grasp. *She.* Another woman? Was Rick cheating?

Not anymore, she thought. And then hated herself for thinking it.

Miriam turned to her. Held both her hands in a firm grip. "I'm so sorry. I don't know how to . . . oh God. The other passenger was your *mother*."

Time stopped. Everything stopped—breath, heartbeat, the turning of the Earth, the wind through the trees, the swarm of approaching personnel. Natalie forced herself to listen to Miriam's explanation, struggled to take in the words while at the same time feeling everything inside her rise up in furious denial. This couldn't be happening, but as more people drew around her, she felt the devastating electric shock of certainty.

She stared at the woman who had just said her mother was dead, but she really couldn't see anything through the blindness of shock. And then it came, a pain so excruciating that she was flash frozen in white numbness, shot through the heart.

3

"Grandy." Natalie spoke her grandfather's name softly, with as much gentleness as she could muster. "It's time to go."

As she stepped through the door, Andrew Harper rose from his favorite wingback chair in his tiny apartment at the back of the bookstore. He could no longer navigate the stairs in the old building and had moved to the new space from the upstairs apartment where he'd lived nearly all his life. The small ground-floor studio had been reclaimed from a storage room. The hurried arrangement wasn't ideal, but it spared her grandfather from having to leave his lifelong home. Though the space was cramped, there was a picture window with a view of the tiny rear garden, now bright with the last of the season's hollyhocks and roses.

Curving a hand over the top of his cane, he turned to her. A sweet smile lifted the corners of his mouth. "Ah, there you are, Blythe. I've been waiting for you. How nice you look. Is that a new frock?"

Natalie's heart swelled as she crossed the room to him. Grandy had always been an immovable fixture in her life. From earliest memory, he had been present, restoring old books in the basement or chatting up customers in the shop. In the evening, he read stories aloud to her while she snuggled up to him, breathing in his comfortable scent of shaving lotion. She had learned wisdom and kindness through his gentle example.

And now he needed her. In the past week, he had frequently mistaken Natalie for her mother. Maybe the grief was too enormous to bear, and his failing mind had embossed Natalie's face with her mother's features. Though several days had passed since the shattering news, there were many moments when he refused to accept that his daughter—his only child—was gone.

Now that Natalie was here, she could see how full her mom's hands had been as Blythe tried to look after Grandy. Somehow, Natalie would have to take over his care. He insisted he could manage on his own, but she wasn't so sure. There were appointments to be kept with his doctor and various specialists. Meds to be dispensed. Meals to be prepared. Housekeeping to be done. Looking around, she spied a half-dozen projects that would make the room nicer. A bright coat of paint. A bookcase within reach. Maybe do something about the hulking old radiator that reluctantly groaned to life in winter.

In the light from the garden window, her grand-father looked wonderful to her—tall and dignified, timelessly handsome in a tailored suit and crisp white shirt she'd stayed up late ironing the night before. She knew he wanted to look his best for the service. He tugged ineffectually at his necktie. "Help me with this, Blythe. I can't . . . I don't know how . . ." His words evaporated into a cloud of confusion.

"Let me help." Standing in front of him, she looped the tie in a Windsor knot, something Grandy himself had taught her to do years before. The tie was vintage Hermès, a brilliant silk print in a sundial pattern. It was probably something her mother had found in a re-sale shop with her unerring nose for high-end fashion at low-end prices.

"It's me, Natalie," she said, her throat raw from crying. "Natalie. Your granddaughter." It felt strange and horrible to have to explain who she was to a man who used to know her better than she knew herself.

"Of course," he said agreeably. "You look just like your mother, only sometimes I think you're even more beautiful. And my lovely daughter would be the first to agree with me."

"Today is her memorial," she reminded him, finishing the tie with a gentle tug. The idea was still too enormous to grasp. She felt as if she were swimming through a fog of grief and guilt, just trying to stay afloat. If only she hadn't assumed her stupid company party had warranted a visit from her mother. If only she had been honest with Rick instead of waiting for him to conclude that their relationship had run its course. Instead, she had orchestrated the demise of her mother and a good man in his prime.

"There's a car waiting out front."

"A car . . . ?"

"The memorial," she said again. "That's why we're all dressed up."

He touched his necktie and gave her a blank look.

"Mom died, Grandy. I came as soon as I found out, and I've been here all week." After learning the stunning news at Rick's office, Natalie had jolted herself into a strange, mechanical fugue, getting into her car and driving straight down to the city to be with her grandfather. Though she scarcely remembered the drive, she kept reliving the moment she'd had to tell him. His face had lit up when she'd come through the door, and for a few precious seconds, she'd let him delight in a visit from his granddaughter.

Then she'd said the words that still didn't seem real—*Mom died in a plane crash.*

Grandy had been uncomprehending, just as Natalie had been. Blythe couldn't be gone. How could she be gone? How could she be stolen from the world, just like that?

It had taken several explanations before the understanding and deep horror penetrated his denial. A crack opened up—an earthquake. A great, unbreachable fissure. She could hear his poor heart shatter into pieces.

They had wept together, torn to bits by their shared grief. Days later, she still felt the aftershocks of the emotional devastation.

Andrew's memory issues made a terrible situation worse. He had begun losing bits of himself—short-term memory, fine motor control, rational thinking. The doctors characterized the dementia as a mild form. Intermittent. Early stage—the awful implication being that it would progress. Increasing memory loss, disinhibition, hallucinations. Natalie's mother had said Grandy got scared and confused sometimes, and other times, he seemed like his old self. He'd lost weight and suffered from headaches, tremors, and fatigue, which the care team couldn't explain.

Natalie had not been prepared for how hard it was turning out to be. It made the current situation a fresh horror to him every time he forgot his daughter had been killed and had to be reminded. Did he feel the same wave of shock and grief all over again? Did he have to keep feeling that fresh pain? She couldn't imagine having to experience the initial overwhelming stab of that first detonation of news, again and again.

Andrew took a breath. His face didn't change. He scarcely moved. But his dark eyes reflected such an inexpressible sadness that Natalie flinched. "I know," she whispered, taking his hand and leading him to the door. "It hurts all the time. Every waking moment."

"Yes," he said. "The pain is a reflection of how much we loved her."

"You've always had a way with words."

"Blythe said it runs in the family. She's been reading Colleen's journals."

"Colleen. You mean your ancestor, the one who died in the 1906 earthquake?"

"The grandmother I never knew. My dear father was just seven years old when he lost her and was sent to an orphanage. He rarely spoke of that day, but I believe it haunted him all his life."

Lately, Grandy had clearer memories of the distant past than he did of events that occurred five minutes ago. "I didn't know about Colleen's journals."

"Blythe found them not long ago. I don't know what she's done with them."

It was possible that the journals were a figment of Grandy's imagination, since all they knew of Colleen O'Rourke Harper was that she'd immigrated from Ireland, had one son—Grandy's father, Julius—and disappeared when the earthquake struck. The family history had been altered forever by a mysterious twist of fate.

Was that what happened to you and Rick, Mom? Natalie wondered. *A twist of fate?* Or had Natalie herself orchestrated it when she'd invited her mother to the company party? Every day, she wished she could snatch back that moment.

She paused at the hall tree by the door as her grandfather went through his familiar going-out routine. First, the soft, wispy neck cloth. Then the overcoat, the black fedora, and finally the cane. No umbrella needed today. It was foggy and damp but not raining. The bright yellow leaves of early autumn were decoupaged against the pavement.

He held the door for her and she stepped through. "Do you want the wheelchair?" she asked.

He hesitated, looking down at the chair, his face creased with pain. "No," he said. "I'll walk into my daughter's memorial and stand to speak at the podium."

The dignified response tore at her heart as she slowly led the way down the narrow hall, past a storage room stacked with books, through the back office, and then into the bookstore showroom.

When she was a girl, Natalie used to start each day by skipping through the shop, calling good morning to her favorites as she passed them—Angelina Ballerina, Charlotte and Ramona, Lilly and her purple plastic purse. Then she would let herself out to catch the bus to school. Now a big portion of the shop was littered inside and out with tributes and notes of sympathy from the many people who had known her mother.

The front door was hung with a Closed sign and a printed announcement of the memorial. A CELEBRATION OF THE LIFE OF BLYTHE HARPER.

Why was it called that when the last thing a grieving daughter wanted was a celebration?

She opened the door and cleared a path through the piled tokens that had been spontaneously left there— bouquets of flowers, dog-eared novels and memorabilia, candles and handmade sketches and cards. The Lost and Found Bookshop had been a fixture on Perdita Street for as long as Natalie had been alive, and the sudden demise of its owner had inspired a huge, loving, and immensely sad reaction.

One thing Natalie had never wondered about until now: After the explosion of tributes, then what? Who picked up the wilted flowers, the rain-soaked poems, the blurred photos, the jarred candles?

The waiting black car smelled of canned deodorizer. The driver helped her grandfather into the back seat. Traffic was heavy even on a Saturday morning, and the drive to the Flood Mansion crawled along through wispy snakes of fog, past trees twisted and shaped by the wind, and along the slanting rooflines of the city's Victorian Painted Ladies. Ringing cable cars lurched past bustling cafés and shops. As they wended their way upward, they broke through the fog and entered another microclimate, a sky of eye-smarting clarity that illuminated the city's most splendid panoramas.

This had been Blythe Harper's city, this peninsula crowned by forty-three "official" hills and surrounded by water, a place she swore she'd never leave. Yet she had left it, never to return, and now Natalie and Andrew had to scramble through the dark maze of unexpected grief.

"She told me she would be back on Friday night," said Grandy, his eyes once again misted with confusion.

"That was her plan," Natalie acknowledged.

"What the devil happened?"

Her mouth went dry. She said nothing.

"Natty-girl," he said, using her nickname, "I know I'm forgetful, but I deserve to hear the truth."

She nodded. She'd already told him. He needed her to go through it again. "I'm sorry, Grandy. It's hard for me to talk about, because I feel as if I caused it. I wanted Mom to come up for some stupid company thing. I didn't realize she and Rick were planning to surprise me by showing up together. He told me he had a test flight, but that was just a ruse. Instead, he flew down here and picked her up at Pier Thirty-Nine. They would have landed at the Archangel airstrip at around three that afternoon. But something went wrong during the flight."

"Your Rick is an expert pilot."

She folded her hands together and squeezed until it hurt. "He was. Oh, Grandy." She remembered the fleeting thought she'd had that the female passenger in his plane had been someone he was cheating with. What a horrible thing to think about a man who was only trying to make her happy.

The memorial for Rick had taken place in Petaluma the day before. Natalie had dragged herself there, enduring a virtual gauntlet of headshaking and consoling friends and acquaintances. Every tribute and eulogy had attested to his expertise, his professionalism.

"If he was such an expert, then how could he have crashed?" Grandy wondered.

"The NTSB is still investigating," she said, hoping she wouldn't need to explain the details yet again.

She had culled through the preliminary reports, as if knowing exactly what had gone wrong would make the tragedy less cataclysmic. According to the report, the amphibious light sport aircraft was flying too low and—probably due to fog—mistakenly entered a canyon surrounded by steep terrain. Investigators postulated that the pilot thought he was in a different canyon that led to the larger, open portion of the lake. Right before the crash, a local man who was fishing in a boat spotted the plane about fifty feet over the water.

"As the plane swooped low, I waved to the pilot and he waved back," the witness had said. "Everything seemed normal. I figured they were just buzzing over the lake or coming in to land on the water. A few seconds later, I heard the engines rev up and accelerate hard. Guess he was trying to turn."

Once Rick realized there was no exit from the canyon, he attempted a 180-degree turn to escape. Based upon performance limits, the airplane would not have been able to climb past the steeply rising terrain.

The plane flew behind a point and then the man heard a loud crash. He sped in his boat to find the site. Approaching a cove, he spotted the wreckage and yelled out, but there was no response. He called 911.

Officials from the sheriff's office, the Federal Aviation Administration, and rescuers from Cal Fire and the U.S. Bureau of Reclamation were led to the crash site. They speculated that the marine layer had caused Rick to mistake one canyon for another. By the time he figured out his orientation, there wasn't enough space to pull up.

Natalie shuddered, haunted by the image. Over and over, she pictured those final seconds, imagining what her mother must have been feeling—the flash of realization, the panic, the terror. She told her grandfather what she'd learned but didn't share the further details in the report. The blood. The motionless bodies found by the fisherman.

"They were both gone on impact," she told Grandy.

He reached over and covered her hand with his. "I never met your Rick in person. I wish I had."

He was never my Rick, thought Natalie. "At the memorial yesterday, his sister gave me something," she blurted out.

"What's that?"

She reached into her handbag. "This was zipped into a pocket of his flight vest." She handed the small box to her grandfather.

"A diamond ring," he said, taking it in a hand unsteady with tremors.

"Rick was going to surprise me with a marriage proposal," Natalie said. "I assume he wanted my mom there when he asked me."

"Yes, that was his plan," Grandy said. "When we spoke on the phone—"

"You spoke with him?" Natalie felt nauseated.

"Indeed I did. He told me what he intended to do. He wasn't exactly asking my permission, but he wanted me to know that he loved you. He wanted to make a life with you."

Her throat clogged with inexpressible grief. Then she choked out, "He told you and Mom? You knew?" Surely not. Maybe this was one of Grandy's episodes— *delirium* was the doctor's term for it.

"Rick had a lovely plan," Grandy continued. "He was going to ask you to marry him, and then fly you and your mother back to the city. He had a suite booked for the two of you at the Four Seasons on Nob Hill. It made me supremely happy to know such a fine young man wanted to marry you. I never dreamed it would go so wrong." His hands shook as he straightened his tie. "Blythe never found anyone, and she always feared it would be the same for you. She believed Rick would be the one."

Natalie put the ring away. "When I told her I was having doubts, she didn't want to hear it. I don't know what to do, Grandy. What should I do?"

He regarded her blankly. This was one of his lost moments. She was beginning to recognize the signs—the distant stare, the agitated hand movements, the impenetrable expression.

Realizing she was truly on her own with this, she gazed out the car window. While Rick had been plotting a surprise proposal and a romantic getaway, she had been contemplating the most civil, low-key way to break up with him. The very moment he'd been flying with her mother, a gorgeous engagement ring tucked into his vest, Natalie had been imagining life without him.

She kept expecting him to be the first to call it quits. Instead, he was buying a diamond ring, secretly plotting a marriage proposal and a whisk-you-away couple's weekend. *Marriage.*

It would have been a surprise, all right. In the most terrible way. How could she have read the situation so wrong?

Attending his memorial had been painful and teeth-grittingly awkward. His family was made up of very nice people who had assumed Natalie, too, was very nice. She wasn't nice. Couldn't they see that? She felt especially not-nice when Mandy appeared at the service, her expressions of sympathy as hollow as Natalie's heart.

His sister had handed her the ring box. "He loved you so much. He would have wanted you to have this."

Natalie hadn't dared to touch the ring, nestled on its bed of velvet. "Please. I couldn't."

"I realize you're emotional now. You're not thinking straight." Rhonda had dropped the box into Natalie's purse. "You don't ever have to wear it. Or you could repurpose it, maybe have it made into something else. Or sell it and use the proceeds for something you care about. Rick would've liked that."

"It doesn't seem right," Natalie had said.

"Nothing about this whole situation seems right." Rhonda's voice caught on a sob and she gave Natalie a brief hug. "I'm sorry we never got the chance to be sisters."

Natalie felt like a monster.

She *was* a monster.

The town car drew up at the mansion, a sumptuous crown atop a hill overlooking majestic views of the Bay

Area—the bay itself, the Golden Gate Bridge, and the hills of Marin County.

"This building has a romantic story," Grandy said, seeming to snap out of his silence. "After the great earthquake, Maud Flood was so afraid of fire that her husband built her a grand house of marble atop this granite hill. He wanted to give her a new place made entirely of stone, so she would feel safe."

"Now that," Natalie said, "is a good husband." *Rick would have made a good husband,* she thought, immersing herself again in guilt. He had been caring, and cautious, and he knew how to look after things. He was steady and stable, her two favorite qualities not only in people but in life itself.

A pair of white-gloved attendants held the door for her and Grandy. Someone in the foyer took their coats and Grandy's hat to the cloakroom. A beautifully rendered poster on an easel welcomed guests to the celebration.

Bryan Ferry's voice crooning "Avalon" drifted from unseen speakers. Mom had loved Roxy Music. On a sleepless night a few days before, Natalie had put together a playlist from Blythe's digital music library.

Natalie nearly stumbled as they passed the gallery of enlarged photos on display in the rotunda. The grief was like a punch to the gut. Breath-stealing agony made her want to crawl out of her skin. Her knees would have given out if not for her grandfather. Though he moved slowly and leaned on the cane, he was strong. With her careless father so notoriously absent, Grandy had been the key man in Natalie's life, a fact she was grateful for every single day.

She, Grandy, and the staff and friends of the bookstore had collected pictures of her mother, raiding old albums and digital files and sending them to a gallery that specialized in large-scale renderings and displays. The result was a beautiful frieze of images that captured Blythe's energy and beauty and spirit.

There she was, a girl in the seventies, picking berries on a farm somewhere. A young woman proudly posing in her cap and gown in Berkeley blue and California gold. An impossibly young mother, surrounded by gauzy light through a window, holding her infant daughter in her arms, her expression a mixture of pride and terror. A woman standing with her cat at the grand open doorway of the Lost and Found Bookshop, in all her glorious vivacity. A soft-eyed daughter sweetly hugging her aging father.

The final portrait was Natalie's favorite picture of her mother. No one knew who had taken the photo of Blythe standing on the beach at Fort Funston at the southwest edge of the city, gazing off into the distance, her expression enigmatic. To Natalie, beneath the joyous spirit everyone had loved, Blythe had always seemed just a bit sad. Sometimes, growing up, Natalie had been struck by the thought that she didn't really know her mother. And now it was too late.

Even more moving than the photo gallery was the size of the crowd. As Natalie accompanied her grandfather to their seats in the front, he said, "I always pictured walking my daughter down the aisle at her wedding, not her funeral."

She nearly stumbled when she heard those words. Only her determination to support him kept her steady. The assemblage was packed to the walls already, and more people were still streaming in. A velvet rope hung across a section in the front, demarcating a few seats with a card that read *Reserved for Family*.

In the strictest sense, they only needed two seats—one for her and one for Grandy. Blythe's mother was long gone. Lavinia had gone away when Blythe was a baby, leaving disaster and scandal in her wake. As for Natalie's father, Dean Fogarty, he likely had heard about the memorial, but he was as much of a no-show today as he had been for Natalie's entire life.

Her family had consisted of the three of them. And now, all of a sudden, there were two. Natalie and

Grandy. And her grandfather seemed to be leaving her in small, heartbreaking pieces.

She recognized many of the attendees—her mom's friends, customers who had frequented the shop over the years, even salespeople from New York, publishers and colleagues in the book industry—people who had depended on her taste and opinions. There were authors whose books had graced her shelves, local merchants and neighbors from the tree-shaded enclave of Perdita Street.

Guests on both sides of the aisle offered tentative waves, mouthed expressions of sympathy and hand-over-the-heart gestures.

No one knew what to say to people facing a grief so big and shocking. Natalie wouldn't know, either. She had a hard time meeting their eyes, feeling irrational shame, or perhaps guilt.

She and Grandy took their seats facing the podium, festooned with sweet-smelling native lilies and autumn mums from the Bonner Flower Farm up in Glenmuir, organic and sustainable, the way Blythe would have wanted. A swag of Buddhist prayer flags hung overhead. Her mother had never subscribed to a particular dogma, claiming organized religion was the cause of too much violence and strife in the world. But she often

spoke of her favorite spiritual books, including Buddhism's *The Noble Eightfold Path*, and admitted happily that she was drawn to the all-loving and nonviolent
tenets of Buddhism.

The smooth-sided urn was overshadowed by another portrait of Blythe Harper, this one larger than
all the rest in the gallery. Natalie had chosen it herself.
Blythe was in her favorite spot in the bookstore—a
cushy chair littered with throw pillows, angled near the
lace curtain of the shop's front display window. The
natural light, filtered through the antique lace, illuminated the fine features of her mother's face, framed by
wispy dark curls, smiling lips, and eyes that were bright
with ideas. The book in her lap was a poetry collection
of Mary Oliver, which most people knew was a favorite of Blythe's. The caption under the photo was a line
from a well-known poem: *Tell me, what is it you plan
to do with your one wild and precious life?*

Natalie had chosen the quote, too. She settled back
and tried to focus on the display. The images blurred
together like a ruined watercolor. She checked her
bag, touching the folder with her eulogy notes. There
was no way to express this terrible goodbye, but she'd
scraped her soul to find the right words.

Grandy leaned his cane on the seat back and stared
straight ahead.

Natalie tucked her arm around his and wondered when she would stop feeling like she was on the verge of tears. "How are you doing?"

"I'm maintaining calm," he said simply.

His lifelong friend, Charlie Wong, in a fine black jacket with a Nehru collar, arrived and sat down next to Grandy. A talented diorama artist, Charlie had known Andrew when both were young boys running around the city. Many years ago, Charlie had created an art piece based on the bookstore building, which was then Grandy's typewriter shop. Now the two old men got together several times a week, going to dinner at one of Charlie's daughters' homes or attending game night at the local senior center. Charlie's usual smile was in place, yet dimmed by the sadness in his eyes.

Tess and Dominic slid into the row behind Natalie. Tess leaned forward and gave her shoulder a squeeze. Natalie acknowledged the touch with a pat of her hand.

Cleo and Bertie, who both worked in the bookstore, arrived and took their seats on Natalie's other side.

"Hi, guys," she whispered. "Thanks for being here."

"How are you holding up?" asked Bertie. "Sorry for speaking in clichés, but I really want to know, sweetie." An aspiring actor, he was lithe and graceful, his whole body expressing feelings without words—in the angle of his head, the slant of his shoulders. Bertie was smart and funny and melancholy, chasing his dream of starring in a major theater production. He'd loved her mother, who had encouraged his acting career by giving him time off for auditions and rehearsals whenever he needed it.

"Grandy and I are keeping each other company," Natalie said. "Honestly, I've never had my heart ripped out of my chest. But I imagine this is what it feels like."

Cleo's eyes were as dim as twilight, gleaming with a mist of sadness. She nodded and dabbed at her cheeks with a tissue. "Damn. You remind me so much of her."

"Do I?"

Bertie leaned forward. "Hell, yeah. In the best possible way."

Cleo was Natalie's age, and had grown up in the neighborhood. The girls used to play together in Portsmouth Square, surrounded by Chinese grannies sipping their milk tea and playing board games. They'd snack on soft buns filled with sweet coconut, and when it rained, they'd duck into the curio shops or the Golden Gate Fortune Cookie Factory, their senses dazzled by the delicious, sugary aroma.

Cleo was Blythe's second-in-command, helping manage the shop and, in her downtime, writing plays.

Frieda Mills, Blythe's longtime friend, had volunteered to officiate the service. Now she stepped up to the podium. Her defiantly unkempt hair, threaded with gray, formed a nimbus around her small, drawn face.

The music subsided as Frieda adjusted her mic. "Good morning and welcome," she said. "On behalf of Natalie and Andrew Harper, I want to thank you for coming."

She gazed out at the crowd. "I've known Blythe since we were freshmen in college. She was the roommate I dreaded having—messy and talkative, better looking than me, never on time, constantly in motion, cluttering every space she inhabited." She said this with a smile, and the smile trembled as she paused and took a deep breath. "In spite of all this, or maybe because of all this, I loved her like a sister. We celebrated holidays together, raised our kids together . . ."

Frieda's two boys had each, on occasion, asked Natalie to dances and parties. She—and probably the boys as well—suspected they were being nudged together by their mothers.

"And then there were the books," Frieda said. "Even in college, she had so many books that we used them for furniture—step stools, benches, nightstands, shelves for other books . . ."

Natalie could so easily picture that. When she was very small, her mother used to tell her that books were alive in a special way. Between the covers, characters were living their lives, enacting their dramas, falling in and out of love, finding trouble, working out their problems. Even sitting closed on a shelf, a book had a life of its own. When someone opened the book, that was when the magic happened.

"My friend Blythe often said her life was a grand adventure," Frieda continued. "Books were her passion, so I wanted to share one of her favorites." She put on a pair of wire-rimmed reading glasses and opened a well-worn copy of *Charlotte's Web.*

The passage from the classic novel was filled with lovely prose that took on new poignancy and concluded with Charlotte's famous words: "After all, what's a life anyway? We're born, we live a little while, we die."

Natalie had heard the reading many times, but now she clung to Charlotte's wisdom, hoping with all her heart that her mother had left with that same calm, matter-of-fact acceptance. Haunted by images of those last moments, Natalie reflected that this did not seem possible given the way Blythe had died.

Other speakers reminisced about her mother. In cracked voices, they recounted memories of browsing the stacks with the well-read bookseller, or relaxing in the tiny café and basking in the sense of community Blythe cultivated. The tributes were lavish and heartfelt, a clear indication of the many lives she had touched. Through her shock and grief, Natalie felt a sad glimmer of understanding of why her mother had been so devoted to the shop.

The readings and tributes were followed by a song, and they were all invited to join in. The lyrics were printed in the program. "No Rain" by Blind Melon had been a favorite of Blythe's, expressing the glory of escaping into the pages of a book. The woman playing guitar was a frequent patron of the shop. She had contacted Natalie and Frieda as they were organizing the program and asked to perform in Blythe's honor.

As the lyrics of the song came out of Natalie on a shaky breath, she wished she could do exactly as the words expressed—*Escape, escape, escape.*

Andrew Harper felt the soft caress of the music on his face as he waited. Waited for what?

His mind darted away in search of the answer. It was a slippery process, like trying to catch polliwogs in the pond shallows in springtime. He glanced over at the young woman sitting beside him. She had pale skin and dark curly hair, and a face so beautiful and so sad it cracked his heart in two.

Now that he was old and plagued by strange fugues of forgetfulness, Andrew was learning to pay attention to certain details he used to filter out—sounds and smells, colors and fleeting images. Focusing on one thing—the timbre of a voice, the narrative on a page in a book—was increasingly difficult and disturbing. Walking out onto the street was like entering an amphitheater into an overwhelming and deafening cacophony of confusion.

He shored up his thoughts. He had to teach himself to think in a different way.

Although he knew Dr. Yang would disapprove, he had skipped taking his tablets this morning. Supposedly the pills were keeping him from feeling anxious. Perhaps that was indeed the case, but he needed a clear head to face the day, and the meds made him drowsy. He must not face this day in a state of drowsiness.

It was an important day. He couldn't remember why.

He felt the sad young woman watching him through eyes bruised by grief. He looked down at the printed program card in his hand. It was beautiful, the thick stock imprinted by the letterpress machine in the basement of the bookshop. After he'd closed down his typewriter repair business and founded the bookstore with Blythe, no one had wanted to move the heavy machine, so they kept it and occasionally used it for special printings—a birth announcement when Natalie was born, the grand opening of the bookstore three decades ago, a gallery showing for Charlie Wong.

Andrew used to tell Blythe he was getting old while waiting to print an announcement that she was finally getting married.

That always made her laugh and say he'd raised the bar too high; she would never find a man who could measure up to him. After what had happened with the fellow who had fathered Natalie, Andrew was glad she could laugh at all.

Then, in a blink, the situation came clear to him. The young woman beside him was Natalie, his granddaughter, Natalie. Her regard felt like a whir of moth wings against his cheek, powdering his skin with a residue like May Lin's dusting powder, back when she had lived with him and they were happy.

He summoned a smile for Blythe. No, not Blythe. Natalie. Blythe was gone, suddenly and irretrievably, like a zephyr shooting into the night sky, leaving a trail of moonlit particles that swirled in brief, unspeakable beauty, and then faded into nothing.

The very sweet pop song was one he'd heard on Blythe's radio many times, so he knew when the melody was winding down. He took out his handkerchief again and checked on Natalie, the silent sadness beside him.

His granddaughter's face was a portrait of everything they were both feeling. Her eyes mirrored his pain. The shock and grief of losing Blythe were so deep and intense that it felt as if a new and devastating emotion had been invented just for them.

Natalie noticed his attention and tucked her hand inside his. Leaning over, she whispered, "Are you doing all right?"

No, he thought. *A man is not meant to outlive his daughter.*

"Yes," he whispered back, the lie hissing through his teeth.

"If you don't want to speak . . . if it's too much for you—"

He squeezed her hand. "I know what I want to say. I'll get through it."

"You're incredible, Grandy. I'm so glad I have you."

"And I you." He sat still as the officiant did another reading. He tried to think about what he wanted to say. What he needed to say.

How did one honor a woman's life in a five-minute speech?

He had suffered losses through the years, certainly, as anyone his age had. Long ago, Lavinia had walked away from him and into the arms of a man who promised her something better. May Lin had come back into his life briefly at the end, bringing latent joy that was all the sweeter for having been delayed, and she had died in his arms last year.

Maybe that was the start of his decline. Dr. Yang called it a decline. A gradual slide down a hill into a pile of nothingness.

Andrew could not pinpoint the precise moment his memories had begun to slip and his thoughts turned to a jumble. Sometime after the hip debacle, he supposed. Before then, and even during his stay in the hospital and rehab, everything had been clear to him.

Then, once he'd finished with the rehab and returned to Perdita Street, Blythe had moved his living quarters to the main floor. Stairs were out of the question now. The room by the garden used to be a storage area for his father's apothecary infusions, medicines, and herbs. Later, Andrew had cluttered the space with the tools of his own trade—Stoddard solvent, brushes, tiny pincers and lubricants and cleansers for repairing typewriters.

As he'd settled into his new quarters, which were not unpleasant, the fog had closed in, bit by bit. Fatigue dragged at him, and his stomach was upset by everything he ate. Food tasted like metal. His days started to fade, and his life turned as thin as lukewarm water. He was a ghost in a world that appeared through a glass that was ash-colored and wavy.

At some point he'd lost the proud man who used to swagger around the neighborhood, a regular cock of the walk. These days, he wandered, seeking a way out, and then he asked himself—out of what? He wanted to go home. Then he would remember that he was home.

He was Odysseus one moment, the Ancient Mariner the next, an ordinary man like Tom Joad or a seeker like Douglas Adams's hitchhiker. He wandered in search of a past that existed only inside himself. He sought fields of flowers and towering cliffs that jutted out over the ocean and mountaintops that pierced the clouds.

Maybe he wandered because he had spent his entire life in one place—the shop on Perdita Street. He used to live upstairs, first with his parents when he was a boy. Then with Lavinia, the wife who had betrayed him. Then with Blythe, whom he had raised with no help from Lavinia. And now he was obliged to bury his daughter with no help from anyone at all.

The reading concluded and soft music trailed from hidden speakers. And then it was Andrew's turn. With Natalie at his side and his cane in hand, he made his way to the podium. He turned slightly, letting his granddaughter know he was all right standing on his own. Then he set aside the cane. The least he could do was stand for his daughter.

Then he took off his glasses and tucked them into his

breast pocket. He didn't need to look at any prompts. Notes were not necessary when speaking from the heart.

"On the day she was born, my beautiful daughter, Blythe, became a part of my life's journey, and we followed our common path until . . . until . . . the unthinkable happened. So let us not dwell on the way she died. Let us celebrate the way she lived." He had to pause, then, as despair took his breath away. Recalibrate. Speak of Blythe, who could no longer speak. "What can I tell you about my child who died?"

He heard a few gasping sobs. "I can tell you that she had a happy life. I can tell you that her life was too short and mine is too long. At my age," he explained, "I thought I knew what grief is. In all my years, I have known loss—my parents, dear friends, the woman I loved. But until the day my daughter was taken from me, I had no idea that grief could cut so deep or feel so painful."

He paused, hearing Natalie's soft, broken breaths. "And that is all I shall say about my feelings, because today is not about me. It's about my daughter, Blythe Harper. On the day she was born, she changed my life. And the day she departed, she left an indelible mark on us all. And in between, she led a remarkable life."

4

Andrew Harper's wife left him on a Monday. He would always remember it was a Monday, because that was the day May Lin delivered the finished laundry, crisply folded and wrapped in a paper parcel. Then she would pick up the week's bag, marked *Harper* and tagged with Chinese characters.

The bag of soiled items was considerably smaller without Lavinia's clothing. She had packed everything in a battered steamer trunk she'd made him drag up from the basement. The trunk was a mysterious family heirloom that had once belonged to Colleen O'Rourke, the grandmother he'd never known. Colleen had migrated from Ireland in the 1880s, arriving at the age of fifteen. She had found work as a maid in the very building that was now the bookstore, somehow making her way in the world alone.

Now her trunk would be traveling with the gloriously beautiful Lavinia, not on a steamer but on a train to Los Angeles, where her rich lover had promised to give her the life she always claimed she deserved.

Her farewell to Andrew and Blythe had been terse. "I can't be happy here," she had said that Monday morning as the taxi driver loaded the trunk into his bulbous Plymouth van. "You'll be better off without me."

Blythe, less than a year old and still in diapers, had gurgled and clapped her hands, a string of teething drool pooling on Andrew's sleeve. The radio was playing that inane Sonny and Cher song, "I Got You Babe." The baby reached both starfish hands out to her mother. Lavinia paused, but the brief flicker of hesitation in her eyes quickly hardened into icy resolve.

"Be well," she said, and then she was gone.

A few moments later, May Lin arrived with the laundry delivery. Andrew was still standing in the middle of the shop, frozen, surrounded by his customers' typewriters, cash registers, and adding machines, with Blythe snuggled against his chest.

The sight of May thawed him out. He and May had fallen in love as teenagers, but her family forbade her to be courted by Andrew, a *gweilo*. His own parents had not forbidden it, but they'd warned him that there could be no easy future with a Celestial—their archaic term for Chinese people in America. May Lin entered an arranged marriage to an older man from her father's district in China. He had a laundry, he needed a wife, and that was that.

Heartsick, Andrew had sought solace in the arms of Lavinia. She was stunningly beautiful, and when she got pregnant, he was foolish enough to believe the sense of obligation that bound him was a kind of love.

Each week, when he and May saw each other, they rarely spoke. They didn't need to, because they knew each other's hearts without words.

And little Blythe became the center of his world. His ray of sunshine, he called her, a black-eyed Susan of a child who sang songs and read stories all the live-long day. She had a little rocking chair right next to his by the dormer window in the sitting room, and he could still remember the way the evening light used to slant through the window, settling over her like a benediction while she was absorbed in a book.

As the years passed, they had their ups and downs, but the core of their relationship was a fierce, protective love. He taught her touch-typing and watched her win spelling bees. Though the teenage years mystified him, he indulged her yearning for pretty clothes and baffling tubes of makeup. For the father-daughter dance in high school, he'd taught her a passable foxtrot, and she had lamented that he'd set the bar too high for any boy to reach.

He harbored no regrets about the way things had unfolded. He had the world's most wonderful child and enough common sense to know, finally, that love took the heart by surprise. Lavinia was gone, but she had left behind the very best part of herself. Of them both.

"It was just the two of us," Andrew told the gathering at Blythe's memorial. Their faces were a distant blur, but memories stood out clearly in his mind. "She was my daily joy. It's probably hard for you to imagine, but there was a time when the Lost and Found Bookshop was a typewriter showroom, with a letterpress printing operation in the basement. I made my living by fixing the very things a writer uses every day. Founding the bookshop was Blythe's idea, and it was a great adventure for us both."

The day Blythe went away to college, Andrew thought he might die from missing her. It was just across the bay in Berkeley, but it might as well have been in Timbuktu for all his lonely heart knew. He lived for the weekends when she would come home with high-flown ideas in her head and a collection of dirty laundry in a faded cloth bag, still stenciled with their name and Chinese characters. His typewriter business was in sharp decline thanks to the computer revolution, and he spent most of his days reading the antique books someone had left in the basement decades before. He became an expert at restoring the rare volumes, which he displayed in a glass-front barrister case. Every once in a while, a collector would come in and buy one of the books, and the enterprise became more than a hobby.

Four years later, Blythe returned home with a bachelor's degree, a broken heart, and an unexpected pregnancy. She tearfully confessed that she had fallen in love with a teaching assistant who had promised her the world. She'd believed him, in her hopeful, romantic way, imagining a life of adventure with the young doctoral candidate.

Then she discovered in the most hurtful of ways that the man was already married and had three children.

Andrew's private, selfish secret was that he couldn't thank Dean Fogarty enough. The man who had broken his daughter's heart had given Andrew a new purpose. Blythe had needed a way to provide for herself and her child. Andrew needed a fresh direction in life. Together, they had founded the bookstore, both energized by the prospect of creating a future for themselves and little Natalie.

He looked out at the gathering once again and brought the present moment into focus. Familiar faces, names lost in the cobwebs. There were ghosts as well, people who had left, yet remained a lingering presence in his mind. He had a fanciful thought that somehow they offered Blythe a loving welcome into their midst.

Please let it be true, he thought.

The rest of his eulogy was brief, highlighting the things he loved best about Blythe, the things he would miss the most. He knew the words were not enough, but they were all he had to pay tribute to his one and only child.

"I am quite certain I will never laugh without hearing her laugh. I will never smile without seeing her bright smile. I'm grateful to all of you for being a part of her brilliant, precious life. I feel sorry for those who missed out on knowing this exceptional person." A gasp of sorrow built in his chest and he paused, then spoke again. "In a moment, you'll hear from another exceptional person. Of all the gifts my daughter gave to the world, the greatest is her own daughter, Natalie."

Andrew kept himself steady as he stepped back, though his knees threatened to give out. A new song started up, Natalie accompanied him back to his seat, and he sank down with as much dignity as he could muster.

"I'm up next," she said, "and I have no idea how I'll follow that."

Her tears were silver tracks of grief salting her achingly lovely face. Blythe's face. One and the same, and maybe this was the reason he was confused sometimes. He held tightly to the top of the cane as "What a Wonderful World" filled the hall. He didn't really need the cane, but by now it was a habit. And maybe a way to keep himself from drifting away forever, on a raft of unutterable sadness.

Natalie didn't sing along with the rest of the gathering as she awaited her turn at the podium. Instead, she time-traveled, trying to visit her mother in a different era, trying to bring her back to life.

When Natalie was little, her mother had dwelled at the bright center of her world, an incandescent force organizing their lives around books and ideas.

Even at a very young age, Natalie had understood that this was unusual. That their family was unusual.

She remembered a time when she was in the fourth grade—Mrs. Blessing, California History—and came home in a quandary: "We're doing family trees in school," she told her mother, "and I feel weird about mine."

"Why do you feel weird about it?" Blythe quite frequently responded to Natalie with a question about her feelings. She read tons of parenting books and got all kinds of ideas from them.

"Kayla says we have an alternative lifestyle. She told everyone at recess that means we're freaks."

"You say that like it's a bad thing," Mom remarked, smoothing her hand over the pages of an antique book. She liked to display the most special collector's items in a lighted glass case under the counter. People who wanted a closer look had to ask, and they had to wear white gloves when they touched the pages.

"Is it a good thing?" asked Natalie.

"What it is," Mom said, finally looking up, "is none of her goddamn business."

Natalie always felt a little forbidden thrill when her mother swore. She didn't do it often, because she said too much swearing watered down the effect.

"Can I tell her that?"

"Sure, but brace yourself for the reaction." Mom carefully placed the book in the case, laying it open to a page with an illustration of a bird. Then she went over to the coffee area and gave Natalie a cookie from

Sugar, the bakery across the street, and poured her a glass of cold milk. It was their afternoon ritual each day when Natalie got home from school.

Blythe set the tray on a tiny table in the coffee area. She often said she wanted to make more room for coffee to serve to customers but didn't want to sacrifice shelf space for the books. "I love our family. And I know you do, too. Just because it's not like other families doesn't mean a thing. It certainly doesn't mean we are freaks."

Natalie took the city bus to school. Her friends had carpools, some of them with drivers in polished chauffeur's livery. Mom didn't even have a car. Natalie's friends all had fathers. Or stepfathers. Or two mothers. Or two dads. She had only ever met her birth father a couple of times. His name was Dean Fogarty, and she didn't like him much. Mainly because he didn't seem to like her. Mom called him her biggest mistake that had resulted in her greatest accomplishment. "He gave me you, Nat," Mom would say. "So I can never have any regrets."

Natalie took a bite of the soft, sugared ginger-molasses cookie. She wasn't sure being someone's greatest accomplishment was as important as it sounded.

"We had to draw a picture of our family and I felt weird about it." She took her sketch out of her backpack and laid it on the counter. She had drawn the people as precisely as she could—her mother's wavy black hair, Grandy's wonderful height, her own missing front tooth, May Lin's half-moon smile, and Gilly the shop cat, curled into a marmalade-colored ball.

"What made you feel weird?"

In her mind's eye, Natalie envisioned the other kids' drawings. Most of them featured a mom, a dad, and a brother or sister or two, always with a lovely house in the background. There were a few Mrs. Blessing called "blended families," which sounded very nice, like a special drink at the Rainbow Soda Fountain down the street. And then there was Calvin with his two daddies, and Anson with his two mommies, which wasn't a big deal on account of this being San Francisco and all. No one would ever say anything mean about families like that. Mom was always pointing out that lots of kids had single moms. Still, when it came to Natalie, there were questions.

"How come you have a grandfather but no father?" she'd been asked.

"Who's that Chinese lady?" Kayla had demanded.

"She lives with us," Natalie explained.

"Is she, like, your maid? Your nanny?"

Most of the kids at Natalie's school had both maids *and* nannies, because this was an Expensive Neighborhood and they all lived in houses or even mansions, not apartments tucked above a bookshop.

"Well?" Kayla had prodded.

Natalie had wanted so badly to lie, but she was really bad at lying. "She's my grandfather's friend."

"Like his girlfriend?"

"I guess so." For some reason, she had been embarrassed by the conversation. She looked up at her mom and decided not to mention that particular exchange.

"No one gets to tell you what to think or how to feel," Mom said. "That's your choice."

"Then why do I feel like a freak? 'Cause I sure as heck wouldn't choose *that*."

Her mother looked at her. Then a spark lit her eyes. "Over here," she said, gesturing at the children's section.

Oh boy. A Book Talk, her mother's specialty. Natalie finished her cookie and chased it down with a final gulp of milk, then washed her hands at the sink. She did like books and reading, but sometimes she just wanted to talk to her mom. She listened, though, because her mother never failed to find the exact-right perfect book, and she read it in a way that made you want to listen forever.

As always, her mother was right. There was a book

for everything. Somewhere in the vast Library of the Universe, as Natalie thought of it, her mom could find a book that embodied exactly the things Natalie was worrying about.

And sure enough, *Maya Running*, about a girl from India whose family didn't fit in, did make her feel better. Like she wasn't the only kid in the world with a different kind of family. *You're never alone when you're reading a book*, Mom liked to say.

At the end of the song, Natalie returned to the podium carrying a book and her folder of notes, along with a packet of tissues. With an excess of care, she opened the book and lowered the mic. "I'm Natalie," she said. "Blythe's daughter."

Almost immediately, her throat was clogged by tears that scalded her with pain. She started to panic, because she desperately wanted to be heard. Big swallow. Deep breath. She had awakened early this morning in order to practice getting through her piece without falling apart. One recommended technique was to squeeze the flesh between her index finger and thumb as hard as she could, letting the pinch remind her to keep it together.

"Books were my mother's world, but she was mine.

We lived in the apartment above the shop, and every day with my mom was an adventure. We didn't travel far on vacations because of the shop."

Natalie used to beg to travel the world the way her friends did on school holidays—Disneyland, Hawaii, London, Japan. Instead, her mom would take her on flights of the imagination to Prince Edward Island, to Sutter's Mill, to Narnia and Sunnybrook Farm, to outer space and Hogwarts.

She tried her best to bring her mother back to life with a few key anecdotes and memories smeared by tears. And then she looked down at the page she'd read many times growing up—from *The Minpins* by Roald Dahl. "The first time my mother read this book to me was after a visit to the Claymore Arboretum. I was five years old, and I believed the dragonflies were fairies, and that tiny sprites rode around on the backs of song-birds. She let me go on thinking that for as long as I pleased. And as far as I'm concerned, that's the best parenting advice ever."

She breathed in, imagining the comfortable scent of her mother's bathrobe as they snuggled together for their nightly story. She breathed out, hoping her words would somehow touch her mother one more time.

"'And above all, watch with glittering eyes the whole world around you because the greatest secrets are always hidden in the most unlikely places. Those who don't believe in magic will never find it.'"

Natalie closed the book and hugged it to her chest the way she used to do as a child. When she spoke again, her voice was surprisingly, gratifyingly steady. "I could keep you here all day with stories about my mother," she said. "Mom wouldn't have liked that, though. She always believed we're all capable of living our own stories, and nothing else can compare to that. So I will leave you with this: thank you."

5

Amid the babble of music and conversation that followed the memorial, Natalie was swept up in a wave along with everyone else. At the catered reception, she was buoyed by the energy of the mourners. She rode that wave, even though she knew that its power came from the deepest sadness. She let it catch her, pulling her along like a leaf dropped into a swift river current.

At the end of the day, the energy dwindled. People promised to stay in touch—a promise she doubted. They urged her to reach out if she needed anything— anything at all. Everyone went back to their own lives, their work and their worries, their families and friends. When they walked into their homes or offices or boarded a plane or train, they returned to the same world they had left.

For Natalie, this was not the case. For her, nothing would ever be the same. She now knew that the aftermath of acute and sudden grief was different, a horrible realm she'd never explored, like an unread book on the shelf. When she stepped into the shop that evening, she felt an emptiness so vast that she almost couldn't breathe. Everything had drained out of her.

"It's exhausting, isn't it?" asked Grandy. "A sadness like this. It's physically exhausting."

"You're right," she said, watching him through the dim security lights of the shop. "Let's both turn in early."

As he made his way down the hall, he seemed diminished. They had not yet talked about what would happen now that Blythe was gone. Natalie knew it was going to be a difficult, painful conversation about decisions they weren't ready to make.

After a few minutes, she tapped at his door and stepped into the room. He was in his flannel pajamas with the piped edges and a pair of old leather scuffs. There were pills and a glass of water on the nightstand along with a stack of books. In the corner, the old iron radiator served as a shelf for the collection of literature and keepsakes from the ceremony.

"Can I get you anything?" she asked.

He sat on the bed. "No, thank you."

She wished there were something she could say to comfort him, but she couldn't think of a single thing. "I'll be upstairs," she said. "Holler if you need anything at all."

Leaning down, she kissed him on the forehead, then lingered in the doorway as he sat motionless for a moment. Then he cupped his face in his hands and his shoulders shook. She had an urge to go to him, but there was something private and unreachable about him. A moment later, he carefully took out his hearing aids and set them in a box on the nightstand.

Natalie quietly left the room. She returned to the shop, took down the placard announcing the memorial, and put it in the recycle bin. The mounds of flowers and tributes around the door could be dealt with in the morning.

As she turned to make her way up the hall stairs to the apartment, a knock at the door startled her. Someone else offering condolences? Another vegan quinoa casserole or batch of cookies?

Glare from the inside lights obscured the visitor. He

or she was in the main entrance to the shop rather than the residential entryway next door.

She unlocked the door and came face-to-face with a person she scarcely recognized. Dean Fogarty was older now, but still tall and well-built, his blond hair faded though styled with an expensive-looking cut. Back in the day, when Natalie's mother had been swept into an illicit romance with this man, he must have been quite a looker.

"Natalie," he said. "I read about Blythe in the *Examiner*. I'm . . . what a shock. I'm so sorry."

She wanted to be alone with her heavy, exhausting sadness. No, she wanted her mother. And that made her even sadder. With a vague gesture, she invited her father in.

They didn't hug or shake hands or touch other than with a glance. Their status was too undefined for anything more. When she was a little girl, Dean had paid her the occasional visit, but even then, it felt awkward, as if they were strangers forced together in a too-crowded space.

"Do you want to sit?" She indicated the shop's coffee nook.

"Thank you."

She took the cover off a plastic dish. "Help yourself to cookies. People have been bringing food over for days."

"How are you doing?" he asked.

She'd been in a fog since the moment she learned of the crash. But he was not the person to share her burdens with. "Still in shock," she said. "I'm trying to focus on my grandfather now."

"I'm glad you and Andrew have each other. I've never been there for you and your mother. I wish I had been. You both deserved better."

Natalie hesitated. *Now?* she thought. *You want to unburden yourself now? Oh, dude . . .*

"Mom did," Natalie agreed.

"I'll always regret that I never found a way to have you in my life," he said.

"Yeah, kind of hard when you have a wife and three kids at home."

He winced. "I was so fucking stupid. I have so many damn regrets." He paused, then asked, "Did she . . . did Blythe ever speak of me?"

"Let's not do this," Natalie said. "Let's not make this all about you. You could have asked Mom anytime in the past three decades. What do you suppose she would have said—that you're the guy who banged her and gaslighted her about wanting to spend the rest of your life with her? She didn't pine for you, Dean." Guys wanted to imagine their exes pining for them.

She studied his face, still aging-movie-star handsome. Begging for absolution. Yearning to believe he had not done the damage they both knew he'd caused. Natalie was too exhausted to summon bitterness now. "Look, if you're here for some kind of redemption, it's not mine to give. Mom found her happiness. She loved the store, and judging by the turnout at her memorial, she was surrounded by friends."

"She was a fantastic person, and I know she was a great mother to you." He flexed and unflexed his hands. Looked around the shop at all the trinkets and tributes people had left.

Natalie sensed that he wanted to talk more. She didn't. "It's been a long day," she said.

He took the hint and got up. "Could we . . . maybe get coffee sometime?"

"I've got a lot on my plate," she said.

"I get it. Take care, Natalie," he said.

"I will."

She stood motionless as he let himself out, disappearing into the shadows. The man was walking, talking proof that relationships were nothing but uncertainty. The only thing certain about a relationship was that it would end. Could be that was the reason her mother never bothered getting into one in the first place.

Natalie's earliest memory of Dean Fogarty was just after she had turned five. Her mother had said a man named Dean was coming to meet her. Dean was her father.

"Is he coming to live with us?" Natalie had asked.

"*No.* God, no. You don't have to meet him, baby. Only if you want to."

Natalie had shrugged, unsure of what she wanted, but curious. So she said okay. He had a smiling mouth with very white teeth, and serious eyes that didn't smile at all. He brought her a birthday gift bag, even though her birthday had been the week before. She had accepted it with a bashful *thank you.* He and her mom exchanged tensely murmured words, and he'd thrust something into her hand. After he'd left, she looked at her mother and saw that she was wiping away tears. "Why are you crying?" she asked. It frightened her to see her mother cry.

"I had such a lovely father, growing up. I wish you had a father like Grandy."

"I do have Grandy. I don't want Dean to come back. He makes you sad."

"No, baby, he doesn't. I just want to make sure I'm enough for you."

You were enough, Mom, she thought now. *I hope you knew that. I hope I was enough for you.*

A few years after that visit, she'd joined the Little Kickers Soccer League. At the first practice, she'd seen Dean Fogarty again. He was, to her horror, one of the coach's helpers, and his son was on the team. Getting through that first practice was agony, and when she got home, she told her mother she was never going back.

"I don't like seeing him with his real kid," she explained.

"You're a real kid," her mother had said.

"It's not the same," Natalie said.

Blythe had gathered her into a hug and whispered, "It's not the same. It's better. It's better with just the two of us."

"Does his other family know about us?"

"Do you want them to?"

"No!"

She never went back to the soccer league. Through the years, Dean came with gifts and a smile that was soft with regret, and eyes hungry with wishes, like the shop cat just before feeding time. Natalie tried to think of him as something more than a benign stranger, a customer stopping in for the latest bestseller, but she was never able to picture him as her dad.

Now the scent of flowers hung as heavy as old remembrances in the air. Natalie massaged the back of her neck, aching with sadness and fatigue. She dimmed the shop lights and set the security system. There were two entrances to the building: the grand foyer leading to the shop, and a street-level private door where the mail came in, with a stairway leading to the apartment where she'd lived as a girl.

Natalie used to envy her friends who lived in actual houses with big yards and swing sets and garages filled with scooters and bikes. Now that San Francisco's real estate market had exploded in value, this ramshackle old structure was probably one of the most desired addresses in the neighborhood. With its historic charm and detail, the Sunrose Building, as it was called, was undoubtedly candy corn for real estate developers. The name of the building apparently came from a detail at the roofline—a winking sun. The bookstore's sign and logo incorporated the image. The shop's signature bookmark, printed on the old letterpress and given out with every purchase, bore the image with the slogan *An Eye for Good Books.*

In the kitchen, Natalie tidied up, putting away as much as she could of the food people had dropped off, and packing up the rest to give to a food bank. She understood why people brought food to the grieving, but she and Grandy couldn't possibly use it all.

The finality of her mother's death was still sinking in, slowly and painfully. She wandered through the labyrinth of memories. The small apartment was filled with a pleasant sort of clutter—interesting objects and of course books, furniture that had been in the family for generations, little mending projects piled here and there. It was as if Blythe had just stepped out for a moment and would return shortly. Natalie noticed an unwashed teacup in the sink, a meandering grocery list, laundry waiting to be folded and put away.

The upper apartment featured graceful old-world details. There was an unusual high-peaked ceiling under the front gable, a spot where Natalie used to lie on the antique chaise, watching the sun rise over the park. The old arched windows, hardwood floors, Gothic flourishes, and marble fireplace harkened back to the building's origins—a saloon downstairs, and a rather high-end brothel up, with a big old-fashioned bathroom at the end.

Natalie's mother had always had a knack for putting together lovely fabrics and textures, giving the place a bohemian vibe. The imperfect charm of the apartment had been lost on Natalie when she was young, but now she appreciated her mother's taste and flair. The clutter—maybe not so much. She tamped down a twinge of annoyance. She did not want to feel annoyed at her mother.

When she'd rushed to the city after getting the news of the plane crash, Natalie had slept in the room she'd occupied all through her childhood, a tiny space that used to feel cozy. Since she'd left home the room had become a repository of things her mother didn't want to bother with. The twin bed was piled with luggage that never saw any use. Her high school collection of CDs and books still occupied a shelf just as she'd left it. She had pushed aside some of the clutter and slept— badly—in her old bed.

Last week, she had not dared to venture into her mother's room. She'd kept the door shut, fearful of the emotional storm it would cause when opened. To- night, though, she didn't feel like wading through the effluvia stacked in her old room. Now she was Goldi- locks choosing a bed. Grandy's former room was cluttered with plastic hospital bins and file folders of paperwork. A framed photo of May Lin hung on the wall.

She stepped into her mother's room and nearly drowned.

The entire space was a frieze of her mother's world.

Of a moment in time. A life interrupted. The room was waiting for its occupant to return, slip on her night-gown and scuffs, settle in with her crossword and her novel. Mom was so present here, from the family pictures on the wall to the china dish of mismatched earrings on the bureau. She was always losing earrings.

Her nightgown hung on a hook on the back of the door. The *San Francisco Examiner*, her lifelong favorite paper, lay on the nightstand, folded open to the crossword puzzle, which was only about half done.

Her mom's nightly ritual was to do the puzzle, then read herself to sleep. When Natalie was little, Mom used to let her help. Now she immediately saw the answer to 23 across: carrion bird, four letters ending in *s*—*ibis*. And 39 down: graceful, three blanks followed by -*some*. *Lissome*. She almost reflexively filled them in.

A small stack of books and a pair of reading glasses were in their usual spot on the nightstand. Natalie picked up the top book. *Acts of Light*. Publisher's Advance Reading Copy—Not for Sale. Mom loved her sneak preview books from publishers, and longtime sales reps had come to value her opinion. There was a handwritten note from the author on the title page, thanking Blythe for being a good steward of books and readers.

Natalie opened to the marked page. A shiver went

through her. Was this the last thing her mother had read?

She started reading at the bookmarked page: *"The first person through the wall always gets hurt,"* said *Finn.* All right, who was Finn, and what did he know of walls? For a few blessed moments, she sank into the story and was able to recapture the vicarious pleasure of losing herself in a good book.

Then the inevitable wave of sadness crept in. Her mother would never finish reading this very good book, nor the others stacked around the room, waiting to be cracked open by an eager mind. Natalie set the volume aside, overcome by endless ripples of grief and nostalgia. Had her mother been happy, as Natalie had assured Dean she'd been? Had Natalie been part of that happiness?

She wanted to cry some more, but she was worn out from crying. It was late and she needed to sleep.

She got up and slipped into a nightgown from her suitcase, then went to wash her face and brush her teeth. The bathroom was another still life—big porcelain sink, enormous claw-footed tub. There was some dampness on the floor, which concerned her. As did the rusty hinges and rattling windowpanes, buzzing light fixtures, and probably a host of other undiscovered issues. The old building was in constant need of repair.

Not tonight, though.

Soaps and cosmetics littered the countertop, the scents evoking sweet and painful memories. Propped on the tub rack was a dog-eared book about dealing with dementia. The pages were steam curled, with highlighted passages. *Oh, Mom. Why didn't you tell me more about Grandy's condition?*

The medicine cabinet contained some surprises. Along with the face creams and lip balms, there were prescription bottles for antianxiety medication and another for a sleep aid. *Zero refills remaining.*

"Anxiety? Really? I wish you'd told me," she said to her mom in the mirror. "You should've said something. I thought we told each other everything."

She brushed her teeth and got into her mother's bed. It still had the mom smell, familiar and evocative of the days of her childhood, when she used to skitter into the room in the morning and jump in bed for a snuggle. Then she reopened the novel on the nightstand. She and her mother used to play book games. "The first sentence on page seventy-two dictates your plan for the next day. Or your deepest secret."

Page 72 of the current book said, *The photographer's*

darkroom was the only place she could clearly see, the place where she felt most competent and in control.

After reading for a couple of hours, Natalie set aside the book and went to the medicine cabinet. One tablet as needed for insomnia.

Thanks, Mom.

There were decisions to be made. That was Natalie's first thought after dragging herself up from the depths of Ambien-induced slumber. Then, of course, fresh grief came rushing in like the morning tide, followed by the dangerous undertow of regret, sneaking in to snatch her out to sea and drown her. She wished she could rewind her life to the moment she'd asked her mother to come up to Archangel. Why, oh why had she invited her mom to the stupid company party?

She got up and took a bath, sinking into a raft of lavender-scented bubbles. She read bits of the dementia book, which made her feel frightened and overwhelmed. Then she dressed and went downstairs to check on her grandfather. He was sound asleep, his hearing aids in a cup on his nightstand. She tiptoed out and turned on the espresso machine in the shop's coffee cubby. When she was little, that had been her job. To get dressed quickly and run downstairs and turn on the coffee machine so the water would heat up to

195°F, the optimal temperature for making a perfect morning shot. Regular customers had their own personalized mugs on a rack above the espresso machine.

The soft hiss of the machine, the droning grind of the beans in the mill, the rich, fecund aroma of coffee evoked all the mornings of her childhood. Now the rattle of the espresso machine was a lonely sound. It would not summon her yawning mother from upstairs. There would be no morning glory muffin from the bakery across the way and no joint perusal of the *Examiner*.

Natalie drew a shot, using a promotional mug from some publisher or other that directed her to find her dreams. The book being promoted was called *Swim Story*, with the slogan *Find Your Lane. Find Your Dream.*

She made herself a café cortado, the powerful creamy coffee served in Spain. She had read about this style of coffee in a book and had taught herself to make one perfectly. One day, she thought, she'd like to go to Spain. She'd had the chance to study there during her college semester abroad—Spain had been one of the most enticing options. It would have been lovely to enjoy the soft breezes of Málaga and the glorious Moorish artifacts of Granada. Half a year in Spain had not been practical, though. It was expensive and didn't offer the technical classes she needed. Instead, she chose Shanghai for her semester abroad. It was tailor-made for her degree program. Wending her way through smog and traffic each day, she had learned digital management from the culture that had invented it. Her homestay had been with a family that specialized in antiquities. It had been the greatest adventure of her life, whetting her appetite to do more. But work came first, always. Spain would have to wait.

Still, she could make coffee like the Spanish did.

In the midst of the silence, she heard a soft mew. "Sylvia," she said, feeling a rush of relief. "There you are. Cleo said you'd disappeared." The dainty calico cat was named after Sylvia Beach—not Sylvia Plath, her mom used to insist. Sylvia Beach had had a Paris salon and bookstore—and presumably no mental health issues.

Natalie sat at one of the three small café tables. Sylvia poured herself down from the windowsill and onto the chair across from Natalie.

She gazed into the cat's topaz eyes. "Hello, gorgeous. What's going to become of you now? Will Grandy look after you?" She reached across the table to pet Sylvia. The moment her hand brushed the chinchilla-soft fur, Sylvia scratched her, a clawed lightning bolt shooting out of nowhere. "Hey!" Natalie drew back her hand, examining the broken skin. "What was that for?" She went to the sink and washed the parallel scratches. "Oh, that's right. You're a cat."

Returning to the table, she spooned up a bit of the warm foam from her cortado and held it out for the cat to lick. "I'm glad she had you. You were with her every day. You were good company, I suppose. Or did you scratch her, too? I hope you know better than to harass the customers."

The shop looked the same as it always had. Mom never liked change. Floor-to-ceiling shelves accessed by rolling ladders with brass fittings. Display tables featuring the latest bestsellers. The children's section with a rug and beanbag chairs. Rare books in display cases. Blythe's favorite shelf near the coffee area. She'd labeled it W.O.W. (WORDS OF WISDOM) and it was stocked with her perennial favorites with bookmarked passages.

Natalie used to love browsing that shelf. A book would never betray you or change its mind or make you feel stupid. She took down *The Once and Future King* and found a marked passage: *"The best thing for being sad," replied Merlyn, beginning to puff and blow, "is to learn something. That is the only thing that never fails."*

"There you have it," Natalie said to the cat. "My plan for the day."

The aftermath of unexpected death was a lengthy and complicated ordeal. She opened her laptop and clicked on the document she had started—a list of everything that had to be done. She hadn't known what to call it, so she'd titled the document "Now What."

Gazing at the cat, she added it to the list. Another detail to attend to. What would become of the shop without her mom? Could Natalie count on Grandy to take care of Sylvia? Fill her water bowl? Post her picture on Instagram for all the world to see? What if he forgot to feed her? She added a question mark to the intimidatingly growing list of things she had to deal with.

She gave the cat some kibble, and Sylvia took a few dainty bites, then slipped out through the cat door to the back garden.

A fresh eddy of sadness washed over Natalie, and she shuddered with emotional pain. When would the tears stop? When would the pain subside? It wasn't like a headache or illness that could be cured by swallowing a pill. No, this ache of missing and regret felt like a constant, incurable condition.

In the back office behind the sales counter, she switched on her mother's laptop. This, she knew, was going to add to her pain, but there was no avoiding it.

She had to access her mother's digital life. Natalie was supposed to be good at that—putting things in order.

The opening screen featured a picture of Sylvia preening herself in the shop window, and Good Morning, Blythe. The required passwords and PIN codes were on a handwritten list under her desk blotter. Mom claimed she was an identity thief's dream, because she always used the same codes and never changed them. She used to say it was because she had nothing to hide and couldn't remember codes and passwords anyway.

Culling through her mother's private digital life felt strange and intrusive, and Natalie knew she was only at the beginning of the ordeal. When someone left without warning, there was work to be done.

Her mother probably had a will somewhere. Natalie had a look through the computer files, trying to figure out where to dig in first.

She opened a folder labeled THE LOST AND FOUND BOOKSHOP: A _____.

What had her mother meant to put in the blank space?

She found scan after scan of notes in her mother's handwriting as well as what appeared to be age-yellowed documents. There was a ship's manifest from 1888 with the name Colleen O'Rourke highlighted, and muster rolls from something labeled "Astor Battery" with the name Julio Harper marked. Another file contained a wealth of information about William Randolph Hearst.

There was also a printed report from one of those mail-away DNA tests. She was fascinated by the results. Predictably, her mother was of mostly Anglo-European descent. But the results also showed she was 7 percent Spanish; 12 percent African. Seriously?

Natalie gazed at her face in the wavy glass of the old barrister cabinet behind the counter. Dark curly hair like her mother's. Pale skin and brown eyes—traits she shared with the man who had fathered her. What did the 12 percent mean? How did one determine one's ethnicity? Who were her ancestors?

Oftentimes throughout her life, she'd felt like a stranger to herself. Had Mom felt the same way? Could this be the reason? Natalie burned with frustration over the questions she would never be able to ask her mother—*What were you looking for? And why didn't you share it with me?*

She checked the banking and credit card accounts and shuddered with apprehension. There were enormous bills and care fees related to Grandy's accident and broken hip—including many costs not covered by Medicare. Scariest of all—liens from the city, county, and state for unpaid taxes. Her mother's own business expenses, taxes and fees, the utilities and upkeep on the shop. The amount took Natalie's breath away. If the figures were accurate, her mom—and the shop— were drowning in debt and unpaid bills and had been for quite some time.

She found more bad news stuffed into a ripped envelope and tucked out of sight—a notice of foreclosure. From what she could piece together, a large property equity loan from a private lender had been taken out in Grandy's name, and they were in default.

A snap of anger went off in Natalie. *Really, Mom? Really?*

It wasn't something to deal with right now, thought Natalie. Not this precise moment. But the truth stared her in the face. The shop and all its contents would need to be sold, sooner rather than later.

She put away her coffee cup and checked the time. She and Cleo and Bertie planned to open the shop today. For the time being, in honor of her mother's life's work, they would carry on. Business as fucking usual.

Natalie knew how to open, though she hadn't done so since her college years. The morning routine was both familiar and mournful. Turning on the shop lights, she passed by shelves and table displays her mother had arranged. There were signs hand-lettered by Blythe, highlighting topics and titles of interest. In the café area, her mother had designated the week's five-dollar special—a morning glory muffin and autumn-spiced latte. Natalie checked the supplies and made a note to get the muffins from the bakery across the way.

Last, she switched on the sign—a neon of an open book—and went behind the counter. The stool by the register had been her mother's perch for the past thirtysomething years. Her mom was left-handed, so Natalie had to move the mug full of pens, the mouse and keyboard.

Taking her place on the stool, she was flooded with anxiety. Judging by the contents of her mom's medicine cabinet, her mother had suffered from unspoken worries of her own. Had she fretted about the finances? Had she ever made a plan? Or had she believed that, like the denouement of a favorite novel, everything would work out in the end?

I don't want to be mad at you, thought Natalie. Yet there was no mistaking the burn of frustration trying to make its way through her.

Mom used say, "To find out who you are, remember who you used to be."

Deep breath. Close your eyes. Try not to cry. Natalie opened her heart to her mother, remembering when and how she'd come to the realization that she was a misfit.

Each day after school, Natalie took the city bus home, jumping off at the corner of Perdita and Encontra Streets and running half a block down to the bookstore. The grand entryway had a heavy glass door framed by lacquered black-painted woodwork, and a honeycomb pattern of black-and-white tile on the floor of the foyer.

She burst inside, jangling the bell over the door. Her mother was at the counter, perched on a tall swivel stool, a book open in front of her, a pretty scarf around her head.

"Mama, are we poor?" Natalie asked, shrugging out of her backpack.

"No," said her mother offhandedly, scarcely glancing up. "Why do you ask?"

"Kayla Cramer says we're poor. She called me a bad name—said I was a mongrel."

Her mother's lips twitched a bit. As she often did, she took *To Kill a Mockingbird* from her w.o.w. shelf. "'It's never an insult to be called what somebody thinks is a bad name. It just shows you how poor that person is, it doesn't hurt you.'"

"She's not poor," Natalie insisted. "We are. Kayla

says that's why we never go on vacation even when school is out."

"We go on a grand adventure every time we open a book." Mom handed her a padded envelope from a pile of mail on the counter. "The new Judy Blume book just came in from the publisher, and you can have the first copy."

Natalie eagerly snatched it up. "I can't wait to read it," she declared. "But reading a book is not the same as a vacation, and you know it."

"If you're talking about flying to Hawaii or Paris, then you're right. But just because we can't afford fancy trips doesn't make us poor. Do you have homework?"

"I had math, but I did it during recess."

"You're supposed to play during recess."

"I don't like playing with kids who call me poor."

Mom quirked her brow. "I don't blame you. I wouldn't want that, either. I'm glad your homework is done. We've got plans for tonight."

"Really? What plans?"

Mom grinned at her. "We're going to China. How's that for travel?" She motioned Natalie to the office cubby in the stockroom and grabbed a granola bar from a box on the shelf. "May Lin's taking us to Heavenly Days."

Their favorite restaurant in all Chinatown. "Can I get the Warrior Bowl?"

"Sure." Her mother tucked a stray lock of hair behind her ear. "Listen, we have our health, and a roof over our heads, food to eat, and books to read. We're doing okay, kiddo."

Natalie felt deflated by her mother's logic. It was the kind of thing you couldn't argue with or if you tried, you'd seem silly. "Where's Grandy?" she asked.

"In the basement, puttering around," Mom said. "Always looking for his father's hidden treasure."

It was a family joke that Grandy's father, old Julius Harper, believed there was treasure in the Sunrose Building. According to Grandy, Julius's mother had hidden something, and then she'd died in the 1906 earthquake and Julius went to an orphanage and the treasure was lost forever. Grandy had grown up hearing stories about it, but they were just that—stories. Not real like her friends' vacation trips to places like Manhattan and Mexico.

The bell jingled, and Mom went quickly to the front. "Hi there. Can I help you?"

The customer was a guy with a ponytail and a concert T-shirt. In the olden days, Grandy would have called him a hippie. "Thanks. Taking a look around," he said. "I just finished *The Things They Carried*, and my brain needs to take a breather."

"I hear you," Mom agreed. "It's like wading through a maze. Maybe you'd like a more straightforward narrative? Here's our fiction table."

"Anything you'd recommend?" the guy asked.

"All of them," she said. "Otherwise they wouldn't be on my table. If you like cool, funny entertainment, you might like this one. It's a first novel by a local author." She handed him a copy of *Practical Demonkeeping*. "A very different kind of buddy novel. I thought it was hilarious."

"You're reading me like a book." The guy shook his head as if embarrassed by his own lame joke. Then he looked over at Blythe. Natalie saw his gaze move swiftly over her mother's red V-neck sweater and short skirt. "How can you tell that's exactly what would make me happy?" he asked.

Oh boy. He was flirting. Guys did that a lot with her mom. She was super pretty, and Natalie knew it wasn't only because Mom was her mom and all kids thought their moms were pretty. Even her snottiest friends like Kayla said Blythe looked like a model. Like Julia Roberts. Plus, her mom had a knack for dressing cool and being social—she could talk to anyone and make them like her.

Also, she had a superpower, which was on full display right now. She had the ability to see a person for the first time and almost instantly know what book to recommend. She was really smart and had also read every book ever written, or so it seemed to Natalie. She could talk to high school kids about *Ivanhoe* and *Silas Marner.* She ran a mystery discussion group. She could tell people the exact day the new Mary Higgins Clark novel would come out. She knew which kids would only ever read Goosebumps books, no matter what, and she knew which kids would try something else, like Edward Eager or Philip Pullman.

Sometimes people didn't know anything about the book they were searching for except "It's blue with gold page edges" and her mom would somehow figure it out.

What Mom wasn't so good at was understanding that sometimes Natalie wished they lived in a real house like a regular family.

The shop bell jangled Natalie to the present. With her mother gone, the past felt different in ways she hadn't expected.

"Morning, guys," she said, getting up to give Cleo and Bertie brief hugs. She felt them both scrutinizing her and waved off their concern.

"Is your grandfather up?" asked Cleo, taking their coats to the back office.

"Not yet," Natalie said.

"How's he doing?"

Natalie flashed on the moment she'd told him good night. The sadness in his eyes. "He was really worn out last night. I'll go check on him in a bit."

Bertie gave her a long look. "You're a wreck."

"Tell me something I don't know." Natalie spread some papers on the table. "I've been going through Mom's files. I actually did find her will." It wasn't much of a will, as far as she could tell. It had been drawn up from a boilerplate the year Natalie was born. According to the document, Grandy was her designated guardian. "It hasn't been updated since she signed it, but I suppose it's valid. I'm going to have to set up a meeting with a lawyer to figure out what it all means." A lawyer. What lawyer? She didn't have one. As far as she knew, neither did her mother.

Cleo went over the updated bookkeeping files, which only confirmed what Natalie already knew. "I wish we had better news, but your mom was struggling."

Natalie nodded. "She was always struggling. I didn't realize how much, though. She never told me she was covering so many of Grandy's expenses after his broken hip. Unless there's some secret source of El Dorado, I'm afraid we'll have to close the shop and sell everything. Liquidate the inventory and put the building on the market." A frisson of dread went through her. "I'll try to explain it to Grandy."

Cleo and Bertie exchanged a look.

"There's so much to sort out," she conceded. "I can stay for a day or two, but I'm going to need to get back to Archangel. Will you be able to handle things for the time being?"

"Of course," Cleo said.

"Grandy, too? He tells me he's fine on his own." Natalie looked from one to the other. "What do you think?"

"He does all right in the new downstairs apartment. Your mom was planning to do more work on the place—fix the back railing, install grab bars in the bathroom, that sort of thing. He usually gets dinner from the corner deli and they deliver it. He and Charlie still hang out together almost every day, same as they've always done."

"I'm nervous about telling him we have to close the shop," Natalie confessed. "It's going to be the hardest conversation of my life. How on earth will I explain it?"

"How about you make a plan and then tell him?" Bertie suggested. "You don't have to do it all today."

She sent him a wavering smile. "Thanks. You're right. So . . . Business as usual today? How do we even do that?" Her chest felt tight with apprehension and grief.

A moment later, the bell over the door sounded off again, and in bounced a little girl, bright-eyed and fresh-faced. Yellow straw braids, big blue eyes. The first customer of the day.

Cleo gave her a nudge. "You just do it," she whispered.

Cleo and Bertie slipped away to the back office, leaving Natalie at the counter. Although she'd stood in this spot many times, having helped at the shop all through high school and every summer in college, the moment felt surreal, as if she'd been unstuck in time. Everyone—her mother and Grandy included—had assumed she would join the Lost and Found Bookshop team after college. It had been a difficult conversation, telling them she was taking a different path.

"I thought you loved the shop," her mother had said.

"I do. But, Mom, I don't love the struggle."

Her mother had looked genuinely mystified. "The struggle? Oh, the administrative chores, you mean. It's not so bad. You get used to it."

"You're amazing," Natalie had told her. "I'll never

be as amazing as you. I'm not cut out for it. I'm more the salary-and-benefits type."

"You might change your mind," her mother had said, gesturing around the shop with its lofty hammered tin ceilings and ancient fixtures. "This is all such a grand adventure."

There were times, Natalie conceded, when digital inventory work had threatened to destroy her soul. It was the opposite of a grand adventure. But then she would remind herself about the steady salary, the benefits and pension plan, and decide it was all worthwhile. Stability had its price.

"You pay yourself a smaller salary than you pay the employees," she had once pointed out to her mother. "Your late notices are getting late notices. You've never taken a vacation. Never bought yourself something nice. Your life is all about keeping the shop running."

"You say that like it's a bad thing."

"It's not, Mom. But it's not *my* thing."

The little girl was looking around so eagerly that Natalie was able to summon her first genuine smile since the accident. "Hi there," she said. "Can I help you?"

The girl tilted her head to one side, ropy braids following the movement. She wore jeans and high-top sneakers, and a buffalo plaid shirt with the sleeves rolled up. One elbow bore the faint outline of a recently removed Band-Aid. She was unself-consciously charming, with a crooked smile, a light sprinkling of freckles across her nose and cheeks, skinny legs, and one missing front tooth.

"My mom gave me a gift card for being good at the dentist," she said. "That's why I'm not in school this morning, because I had the dentist. I got a filling, see?" She opened wide and tilted back her head, hooking a finger into her mouth and pulling it to one side.

"Oh, gosh," Natalie said. "Does it hurt?"

"Nope. The Novocain shot did, though." She shuddered.

That explained the crooked smile. "The shot is always the worst."

"And then it sounded like they put a whistle in my mouth." She emulated the sound, her voice making a crescendo.

Natalie felt the first nudge of humor in days. "No wonder you got a gift card. That was nice of your mom."

"Yep." The girl showed it to her. The card had a message on the back. *Good job, Dorothy! Love, Mommy.*

"Dorothy's a cute name. One of the all-time best characters ever is Dorothy Gale. From the *Wizard of Oz* books."

"My dad says that's why he named me Dorothy. He read the first book to me, even the scary bits."

"That's impressive. Are you looking for a book in particular?"

"Yes," she declared, making her way to the children's section. "I know how to find it, too—in the Ds in fiction."

The children's section was a nook in the back corner of the shop, defined by a braided oval rug, colorful pillows, and beanbag chairs, surrounded by shelves and display racks. The old Kennedy rocker was set up for story time next to an easel with the times listed.

The girl plopped down on a throw pillow and made a serious study of the middle-grade readers. She looked young for middle grade, but something about her bright-eyed expression suggested she was an early reader, like Natalie had been. The girl ran her finger along an upper shelf, which contained multiple copies of titles by one particular author.

"Trevor Dashwood," Natalie said, joining the girl in the corner. The man had become a household name in the past few years—that much she knew. Her mother had said he'd burst onto the publishing scene with a series of children's books that sold in the millions.

Dorothy gazed up at her with bright eyes. "He's my favorite in all the world."

"I hear he's very popular, but I've never read his books."

Dorothy gasped. "He's the best! I've read all his books at least three times." Her blue eyes brightened as she selected a book from the shelf. "This one!" She held it up in triumph. "I checked this out from the library and kept it until it was overdue, and now I want my own copy."

Watching the eager child, Natalie had a strange sense of déjà vu. She herself had spent hours in that spot, browsing through books and sometimes agonizing about what to pick. Like an ephemeral breeze, she felt the presence of her mother, who never influenced her choices. *Sometimes you have to let the right book find you*, Mom used to say.

"What do you love about these books?" Natalie asked.

"Everything! See, they're called the *Flip Side Stories* because watch." Dorothy demonstrated. The front of the book became the back and vice versa. "There are actually two stories in every book. It's the same story, only told from two different characters. You read one, and then you flip it over and it tells the other side of the story."

The titles were simple and straightforward—*Cat and Mouse. Rich Kid, Poor Kid. Class Clown, Class Brain. Geek and Jock.*

"Well, that's ingenious," Natalie said. "I can see why you like these books. I'll have to read some of them right away."

"You should! I bet you'd like *Jack and the Giant.*" Dorothy handed her a copy. "Everybody thinks the giant is bad, but when you read what he's really like—well, I won't spoil it for you."

Natalie opened the book, and her gaze fell on the inner flap of the cover, which featured the author's photo. Trevor Dashwood had perfectly sculpted cheekbones, a glorious tousle of hair, a crisp white shirt, and an intriguing, slightly mischievous grin. Either he was the best-looking author she'd ever seen, or this picture was his greatest work of fiction.

His brief bio offered tantalizing details—homeschooled in Northern California, attended Oxford University through a program for exceptionally creative students, avid book collector, founder of a nonprofit fund to help children dealing with addicted parents, winner of the Prix de la Croix in France. The bio concluded, "Mr. Dashwood lives on the California coast near San Francisco."

"I'll start tonight," Natalie said. "He sounds like a wonderful person."

Dorothy hugged *Big Sister, Little Sister* to her chest. "I'm getting this one." She jumped up and went to the counter.

"Are you a big sister? Or a little sister?"

"Nope," said Dorothy. "But maybe soon."

"You'll still have enough left on the gift card to get something else if you want," Natalie told her after showing her the total.

"Oh, good! Sometimes I read a book too fast and then I panic because I need another one right away."

"I can relate," said Natalie. "Would you like a suggestion?"

"Sure!"

Natalie went back to the children's nook and selected a book her mother had specially highlighted with a handwritten card. "*Wedgie and Gizmo*," Natalie said. "I like their names."

"Me too." Dorothy studied the bright, whimsical cover. "It looks really good. Do I have enough to get this one, too?"

"I think you're in luck." Natalie rang up the purchase, and for a moment, it was like old times. A delightful customer, delighted with her purchases. A sale completed. Natalie took extra care, putting the little girl's books in a bag, adding a bit of swag—a bookmark with the shop's slogan and a pin that said *Read All Night*.

"Here you go," Natalie said. "You're all set."

"Thank you."

Grandy came into the shop from the back. He had his cane in one hand and a yellow writing pad in the other. "Is that Dorothy I hear?" he asked.

"Hiya, Mr. Harper!" She favored him with her gap-toothed grin. She was like a cartoon character come to life.

Natalie was gratified by the delighted expression on her grandfather's face. "You two know each other, then."

"Dorothy's a regular," said Grandy. He indicated the writing pad. "Blythe and I have been working on the story of the bookstore, and we must remember to mention how important our young customers are."

Natalie felt a sinking sense of guilt. She was going to have to spoil the ending of that story. Soon, probably.

Dorothy held up her bag. "I got two books today."

"Lucky you. And look what I found." He rummaged

in the pocket of his trousers and pulled out a handful of round glass-topped typewriter keys.

She peered at them. "Cool."

"Here, take the D and the G—your initials."

Natalie was encouraged that Grandy had recognized the kid, even knew her initials. Her mom had said the dementia seemed to ebb and flow, unpredictable and arbitrary. Today might be a good day. She hoped it was.

"Really? Thanks!"

"I have plenty left over from my old typewriter shop," Grandy told her. "That's what this place was before it was a bookshop. I thought it would always be a typewriter shop, but the business went into decline. That means it was failing because of the modern world."

"Good thing you turned it into a bookstore," Dorothy said.

He nodded. "Blythe and I started it with a treasure we discovered in the basement—a box of antique books. And that was how the Lost and Found Bookshop got its start." His brow furrowed. "The business is in trouble again because of the modern world. People are watching nonsense on their phones and ordering books online. If that keeps up, places like this might cease to exist."

Apparently, he did have some understanding of the difficulties her mother had been having.

Dorothy's face drained of color. "No," she said. "Bookstores are magic."

"I must write that down." Grandy shuffled to the small desk behind the counter. "We can all use a bit of magic. Enjoy those books, young lady."

"I will."

"Is someone picking you up?" Natalie asked her. "Your mom, or . . . ?"

"I have to walk to my mom's office on the corner. She works at Century Financial Services."

"All right. I hope you come back soon."

"Okeydokey. Bye!" The girl left with a spring in her step.

After she was gone, a quiet air settled over the shop. It was not a welcome quiet. Natalie wanted a bustle of readers coming and going. Things picked up around midday, starting with a panhandler who shuffled in with a tattered backpack and layers of unwashed clothes. He helped himself to a cookie from the café area, and Natalie didn't say anything. Then, to her surprise, he bought a used copy of *Bastard Out of Carolina*, meticulously counting out his cash from a threadbare billfold.

Several regular customers dropped by to offer condolences. A couple of them bought books.

"I'm sorry for your loss," said one woman, selecting
a vegan cookbook. "The bookstore won't be the same
without Blythe."

Natalie contemplated the mess her mother had left
behind. She liked to hope she would never be so ir-
responsible with her finances . . . yet her mom had
been happy, as far as Natalie could tell. She lived for
the shop, and although it had pounded her into debt,
she had been beloved and connected in ways that had
nothing to do with security.

Natalie wasn't sure she had the nerve to embrace
that kind of risk.

She nodded with a tremulous smile at the sympathetic woman. What Natalie didn't want to tell customers was something that was becoming increasingly,
depressingly clear. Without Blythe, the bookstore would
cease to exist at all.

6

"You can't sell the shop," the lawyer said. "Not the building or the business or its assets."

Natalie felt a twist in her gut as she stared across the table at Helena Hart, attorney-at-law. She was the only lawyer Natalie had been able to find online who was willing to work without being given a giant retainer fee up front. "I don't understand."

"It's not yours to sell."

"It's . . . That makes no sense. My mother left me everything, according to the will I found in her files."

"That's true," said the lawyer, "and the document you showed me is certainly valid. You're the only beneficiary named. But I'm sorry to say that, based on the records provided, the only thing your mother left to you were her personal effects . . . and her debt. A deceased person's debt can be recouped from their estate—assuming there's something of value in it— although you wouldn't be personally responsible for paying for it."

Natalie's stomach churned faster. The deeper she peered into her mother's records, the more little nightmares she discovered. The crushing debt included unpaid back taxes and bills, ignored notices, a scary balloon loan coming due. Her mother had borrowed from a private lending firm at an exorbitant rate. "I'm aware of the debt. There've been some major medical expenses related to my grandfather. The shop's operating expenses are steep. My mother wasn't a bad person," she told Helena. "She just wasn't focused on bookkeeping details. But the physical assets, the bookstore inventory, the building itself—"

"Those did not belong to your mother. Both are in the sole possession of your grandfather, Andrew Harper."

Natalie absorbed this information in silence. "I wasn't aware of that. It never occurred to me that . . . I guess I always assumed she was the owner of the business, if not the building."

Ms. Hart shook her head. "Not even a partner.

From my reading of the records, they never had a formal partnership agreement. Your grandfather is sole proprietor of the business."

"Wow. I had no idea."

"There's a bit of possibly good news. It's a listed building in a landmark district. It's in the National Register of Historic Places. That means it qualifies for a fifty percent reduction in property taxes. You can get further tax relief with a preservation easement, and a large rehabilitation tax credit for restoration work. All the work would have to be done by a qualified restoration specialist, of course."

"Thanks, I'll look into that, for sure. I'm not optimistic, though. 'Qualified restoration specialist' sounds like it comes with a high price tag." She thought about the creaky woodwork, the ancient roof, the clanking plumbing. The depleted bank accounts.

"Then perhaps your best option is to persuade your grandfather to sell."

"I'll have to explain all this to him. But if I know my grandfather, I know he would never agree to sell." Natalie was absolutely certain of this. "He's lived there all his life. Literally. His parents raised him in that very building, and he raised my mom there. It's the only home he's ever known."

"I see." The lawyer cleared her throat. "Not to be insensitive, but . . ."

When someone apologized in advance for being insensitive, it was certain that the next thing they'd say would be insensitive. Natalie braced herself. "But what?"

"How old is your grandfather? And how's his health?"

"He's seventy-eight. He fell and broke his hip a few months ago and had to move to the ground-floor apartment. He gets around with a cane."

"What about his mental health?" asked Ms. Hart.

Natalie paused, feeling in some way disloyal for discussing Grandy with this stern-faced stranger. "He's having memory issues. My mother said he's been different since the surgery. He's forgetful these days. He'll freely admit that—"

"Is there a diagnosis of dementia, then? Because that could actually work in your favor. Showing diminished mental capacity can be a way to take over guardianship and assume general durable power of attorney."

"Take over? It's a legal maneuver?"

"It's a process. A petition is filed, and the court renders a ruling."

"So I'd have to get a court order declaring my only

living relative, a man who has loved and supported me all my life, is incompetent. And then I take everything from him."

"You're assuming responsibility for his well-being and quality of life. Fair warning, though. The legal process of being appointed conservator is time-consuming, intricate, exhausting, and expensive."

"Oh, joy."

"There are good reasons to have a power of attorney. It will protect you and your grandfather both."

The lawyer was probably right. Natalie conceded that. But in the wake of Grandy's loss of his only child, she was not going to take one more thing from him. She stood up and gathered her papers. "Thank you for your time," she said.

She didn't know why she was thanking the woman. She was sure she would get a bill for it.

Natalie took her grandfather to Sunday brunch. It had been a tradition for as long as she could remember—Grandy, May Lin, Mom, and Natalie went to brunch together every Sunday, up until she moved to Archangel. If money was tight, it would be French toast and berry compote at Mama's on Washington Square. If they were feeling more flush, they'd take the Geary bus to the buffet at Cliff House, an imposing concrete behemoth perched above the Pacific between Ocean Beach and the old Sutro Baths.

She used to love going to Ocean Beach, not just for the scary, crashing waves and the throaty roar of the surf, but for the fun they had, rain or shine. In fine weather, she'd run along the beach, and she and her mom would kick off their shoes and wade in the chilly surf. In stormy weather, they'd sit by the massive fireplace, drinking cups and cups of tea while playing Wild Card Rummy. Natalie and May Lin always hoarded their wild cards, while her mom and Grandy played them immediately. Because, Mom would explain, if you don't play the wild card now, you might never get the chance.

They took a taxi to the Cliff House. Not because Natalie was feeling flush, but because she wanted a quiet, beautiful spot to have a serious conversation with her grandfather. Although the place had been updated, the views from the Terrace Room had not changed in decades.

Over fluffy omelets and brioche bread pudding smothered in blueberry compote, she laid out the situation for Andrew. He listened politely as she explained the back taxes, the overdue balloon payments, the looming bills, the needed repairs, and the dire cash-flow situation.

Grandy accepted a refill of his coffee with a smile at the waiter. When he picked up his mug, his hand trembled so much that the coffee spilled. Natalie mopped it up with a napkin. "Are you all right?"

He glowered at the half-full mug. "Hardly. Staying in business has always been a challenge. Even when I had the typewriter shop, there were challenges. My father used to tell me how he scrimped and saved for ten years and then launched his apothecary business at the height of the Great Depression. Somehow, he survived."

"I wish I remembered them better," she said. "Great-Grandpa Julius and Granny Inga. He used to give me root beer barrel candies, and Granny had two canaries in a cage. I was so little when they passed away." Natalie made herself pull the conversation back on track. "I went to see a lawyer about Mom's will," she said. "I never knew you were the sole owner of the building and bookstore."

"It came to me from my father," he said. "It was meant to go to your mother, and, I assume, to you after that. Things did not occur in the proper order."

"I'm so sorry about that. Did you know about the liens? The back taxes?"

"Blythe said she'd work out a payment plan."

"Grandy, I looked at the numbers and there's no

way to dig out of this hole. I think we need to talk about putting the business and the building up for sale." She paused, and when he didn't say anything, she said, "There are some beautiful places for you to live in Archangel, up by me. I would love to be closer to you." She showed him a collection of glossy brochures illustrated with smiling silver-haired people playing golf and bridge and laughing around the dinner table.

He responded with a long silence.

"Grandy?"

"I'm still here. It's a no, Natalie."

"But—"

"A hard no."

She took a breath and spoke softly to hide her frustration. "I don't want to pry you out of your home," she said, "but I'm trying to come up with a strategy here. Foreclosure is a terrible option."

"And I appreciate your concern. However, selling the building is not on the table. The shop has hidden value, and I'm certain we'll manage. It's where I've lived my life and where I intend to finish my days."

Her heart sank. "I want to be able to provide that for you. Mom wanted it, too. But—"

"We'll find it, Blythe, don't you worry," he said, gazing at her but obviously not seeing her. "My father would never lie about such a thing."

She frowned. "Your father? You mean Mom's grandpa Julius?"

"Don't be impertinent. You're talking nonsense." His voice cut like a knife.

She didn't let herself argue further. In some moments, he was uncharacteristically angry. She'd never known him to have a temper before. The medical reports on his condition, which she'd found in her mother's files, indicated recently observed signs of dementia and called for more tests. *The patient might become argumentative.*

"Mom's calendar shows an appointment with Dr. Yang on Tuesday."

"He's impertinent as well. Thinks he knows more about me than I myself do."

"I'm sure he means to help." Her stomach knotted. She felt horrible—guilty for subjecting him to the neurologist. Filled with dread at the prospect of pursuing the lawyer's suggestion—to have her grandfather declared incompetent and taking the decision away from him.

She gazed across the table at his furious, troubled face. *We're not there yet, Grandy.* She tried not to acknowledge the fact that they *would* get there one day. From her reading about dementia, it was progressive and, ultimately, fatal.

"You're sad," he said in a clipped voice. "Natalie's a good daughter. Just different from you, Blythe."

Natalie swallowed. Had Mom discussed her with Grandy? Complained about her? "Can we keep the appointment with Dr. Yang?"

"I'll be ready. I won't forget."

"Count backward by sevens from one hundred," the doctor instructed Andrew.

Andrew looked at the man blankly. Close-cropped hair, clipped fingernails, crisply enveloped in his white coat, the shine on his shoes reflecting the glare of the overhead lights, his eyes like two small mirrors.

Then Andrew looked around the tiled exam room. Blythe perched on a swivel stool, holding her fingers in knots of tension. Outside the window framed by bright steel, leaves turned to gold and coalesced into a flock of finches, then flew off.

It had been a bad night, a night of comets and tornadoes and bellyaches and the strange taste of metal in his mouth. He didn't know this doctor. Did he? The white coat had a name embroidered on the breast pocket: David Yang, MD. Neurology.

"Mr. Harper?" the gentleman prodded. "Can you count backward by sevens from one hundred for me?"

For him? For what purpose? "I'd rather not."

The doc smiled. "It's okay. On my best day, I can't count backward by sevens, either."

Andrew glanced over at Blythe. Her exceedingly pretty face was puckered by worry. "I hate being a bother," he said.

"Grandy, you're not a bother. You're the best person I know and always have been."

He was not a bother, and she was not Blythe.

He felt a sharp pang of sadness, because his daughter was gone. His granddaughter had come to manage things, and she had discovered that the shop was in trouble. Crushing debt and back taxes. She believed the only way to survive was to sell the shop and move away forever. What Natalie didn't understand, what he hadn't been able to make her see, was that they couldn't sell the shop—at least, not until they found the lost treasure.

"Can you tell me the date?" asked the doctor.

"Can I consult my calendar?"

"Of course."

Andrew took out his billfold, neatly organized as always. He took out a card-size calendar, adjusted his glasses, and said, "It's the sixth of October. A Tuesday." In a tiny corner of the billfold lay a small square of cloth. He unfolded the square to reveal a length of faded green ribbon—the one object he kept with him always. His father had given it to him, along with the story of how the slender ribbon tied him to the Sunrose Building and the treasure that lay within.

PART TWO

In San Francisco, two people actually *saw* the earthquake. Jesse Cook, the police sergeant on duty in the produce market, saw it a moment after he became aware of panic among the horses all around him.

—GORDON THOMAS AND
MAX MORGAN-WITTS,
*THE SAN FRANCISCO EARTHQUAKE:
A MINUTE-BY-MINUTE ACCOUNT
OF THE 1906 DISASTER*

7

Andrew closed his eyes and dreamed of his father. Or more probably it was a memory emerging from the far distant past. There was a gray zone that surrounded some moments like layers of fog, the kind of San Francisco fog that rolled in at night and crouched there, hovering around the place where the land met the sea, ready to pounce on the morning and hold it hostage, sometimes all day long.

It was there in the great miasma of remembrance that Andrew lost himself. Or sometimes it felt as though he found himself in that space, the person he'd been at another time. He found a young boy, running along the lido, calling out to his father as they flew a kite or plied a catboat in a sheltered part of the bay. Afterward, a treat of sugared nuts from a vendor's cart.

Papa was the best person in the world. That was how he knew the story about the treasure was true.

"Tell me about when you were a little boy," Andrew used to say. He never tired of hearing the tale, and he heard it a little differently each time Papa told it.

Sometimes Papa recited the story at bedtime, speaking slowly and thoughtfully, as if trying to parse through his own memories. Then he would hold Andrew close and kiss him ever so gently, every single night, same as he did each morning before Andrew went off to school.

Although Papa never said so, Andrew came to understand the reason for this. You never knew when you were seeing a loved one for the last time.

Papa owned that this was so, because long, long ago his entire world had changed in a single moment. His world had been a small basement apartment with his beloved mam, who worked upstairs all day and in the evening smoothed her chapped hands with oil and drew lovely pictures and told him stories. Sometimes she'd take out her prized bird books, teaching him to recognize birds by sight—grebes and cormorants and quail.

His sparse recollection of that last day was that he and his mother had been jolted from bed in the dark. As the whole building trembled, Mam scooped him into her arms and spirited him up the stairs while screams came from the other residents. Timber and glass flew everywhere, horses and dogs adding to the noise. They choked on dust and smoke.

"My angel mother saved my life," Papa told him. "She lost her own in the process. During the great fire, she rushed to the waterfront and placed me aboard a barge. I remember seeing her bloody footprints, as she had no shoes to wear. The barge was filled with other children and elderly folk, all of us crying and panicked. My mother tied a green ribbon around my wrist and the same around her own. I didn't understand why she loaded me aboard the barge and then rushed back into the city. Later, I always wondered if she went back to save her belongings, or perhaps another person. We saw rockets in the sky—the dynamite used by fire-fighters trying to stop the advance of the conflagration. City Hall was a shattered dome. The great buildings crumbled or burned to shells. Smoke was thicker than fog, and someone put a handkerchief over my nose and mouth, and my eyes stung. I recall very little after the barge was brought ashore. Impressions, really. Terror. Scattered milk cans everywhere. The dead being hauled away. Troops marching through the streets and shouting orders. Electric poles toppled every which way. Someone asked questions, leading me along by the hand. I told them my name and my mam's name, but no one knew her. I did not know the place where I lived. All I knew was my name, and that I lived with my mam in the basement of a building with a winking sun on the roofline.

"I was taken to the great orphanage west of Van Ness. The massive building looked like a haunted castle, and since it was damaged by fire, we camped in tents. I waited and watched. I was told my name was posted on rolls around the city. So many children were joyously reunited with their families.

"But my mother never came. After the cataclysm, the unclaimed children were moved to the orphan asylum and later to the State Normal School. There was a terrible sadness. A loneliness. Those who cared for me were kind indeed, but I yearned to see my mam again, always praying she would come back, singing the songs she'd sung to me as a babe, and working so tirelessly at her drawing. She toiled upstairs from dawn until dusk, I recall, but at the end of the day, she always had time for stories and songs while she drew pictures of birds and animals, and of me."

"Did you ever try to find out what happened to her?" Andrew once asked his father.

He still remembered the sad, haunted look on Papa's face. "I did, when I was older. I combed the archives of the army relief operations, but I never saw her name. There were hundreds of 'unidentified females,' and I suppose one of them was her." Papa looked so sad when he said this that Andrew never asked the question again.

Papa told him that the orphanage had been taken down for good in 1919, and of course by that time he was a man on his own, a veteran of the Great War with his life ahead of him.

"I grew up inspired by soldiers in the military," Papa had said. "At the start of the war, the young men enlisted and it was an honorable thing, but due to my leg—I was born with a turned foot—I served as a medic."

"Tell me how you found the shop again," Andrew used to prod, enchanted by the tale. His father had no clear memory of his childhood home, only that it was a basement room with windows level with the street. He used to watch pedestrians' boots passing by. And of course, after the disaster, it was impossible to recognize the neighborhood. There was one clue he recalled, and that turned out to be the key to finding home.

"I came back from the war with a bride—and a purpose," Papa was proud of saying. He was a skilled healer and apothecary, and he eventually went looking to establish a place of business in the city. After the fires, San Francisco rebuilt with a vengeance, and it was full of bustling newness. Julius Harper found home by chance one day. He was walking along Perdita Street on an errand when he saw the winking sun symbol at the top of a derelict, abandoned building.

The sight awakened a slumbering memory in Papa. His mother told him when he was a very little boy that if he ever lost his way to look for the building with the winking sun. It was a distinctive feature on the facade, a sun with a face and one eye open, the other eye shut. In olden times many people didn't know how to read, so they looked for symbols instead.

"Mam drew a picture of it for me," Papa said. Years later, when he saw that symbol, he realized he was looking at the place where he had lived when he was a little boy.

He broke down weeping as memories thundered through him.

That day, Julius Harper found an opportunity. He acquired the neglected building and made it his home once again, laying claim to it by paying its back taxes. He and his bride repaired the place and founded the apothecary shop, the Perdita Drug Company.

"My father was a good man but a troubled man," said Andrew, looking at the strange doctor as the past melted into the present. "He was so young when he went to war, an ambulance driver and medic. He always said that in war and in peace, it is the lives you save that give your life meaning. My mother, Inga, was a nurse, and they came together much like the love story in that Hemingway novel.

"I believe he spent much of his life searching for the lost pieces of himself that never seemed to materialize—the mother he scarcely remembered, the young man whose innocence was destroyed by a brutal war . . . When he was present, he loved my mother and me and he worked hard. Sometimes, though, he would fall silent and descend into dark places. But we were a happy family and he indulged my affinity for taking things apart—clocks and adding machines and scales, anything with moving parts. When I took over the business, that was the passion I followed.

"It's probably mere sentiment, but when my father reclaimed the building as his own, he felt as if he had found his lost mother."

Andrew tried to see his long-gone parents through the fog. He carefully folded the faded green ribbon and put it back into his billfold. "The Sunrose Building is part of my blood and bone. It is a repository of treasures seen and unseen. I need to stay in order to keep my mind from wandering away. It is the only way to keep the world intact." He looked at Blythe—no, Natalie—whose eyes were misted with grief. "And so perhaps that is why you must understand—I will never leave it."

When Natalie returned to work at Pinnacle Fine Wines, no one at the firm appeared to know or care that the world had changed irrevocably.

A few of her coworkers made sympathetic noises. For the most part, they avoided her. It was probably awkward being around her. When someone suffered a loss so shocking and so enormous, it was impossible to know what to say.

Saying anything at all probably seemed risky to acquaintances at work. They were likely worried they might set off a storm of hysterical tears and then they'd have to figure out how to deal with the breakdown. And at the end of the day, there was nothing that could be said that would help.

She disliked being viewed as a wounded bird. Now that she knew how her coworkers felt about her, she sensed an even deeper ambivalence with her job situation. Amplified by grief, the discontent rang through every moment of the day—the meetings, the filings, the projections, the account maintenance. Her weekends were shot, since she had to make trips to the city to look after her grandfather. Between visits, she pictured him alone, reading, missing his daughter, drowning in memories of his father and his mysterious past.

Her usual laser focus at work was lacking. She frequently caught herself ruminating on the dilemma of what to do about the shop. And her grandfather. And her mother's debt. And the old building that had fallen into disrepair. Cleo and Bertie had agreed to keep an eye on things and on Grandy, but the arrangement was temporary. There was no long-term plan in place.

In unguarded moments, Natalie felt a terrible anger at her mother for leaving her in the midst of the storm. Maybe old Julius had felt that way, losing his mother in the maelstrom after the earthquake.

She contacted a placement agency about hiring a general manager to run the bookstore. Neither of the two candidates was a good fit. The first one didn't make it past the second page of the profit and loss report. "Not only can you not afford me," he said, "you can't really afford anyone."

The second candidate created an elaborate plan involving angel investors and high-interest loans. To Natalie, it sounded so risky that she nearly hyperventilated.

She was mulling over other options when an urgent interoffice message appeared on her screen.

Another Mandy disaster. She'd screwed up a report and it needed to be redone.

Knowing Mandy's opinion of her made it hard for Natalie to want to bail the woman out, but the habit was ingrained: redo the document correctly and get it done on time. It was such a simple thing.

Natalie sighed. She was about to tackle the report herself, correcting all the errors and updating the totals, when she remembered something Tess had said. *If you keep rescuing people from their mistakes, they'll never figure things out on their own.*

But what if this was the mistake that would get Mandy fired?

Natalie spun slowly in her expensive ergonomic desk chair. She looked out at the Sonoma landscape, beautiful and unreachable.

Then she swung back and looked at her desk with its neat, organized stacks and files, and a concise spreadsheet displayed on her computer screen. There was a framed picture of Rick, another of her mom and Grandy.

God, I hate this job, she thought.

A single day at the failing bookstore had made her happier than a year at this grind.

Her fingers flew over the keyboard, highlighting Mandy's errors and suggesting revisions. The pages of the spreadsheet whispered from the printer. She collected the still-warm job from the printer. Then she went down to the department to find Mandy.

Her colleagues were all hanging out together, chatting and sipping their afternoon kombucha or cold press coffee or whatever the beverage du jour happened to be. Mandy was regaling her friends about trying an aerial yoga class. When Natalie approached, Mandy stiffened. "Oh, hey, Natalie." Her expression instantly softened into a pucker of concern. "I still can't get over what happened to Rick. How are you doing?"

A part of Natalie wished the inquiry were sincere. She would like to confess that she felt like shit. She was sad all the time. She couldn't sleep. She worried constantly about her grandfather. But there was no comfort in seeking solace from someone who didn't care. She offered a noncommittal shrug.

"What can I do for you?" Mandy asked.

This was the moment Natalie was supposed to bail her out. She was supposed to pretend this job was not above Mandy's pay grade. She was supposed to correct the mistake and cover up for the woman's incompetence. She had been doing it for months and months.

"Did you do a final check on those numbers?" she asked.

"Sure," Mandy said breezily. "I wouldn't have sent it in if it wasn't final."

Natalie hesitated a few seconds longer. She was about to hand over the pages with her corrections. And once again, Mandy would be saved.

On the other hand, she could accept the woman's word that the document was final, and Mandy would be toast. Out.

She was about to point out the errors when she hesitated again. No. Fuck it.

Then she said simply, "Okay," and walked away.

And for some reason she didn't understand, she took a deep breath and felt better. She remembered reading something she'd come across in her mother's favorite Mary Oliver book when she was looking for a piece to read at the memorial. *Listen—are you breathing just a little, and calling it a life?*

Natalie knew she'd been too afraid to live her life. She had sold it to the firm for a big salary. But what she'd really sold was her own happiness. Despite her need for steadiness and predictability, she couldn't stand her own life anymore.

She was furious at her mother for leaving her with nothing—no words of wisdom, no path to guide Natalie along the journey. Now she understood, finally, that the lesson was in the way Blythe Harper had lived her life.

She walked straight into Rupert's office. He was bent over his golf putter, aiming a golf ball at a cup on the floor. "Hey, Rupert."

The shot rolled past the cup. "Dang," he said, straightening up and turning to face her. "You made me miss."

"Sorry—" *Don't apologize.* "I've decided to leave," she said. "Right away."

He glanced at the clock. "It's only three thirty, and I still need those warehouse reports from your team."

"I imagine you do," she said.

"But whatever." He waved a dismissive hand. "We might be able to spare you this afternoon. Get them in first thing tomorrow."

"No, I mean I'm leaving. Today. For good."

His brow furrowed. "You mean you're quitting?"

"Yes." She nearly hyperventilated as she said it.

"What the hell? You can't quit. We're in the middle of our biggest project of the year. The state wedding's in two weeks, and I need you to manage the inventory for Cast Iron, and— Why would you ditch me now?"

She could give him a hundred reasons. All the ways she'd been slighted in the office. All the times she'd picked up the slack, not just for Mandy but for her whole department. For Rupert himself. The list could go on and on.

"You'll have to manage without me," she said calmly.

"For Chrissake, Natalie. *Why?*"

"Because fuck you," she said, and walked out of the room. She went straight to her beautiful new, perfectly organized office. She didn't even bother to take one last look around. Her departure was sure to inspire gossip—she'd lost her mother and Rick *and* her mind.

She grabbed her few personal items—so few they fit in her tote bag—and walked out without a backward glance. Natalie, who didn't have an impulsive bone in her body, drove away from stability, from safety, from everything she had worked for and focused on for the past decade.

A strange lightness enveloped her as she drove to her apartment, past the shady village green, the trendy shops and cafés and galleries and tasting rooms. Her favorite spot in town was the White Rabbit Bookstore with a sign over the door—FEED YOUR HEAD.

Yet despite the town's charms, she had never quite set down roots in Archangel, a place so inviting it drew tourists from all over the world. But it wasn't her town.

Rick had once hinted that they could move in together. He had a rustic but well-appointed cabin on the banks of Angel Creek, the sort of place people pictured when they dreamed of getting away from it all. It had a deck with a hot tub, a massive bed of peeled timber piled high with pillows and quilts, and windows that opened to the fresh scent of juniper and rushing water.

But no books. Rick wasn't really a book person. And although that seemed like a lame rationale for Natalie's hesitation, she had never been able to fit herself into that romantic picture. It was her failing, not Rick's. She craved security, which was exactly what he had to offer—yet she couldn't embrace a life of security with him. *Why?*

Now she wrapped up her life in Archangel with a few phone calls—to a moving company that could pack everything up in a matter of hours, to the management company that would terminate her lease.

What did it say about her that she could shed this life like a skin that had never fit in the first place?

The question haunted her as she drove south. She arrived in the city late at night and crawled into her mother's bed. She hated that this was her story. She hated that her mom's story ended this way. Maybe this was the reason she was so determined to turn the shop's fortunes around—to give her mother a better ending.

She picked up the book on the nightstand—*Acts of Light*. The book her mom had been reading before she died. Mom had had a habit of marking passages she liked or wanted to remember. Natalie paged through several. One of them, tagged with a stick-on page marker, jumped out at her: *How would you live your life differently if you could start over, what would you do, who would you be, where would you go, what would you embrace?*

Natalie sat in the bookstore back office with Bertie and Cleo, trying to stave off a full-blown panic attack.

"We're staying open," she said. "I'm going to figure out a way to make it work. Grandy won't sell, and he refuses to move, and I'm not going to force him. So I'm going to make this the best damn bookstore on the West Coast."

The show of bravado sounded strange and hollow, coming from a place of desperation. She wished she felt more conviction.

The impulse to walk away from her life had been the most momentous decision she'd ever made. And yet she'd made it on sheer whim, like switching from soy milk to cream in her latte. Normally, she would analyze a decision to death. Not this time. She had thrown away a stable, lucrative job to embrace a failing enterprise with no safety net.

In between the anxiety attacks and sleepless nights, she felt a soaring sense of elation, as if she could fly. It was probably the sense one felt after jumping off a cliff.

Leap, and the net will appear. That had been her mother's motto, copied in calligraphy from a Julia Cameron book. Judging by the shape of her finances, Blythe had lived her life that way. In the end, there was no net—in the most literal sense of all.

"There's no turning back," Natalie told the two of them. "I quit my job, and now I'm doing this thing and it's terrifying but I'm determined. I'd love it if you could stick with the shop. I'll do my best to make it worthwhile. If you can't stay, I'll understand."

Cleo and Bertie exchanged a glance, then looked at her. They were both such kind people. Natalie was glad they were in her life. And that reminded her of how small her life had shrunk. Her grandfather. A few friends. And yet it felt rich. Meaningful.

"I'll tell you the same thing I told your mother," said Bertie. "If my breakout role comes along, I might need to move on. Otherwise, I'm here."

She paused, studied him. Bertie Loftis was a striver and a romantic. He'd won roles in productions, everything from *Rent* to Samuel Beckett. He had a huge talent and a passion for acting. In the heartbreaking profession to which he'd devoted his life, that wasn't always enough. "You're so talented," she said. "Your acting gives me chills. I'm amazed you're not headlining somewhere."

"Just haven't found that sweet spot—the right role at the right time. And a giant helping of pure, unadulterated luck." He braided his fingers together and stared down at his hands. "My acting coach says it's fear. Acting in a role forces you to show the world who you really are. He says I have a block against going there." He leaned back in his chair. "Could be my breakout role is right here, reading *Horton Hears a Who!* to the Tuesday Tots. And there are times when I could be completely happy with that, I swear. If the rent wasn't so damn high in the city, I probably would be."

"Blythe used to say you'll never be happy with what you want until you can be happy with what you've got," Cleo said.

What Natalie wanted was unreachable—for Grandy to be all right. What she had was a man whose memories were fading and who was suffering from mysterious physical symptoms the doctors couldn't explain. "Moving right along," she said. "I've been looking for ways to get our revenues up. Contrary to the naysayers, bookselling is not dead. We need the bookstore to be more than a bookstore. Mom relied so much on the long-term customers she loved. I think we can build on it."

"Cool," said Bertie.

"How can we help?" asked Cleo.

"I've been doing the analytics on revenues. And I think I see a way to bring in more sales." Digital inventory management was not sexy, but it did come in handy. Her skills had kicked in as she took a deep dive through the shop records. She had stayed up late, checking for trends to see if she could find a way to improve the numbers.

"I found a pattern that makes sense to me. A spike in sales occurs when a much-anticipated book is published. We need to settle the unpaid accounts with publishers and get those books on the shelves. I also noticed a spike when there's an author event. And obviously, the more popular the author, the higher the sales."

Cleo nodded. "So let's organize an author event."

"Specifically, a children's author. We can vouch for that," Bertie said. "Kids come with adults. So that means the adult might buy a book, too."

"Exactly. I want to kick off this new phase with a major author event." In spite of everything, she felt a soft uptick of optimism.

"Right, then. All we need is a major author," said Cleo. "Who did you have in mind?"

She remembered the sprightly Dorothy. "Trevor Dashwood," she said. "He's perfect, right?"

"And impossible to book," said Bertie. "We'd have better luck getting Harry Potter himself."

"Harry Potter is fictional."

"And easier to book than Trevor Dashwood. Seriously, the guy is on fire."

Natalie took out a number and dialed. "I have the name of his booking agent. I'm going to give it a try."

After a few rings, someone picked up. "Candy and Associates."

Natalie had to make her way through a few of the associates. Then she found someone named Emily and made her request. "We're a full-service bookstore in the heart of San Francisco, and we'd like to organize an event with Trevor Dashwood."

"He's scheduling events two years out," said Emily. "I can send you a request form—"

"Oh, gosh." Natalie's heart sank. "I was hoping for something later this month. It says on his webpage that he lives in California, so—"

"I'd love to help," said Emily. "But honestly, he's fully committed for the next two years."

"But—"

"I'll email you the request form. I'm sorry. It's the best I can do."

The rest of the day revealed more frustrations as it unfolded. Natalie contacted publishers about other authors, but the ones who could draw a crowd were booked up as well. She also discovered more unpaid bills from publishers.

"My God, Mom," she muttered. "How the hell did you manage?" She rolled her chair back and glared at her mother's desk, a bright collage of Post-its and pinned notes, stacks of books, a bin of still-unopened mail. The spines of the books displayed tantalizing titles: *The Never-Again Club. One Hand Clapping. Life Among the Elephants.*

She noticed a slip of paper protruding from a book like a sliver of hope. She extracted the book and set it in front of her. *Maybe, Maybe Not* by Quill Ransom. A pen name, probably. No author photo. The cover art showed a person on a tightrope, but more importantly, an embossed medallion designating a literary prize.

Natalie opened the note. It was a personal letter from the author. ". . . scheduling bookstore events this fall" were the magic words she was looking for. She looked up the account with the publisher and it appeared to be paid up. It wasn't a children's book, but it checked all the other boxes. Encouraged, she sent an email to the author and publicist.

Most of the customers who stopped in were just browsing or needed the bathroom. This reminded Natalie that the building itself added its own set of worries. A pipe in the wall was making a funny sound when the hot water ran. She worried about her grandfather, too. Yesterday Grandy had dropped a glass bottle in the shower and cut himself.

She used up the last of her mother's sleeping pills and still tossed and turned most of the night.

Natalie was jolted awake by the wind rattling a windowpane that should have been replaced decades ago. She was filled with a what-have-I-done sense of dread. How could she even think there was a way to rescue this situation? She had lost her mother and Rick. She'd thrown away her job and was now faced with running a business that was deeply in debt in a falling-down building, with her elderly grandfather slowly losing himself. Trying to keep the bookstore going was a horrible mistake.

She yanked on her clothes, shoved a few more into a bag, and rushed downstairs. Maybe if she went back to Pinnacle Fine Wines and recanted her quitting, they would take her back. It was an awful job, but at least it wouldn't send her and her grandfather off a cliff.

She went outside to throw her bag in the car. Standing at the curb, she looked left and right, then froze. No car. Where the hell was her car? In its place was a panel van covered in morning dew.

She took out her phone to report the car stolen. Her screen flashed the daily affirmation from the app she'd installed: Happiness isn't a moment in the future. Find something to be happy about right here, right now.

"Bite me," she muttered to the universe. Who would steal a nine-year-old compact sedan? Then she spotted a sign spelling out the on-street parking rules—NO PARKING M-W-F ON EAST SIDE EXCEPT . . . The rules were so complicated and restrictive that her eyes glazed over. Obviously she'd violated one of the intricate restrictions. The car had been towed, then. Wonderful.

She tipped back her head, addressing the universe again. "All I need is a glimmer," she said. "Just one goddamned glimmer of hope. Is that too much to ask?"

An oversize work truck trolled past, its engine growling ominously. It wasn't a tow truck, though. Just some workman looking for a parking spot. *Good luck with that, buddy*, thought Natalie. A magnetic sign on the door depicted Michelangelo's David wearing a strategically placed tool belt and HAMMER FOR HIRE with a phone number.

Really? she thought, batting away a cloud of diesel exhaust. That was not the glimmer she was looking for.

A Radiohead song blared from an open window. She covered her ears to block out the noise as she called the posted number of the towing service. After an annoying sequence of automated responses, she figured out that there was actually no simple way to pay the fine and reclaim the car.

Good job, Natalie, she thought. *Now what the hell are you going to do?* While she stood there pondering the feeling of utter defeat, a woman came out of the gallery a few doors down, climbed into the panel van, and pulled away from the curb.

What next? Natalie wondered. What new disaster awaited her?

8

Peach Gallagher was amazed when a parking spot opened up right in front of the job site—a bookstore in a funky old building. That almost never happened. Parking was a bitch in this section of town, one of San Francisco's historic districts. That was code for "no place to park and unaffordable real estate." But this morning, luck was on his side, and he glided the truck smoothly into the nice big spot.

He could use a little luck this morning. It was changeover day for Dorothy, when his kid had to go to her mom and Regis for the rest of the week, leaving a giant gaping hole of loneliness in Peach's life.

On the sidewalk near the bookstore, there was a homeless woman with wrinkled clothes and messy hair and an overstuffed bag. He made sure he had a couple of bucks in his pocket to give her if she panhandled him. He wasn't exactly made of money, but he could always spare a little something.

Adjusting the bill of his baseball cap, he jumped out of the truck, went around to the back, and lowered the tailgate. He heard the woman talking, maybe babbling to herself. Then he realized she was talking on the phone, pacing the sidewalk. So maybe not homeless.

She hung up, jammed the phone into her pocket, and finally seemed to notice him.

"Morning," he said, flashing a grin.

"Morning," she said, and brushed a hand through her hair. Dark and curly, tumbling over a frown that appeared to be more angry than troubled. "This is a tow-away zone, by the way," she said.

He strapped on a tool belt and clicked the buckle. Then he added a nail bag to the belt. "Yeah?"

"I just got towed."

That accounted for the frown and the pacing. "Bummer," he said, then took out his battered notepad, double-checking the numbers over the shop door.

"Looking for something?" she asked, her voice tinged with suspicion.

"I'm looking for Ms. Harper."

The frown deepened. "What? Ms. Harper?"

He glanced at the address on his notepad again, then

back at the woman. "Pretty sure this is the right place. Do you know her?"

"Yes," she said. Then she shook her head. "I mean, no."

He paused, eyeing her up and down. She was small and cute in spite of the rumpled clothes and distracted air. Amazing eyes, nice lips that needed to smile more, the kind of interesting face that might inspire a song. "Which is it?"

"I'm Natalie Harper. But I think you might be looking for my mother."

"Gotcha. So is she—"

"Dead," the woman named Natalie blurted out. "My mother's dead."

Whoa. Dead? He adjusted his cap and absorbed this information, hoping he'd heard wrong. "Oh, uh, oh, man." Shit, what the hell did you say to that? "What . . . I mean . . ."

As he floundered for words, the woman leaned back against the black enamel facade of the building, put her hands to her face, and, to his mortification, began to cry.

What the hell? Jesus.

Peach set down his toolbox and strode over to her. "Damn, I'm sorry. I spoke with her about a job and— *Damn.* What happened?"

She used the tail of her shirt to wipe her face. He had a swift, inappropriate thought about her toned, bare midriff.

"It was an accident. A plane crash."

"Holy shit. I mean, I'm sorry . . . Natalie, right?"

She nodded. "That's me."

"I'm Peach," he said. "Peach Gallagher."

She blotted her eyes with her sleeve. "Peach." She gave herself a little shake. "My mom wrote that on her calendar, underlined. I thought she was starting a shopping list or something. And you're here to . . ." Her voice trailed off as her gaze wandered to the tattoo on his upper arm—one of several bad decisions of his youth.

"Are you all right?" he asked, feeling way out of his depth. He was a contractor, not a grief counselor. "I mean . . . Sorry. Dumb question."

She leaned against the building, hugging her arms around her middle as if she were cold. Peach felt an urge to touch her, pat her shoulder or something, but he knew better. "I'm really sorry." The tragedy put his crappy morning into perspective. "I just don't know what else to say to you."

She conceded this with a nod. "No one does. I get it. I wouldn't know, either." Then she looked up at him, enormous brown eyes beneath that tumble of curls, her lashes damp spikes. "So you had an appointment to . . ."

He flipped the page in his notes. "She had a list. There's a doorway that needs widening, a light switch that needs to be moved, and a wheelchair ramp installation. Grab bars in a bathroom? Does any of this sound familiar?"

"I feel so out of the loop. I live—*lived*—up in Sonoma until all this happened. My mom was planning to make the apartment safer for my grandfather. He had a fall recently and broke his hip, so he moved from the upper apartment to a studio on the main floor."

"She mentioned some other repairs in addition to the accessibility modifications, but didn't specify. Said she'd walk me through it all when I got here. Listen, if you want to reschedule, we can do that," Peach suggested.

"No," she said quickly. "Grandy—my grandfather—needs those safety features. I have to take care of my mother's shop. And I need . . . oh God." The tears came again. The shirttail. The undeniably cut abs, the kind you saw in a yoga studio if you were lucky enough to see the inside of a yoga studio.

He cautioned himself to quit checking her out. Clients—even potential clients and especially cute, grieving clients—were off-limits. "I can't imagine how hard this must be," he said. "You had a terrible shock. I'm sorry for your loss. I didn't know your mother, but my daughter loves this bookstore. Dorothy comes here all the time."

"Dorothy with the yellow pigtails? About yea high?" She sniffled, then gestured with her hand.

"Sounds like my girl."

"She came in the other day and bought herself a couple of books. She is adorable."

He flashed a grin of pride. Everybody said that about his kid. And everybody was right. "Thanks. So do we reschedule, or . . ."

"Please. Come on in. I was just . . . My plans for the day have changed." She took a breath. Squared her shoulders and tipped up her chin. "When all this happened, I left a good steady job up in Sonoma, thinking I'd take over the shop. I woke up this morning and realized I'm never going to make this work, so I came out here to jump in my car and drive to Archangel and ask for my old job back. I left in a fit of pique and I shouldn't have."

As the words rushed out of her, he tried to imagine her in a fit of pique. For some reason, that sounded sexy to him. He'd been living like a monk for so long that pretty much everything sounded sexy to him.

"Then I saw that my car had been towed," she said, "and I've decided to take it as a sign."

"A sign of what?"

"I'm taking over the bookstore, and I intend to make it work, after all." For the first time, something approaching a smile softened her face. *Damn*, he thought, *she's a looker.* "Recognize that burning smell?" she asked.

"What?"

"A bridge, maybe?"

"Sounds like you're committed."

"At this point, my options are limited." She showed him the street-level door to the residential foyer. Next to that was the bookstore entrance. She unlocked it and they walked through the darkened shop. She stopped at the coffee station to turn on a gleaming silver espresso machine. It came to life with a steamy sigh. She poured roasted beans and turned on the coffee mill. Over the gnashing of the grinder, she asked, "How do you like your coffee?"

He regarded her blankly. When the mill stopped, he asked, "You're making me a coffee? With that thing?"

"Sure. Nowadays, you really can't have a bookshop without coffee."

He couldn't remember the last time a woman had

made him a cup of coffee. "I may never leave," he said. "Americano, black. Please."

"My grandfather will be up in a while. Have a seat and we can go over your list."

When the machine was ready, she expertly drew the Americano and fixed some kind of small latte for herself. He took a sip and looked straight at her. "Damn. That might be the best coffee I've ever had."

"My mom dated an Italian guy for a while, decades ago, and he gave her this amazing machine. Customers love it."

"Gives people a reason to shop local," he said.

She nodded, and her shoulders tensed. "So . . . anyway, you'll have to forgive me. I'm still in a fog."

"Nothing to forgive." He studied her face, soft and sad in the morning light. "A plane crash," he said. "What happened? Or does it suck too bad to talk about it?"

"It sucks whether I talk about it or not," she said.

"Up to you, then."

Several seconds passed. She looked at him through eyes that seemed bruised with pain and exhaustion. "What happened was . . . well, there was this work thing. At my firm in Archangel, up in Sonoma."

"The one you walked away from. In a fit of pique."

She threw him a sharp look, as if surprised that he'd

listened to her every word. "Mom was planning to come up for an event, and she never showed. It wasn't a big deal. She tends to—tended to—change her plans a lot. Later that day, there was a report on the radio—a small private plane went down." She faltered, pressing a hand to her chest.

"Damn. I don't even know what to say."

"There's nothing . . . We had an amazing memorial service. And people have been coming by, leaving notes and expressing sympathy." She indicated a collection of flowers and cards, a scattering of dropped petals on the floor.

"I hope that helped. Just a little."

"It's nice. But . . . gone is gone."

As they finished their coffee, a cat sidled over and perched on the windowsill, tail twitching to and fro. "That's Sylvia," Natalie said. "She hates me."

"This girl?" Peach held out a hand. The cat bowed her head and rubbed it against Peach's knuckles.

"Watch this." Natalie put her hand out. Sylvia glared at it and bared her teeth. "See?"

"You never know about cats." It sounded like the start of a song. Peach had been writing since he was a kid, and sometimes his mind hooked onto an idea like that. He finished his coffee and opened his list. "Let's go see about these repairs. A plumbing issue in an upstairs bathroom . . . She also said there was a damp spot on the wall on the main floor . . ."

"Maybe she meant this section over by the travel books," Natalie said. "It looks like water damage. Is it, like, really bad?"

"It's not good." He bent down to inspect the crumbling plaster. "But I am. I'll figure out what's going on and fix it."

"Is it going to be expensive?" Her voice thrummed with tension. "Sorry to ask, but the shop's having budget issues."

He sat back on his heels. "It won't be cheap. But it's not going to get better if you don't fix it. I'll have a look and give you an estimate."

"Fair enough," she said. "Thanks."

He went out to his truck and returned with some tools. Then he spread out a drop cloth. "This is going to make some noise," he said. "Want me to wait until your grandfather's up?"

She shook her head. "He's really hard of hearing until he gets his hearing aids in. Do what you have to do." She went to the main counter and turned on some lights and a computer. "And thanks for showing up," she added.

9

As Mr. Peach Gallagher got to work, the energy in the shop shifted in some subtle way. Silhouetted by the light through the front display window, he moved with a curious grace, reaching and measuring, searching for flaws. Natalie kept catching herself sneaking looks at his faded jeans and tight black T-shirt, baseball cap, ponytail, and big, battered hands. And—it had to be said—the physique of David. The hammer for hire.

When he noticed her staring, he looked back with something a bit warmer than friendship, which she didn't much like. He had a wife and kid.

Maybe she was reading it wrong. Maybe he was being nice because she'd had a breakdown on the sidewalk this morning. He probably hadn't expected to start his day like that, but he'd taken it in stride. In fact, he seemed to be a pretty good listener. For a guy. For a hammer for hire.

After making an inspection of the moldy wall, Peach motioned her over. "I think I found your problem."

He'd placed a drop cloth on the floor to catch the loose plaster. The exposed horizontal laths spanned the hole like a set of broken ribs. He'd cut away several of the wood strips to reveal a cracked pipe. "There are three things that are the enemies of an old building— human beings, fire, and water. You've got some water damage here."

She inspected the mineral-crusted pipe. "A leak," she said. "I suppose that's bad."

"Definitely not good."

"Do I need to call a plumber?"

He shot her a wounded look. "Please." He stuck his hand into the wall and groped around. "I'll need to find a shut-off valve. You might have to do without water while I investigate. Could be— *Hello.*"

"Now what?" She leaned over his shoulder while he groped around some more.

"There's something else in here."

She took a step back. "Is it alive?"

"You do seem to have a rat problem."

"How can I have a rat problem? I have a cat." She shot a glance at Sylvia. "Lazy old thing."

Peach loosened more plaster to reveal a gap in the laths. "I can put out some bait stations, but this is something else." Reaching deeper, he pulled out a long, flat metal box and set it on the drop cloth. "What do you suppose that is?"

The box was covered in plaster dust and cobwebs. It had latches on each end and rusty hinges along the back. Flaking stenciled letters spelled out WOODRUFF'S CELEBRATED HEALING OINTMENT, and someone had scratched *A. Larrabee* in one corner of the metal.

"No idea," Natalie said. "I wonder what a box was doing in the wall."

"How old is this place, do you know?"

"Dates back to the gold rush days."

"Maybe it's buried treasure."

"That would be nice."

"Let's have a look, then." He pried open the latches and squirted the hinges with oil. The top flipped up, raining flakes of corroding metal and paint and revealing a collection of objects.

They both leaned forward to peer at the odds and ends—faded photos, buttons, a monocle, some keys and old ribbons. "Ancient mementos," said Natalie. "These look like medals. War medals?" She held one up. It was heavily tarnished, but she could make out a couple of the words. *War with Spain. Philippine Insur-*

rection. Then she grabbed her phone and sent a picture to Tess. "One of my friends is an antiquities expert. I bet she can find out more information."

There was a faded postcard depicting a bay of some sort. A printed description identified it as the Old Gateway. Someone had written a note on the card, but the ink was too washed out to decipher.

"That must be Manila," said Peach. "The Americans destroyed a Spanish fleet there in 1898."

She looked at him in surprise. "You just had that on the tip of your tongue?"

He shrugged. "I know stuff. Sometimes."

She was embarrassingly ignorant of the Spanish-American War, not to mention an insurrection in the Philippines, which she knew was related but didn't know how. Her phone pinged her. "You were right. Tess says it's a medal from the Spanish-American War. She wants the serial number on the edge." Natalie picked up the medal and squinted, trying to make out the tiny numbers. Peach rummaged for something in his tool belt and handed her a polishing cloth. She caught his scent of rain and motor oil, which she found oddly appealing. Unsettled, she moved away from him and used the monocle to magnify the print on the medal.

She sent the numbers to Tess. A brittle, yellowed

newspaper clipping lined the bottom of the box—an article from the *Examiner*. She sat back on her heels. "I wonder why someone would hide these things in the wall."

"It wasn't an uncommon practice," said Grandy, shuffling into the room.

Startled, Natalie got to her feet. "Good morning," she said, giving him a quick hug. "I didn't hear you get up." She introduced him to Peach, hoping her grandfather was having a good day. She never knew if he would be with her, or if he would mentally wander off to places she couldn't follow.

"Peach?" Grandy studied him. "A nickname, I assume."

"My given name is Peter. I grew up in Georgia, and when I was in the Marines, the name stuck."

"I see. Well, then. Thank you for your service."

In one exchange, her grandfather had already learned more about the guy than Natalie had. Maybe her mother was right. Maybe she was too closed off from people instead of extending herself and inviting them in. She thought she'd done that with Rick, yet they'd hit a dead end.

Dead end, she thought. *You're a horrible person, Natalie Harper.*

". . . a while ago," Peach was telling Grandy. "I got to see the world when I was in the service."

With the ponytail and pirate earring, he didn't look like a marine at all, Natalie observed. He looked . . . She shut down the errant thought. She shifted focus and turned to Grandy. "So you know something about things hidden in the walls?" She brought the old box over to the coffee area, placing it on a table while she fixed him a coffee.

He offered a vague, sweet smile. The morning light played softly across his features and his neatly combed white hair. He had always paid attention to his grooming. Maybe this meant he was having a good day. Natalie had been dreading the day when he would be broken beyond repair, a day the books she'd been reading said would inevitably come.

Please, not today, she thought.

"Soldiers who had no home needed a place to leave their keepsakes when they were being shipped out, so they sometimes hid things in the walls of their favorite haunts."

"Well, that's remarkable. I had no idea." She wondered what her mother would have said about the false cupboards and artifacts. She wished Mom were here to talk to. One of the most alarming things about losing her so suddenly was that Natalie questioned her own recall. Had she listened closely enough? Filed the memories away like digital documents?

"This building started out as a public house," Grandy said. "We think the counter there was once the bar. Actually, this place was originally a saloon with a brothel upstairs."

"You don't say." Peach looked around, taking in the high ceiling of hammered tin, the wainscoting with its many coats of paint, and the rolling ladder for reaching the top shelves.

"It's referred to as a boardinghouse in old county records. And of course, 'boardinghouse' was a code word for brothel. It was nicknamed the Ten-Foot Ladder. Apparently that was the way some dandies accessed the upper floors if they didn't want to be seen. I've always thought the rooms upstairs are so small because it was a brothel. All that was needed was a bed and a wash-stand and a hook to hang your hat on."

Natalie looked around the shop, trying to imagine an old-time bar and the goings-on upstairs. "I was a kid when you first told me about that," she said. "I pictured women lined up like books on a shelf. It was a bit confusing. And gross." To Peach, she said, "In the historical register, it's listed as the Sunrose Building. There's an ornament at the roofline."

Andrew went on, "My father told me about the

saloon. *His* mother, Colleen, worked as a chambermaid and had rooms in the basement. He never mentioned the brothel. Blythe and I found that out later." He took an unhurried sip of his coffee. "Where is Blythe this morning?"

Natalie winced. She felt Peach watching her. "Grandy, she's gone."

"Gone where?" He blinked, his expression mild with bewilderment.

"Mom died. Remember? You spoke at her memorial."

He turned his head and stared out the window. His shoulders came up as though hunched against a cold wind.

"I'm sorry," she said. "It was a beautiful service and you spoke of her with so much love." It was awful enough getting the news for the first time. Each time he forgot, she had to remind him, forcing the words from her mouth and bringing on a fresh wave of hurt.

"My wonderful Blythe," he said. "She was killed in a horrible accident. A plane crash. I hope she didn't suffer. I miss her terribly. We had so much more to do . . ."

Natalie wondered if the exchange sounded strange to Peach. She tried to move ahead with the conversation. "So you said you and Mom found out more about this building?"

"We've been putting together a history of it. Blythe thought the project would help unscramble my brain."

Natalie winced and touched his hand. It must be frightening to feel the memories slipping away, always wondering if he'd ever get them back.

"It's a remarkable building," Peach commented. He seemed to be taking Grandy's confusion in stride. "I can see why it's listed in the historical registry. The facade in front is made of cast iron. That might be one reason it didn't burn after the earthquake."

"Blythe and I found references to this place in the county records and in early issues of the *San Francisco Examiner.*"

"Grandy's father had a drugstore here," Natalie told Peach. "Grandy turned it into a typewriter repair shop. And now this." She gestured around the bookstore, wondering what it looked like through Peach Gallagher's eyes. It was worn and sad in too many places. Some of the walls bore road maps of cracks. She touched her grandfather's hand. "I saw the notes on Mom's computer files. We can keep going with the history project if you like, and—" A text message appeared on her phone. "Oh, here's more information from Tess. She says the medal with the palm trees is probably worth something, and the others might have sentimental value to someone."

Grandy looked over at Peach. "Are you here about the plumbing?"

Peach Gallagher's eyes were a compelling shade of blue-gray, like sea glass with the light behind. And even though he was a stranger, she somehow got the impression that he understood and empathized.

"He's here to fix some things around the place, and to do a few projects in your apartment," Natalie said. "I told you that a few minutes ago."

"You probably did," he agreed, and took a sip of coffee.

Natalie got up from the table. "Let's have a look at what needs to be done." She led the way to the back apartment. "Mom wanted to make sure it's safe for you in here," she said to Grandy.

"She was a good daughter when she remembered to be," he said.

Natalie was startled by the comment but said nothing more. Peach unclipped a tape measure from his belt and took some measurements. "You need grab bars in the bathroom and a ramp going down the back steps."

"I so enjoy the garden on a nice day," Grandy said. "May and I spent many happy hours there. And you," he added with a smile at Natalie, "you were a veritable Mary Lennox in those days. There's nothing like a garden in the sunshine."

"Then I reckon I'd better get that ramp done soon," Peach said.

Grandy's favorite typewriter, an Underwood Excalibur, sat on the table next to a stack of typed pages. Natalie recalled him using it for as long as she could remember. Beside it was a stack of books, papers, and handwritten notes.

"More of your project?" she asked.

"We worked on it nearly every day. I do the research and type the notes. Blythe was transcribing everything on the computer." A wave swept over him—invisible, but it seemed to leave him diminished. "I suppose we'll never finish now."

"Like I said, I'll help you," Natalie reminded him. "I can take over for Mom."

He gave her a vague look, signaling the confusion that overtook him all too frequently.

"Who's that?"

She looked over at Peach. Then she crossed to Grandy and gave his shoulders a squeeze. "Let's let Mr. Gallagher get to work. I need to open for the day."

Peach hummed as he worked. He had a pleasant voice, she thought. On key, unusual for a workman. He said he'd draw up estimates for the repairs that needed to be done. His tone had sounded like a warning— historic buildings could be complicated. And by complicated, he meant expensive to maintain.

Trying to stave off a sinking sense of doom, she busied herself by texting back and forth with Tess about the found medals and other mementos. "Well, what do you know," she said to Grandy. "My friend was able to trace the numbered medal to the recipient, and she says his ancestors might still live in the city. The soldier's name was Augustus Larrabee, and there's someone by that name who lives in the Mission District. Suppose we found them and gave them the medals?"

"It would probably mean a great deal to them."

When Cleo came in later that morning, she raised her eyebrows at the sight of Peach at work on the leaky wall. "Dorothy's father," Natalie said, introducing them.

"Nice to meet you, Peach. You have the coolest kid," Cleo told him.

"Thanks. I think so, too."

Natalie pictured him as a family man with a lovely wife and cute daughter. A man who hummed while he fixed things. He worked through the day on the leaky pipe, which entailed numerous trips to the basement, from which he emerged with more dire news about repairs. Old wiring and corroded plumbing. Her grandfather's apartment had multiple issues as well.

"You need a king stud," Peach told her.

"I beg your pardon."

"In your grandfather's room. That's why the door doesn't close all the way. Whoever put in the stud-framed wall didn't do it properly." He went into an explanation about jack studs and headers until she held up her hand and told him to fix the door. *Please.*

Customers came and went. Grandy walked down the street to the senior center for lunch and bingo, and Natalie made several halfhearted calls to publishers, hoping to set up book signings—to no avail.

In the late afternoon, a woman stopped by looking for Blythe. She wore a crisp business suit, sharp shouldered and nipped in at the waist, and she carried a no-nonsense but expensive-looking bag, perfectly matched to her shoes with a subtle houndstooth pattern. She hardly resembled one of Blythe Harper's close friends.

Natalie got flustered, choking out an explanation. She felt strangely like a fraud, saying the words she'd never pictured herself saying: *My mother died. She passed away. She was killed in a plane crash.*

The shock on the woman's face made Natalie want to apologize. *Sorry for ruining your day.*

"Here's my card," said the woman. "I was going to set up a lunch with Blythe, but . . ."

Natalie took the card. *Vicki Visconsi, Equity Advancement Specialist, Visconsi Development.* "Thank you."

After the woman left, Natalie showed the card to Cleo. "What's equity advancement and why did my mom need a specialist?"

"No clue. Blythe never mentioned her."

Natalie tucked the card under the desk blotter. She searched the web and found out that the firm had developments all around the Bay Area. Could her mother have been thinking of selling? *No way,* thought Natalie. The shop had been her mom's life.

By the end of the day, Peach had made a list of repairs, ranked in order of urgency—safety features for Grandy, things that were on the brink of disaster, followed by matters that probably needed attention sooner rather than later. Natalie walked outside with him as he loaded tools and gear into the truck. She studied the list, picturing a river of cash flowing out the door.

"You can take your time and let me know how you want to proceed," said Peach.

"I will. Thanks for helping today. I'll call you, okay?"

"Sure." He dug his keys from his pocket and then paused, studying her face and looking as if he could read her thoughts. "Once again, I want to say I'm real sorry about your mom. Nothing quite prepares you for something like this."

She looked at his eyes, soft and thoughtful, like Dorothy's. "It's hard to describe. The sadness feels so . . . pervasive. It takes up all my headspace, and I'm supposed to be taking care of things. The shop. The building. My grandfather."

"If you want to put off the work for a later time, we can do that."

"No." She was surprised at how quickly that came out. "I mean, these things are not going to get better on their own, right?" She knew the repairs wouldn't be cheap, but she had money put by. Her savings. She could sell her car, which was a liability in the city anyway, impossible to park. And the damned diamond ring she would never, ever wear, because it was an albatross of guilt. She could cash in her 401(k), the retirement fund she'd been nurturing since the day she'd landed her first grown-up job. Not so long ago, that would have been unthinkable. Now it seemed like the best option.

You're young, she told herself. *You'll replace those funds once you* . . . What? That was the trouble. Once the shop was profitable? When would that happen?

"Can you get started on my grandfather's apartment?" she asked Peach. "I worry about him. He's . . . ever since he broke his hip and then got back from rehab, it seems like he's aging so fast."

"Sure. I'll get right on that."

Natalie studied the list she'd found in her mother's handwriting. "God, I wish I could talk to my mom. Do you talk to your mother, Peach? Because if you don't, you should. And if you do, you should do more of it. When I think of all the conversations Mom and I could have had . . ." She shook herself. "Sorry—"

"Don't be. This must be really damn hard."

"It . . . yes. The building is only part of it. I need to figure out how to help my grandfather. If it was just his hip, I'd know how to help. But the other symptoms are so unpredictable. Every day, I wonder what he'll forget, or if a memory will come back to him. What if he forgets who I am? Or worse—what if he forgets who *he* is?" She felt like babbling on, but stopped herself.

Peach was quiet for several seconds. "I'll be back

first thing in the morning," he said. "If that works for you."

"Yes. And . . . thank you for coming."

He hoisted himself into the truck. "Yep. You take care now."

The day ended as it had begun, with her standing at the curb in tears in a cloud of diesel exhaust from Peach Gallagher's truck.

10

After the divorce, Peach had ended up with only his work truck for a vehicle, and Dorothy had insisted on being dropped off for school on the corner rather than in the carpool pull-through. Eventually, he'd persuaded her to explain why, and she'd shame-facedly confessed that certain kids made fun of her for arriving at school with a "workman."

Yet another dart from Regina, whose biggest com-plaint in the marriage had been not having enough. They didn't make enough money. The house wasn't big enough. The car not new enough. The school not exclusive enough. The husband not ambitious enough.

Discovering her affair with Regis should not have surprised Peach. Should not have laid him flat. Regis was getting his MBA. Regis was going places. Regis was going to give Regina the life she deserved.

And stuck in the middle of her mother's discontent and her father's desperation was Dorothy, objectively the best kid in the world. Neither he nor Regina deserved her. The parenting plan had them dividing their time with surgical precision, down to the minute, so he dedicated himself to giving this incredible little person the best he had. That included parking the truck and walking inside with her.

Friends asked him why he didn't find a cheaper place to live outside the city. Why he lived with his bandmates, Suzzy and her husband, Milt, in a neighborhood where rent was charged seemingly by the square inch, where he had to juggle two jobs and share housing just to make ends meet. The answer was simple. The answer was right here next to him, holding his hand.

She bounced along, nattering away about koala bears, the topic of her science report. *A koala's not actually a bear but a marsupial. It eats only eucalyptus leaves—two pounds a day. A koala's fingerprints are indistinguishable from human fingerprints.*

"You don't say," he remarked. "That's cool."

"Did you tune my uke for me?" she asked. The

tiny instrument was tucked in its case in her back-pack.

"I taught you how to tune it yourself," he said.

"What if I get nervous at Show and Tell and for-get?"

"You won't forget. And what'd I tell you about get-ting nervous?"

"Breathe, slow down, and remember I play like a boss."

"Exactly. You're gonna dominate Show and Tell."

"Can we do something fun after school today?"

"Heck yeah." He lifted his face to the sky. Autumn was San Francisco's summer. The days were bright and warm, scented with drying leaves and fading flow-ers and the ever-present salt air. He tried to knock off work early on the days he had Dorothy. "How about we go get you a kite in Chinatown and take it up to Kite Hill?"

"Yes! Yes yes yes yes *yes*." She danced in a little circle around him.

He nodded a greeting to Amber's mother, who was single and kept wanting to go for coffee. *Thanks, but no, nice lady*, thought Peach. Since the divorce he'd gone out with a few women—enough to convince him he wasn't ready to hand his heart over to somebody.

"Got your lunch?" he asked Dorothy.

"In my backpack."

"Library book? Permission slip? Water bottle?"

"Yep. Yep. Yep."

"Okay then. Love you, squirt."

"See you when I come back around," she said. Her smile lit the world even as her words broke his heart. *See you when I come back around.*

Natalie struggled up the hill with her grandfather in his wheelchair. She was learning to find accessible routes to their favorite places, but this one might be a fail. She was determined, though. Getting out and about seemed to be good for his head.

Dr. Yang was concerned about symptoms that appeared unrelated to Grandy's dementia—digestive issues, respiratory troubles. He was bringing in more specialists and ordering more tests. He had shown her pictures of Grandy's brain. He'd given her brochures with information about the different types of dementia and the path it might take, none of them encouraging. He'd increased the dosage of meds for the condition and scheduled another appointment. The pills might decelerate the process, but her grandfather's memory was in danger of being slowly erased.

Sometimes he woke in such a state of disorientation he couldn't find his way to the bathroom. Other times he insisted his dinner tasted like scrap metal and that he heard the wind in his ears.

The doctor encouraged her to do normal things with him, to help him keep the chaos in his mind at bay.

Grandy himself sometimes seemed to understand what was happening to him. He said he wanted to stay "intact," and she understood that to mean he didn't want to sell the building and try to create a new life for himself somewhere else.

She stopped in front of Corona Jewelry & Loan. There was a sign on the door: QUICK CASH—NO CREDIT CHECK. She stood for a moment, studying their reflection in the plate glass. She looked small behind the wheelchair, curls escaping her beret and her cheeks red from exertion. Grandy sat calmly, studying the window display.

He turned and looked up. "A pawnshop?"

"It's supposed to be a good one. I looked up reviews online." Taking a deep breath, she pushed a button by the door. A woman with streaked hair and bony cheeks held the door and greeted them. Her stiletto half boots, with telltale red soles, made no-nonsense clicks as she stepped aside and welcomed them.

"How can I help you?" she asked. She had an accent, like Natasha in those old cartoons.

Natalie was tempted to flee. *Deep breath,* she thought. *Just because she looks and sounds like a cartoon villain doesn't mean she is one.* "I have a piece of jewelry," she said.

Natasha led the way to the counter. A lighted display glistened with pirate's loot—watches and rings, necklaces, vintage pieces, old coins and weapons. A barred window to a back room framed a guy who was gazing at a computer screen with a bored air. Security cameras were pointed everywhere.

Natalie set the wheelchair brake and opened her bag. The small box was nestled against an envelope stuffed with invoices, along with the estimate from Peach Gallagher.

She had tried to get Rick's family to take back the ring. They had refused. *He meant it for you, Natalie. It wouldn't be right for us to take it.*

Five minutes later, they left with a scary amount of cash zipped into her coat pocket. It wasn't a loan but an outright purchase. She never wanted to see the ring again. She had an urge to rush to the bank with the cash but forced herself to calm down.

"People do stuff like this every day," she said.

"How's that?" Grandy asked.

"People," she said. "Pawn stuff." She gritted her

teeth and headed up a steep hill. The deed was done. And today was Grandy's birthday and she wanted to take him to a place she remembered with fondness.

The question was, would *he* remember?

The small park crowned a hill overlooking the city, and the late-afternoon sun gilded the scene. People whiled away the time on benches, or walked their dogs, or watched their kids play and fly kites. The grass was parched and golden brown, thirsty for the winter rains.

"How about this spot?" Natalie said, trying to catch her breath. She parked the chair next to a bench and set the brakes.

"Lovely," he said. "When I was a lad coming up, this was called Solari Hill. A farmer named Solari used to graze his cattle here. The grass was so abundant, waving in the breeze." Shading his eyes, he scanned the skyline. "How this view has changed."

"It's still quite a view, isn't it?" Deep autumn gold swept the panorama of Market Street and Sutro Tower, distant Twin Peaks and Diamond Heights. Natalie sat down on the bench and took a long swig from the water bottle she'd wisely brought in a hamper with the birthday cupcakes. With a deep breath, she patted his hand, taking in her surroundings. "It's so nice here," she said. "I'm glad we came."

"I'm impressed that you made it up the hill. I hate being a burden."

"Stop it. Never say you're a burden. Ever."

"You changed your life completely for my sake," he said. "Don't think I haven't noticed."

"I needed a change, Grandy. My life up in Archangel was all about a job I didn't much care for. Coming back here . . . I love this city. I'd forgotten how much I love it. This is the only place that really feels like home to me. Being back has been good for my soul. I hope it's good for us both. I've missed you."

She was not just saying that. She was finally remembering who she once was and what she loved, and it was more than a geographical change. She had come home to that person, the one who still remembered how to find something to feel hopeful about—her grandfather's smile and the way his scarf fluttered in the wind. Kids and dogs playing in the park. The view from this small hilltop.

"I've missed your smile," he said. "You should show it off more frequently."

"I'd been feeling as if it was somehow disloyal to Mom to be happy," she said. "I can't do that anymore. I'm through feeling guilty for being happy, Grandy."

He said nothing for a moment. His somber expression didn't change. Natalie started to worry that she'd offended him.

"Grandy, I swear, I miss her so much, but I just can't—"

He held up one hand to silence her. "Natalie. Natty-girl."

"What?"

"I simply wanted to tell you that this is the best thing you could have given me for my birthday. To know you're able to be happy is all I need right now."

She felt a lump in her throat. "Yeah?"

"Yes."

"Well, you haven't tasted these cupcakes yet." She unhooked the bag from the back of the wheelchair and set the bakery box on the bench. "I think you were the first person to bring me up here," she said. "Remember?"

"You were missing a tooth. You made a sled from a cardboard book box and you went down that slope over there." He pointed to a spot near a wind-sculpted cypress tree. There was a fringe of silver puffs, dispersing their seeds like tiny paratroopers.

"I guess you remember it better than I do."

"Perhaps because I recall how brave you were despite two scraped elbows. When your mother was a child, I brought her here as well," he said. "She never had your sense of adventure, though."

"Mom?" Natalie frowned. "I always think of her as the adventurous one."

"Blythe was too eager to get home to her books," he said.

A gust of wind snatched his hat and tumbled it along the grass. Natalie jumped up and gave chase, dodging kids with their kites and jump ropes. The hat kept blowing just out of reach, and she feared it might go over the edge. Then a big hand snatched it up. "You lost something," said the guy.

She stopped and looked up. For a split second, she couldn't place him. Tall, cool shades, baseball cap folded into the back pocket of his faded jeans. "Peach? Hey."

"Funny meeting you here," he said, handing her the hat. "What's up?"

"I brought my grandfather up here on a walk. One of our favorite spots in the neighborhood." She noticed the way the wind toyed with his hair. "How about yourself?"

"Dad look, Dad look, Dad look!" said a high-pitched voice. "It's *swooping!*"

Dorothy ran backward, her eyes trained on a brightly colored kite dancing high overhead.

Peach put his hands on her shoulders. "Whoa there. Watch your step, squirt."

She turned and looked up at him, her eyes shining. "If I had more string, it'd go all the way to the clouds."

"You think?"

She nodded, then seemed to notice Natalie. Her smile contracted a bit. "Oh. Hi."

"Remember Miss Natalie from the bookstore?"

The smile expanded again. "Oh," she said again. "Hi!"

"I like your kite," Natalie said.

"Dad and I picked it out after school."

"It's really pretty. I used to fly kites here when I was your age. My grandfather would bring me when the weather was nice. Today I brought *him* here because it's his birthday."

"Oh!" She was like a little animated character, springy with excitement. "I want to show him my kite."

"Over there." Natalie gestured toward the bench.

Towing the kite, Dorothy went over to Grandy.

"I like her energy," Natalie said to Peach.

"Yeah, where that comes from after a long day of school, I'll never know."

Dorothy showed Grandy the kite and they watched it for a few minutes. Then the wind changed and the kite came down, fluttering on the ground. She ran over and collected it, showing him the rainbow design.

"That's a beauty, Miss . . ." he said. He took off his glasses and polished them with the end of his scarf. "I forgot your name."

"It's Dorothy. Dorothy Gallagher."

Grandy put his glasses back on. "I'm losing my memory."

She pushed a finger at her chin and studied his face. "Where'd it go?"

"Like those seeds." He gestured at the silver puff hedge. "Carried off someplace far away."

"Maybe they'll grow in a new spot."

"I like that idea. Yes, indeed, that's a fine idea, Dorothy."

"I didn't know it was your birthday, Mr. Harper. I don't have a present for you. But . . ." Her eyes lit. "Hey! I have a *surprise!*" She ran and got her backpack and took out a little guitar.

No, Natalie realized. A ukulele.

Dorothy exchanged a look with Peach, who gave her a slight nod. She sat on the bench facing Grandy's wheelchair. "I brought my uke to school for Show and Tell today. Ready?" she asked.

"I'm all ears, young lady."

She adjusted the tuning, her head tilted to one side.

Natalie glanced at Peach, then took a seat on the dry grass in front of the bench, and he joined her there.

Dorothy strummed tentatively and gradually seemed to gain confidence as she repeated a series of chords. Then she sang "Somewhere Over the Rainbow," the gentle Hawaiian version, sweetly soothing. Her voice was breathy and pure and unschooled. Passersby slowed their pace, and a few lingered to listen. Natalie watched the interplay between Dorothy and Grandy, and her heart melted.

At the end of the little song, Grandy applauded, smiling from ear to ear. "That was the nicest birthday surprise of the day," he told her. "Thank you, Dorothy."

"Welcome! I played it at school today, and I think I did real well." The little girl looked up at Peach. "Aw, Dad. *Really?*"

Peach dabbed a bandanna at his cheeks, his sentiment on unabashed display. "Can't help it, squirt. Whenever I hear you sing like that, it makes me cry big giant man tears."

Dorothy put away her ukulele. "Good to know."

What a lucky woman Peach's wife was, having these two, thought Natalie. She jumped up. "I have a little something for all of us." She opened the box from Sugar. "Birthday cupcakes!"

"Really? For us?"

"Really. I got a couple of extras for Bertie and Cleo. But . . . first come, first served, right?"

"Right!"

"There's chocolate, vanilla, strawberry, and rainbow unicorn."

Dorothy's eyes devoured the gorgeous little cakes. Then she glanced over at Grandy. "It's your birthday. You pick."

"Well, chocolate for me," he said, helping himself.

Natalie glanced at Peach, and somehow knew. "I'll take the strawberry and we'll give your dad the vanilla one. Guess that leaves the rainbow unicorn for you."

11

While working on restoration jobs and repairs, Peach often found himself privy to bits and pieces of people's lives. Something about the work he did tended to make him invisible to clients. At various stages of a job, he'd encountered closets full of hoarded things, priceless artifacts on display, careless messes not meant to be noticed. He'd overheard heated arguments and inane, rambling conversations, silly jokes and words of kindness, kids being scolded, music blaring, disasters being navigated, tragedies playing out: people living their lives.

Many projects took weeks or months, and he became a fixture, like part of the woodwork or a tool left lying out. People didn't forget he was there, but as they acclimated to his presence, pretenses were dropped and they became more like themselves around him. A silent observer, he didn't want to intrude, but sometimes it couldn't be avoided. For the most part, people's day-to-day lives revolved around mundane matters, yet there were occasional flares of drama, humor, or poignancy. Sometimes bits of his observations made their way into the songs Peach wrote. He once composed an entire ballad about a woman putting her late husband's shoes into a charity box.

You never knew what would spark inspiration.

He suspected he would probably write a song about Natalie Harper. She was stressed to the max, in the middle of a multiact shit show, inheriting the shop as well as old Andrew, who was clearly having serious memory problems. Based on the calls he overheard, she'd also inherited a load of money troubles, not to mention a building that was dying of neglect.

Something about her touched him in a soft spot. It had been a surprise to run into her in the park the other day, but San Francisco was like that, a big city made up of small towns where people knew each other. With her old granddad, she'd been as sweet as those cupcakes. With customers, unfailingly polite. With Peach—hard to read.

And she was so damned pretty—small and graceful, with tender-looking skin and enormous eyes that hid nothing. She was a mixture of delicate and fierce. Dainty hands that flew over the keyboard, particularly when calculating spreadsheets. She dressed plain, like in a navy skirt and sweater and flat shoes—a sexy librarian. He could watch her all day.

She seemed like a nice woman. Nice, but troubled. Suzzy—his always-opinionated housemate and cowriter—would call that a red flag. But it wasn't Natalie's fault her mother had died and she had moved to the city to help her grandfather and was somehow trying to have a life.

Red flags or not, Peach wasn't interested in a relationship. He had learned his lesson soon after the divorce. He'd dated a woman who had checked all the boxes—kind, beautiful, smart—yet she'd failed to hide her resentment of Dorothy, which was a deal killer. Another girlfriend had seemed nice enough, but she wanted kids of her own, and she wanted them right away.

Peach had shied from that. He never, ever wanted Dorothy to think she wasn't enough for him. In the unlikely event that he ever felt like going down that path again, he planned to take his sweet time doing it.

These days, he was a monk. No drama. No complications. Work and the band and Dorothy kept him busy enough. Natalie Harper was tempting but would only ever be a client.

He didn't want to add to her stress, but the repairs and restoration on her place were going to take a while, and the project wouldn't be cheap. He felt bad about how much work would be needed to rescue the venerable old building. She was in good hands with him. He knew what needed to be done, he knew how to do the work, and he wouldn't overcharge.

Suzzy sometimes chided him for charging reasonable rates here, in the heart of the wealthiest city in America. "Dude," she would say. "It's one of the perks of living in San Francisco. You're surrounded by people who rake in the dough. You should feel free to share in the bounty."

"Don't call me dude. Nobody says dude anymore."

"I do. Some dude gave me a hundred-dollar tip yesterday morning, and all he had was an egg white omelet. And I was like, 'Thanks, dude.'"

Peach suspected the tip was more about her tight skirt and red cowboy boots and the treble clef tattoo on her dainty collarbone than it was about the omelets she served at Spotters, the buzzy breakfast place where she worked while waiting to be discovered. Suzzy didn't advertise the fact that she was happily married to Milt,

210 · SUSAN WIGGS

their drummer, because she swore the tips were better that way. She and Peach had even done a song about it—"Color Me Regressive."

It was pretty clear that Natalie Harper was not going to be the kind of client he often encountered, the kind with more money than sense. He had recently finished a job for a couple who had spent a small fortune importing a set of library doors from London because they matched an antique mantelpiece in their Nob Hill home. Another client had commissioned a glass countertop so big that they had to take out part of a wall in order to get it inside.

Natalie Harper was not that client.

She was always hard at work when Peach showed up in the morning, and she was still working when he left each day. She and her staff were looking for ways to improve the bottom line, like expanding the coffee service and putting on events for readers.

She was good at her job, greeting customers who came in and helping them find what they were looking for. During slow periods—and there seemed to be too many of those—she worked efficiently at her computer station. She stayed calm through phone calls that would drive most people crazy—*I don't have a certified copy of the death certificate yet. I can't access those documents until there's a court appointment making me her personal representative. The official cause of death is in those papers . . .* Each time she had to reexplain the situation, her voice sounded thinner and more weary. Each time her grandfather mistook her for her mother or treated her like a stranger, the heartache showed in her haunted eyes.

While Peach patched the wall he'd broken into, Natalie fielded a call from some lawyer, which she took on speaker while shelving books. The lawyer suggested she sue the aircraft company and plane manufacturer.

Her eyes took on a glassy haze. "What, sue them because my boyfriend was bringing my mother to watch him propose to me?"

Stabbing her finger at the phone to end the call, she looked up and noticed him. He set down his trowel and wiped his hands on a rag.

"I'd ask how your day's going, but I overheard your conversation."

"In my wildest dreams, I never imagined getting a call like that."

"So, uh, I didn't realize you'd lost your boyfriend in the crash, too."

She shivered slightly, folded her arms. "Yes, he's . . . he was a pilot. A good one, and the thought of suing . . ." She tightened her folded arms. "It's complicated. Or maybe not. Maybe I'm just a horrible girlfriend. Even after he died I was horrible. I hocked his ring to pay bills."

Oh.

"It's no crime to be practical," he said. "You're looking after your grandfather. Doing what you have to do."

She stared at the floor, then back at him, her eyes soft with sorrow.

"I sure wish I could help more."

She looked at his plaster trough and the trowel. "You're helping," she said.

He offered a slight smile and went back to work. *You're helping.* He wished he could patch up her heart.

Later that day, she made several calls to publishers, some to work out a plan to settle bills, others to see about scheduling book signings with famous authors.

He had to admire her persistence and patience, even when she had to explain—repeatedly—that the well-known proprietress of the Lost and Found Bookshop had died. Cleo, her coworker, came in to work and asked if she'd had any luck setting up events.

Natalie scanned the shop—empty except for Peach—with a wistful glance. "Maybe writers are like guys," she said. "All the good ones are taken."

"You'll find someone," Cleo said. "Several some-ones."

"I've left a dozen voice mails," Natalie said. "No-body returns calls anymore."

Peach didn't know anything about running a book-store, but he figured any writer would feel lucky to sign books here. For all its faults, the place was a gem—great atmosphere, a treasure trove of old and new books, a staff of folks who knew and liked litera-ture.

He motioned Natalie over. "Can I show you some-thing?"

"Good news or bad news?" she asked him, her voice thin with weariness.

"I feel like the grim reaper." He led the way to the upstairs bathroom, an excessively feminine space dominated by an impressive antique tub with high sides and claw feet. The room smelled like flowers and candles. Hunkering down, he aimed his flashlight at the pried-up floorboards in the space under the tub.

"If anybody deserves a break," he said, "it's you. But this needs to be addressed." He showed her where galvanized pipe had been improperly connected to copper pipe. A slow fiasco was unfolding beneath the floorboards.

"This is bad, right?" Natalie asked quietly. "How bad?"

"Is the bathtub going to go crashing through the floor today? Nah. But the longer it goes on, the more it'll take to fix it."

She sat back on her heels and nodded glumly. "You'd better fix it."

He extended a hand and helped her to her feet. It occurred to him that he hadn't held a hand other than Dorothy's in a long time. They went to the main room of the apartment, which was filled with light slanting through the dormer windows and playing with the angles of the roof. The millwork had details from the Gilded Age—fretwork and corbels, flourishes from a bygone era.

"What?" she asked. "I can see you're having thoughts."

"You can, eh?"

"The way you're looking around. Is something else falling apart?"

"You can always find something in a building this old. But that's not what I was thinking. This place is really beautiful. Tons of original historical detail, and it hasn't been ruined by a bad remodel job."

She set her hands on her hips and slowly turned.

"That's kind of you—to say something nice about this old place."

"Seriously, it's a classic. I love the character of it."

"As far as I know, it's never been touched. We were either averse to change, or too broke to upgrade."

"It's pretty great." He noticed a guitar case in the corner. "You play?"

"Not really. Mom got that at a rummage sale when I was a kid, and we taught ourselves a few three-chord songs." Her expression softened with remembrance, but then the worry frown reappeared. "I guess you could say I have a love-hate relationship with this place. I love that our entire family history lives here, and I hate that we can't afford to keep it."

"Not that it's any of my business, but you'd have buyers lining up. It's in a prime location, has the kind of vintage appeal people can't get enough of. I see places like this selling for cash, as-is."

She sat on the rolled arm of a comfy-looking sofa and knotted her hands together until her knuckles turned white with stress. "That was my first inclination after the crash. The bookshop was my mother's reason for living, and I thought without her, it couldn't go on." She brushed her hand across a soft blanket on the back of the sofa. "It's not mine to sell, though. It wasn't even my mother's. Everything belongs to my grandfather, so it's his call, and he won't budge. He was born here, grew up here, made his living here. I want him to enjoy his retirement in a place he loves. Uprooting him now would break his heart."

What about your heart? Peach wondered, but not aloud.

"He's lucky to have you," he told her.

"I'm the lucky one," she said. "He's my only family, and it's a privilege to look after him. I'm going to do what it takes to keep him here."

"Now that," said Peach, "is something I can help you with." He wanted to say more, ask her more. Instead, he said, "I'd better get to work."

In Andrew's apartment, Peach had already finished installing sturdy holds in the bathroom. Now he built a ramp leading down to the garden in back. While he worked, the old man seemed absorbed in reading yellowed pages and documents from a big folder, turning the pages with his unsteady hands. Sometimes the tremors were so bad, he would press his hands flat on the table, an agonized expression on his face. Every now and then, he would glance up with a benign gaze and make some comment or other, drifting in and out like the window curtain blowing in the breeze. Peach realized he was seeing the symptoms that kept Natalie up at night.

He found things like a jar of peanut butter in the bathroom cabinet. The old guy asked the same questions over and over again—What's your name? Where are you from? Are you here about the plumbing?—until Peach realized that no answer would seat itself in the guy's head in any meaningful way. How did it feel to forget everything? Did Andrew know he was losing it? Did he fight to keep his sense of self? Did he feel it eroding, or did it ebb and flow?

Man, thought Peach, *I wish I knew how to talk to you*. It was a bit like being with someone who spoke a different language. But sometimes he imagined he could actually sense Andrew's panic and disorientation. And now his self-loathing when he pissed himself and stood glaring at his feet. "Hey, this is a good time to check out the shower bars," Peach said when he noticed the wet floor. "Let me give you a hand." He set aside his tools and held up a towel while Andrew undressed and moved to the shower bench.

Peach turned on the shower and handed the wand to Andrew. "Rinse yourself off and I'll find you something to put on."

Andrew simply held the shower wand against his

bony chest and regarded the stream of warm water with a sense of wonder. Peach grabbed a change of clothes from the closet and set them by the tub. When the shower stopped, he handed over a towel and went to clean up the mess.

A few minutes later Andrew came out, dressed in clean clothes, looking slightly chastened. "I'm sorry to be such a burden."

"Don't worry about it."

"I'm old."

"We'll all get there one day, buddy," Peach said, "if we're lucky."

"I've far outlived my usefulness," Andrew said.

"Listen, I don't know you guys so well, but I know this. Natalie needs you. And you're damn lucky to have her. Everything she does shows you that you mean the world to her."

"I shall keep that in mind, young man," Andrew said. "But if I forget, you must remind me."

Peach nodded, then went back to work. When he finished for the day, he took his tools to the truck and loaded up. "I'll be back in the morning," he said to Natalie. "Eight o'clock okay?"

She nodded. "I'm an early riser." She paused, then said, "I heard you talking with my grandfather."

"He's good company. Hope that's okay."

"Okay? It's wonderful. Thank you. Some people . . ." She bit her lip, looked down. "Some people don't have the patience. It's hard. There are times when I have to remind myself that he's still there."

Peach realized by "some people," she meant herself.

"Have a good evening, then." He hesitated, a hairbreadth from inviting her to get a drink and maybe a bite to eat. She looked so damned lonely in the empty shop.

12

"Grandy?" Natalie partially opened the door to his apartment. "Charlie's going to be here at nine to take you to breakfast."

Silence. She pushed the door open and stepped inside. "Hey, Grandy."

As usual, his bed was neatly made, the small table carefully arranged with his typewriter and pages about the Sunrose Building. He'd always been fastidious. The wheelchair was parked over by the radiator. The scent of witch hazel still hung in the bathroom. But her grandfather was gone.

A jolt of panic sent her rushing to the back door. Opening it wide to the garden, she ran down the ramp and looked around but saw no sign of him. Then she hurried back to the shop, where Peach was setting up for the day's work. Today's challenge was to tackle the electrical panel, now open like a tangle of exposed nerves. The old building's antiquated wiring was objectively dangerous and probably wildly out of compliance. The attic space was swagged with ancient knobs and tubes from times long past, and the whole panel needed to be reconfigured. Peach had warned her that inspectors were notoriously picky.

"Have you seen my grandfather?" she asked.

"Today? Nope." He had the panel box open and was studying the breakers as if they held the day's winning lottery numbers.

"He's gone," she said. "I'm afraid he wandered off." Her stomach knotted. Grandy's care team, still baffled by his symptoms, had mentioned the possibility that he could leave the house—"exit-seeking," it was called—and lose his way. "It's all my fault," she said. "I meant to set an alert on the security system but I haven't done it yet. Oh my God, if something hap—"

"Easy," said Peach, heading for the front door. "We'll find him. He couldn't have left this way. I let myself in this morning with the code and locked the door from the inside behind me."

She felt the color drop from her face. "The back door wasn't locked."

They both made a dash for it. She called Grandy's

name and got no response. Peach checked the back gate. "Good news," he said. "This is still locked. I doubt he's spry enough to jump the fence."

She was about to call 911. "Then where—"

"There," he said, pointing to a small space at the side of the building. "Isn't that his cane?"

It was leaning next to the panel door that provided outside access to a long-neglected crawl space that May Lin had used as a shed to store her gardening tools and supplies. "Grandy!" She ducked her head and poked it inside. "What are you doing?"

Andrew shone a penlight into her eyes, and she flinched. "I thought Natalie would enjoy seeing the bird books," he said.

"Oh, Grandy." She stepped forward and put her hand on his arm. "It's me. Natalie. You're looking for something?"

"We've been searching for years," he muttered, following her. "Papa was always looking for his books."

"Papa. You mean your father, Julius."

"After he lost his mother, after he lost everything, he still remembered those treasured pictures with all the birds."

She could only imagine the wrenching trauma of seven-year-old Julius, alone and lost after the city's deadly earthquake and fire.

"Everything all right?" Peach asked, ducking as he came through the low door.

She nodded, offering a fleeting smile. "He always seems to be searching for something." If this was where old books had been stored, she thought, they'd probably been ruined by the damp air.

Using the flashlight on his phone, Peach inspected the cramped, dusty space. An old rake, a sack of fertilizer, plant pots in a lopsided stack. She could see a small army of spiders hanging in the corner, their webs like trapeze nets, and the sight made her shudder. "Oh my God," she said, pulling her grandfather toward the door. "I'm terrified of spiders. Let's get out of here."

"What do you suppose that is?" Peach asked, aiming the beam at an old wood-and-metal box.

"Do you recognize it?" she asked her grandfather.

He frowned and shook his head. Shadows from the doorway flickered across his face. Natalie felt the ghost of a cobweb brush her cheek and shuddered again. "Come on inside, Grandy," she said. "I'll fix you a coffee to drink while you wait for Charlie. Now, watch your head." Taking his hand, she steadied him as they stepped outside.

Grandy looked around the garden. "We used to have an apple tree. I liked to climb it and peer over the fence at the neighbors. At some point, it was cut down. I believe it had some sort of disease."

"Want me to grab this box?" asked Peach.

"Yes, bring it inside," she said.

"No problem."

Even though Peach was here for work, he already seemed like a friend to her. Looking after Grandy and the shop and the building felt overwhelming sometimes—most of the time—and she appreciated Peach's calm, matter-of-fact demeanor.

Back inside, she made cortados for herself and Grandy, and an Americano for Peach. With all the work that had to be done on the building, he was a constant presence, and she relied on him more than she was willing to admit. He had a calm sort of energy, the bearing of a man who knew what had to be done and was doing it, simply and competently.

Charlie arrived for their morning walk to the senior center. Exquisitely neat in his white cotton jacket and canvas sneakers, he regarded Grandy with gentle affection. Peach came in with the old crate from the crawl space, greeting Charlie with a nod. "Your buddy was on a treasure hunt," he said, indicating the dusty collection.

Charlie removed a few rusty tools and stoneware pots, then took out an old vase and rubbed off the dust. "This is beautiful," he said, holding it up.

Natalie had seen similar vases in the curio shops of Chinatown. "Pretty. I'll clean it up and put some fresh flowers in it, assuming it doesn't leak."

Charlie nodded. "Handle it with care. Might be another of your treasures."

She grinned and took it from him. "Right." As she upended the vase, a large, hairy-legged spider scuttled out. Natalie screamed, flinging the thing away from her. Peach's hand shot out and grabbed the vase before it shattered on the floor.

"Damn," he said, "you really don't like spiders."

"Sorry." She sagged back against the edge of the counter. "Nice ninja move, by the way."

Peach stooped and picked up a dusty object tied with twine. "This fell out of your vase."

It was an old folio the size of a playing card. Natalie opened it carefully to reveal several onionskin pages covered in Chinese characters. She showed it to Charlie. "Any ideas?"

He studied the paper, then shook his head. "My Chinese reading ability is not strong enough."

Natalie sent a picture of the vase and folio to Tess—Another treasure? Or someone's Chinatown souvenir?—and then put the items on a shelf above the espresso machine.

A few minutes later, Tess returned the text. Could

be something, could be nothing. I'll send someone around from Sheffield's to pick it up.

After Grandy and Charlie left, the day was quiet in the shop. Too quiet. Bertie had an audition for a revival of *Waiting for Godot*. Cleo had gone to work a school book fair. Natalie busied herself with ordering books. The shop featured about seven thousand different titles, but a steady stream of new material was needed to keep the inventory fresh. The budget didn't allow for mistakes. It barely allowed for the requisite numbers of new books. Making a living as a bookseller was entirely possible, but only if the inventory was skillfully managed. Sometimes she looked at her mother's bookkeeping and wanted to scream.

Agitated, she got up to stretch her legs and wandered over to her mother's W.O.W. shelf—the "words of wisdom" Blythe had marked in favorite books. Natalie's eye fell on a volume of Thoreau's letters, and she opened it to a passage marked with a sticky note in her mom's handwriting with an arrow pointing to the words: *I am grateful for what I am & have. . . . It is surprising how contented one can be with nothing definite—only a sense of existence. . . . O how I laugh when I think of my vague indefinite riches. No run on my bank can drain it—for my wealth is not possession but enjoyment.*

Natalie's frustration ebbed as sadness returned. Trying to channel her mother's optimism, she focused on the heady pleasure of deliberation. Which books would catch someone's eye? Which would captivate their imagination? What brand-new title would get people talking? She'd made a spreadsheet—of course she had—detailing sales patterns, review and media attention, and reader affinities, and made a plan for each major category.

The king of the spreadsheet, week in and week out, was the elusive Trevor Dashwood. People couldn't get enough of his books. Natalie ticked the box next to his recent title, knowing the copies would sell quickly, whether or not he'd deign to visit her shop two years from now. She was actually more excited to find the *next* Trevor Dashwood—the incredible author no one had heard of yet but who would one day capture the hearts of readers.

She'd been staying up late every night, devouring new offerings from publishers, and there were several she couldn't wait to put on display in the shop—gripping memoirs, soaring romance, irresistible cookbooks, twisty thrillers, exuberant children's books. This part of the process was catnip to her. Still, studying the spreadsheet and her own notes on the distributor's order sheet, she felt a wave of uncertainty.

There was no algorithm for predicting which books would sell. That took judgment and taste. She only hoped she had adequate supplies of both.

This had been her mother's singular expertise and probably the reason the shop was still afloat despite Blythe's haphazard management. She'd called herself a book evangelist. Natalie could still remember her mom's look of utter pleasure when she hand-sold a book to an eager customer.

In the late afternoon, a bright spot appeared—an email from Quill Ransom's publicist. Since she was local, the author was available on short notice. The publicist proposed a date for the book signing. Natalie knew one event wouldn't reverse the shop's fortunes overnight, but it was a start. She went straight to work planning and even had an excited call with the author, who sounded utterly charming.

An older couple wandered in to browse, and despite Natalie's sales pitch—*This story is like a conversation with a trusted friend. That one kept me up all night. Even though science fiction isn't always my thing, I loved this time travel novel*—they left with a single paperback. Three teenagers came in, but only wanted to take selfies with books to post on social media. Even Peach, who generally didn't interact with customers while he was working, couldn't suppress a comment as they jostled their way through the aisles.

"Is there a point to that?" he asked Natalie.

She shrugged. "To make them look smart online, maybe."

"Is there a point to that?" This time Peach asked one of the jostling kids.

The boy shoved his phone into his back pocket. "Not really, man."

Natalie cringed, hoping Peach wasn't going to start something.

"Tell you what," Peach said. "I was a giant loser in high school until I read this book." He showed them a copy of a Dave Eggers book. "It raised my IQ like forty points after I read it."

"Really?"

"Nope. But it's an awesome book and you should read it."

"Yeah?" The kid struck a pose with the book and his friend took a picture. "I'll get it on my phone, then."

To Natalie's surprise, he already had the app, and he purchased the digital book from her.

"Thanks," she said. "Let us know how you like it."

After they left, she turned to Peach. "I keep wondering if there should be some kind of etiquette around taking pictures in bookstores."

"How about you put up a sign saying this is a phone-free zone?"

"I don't think so. Seems bossy to me."

"You're the boss." He turned the bill of his baseball cap backward and marked something on the wall he'd dug into.

"I was a toxic boss in my last job," she said. "My coworkers hated me."

He chuckled. "You? Naw."

"You laugh. I overheard them talking about how awful I was. Really, they couldn't stand me." She liked the fact that he found it hard to believe that she could be toxic.

"You were working with the wrong people, then," he said.

"I might have been in the wrong job. Didn't love the work, but it was stable and predictable." She looked around the shop, illuminated by the late-afternoon sunshine. "Unlike this."

"Regrets?" he asked.

"Ask me after I meet with the county auditor's office." She needed to work out a plan to pay the back taxes.

Two women came in, their cheeks bright with color

from the chill air. They looked like affluent young professionals in their luxurious infinity scarves, well-cut blazers, half boots, and expensive shoulder bags. Since moving back to the city Natalie had observed changes in the neighborhood of her youth, and these ladies were a prime example. There were still traces of the bohemian vibe here and there—a new age school for interpretive dance, a psychic healer, a crystal peddler—but the majority of businesses and shops were now decidedly posh, catering to a stylish, well-salaried clientele. Natalie wasn't quite sure how to make the bookstore posh, or if she even should.

The women scanned the displays, their eyes lighting on intriguing covers and handwritten book review cards from the staff and regular customers. There were several in Blythe's urgent scrawl, with an overabundance of exclamation points. As time went by, Natalie would probably need to retire the cards, but she couldn't bring herself to do so yet.

"Let me know if I can help you find something," she said to the newcomers.

"Thanks," said one of the women, checking her phone. "Just browsing for the moment."

Great, thought Natalie. *More cell phone pics?* Maybe she ought to consider Peach's suggestion—an outright ban.

The buzz of a power tool shrieked from the corner where Peach was working. He leaned around a shelf and waved. "Sorry about the noise," he said. "I'll be done in a sec."

"No problem," the other woman murmured, slipping on a pair of couture glasses and picking up a novel with a vibrant red-and-white cover.

The friend gave her a nudge and jerked her head toward Peach, then fanned herself. The first woman wandered over to the travel section, feigning interest in a pictorial guide to Estonia.

The drill buzz stopped. "Hello," Peach said. "Am I in your way?"

"Oh no," she said quickly. "Being nosy, is all. Looks like a pretty major repair you're doing here. I love these old buildings."

Peach nodded affably. "They can be high maintenance."

"Well, you look like you know what you're doing," she said, not quite batting her eyes. "I've always got something around my place that needs fixing. Do you have a card?"

He's married, Natalie thought, trying to concentrate on her inventory chores. *He's got a kid.*

"Sure." He set down his drill and straightened up. At his full height, he was even better looking.

"I'll take one, too," said the woman with the glasses. "I'm hopeless when it comes to home improvement. I just bought a place on Russian Hill, and I'm renovating. Or I should say, I'm begging for contractors who can do the renovation. You gentlemen are hard to find."

He handed out the cards. "P. Gallagher," the blond woman said. "*P* as in Peter, like the actor? Or Philip, like the best character in *Shameless*?"

He looked slightly mystified. "*P* as in Peach, like the fruit." Flashing a grin, he hefted his drill. "I'd better get back to work."

"Peach." The glasses woman looked intrigued. "I bet there's a story there." Her words were drowned by the whir of his drill. She went back to the New Releases table. "How about this one, Taylor? 'A searching memoir of turbulent times,'" she read from the flap copy.

"We did a memoir last month," the woman called Taylor said. She looked over at Natalie. "We're looking for our next book club pick. Any recommendations?"

Natalie smiled. "I thought you'd never ask. What's your group like?"

"We do wine and nibbles once a month. There are nine men and women. I'd say we have eclectic taste in books."

"And wine," the other woman said. "And men, for that matter."

"Sounds like fun." Natalie introduced them to a few new releases and a couple of classics, offering her best pitch each time. Both women agreed that the new Stacy Kendall novel, about twins growing up separately and unaware of each other until one is accused of murder, would give the group plenty to talk about. "Sounds like a great one for our next meeting," Taylor agreed, admiring the intriguing cover art. Instead of buying the book, she set it aside.

The other woman didn't buy it, either. "I read everything on my phone app," she said, offering an apologetic look.

"Oh, you can get a download right here in the shop," Natalie said. "You purchase a unique code, and then—"

"Thanks. Maybe I will later on your website . . ."

Natalie recognized the signs of a failed sale. The two women edged toward the exit in that way customers had when they didn't intend to buy anything— checking their watches, suddenly remembering they needed to be somewhere.

Natalie offered a smile of understanding—never make a person feel bad for visiting the shop. "Well," she said. "Thanks for stopping by."

"I'm a sucker for stories about twins," Peach said in a conversational tone. "Sorry for eavesdropping, but it sounds really good. I'll buy a copy."

"Great," Natalie said, trying not to sound surprised. "I'll ring one up for you."

"*The Man in the Iron Mask* is probably my favorite look-alike story," he added. Wiping his hands on a bandanna, he took a volume from the Vintage and Collectible shelf. "This is the exact edition I had when I was a kid." The volume featured bold illustrations and an old-fashioned dust jacket.

Suddenly the women didn't seem to be in such a hurry. "Oh my gosh, I might need that for my nephew," said the glasses woman. "He's obsessed with action comics and I've been looking for ways to get him to read more books."

Peach handed it over with a flourish. "That'll do the trick, I bet."

"I always loved *The Prince and the Pauper*," Taylor said while her friend bought the book. "There's something about the idea of switching roles, living someone else's life . . ."

"We've got a copy of that," Natalie said. "It's in the case, though, because it's a first edition."

"Really? That's cool. Mind if I have a look?"

Natalie took the Mark Twain out of the rare books

case. Over the years, her mother and grandfather had created a special collection of books by authors in the San Francisco literary circle known as the Bohemians, which included Mark Twain. Rumor had it they'd frequented the Ten-Foot Ladder.

Slipping on her mom's white archivist gloves, she opened the book and laid it on the display counter. "This is in wonderful condition," she said. A note in her mother's handwriting had been tucked inside the dust jacket. *First U.S. edition, 1882. $1,200.*

"Well, that's something," the blond woman said. "A regular museum piece. Thanks for showing me."

"There's a facsimile edition with the same binding and illustrations for $16.95." Natalie showed her the replica.

"Now that I can handle. This is really nice. Brings back memories." The woman set the book on the counter and took out her wallet. Then she grabbed a copy of the Stacy Kendall. "I'm going to get this one in hardcover after all."

"Sounds like you're quite the reader, then?" the other woman asked Peach.

"I like reading." He seemed distracted as he went back to measuring something on the wall.

"Maybe you'd like to join our book club," she suggested, scribbling something on the back of a business card. "We meet the first Thursday of every month."

"Hey, that's nice of you to ask," he said. "Unfortunately, all my Thursdays are booked."

She cocked her head and silently questioned him.

"I play in a band, and Thursdays are practice nights for us."

"You're a musician." She sent him a melting look.

He grinned. "I've been accused of worse."

He was in a band. For some reason, Natalie resented the fact that these flirty women were getting to know him better and more quickly than she had. Then she felt ridiculous for feeling that way. What he did when he wasn't repairing her shop was none of her business.

"So do you play locally, or . . . ?"

"We do, yeah. The group's called Trial and Error. I think the next gig is at the Smoke and Fog Tavern."

"I love going to live music. Maybe we'll check it out," the woman said, tapping a note into her phone. With a lingering look at Peach, she smiled, then turned away. She and her friend left with their purchases.

Natalie let out a sigh and started to straighten the table display. Though grateful for the flurry of sales, she reflected that getting a few bucks in the till should not have to be so hard. She glanced at Peach. "Hey, thanks for your help. They almost left empty-handed. That was some quick thinking."

He went back to feeding some electrical wires through a long tube in the wall. "Glad to be of service."

"If I could afford you, I'd add you to the staff."

He glanced at her over his shoulder. "You're the bookseller, not me."

"My bookselling skills are rusty," she admitted. "I need to up my game. I used to be pretty good at it, back when I worked here through high school and summers in college. Never thought I'd be at it again, though. Used to be, we could recommend a book, and the customer would buy it and go home happy. Nowadays, we recommend a book, and they might buy it, just not from us."

"Because of online sales?"

"And digital downloads. And gigantic volume discounts from the big club stores. It's hard to compete, day in and day out. And yet, here I am. Crazy, huh?"

He connected the wires to a wall outlet. "I've seen crazier."

"You don't have to buy the Stacy Kendall if you don't want."

"I want. It wasn't a stunt, Natalie. I like reading and it sounds like a hell of a book. I read all the time growing up, and even more when I was in the service, overseas."

"In that case, thank you, and you're getting the employee discount." She finished with the display on the main table, then put away the Mark Twain book.

She heard Peach's phone ping. He glanced at a text message, and something about it made his ears turn bright red.

"You got a text from one of the book club women, didn't you?" she asked.

The ears turned a deeper shade of red.

"Oh my God, I'm right."

"Don't you have bookkeeping to do? Or book shelving?" He turned his back and resumed working.

He probably got that a lot, she speculated. Women were drawn to guys who looked like that in a pair of jeans, and who were good at fixing things. And this one played in a band. The trifecta of attractiveness. She wondered how he would respond to the text. *Sorry, I'm married?*

She hoped he would. *Please don't be a cheater*, she silently urged him. *Don't shatter my illusions about you.*

On the Saturday of the Quill Ransom book signing, the sun shone with the kind of golden clarity that made people fall in love with San Francisco in autumn. Natalie had worked tirelessly to prepare: a poster in the window, a special table display, printed flyers, an email blast, chirpy reminders on social media, a tent sign on the sidewalk in front of the shop. She'd sent out press releases, but the local media hadn't picked up on anything.

Still, she was optimistic. The book was wonderful, and the author's past titles had been praised by readers and critics alike. She splurged on a tray of assorted cookies from Sugar and put out a samovar of warm spiced cider. She and Cleo set up folding chairs for the readers and stacked the books on a table decorated with a pretty autumn floral arrangement and a pitcher of water.

When the author arrived, Natalie stood in the doorway and smoothed her hands down her A-line skirt. She didn't dress with her mother's colorful flair, but she wanted to look nice for the event.

Quill Ransom appeared to be a kindred spirit. Middle-aged, with intelligent eyes and salon-shiny hair, she greeted Natalie with a warm and friendly smile. "I've been looking forward to this," she said, handing over a small gift bag. "Thank you for having me."

"Thank *you*. We love your books, and I know our readers are going to love the new one."

"Here's hoping," said Quill. "I was so sorry to hear about your mother," she added.

Natalie nodded, acknowledging the condolence as she had so many times in the past few weeks. She showed the author around the shop and set her up at the table.

Quill glanced at the clock. The look was not lost on Natalie. "Things have been a bit slow around here," she said.

"It's such a lovely day. People are probably out enjoying the weather." Quill took a dainty bite of a cookie and checked for crumbs. "Delicious," she said. "Thanks for going to all this trouble."

A few customers came in and browsed around. Natalie perked up. "We're having an author signing today," she said. "This is Quill Ransom, and she'll be reading from her new book. *Kirkus* gave it a starred review."

"Oh! I was just looking," said one woman. She eyed the empty chairs. Her gaze skated away from the author.

"Well, let us know if we can help you find something," Natalie said, wilting.

Cleo pitched in, trying to steer people over. Several helped themselves to cookies and cider. No one took a seat. Natalie nearly drowned in mortification.

Quill was charming as she circulated around the shop, since no one gathered to hear her read. One hesitant reader asked for a signed book. Natalie prayed silently for a dozen more. Even one more.

Her mother's friend Frieda came in, cheeks bright from the autumn air. "Oh, good, I'm not too late," she said, giving Natalie a hug. She bustled over to Quill. "You're one of my favorites. Did I miss the reading?"

Quill laughed. "I think we decided to skip the reading. But I'm happy to sign a book for you."

"Sign two," Frieda said. "One for me, and one for my daughter-in-law."

The author gamely inscribed two books.

"I thought—I really expected a better turnout," Natalie said. She remembered her mom's events, readers streaming in to meet the author.

"Don't feel bad," Quill said. "I'm a writer. Rejection is my life."

"I just don't get it," Natalie said.

"Oh, I do. This is my thirty-first book. Over the years, I've learned to adjust my expectations. Judging by my sales figures, my readers are many, but they do tend to stay away in droves."

"Your books are fantastic. *You're* fantastic. Did I get something wrong in the planning?"

"Nah." Quill sank her teeth into a chocolate chip cookie, ignoring the crumbs. "Some authors have the X factor, and they draw a crowd. Others just have readers. And frankly, I'd rather have my readers. They're all home waiting for me to finish my next book. Which—if I'm being perfectly honest—is my favorite place to be."

"Shoot. I'm really sorry," Natalie said.

"It's all right. I'll sign a stack of books so you'll have some on hand." She scrawled her name in the books and ate another cookie.

"Thanks for being a good sport," Natalie said.

"Thanks for being a good bookseller," Quill said. "Mind if I take some of these cookies with me?"

"Of course. Help yourself."

The author left, still unfailingly cheerful. Natalie turned to Frieda. "I'm mortified."

"Don't be. She's lovely. I can't wait to dive into her book."

"God, Frieda. I wish I could clone you."

"Ew. No. Listen, your mom would be proud. She endured her share of book signings where she and the author just sat there with egg on their faces."

"Really? I don't remember that."

"She was a trouper, your mom. I miss her every day."

Natalie nodded. She was getting a sugar high from all the cookies. "Why didn't Mom ever fall in love?"

"Blythe? She did, all the time. Just didn't stay in love. She finished with guys the way she finished books—closed them with gratitude and moved on to the next."

"Dean Fogarty came by after the memorial."

Frieda's eyebrows went up. "Did he, now?"

"I'm not sure why. We've never been close."

"I think—and with all due respect to your mother— that Blythe wanted it that way. He wanted to be more involved, but she didn't let him. She was grateful for the tuition payments, but—"

"*What?*" Natalie nearly choked on her cookie. "Tuition payments?"

Frieda fell still. "Oh, shit. You didn't know."

"I didn't know. Now you need to tell me everything."

"It's . . . I wasn't privy to all the details, but Dean paid your private school tuition. He set up a 529 plan for college, too. That's what Blythe told me."

"She didn't tell *me*," said Natalie. "Why didn't she ever say anything?"

"Blythe had her pride. And her secrets. Shoot. I betrayed a confidence."

"I don't know, Frieda. Mom's gone, so it's okay that

you told me. I'm glad you told me." She started folding up chairs and putting them away, and Frieda pitched in. "Now what? Do I contact Dean?"

"That's up to you, sweetie. Take your time, okay?"

"I will." Natalie made a special display of Quill's books and vowed to hand-sell every last one of them.

13

Early the next Saturday morning, Natalie woke up to the ominous beep of an alarm. Tipping her head to one side, she tried to pinpoint the source of the sound. It wasn't the security alarm—that one was silent and an alert would have appeared on her phone. It wasn't the shriek of the smoke alarm, either. Something from Grandy's room? Since he'd wandered away, she'd reprogrammed the building security system to alert her when an exterior door opened.

She threw on a sweater and slippers and took the back stairs to her grandfather's apartment. Through a crack in the door, she could hear the peaceful, soft whistle of his breathing. Without his hearing aids in, he tended to sleep soundly.

The beeping grew louder as she approached the

basement door. Flipping on a light, she went down the stairs, noticing a dank smell. The light fell over the big old letterpress and the workbench where they cleaned up and restored the vintage books. When she reached the bottom step, her feet landed in ankle-deep cold water.

She gasped and jumped back onto the stairs. "What the hell?" she asked, shuddering and peering through the shadows. In a far corner of the space, a red button was blinking. Gritting her teeth, she waded over to it and pushed the button, and the alarm fell silent. "Damn it," she muttered, wading back and then hurrying upstairs to find her phone. She peeled off her sodden slippers, then scrolled through her contacts.

Peach Gallagher picked up on the third ring with a sleepy "Yeah?"

"It's Natalie Harper," she said. "I'm sorry to call you on the weekend, but I didn't know who else could help."

A yawning sound came through the line. She pictured him in bed with his wife, who probably moaned and snuggled deeper under the covers. "What's up?" he asked.

"I've got a flood in the basement. An alarm woke me up. Can you come?"

"I . . . Only if it's okay to bring Dorothy along."

"Of course. She's always welcome. That's no problem at all. Again, I'm sorry to—"

"Hang tight. We'll be there soon."

She rushed to get dressed, glancing at her unkempt image in the bathroom mirror. "I swear, Mom," she said to her mother, "I have no idea how you did this, day in and day out. Did you just run from one disaster to the next?"

She piled her hair into a ponytail and brushed her teeth, then dressed in jeans, a gray college sweatshirt, and flip-flops.

She hesitated, wondering about lipstick and maybe a more attractive top. No. This was hardly a date. A workman was coming over to deal with her flood. He didn't care what she looked like, and she shouldn't care, either.

Across the street, the bakery was just opening for the day. The least she could do was offer Peach and Dorothy a snack. She grabbed some fresh cinnamon rolls and a jug of cider, then went back to the shop and turned on the coffee machine.

Grandy was up, hearing aids in, trousers on, shirt buttoned wrong. He greeted her with a blank-eyed stare. "Did you call the fire department?" he asked.

That cloudy stare always rattled her. It made him seem like a stranger instead of the man she'd known all her life. "Oh—you heard the alarm? There's no fire. It's a flood in the basement. I called Peach."

Grandy frowned. "Peach."

"Gallagher. The hammer for hire. He's been working on the building every day, Grandy."

"Ah, that one. Did the sump pump fail again, then?"

"It's done that before?"

"It has." He paused, and in a brief, subtle moment, his eyes seemed to focus on her face, and the endearing wrinkles of his smile appeared. He held out his arms. "And a good morning to you, Natty-girl," he said, his voice firm now.

She hugged him, taking in his scent of witch hazel and toothpaste, the comforting warmth of his arms. *Stay with me*, she thought, holding on to the moment.

"Have a seat," she said. "I brought cinnamon rolls."

"Lovely," he said. "We used to have breakfast together every morning before you went away to school."

She beamed at him, flooded with relief. Each time he mentally left her, she couldn't be sure she'd get him back. "I remember. You made the best toast, and you let me dunk it in your coffee. Here, let me fix this." He sat patiently while she unbuttoned and rebuttoned his shirt.

"I always shared a silly book with you," he said, "because I wanted to send you off with a smile."

"*The Watchbirds*," she recalled. "*Babar and the Wully-Wully. And I Mean It, Stanley.* We used to laugh and laugh."

"That is the best part of a grandfather's job—making a child laugh." He paused. "You don't laugh much anymore, Natty-girl."

"I . . . Hey, let's see if we can find more things to laugh at. It's hard to find the humor in a flooded basement, but maybe later we can watch something funny on TV."

"*Benny Hill?*"

She tried not to cringe. "*Happy Gilmore*," she countered, handing him a napkin. "There's fresh cider, too. The bakery across the street gets theirs from an orchard up in Archangel, where I used to live." She poured him a glass from the chilled jug.

"Do you miss it, then?" he asked. "Your life up in Sonoma County?"

She set the glass in front of him. "I don't know. Sometimes . . . It's so beautiful up there. I never really liked my job, though," she confessed.

"In that case, you're well rid of it. The way you spend your day is the way you spend your life." He picked up a napkin and stared at it uncomprehendingly.

She reached across and tucked it into his collar for him. *Oh, Grandy.*

"It would be very unfortunate if the water ruined things in the basement," he remarked. "That was Colleen's domain down there. Papa told me she didn't have much, and she was careful with her things. I shall ask Papa why they were never found."

Natalie was learning not to ask Grandy to remember or to try to make him understand what was real and what wasn't. She was learning that it was enough to be with him, to take his hand, tuck his collar, fix him something to eat.

Sometimes he spoke of his parents as if they were in the next room. Maybe it was a blessing for distant memories to be so vivid. She thought about her mother every day, remembered countless details of their life together, but already certain things were fading, like images in a rearview mirror growing smaller and smaller. There were moments when she couldn't picture the exact shape of her mother's hands or the way she parted her hair or the tilt of her head when she was concentrating. Moments like that made her panic. *Don't go. I still need you.*

Well before it was time to open, Peach arrived with Dorothy in tow. The little girl was adorable, even with severe bedhead and shoes that looked a bit like bedroom slippers.

Peach buckled on a tool belt and holstered a flashlight, then swapped his shoes for rubber boots. There was something elemental about him—his approach to a problem, his calm confidence as he ripped into a 150-year-old wall or tackled a flood.

Watching him at work made Natalie miss Rick. Despite her ambivalence about their relationship, she did miss his big manly hands and can-do air of self-confidence. Rick had not filled a pair of jeans in quite the same way Peach did, though. She cut the thought short. She had dragged him from his wife's bed this morning, for Pete's sake. He was, as she often reminded herself, totally off-limits.

"I'm sorry to get you over here so early," she said. "I'm sure you have better things to do on a Saturday than to look at my swampy basement."

"I didn't have to twist Dorothy's arm," he assured her. "She loves this place."

"How about a fresh cinnamon roll and some cold apple cider?" Grandy offered. Just the sight of the little girl caused him to light up. He sat straighter, and the smile lines on his face deepened.

"Mr. Harper!" Dorothy scurried over to him. "Yes, please."

"Oh good, you can keep each other company," Natalie said. "Can the two of you hang out together while I show your dad the basement?"

"Yep!" Dorothy hoisted herself onto a chair and sank her teeth into a cinnamon bun.

Natalie motioned Peach toward the back of the shop and led the way downstairs. "She's really cute," she said. "I love seeing my grandfather's face when he's around her."

"I'm pretty proud of that kid," Peach agreed. He flipped off one of the breakers at the electrical panel. "In the future, kill the power before you go wading in the basement."

"I didn't know I was supposed to do that."

"Standing water and live wires are not your friend."

"Got it."

Rays of light from the street-level windows high-lighted the skeletal hulk of the letterpress and re-flected off the surface of the water on the floor. "Looks bad, right?" she said. "Grandy asked if the sump pump failed again, so I suppose it's happened before."

"Let's take a look." He shone the light at the hot water heater and the pipes lining the ceiling and walls. "There might be a slight bit of good news," he said. "The water doesn't seem to be coming from a leak in your building. This is from the city."

"Can I get them to stop it?"

"You'll need to call the public works department. The pump should be able to handle it if I can get it running. I might need you to hold the flashlight." He glanced down at her feet. "Got any boots?"

"I'm okay with flip-flops."

His look of approval should not have been gratifying, but it was. She rolled up her pant legs, then took the flashlight from him and stepped into the standing water. "Dang, that's cold," she muttered, leading the way to the blinking red light in the corner.

Peach looked into the hole where the sump pump was positioned. Then he peeled off his sweatshirt and hunkered down, plunging his arm deep into the pit. "You're right. That's damn cold."

She held the light steady while he brought up the submerged pump and unplugged it. Taking the flashlight from her, he inspected the pump, which was covered in slime. He used a screwdriver to pry something out of the bottom. "Hello."

"What is it?"

"I think I found the problem." He held out a small metal object—an old key of some sort. "This was caught in the intake. Let's see if that fixed it. I'll plug it back in and you flip the breaker back on."

"Only if you promise not to get electrocuted."

"Yeah, not on the agenda today."

While he replaced the pump, she pocketed the key, went to the breaker box, and flipped the switch. A quiet mechanical hum ensued. "That's a good sign," called Peach.

She rejoined him in the basement. "Is it fixed?"

"Let's check it out." He shone the light, and they saw that the pump was sucking in swirls of water.

Natalie exhaled a breath of relief. "Wow. That's . . . I'm glad I didn't have to buy another pump. Thank you for fixing it."

He looked around. "The water'll subside pretty quickly. Good thing you heard the alarm."

"Miss Natalie?" Dorothy called from the top of the stairs. "Can you come?"

Natalie glanced at Peach, who shrugged. They both went upstairs, leaving flip-flops and boots in the hallway. Natalie was haunted by visions of her grandfather wandering off again. "Everything all right?" she asked.

The two of them were still sitting together in the café area. Sylvia had made an appearance, crouching on the windowsill nearby. Dorothy had a piece of lined paper and appeared to be making a list.

"Yes, indeed," said Grandy.

"What's up, buttercup?" Peach asked his daughter.

"We have a plan to save the bookstore," Dorothy replied, utterly serious.

Natalie felt a twist of anxiety in her gut. She'd been trying to protect her grandfather from fretting about finances. Forcing a smile, she asked, "Save the store from what? Sea monsters? Pirates?"

Dorothy's expression clearly said *I'm not having this.* "Mr. Harper and I are making a list. Number one, get more of these yummy cinnamon rolls to sell to your customers."

Peach washed up at the sink and helped himself to one. "Excellent plan. Dang, that's good."

"That's very smart," Natalie said. "I did the math, and the café makes up about a quarter of our revenues. You must be good at math, too."

"Nuh-uh. I just like sweet rolls."

"Then I'm going to see about having the bakery across the way help us turn the coffee area into a proper café." Yet another project she didn't have time for, but visitors to the shop would love it.

"You need Wi-Fi, too," Dorothy said. "Free Wi-Fi."

"Why do you need Wi-Fi with all these books?" asked Peach.

"I don't. All the grown-ups do. Mom says Wi-Fi runs the world."

Peach took a savage bite of his sweet roll.

"Adding guest Wi-Fi is on my list of projects," said Natalie. "And it's actually something I know how to do. I'm liking this free advice, Dorothy. What else do we need?"

"A book-signing party with Trevor Dashwood," the girl said matter-of-factly. "He's super famous and you'd sell a ton of books. He's magic."

"We could use a bit of magic around this place." She glanced down at the water she'd tracked on the floor.

"Then that's the plan. But we're just getting started. There's more to come." Dorothy tapped the pencil on the list, her eyes bright with excitement. "Trevor Dashwood needs to have a book signing. People will come and they'll all buy books and you'll be back on track."

A laugh of disbelief burst from Natalie. "Well, that would be a dream come true, but I'm sorry to say, I already looked into this, and his schedule is too full."

"That's what Mr. Harper said, too."

Apparently Grandy had been paying attention.

"I did have a book signing last Saturday, but it didn't turn out so well." The Quill Ransom book was selling, though, slowly but surely. "I've been talking to publishers about other popular writers," Natalie assured them both.

"Trevor Dashwood is the *most* popular," Dorothy declared. "I bet he would come if he knew you needed help." She leaned back in her chair and admired her list.

"Your child is very resourceful," Grandy said to

Peach. He beamed at Dorothy. "That's a compliment, by the way."

"Thanks," said Dorothy.

"I like this child, Blythe," Grandy added.

"I'm Natalie," said Natalie.

"I know that." He nodded at Dorothy. "She's not like some of those whippersnappers who come into the shop."

"What's a whippersnapper?" asked Dorothy.

"An impertinent youngster."

"I know what a youngster is, but what's impertinent?"

"The sort of child who makes fun of me because I'm old and have hair growing out of my ears and a forgetful brain. And I'm happy to say that although you are young, you're not impertinent. Therefore you're not a whippersnapper."

She grew quiet, studying him. "How old are you?"

"Seventy-nine."

"Did you have fun, getting that old?"

"What a delightful question. No one has ever asked me this question before." Grandy folded his hands on the table and looked off into the distance, his expression one of grave dignity. "I did have a great deal of fun. I loved this city. Used to run all around with my schoolmates. The Palace of Fine Arts was a wreck of a thing back then, fenced off and crumbling, but my buddies and I used to sneak in and race around scaring each other with a game like hide-and-seek. And we'd go to the lagoon and toss bread crusts to the ducks and have grass wars on the lawn there. When a kid fell into the lagoon, he came out covered in slime."

"Did that ever happen to you?" asked Dorothy.

"It did. My mother made me clean up at the pump out back, and she didn't even care that I was howling from the cold. We used to fly kites at Marina Green, and sometimes the navy would have submarine races and we could watch from the Heights. I had a friend named Jimmy Gallenkamp, and he was the king of the kite flyers."

"I like flying kites," Dorothy said.

"I know that. I saw you up at the park on my birthday." Grandy's expression sobered. "Have as much fun as you can, as often as you can. There were other times that I've endured unpleasantness and outright tragedy. There have been days when it was all I could do to take the next breath of air."

"Breathing is always a good idea," Dorothy stated.

"Indeed it is. When tragedy strikes, I must remember to breathe until I get to the fun part again."

"And if you forget, I'll remind you," Dorothy said.

Natalie rarely considered herself terribly maternal.

Kids were messy and unpredictable, a constant source of worry. They were a wild ride—flashes of utter joy interspersed with long stretches of tedium, often punctuated by disaster. But every once in a while, she came across a child who challenged her notions about kids. A child like Dorothy. She felt a tiny nudge of envy for the little girl's parents. The world could use more Dorothys in it.

14

Tess had not prepared Natalie for Jude Lockhart, her associate from Sheffield Auction House, the San Francisco firm where Tess used to work. Tasked with tracing the provenance of the artifacts they'd found, he was coming in today to let Natalie know what he'd discovered.

He was more stylish than any man had a right to be—flinty-eyed, square-jawed, and dressed in couture slacks, a black cashmere sweater, and a jacket with elbow patches. He stepped into the shop with a swagger and greeted her with a glorious smile. "I've heard about this place," he said, looking around. "Glad to have a chance to visit."

"I'm Natalie," she said, holding out her hand.

He grasped it in both of his, his clear gray eyes taking her in. "Sorry, I shouldn't stare," he said. "You're really pretty. And I'm being totally inappropriate."

Somewhere at the back of the shop where Peach was working, there was a raucous thud and the whir of a power tool.

Nonplussed, Natalie said, "Thanks for coming. I'm excited to hear what you found out about all our artifacts." She introduced him to her grandfather and then Peach when he came up front. As they shook hands, Peach said, "Hey, Jude," then chuckled. "I bet you get that a lot."

What a dork, thought Natalie. Why did she find that charming?

"Not really," said Jude. He scanned the barrister cases and the display under the glass counter. "Rare books?"

"Indeed," said her grandfather. He was shuffling papers, something he seemed to do to calm himself. "That was our very first stock in trade. Blythe and I started the shop with some old books we found in the basement. We've had some exciting finds—a book by each of the four original Bohemians—Mark Twain, Bret Harte, Charles Warren Stoddard, and that lady poet, Ina . . ." His voice trailed off. "I don't recall her full name."

"Coolbrith," muttered Peach, heading to his truck with some old lumber.

"That's correct," Grandy said. "Thank you, Mr. Gallagher."

"You just came up with that," Natalie said.

He shrugged, then used his hip to open the door. "Her name's on a plaque at the library over in Oakland."

She turned to Jude. "My mother specialized in works by California writers. If you know any collectors, send them our way."

"Will do. Let's take a look at your stuff." He followed her to the back office and set down the collection of found objects and artifacts. There were old photos, letters, and ephemera. An opium pipe. There was even a bag of gold marked *For my Annabelle.*

"Fool's gold," Jude told her.

"Bummer. It would be nice if it was real gold," Natalie said.

"Sadly, it's not. I wonder if whoever stashed it away knew."

"Poor Annabelle. Maybe it's a good thing she never found out."

Jude moved quickly through the photos and letters, small whittled objects like mouth harps, buttons, and whistles. There were several stock certificates for things that no longer existed. One of the letters concerned the Levi Strauss company, but according to Jude, it had no worth other than human interest.

"A lot of these things can be catalogued by the local historical society. The medals are a mixed bag. This group here"—he indicated a collection of objects—"is probably only of limited interest and little to no value. They could be donated to the historical society or put on display here in the shop. They could be sold to collectors, or some might be traced to their ancestors. Anyway, most of these things are curiosities. With one very great exception."

Jude took out a velvet-lined jeweler's pad and laid a largish medal on it. "This one is different. It's quite a find—a rare Dewey Medal engraved with the name of the recipient." He turned it over to show her while he consulted his notes. "The medal was authorized by Congress in 1898 for men assigned to the ships of Dewey's squadron that fought in the Battle of Manila Bay. Tiffany struck a limited number with a portrait of Admiral Dewey on the obverse. The name on the rim is Augustus Larrabee, Seaman, a member of the crew of the flagship *Olympia*. It's rare and worth maybe twelve grand at auction."

"That? Really?" Natalie leaned forward and studied the medal closely. She tried to picture the recipient, tucking the box away along with his memories of a war he'd fought in. Was he haunted by memories of the battle? Had he killed someone? Had he been wounded? Had he been proud of his role, or had he hidden the medal away because it was a reminder of trauma?

"There's something else you should know about the Dewey Medal," said Jude. "I found Mr. Larrabee's family."

"Tess mentioned that. You think they're related?"

"Very likely."

"Grandy, did you hear that?"

"I did," he said, his expression thoughtful. "Shall we contact them?"

"That's up to you." She paused, looked over at Jude. "What do you think?"

"According to the standards of provenance, it belongs to the building, which belongs to your grandfather."

"Grandy?"

He smiled. "It only seems proper to contact the family."

Natalie studied the tarnished treasure. To someone, somewhere, the sentimental value might be beyond price, she reflected. People liked knowing where they came from. She thought about her mother's mail-away DNA test. Had she been looking for something? Or just wondering?

Peach liked the bookstore job, and not only because it was a building full of secrets. He liked being around Natalie Harper, watching the way she studied a problem with deep absorption, considering it from all angles. He liked how she was with her old granddad, tender and patient.

Sometimes he wished he knew a way to lift her out of her melancholy, which she wore like a hand-knitted shawl around her shoulders.

Today, though, her mood was different. She flitted around the shop with an air of excitement, neatening the stacks of books and straightening the signs. "I'm glad you're here," she said.

The statement startled him. "Yeah?"

"I mean, because the Larrabees are coming for their medal—that rare one you found."

"That's cool, Natalie."

"Since you're the one who found it, they'll want to meet you."

It was good to see her looking animated. It was good to see her, full stop. She'd cleared off the counter that was usually covered with incoming books and invoices.

Apparently the family coming to claim the medal was into historical artifacts and genealogy, so this find was a big deal to them.

Although he didn't say anything, Peach wondered if the value of the piece—upward of ten grand, according to that pretty-boy appraiser—accounted for their keen interest.

Mind your business, he cautioned himself. Usually he had no problem doing that with clients. He did his job, collected his fees, and moved on to the next. Every once in a while, a lady client would come on to him, but he knew better than to go down that path. Even with the ones who weren't clients, come to think of it. He was so snakebit from the demise of his marriage that he tiptoed around relationships the way he would around a pit of vipers. It was remarkable to him that a love that had once been the center of his world had disappeared without a trace. The one good thing that had come of it was Dorothy, and she was worth all the drama and strife dished out by Regina and Regis.

Suzzy and Milt tried to tell him not to keep the door shut against other women, other loves. They pointed out that there could even be more kids one day, a whole new life. He didn't need a new woman. Or another kid. Or a new life. The life he had was just fine. But since meeting Natalie, he'd been having thoughts.

He'd been writing, too. One day he'd observed Natalie and her grandfather sitting across the table from each other, the vintage typewriter between them, going over the family history her mother had been working on. At one point, Andrew had reached over to briefly cup her cheek. He'd called her Blythe, and she hadn't corrected him. She'd smiled, and it was the saddest smile Peach had ever seen. And that became the basis for a song—a good one, according to Suzzy, who was always bluntly honest about such things.

That afternoon, the bell above the door rang, and Peach craned his neck over the bookcases.

He saw four people come in, and Natalie greeted them at the door. The Larrabees, he assumed. There was an old lady, a middle-aged couple, and a guy in his twenties who homed in on Natalie, checking her out like a wolf that hadn't eaten in weeks. Peach took an instant disliking to him.

At the same time, he conceded that the interest was understandable. There was something wildly attractive about Natalie Harper. It had to do with the fact that she was the absolute opposite of needy, holding herself at a distance, her defenses drawn around her like a wall.

There was a man in the mirror over Andrew's bathroom sink, and for a moment, he lost his place in time.

He felt as if he were looking at a stranger. More and more lately, his thoughts slipped into confusion and sometimes he couldn't find his way back.

Too often, it was hard to tell the difference between what was real and what his mind fabricated. In these moments, he had to close his eyes and breathe until he recognized himself again. He did that now, and felt a welling of gratitude when he opened his eyes and recognized the image looking back at him.

He had dressed carefully for the meeting with the Larrabee family. Pressed pants and a crisp white shirt, just the way May would have wanted. For as long as he could remember, her family laundry had taken care of his clothing. She used to do the pickup and delivery herself, back when she was ensnared in the arranged marriage she'd borne like the heavy canvas bags she transported to and from the laundry.

She would arrive and greet him with downcast eyes, but inevitably their gazes would meet, and the yearning that had bound them as youngsters would briefly flare, then subside into calm acceptance. They hadn't allowed themselves to hope that one day the world would allow them to show their love for each other. That day had come in the twilight of their lives, when her elderly husband had died and she had fiercely claimed her independence. She'd brought the laundry as usual on a Monday, only instead of the drawn and downcast mien, she had looked him in the eye and declared that she was free. The business was sold and within weeks, she'd come to live with him and Blythe and little Natalie in the cozy upstairs apartment.

They spoke of marriage sometimes, but he had never actually divorced Lavinia. He could have pursued a legal proceeding, yet it didn't seem necessary. She and her lover were longtime residents of Chateau Marmont in Los Angeles, which he knew because every once in a while, Blythe received a postcard.

"She's a stranger," Blythe used to say, tossing the card in the trash. "I don't know why she bothers."

But the absence of a mother had left its mark. During her childhood, Blythe had moved through confusion and hurt, then fury and, ultimately, dismissiveness.

May knew better than to try to step into that role, but she was a gentle presence in their lives. His girls, he called them—May and Blythe and Natalie—were sunshine and fresh air, and they created a deeply happy, if unconventional, family.

He clung to memories of May's soft singsong voice and soothing hands gently loving him in the shadowy quiet of the back bedroom. Sometimes missing her seemed like too much, like he should simply die rather than live another day without her. Then he reminded himself that there were those who never found what he and May had—poor Blythe among them. He was grateful for the years they'd had, and the ache of grief was assuaged by memories of a rare and special love. Now Blythe was gone as well, but that pain was still too fresh and sharp to soothe. His mind played tricks; he would see her face when he looked at Natalie. He'd hear her voice and imagine she was in the next room. His daughter was everywhere in this place, another reason he clung to the venerable old building despite its many flaws and failings. Just because something was old and damaged was no reason to abandon it.

Dorothy had asked him if he'd had fun getting old. He feared losing the cherished memories. If he forgot, would that mean his life had never happened at all? That it didn't mean anything? Perhaps this was the reason his mind lingered in the past.

Blythe appeared in the doorway of his apartment. "The Larrabees are here," she said.

Turning to her, he saw his daughter in all her radiant beauty, the large soulful eyes alight with anticipation. She was his greatest accomplishment in life—his daughter, best friend, business partner, and favorite person.

"Grandy?"

Natalie, not Blythe. His heart absorbed the hit yet again. Blythe was gone. "I'm ready," he said.

He was grateful for Peach Gallagher, who tackled the repairs with gallantry and confidence. The renovations revealed so much more than corroded pipes and rotted timber in the walls. Andrew was quite proud of the fascinating artifacts that had been secreted away generations before. This building was a trove of hidden lives—ghosts with secrets waiting to be revealed.

She introduced him to Augusta Larrabee Jones, a woman about his age with a dramatic swirl of silver hair, bright diamond earrings, and sharp polished nails. *Soigné*, she would have been called back in the day. Well put together. "Augustus Larrabee was my grandfather," she said. "My son and grandson also carry the name, but we call them Gus and Auggie to avoid confusion."

"We're all quite delighted to have found you," said Andrew as they filed into the back office.

Natalie took out the medal and the original letter that had been tucked into the tin box with it. Her friend from the auction house had treated the dry, brittle paper with a spray to keep it from crumbling, and it was now encased in plastic. They took a moment to admire the find. Objects that evoked memories had a peculiar sort of power, Andrew reflected. As he and Blythe had sorted through the precious few items Colleen O'Rourke Harper had left behind, he had felt a subtle tug of connection to a stranger he'd never known. Perhaps that was what the Larrabees were feeling now.

"I can't tell you how much this means to our family," said Gus Larrabee. "It's a major piece of a puzzle I've been putting together for years."

"My grandfather spoke with such pride of this medal," Augusta said, "but after the earthquake and fire, he assumed it was lost, like so much else in the city."

"This was one of the few structures left standing," said Andrew.

"Such stories he had," Augusta continued. "When he was under Commodore Dewey's command, he was blasted into the sea during a battle. Half his regiment drowned, but he and several men were rescued by native rebels—they were called Tagals back then. It didn't sound like a good outcome, though. He was taken prisoner, and only managed to escape when the Tagals got into a skirmish with Spanish soldiers."

"My grandfather went to fight in the Philippines as well," said Andrew, "but he never returned and no one ever discovered what became of him."

The woman regarded him with a gleam in her eye.

"When we spoke on the phone, you said his name was Julio Harper?"

Andrew nodded, though he couldn't remember speaking to her. "His name is on the marriage certificate left by my grandmother. Other than that, there was no other information to be found."

"We've brought a few things to show you," said Gus. "When you gave us that name, we knew there was a connection. There was a Julio Harper under Dewey's command."

Natalie looked at him. "Grandy, did you hear that? Julio Harper."

Andrew nodded again. "When he was declared missing in action, Colleen applied for a widow's pension. Yet she never received any funds. She had a letter denying the claim based on a dispute over the validity of the marriage. We never discovered the reason."

"This might explain it." The younger Larrabee, Auggie, placed a photograph on the table. "It's a replica print from the *San Francisco Examiner*."

Andrew leaned in, pushing his glasses against the bridge of his nose. The photograph showed a line of black soldiers standing at attention and gazing straight ahead. The caption read, *Some of our brave colored boys who liberated the Philippines were among the most gallant and soldierly . . .* A list of names under the photograph identified the soldiers in order.

"Look at this one, here." Auggie indicated the man in the middle, staring from beneath a dimpled brimmed hat, white-gloved hands folded around a rifle barrel. "That's Sergeant Julio Harper."

"That's your grandfather?" Natalie looked at Andrew, eyes bright with discovery.

"So it appears." He studied the grainy photo, showing a man of color like all the others in the shot. "He was a Buffalo Soldier, then." Andrew absorbed the information. His father's father had been a black man. It was very puzzling.

"You never knew?" asked Natalie.

"I couldn't have." Could he? Was it something he'd once known? What other memories had been snatched away?

"The pension claim was probably rejected because it was an interracial marriage. It was illegal," said Auggie Larrabee.

"Wow. Just . . . Wow." Natalie gazed across the table at Andrew, and he saw Blythe in her thoughtful smile. "Then how did they get a certificate of marriage?"

"Another matter to puzzle out," Andrew said. "This

is simply delightful, having a photograph of my grand-father," he added, addressing Augusta. "We're very appreciative."

The Larrabees left copies of the documents they'd brought, profusely thankful that they had been re-united with the medal. After learning of its value, Andrew had toyed for the briefest of moments with the notion of selling it. But there was no profit in keeping something that rightfully belonged to someone else.

As they were saying goodbye, young Auggie Lar-rabee asked Natalie if she'd like to go out for drinks sometime. She looked sweetly flustered, then said, "Maybe. I'm a bit busy with the shop. You know where to find me."

After they left, she came back into the office. "Mom did one of those home DNA tests," she said. "Did you know that?"

Andrew took off his glasses and wiped the lenses. "How's that?"

"You send off a saliva sample and it's analyzed to find out your genetic makeup. Mom did that test, and I found the results in her computer files."

"Perhaps she mentioned it. I don't recall."

"According to the results Mom received, most of her DNA was from the British Isles. But nearly an eighth of her DNA is West African, and another sixteenth is Spanish. And there's a small percentage of Native American as well."

He put his glasses back on and studied the grainy photo again. "Now we know why."

"Are you surprised? Shocked?" she asked.

He shook his head. "At what point does one's phenotype change one's ethnicity? It's never mattered to me."

She gave his shoulder a squeeze. "I love that you said that." Then she sighed. "What a world. I feel bad for old Colleen. I guess she wasn't old, though, just a young immigrant trying to make her way in a strange country. It's sad, picturing her raising her little boy alone, being denied her husband's pension. I hope they were happy for a time."

"I like to think they were," Andrew said.

"But your father . . . Did he look like a white man? A black man? Did you ever wonder . . . ?"

Andrew had only a few photographs of his parents. His mother was a blond Norwegian beauty, square-jawed with a determined light in her eyes. She was the one who had managed both the business and family, and she was a strict disciplinarian. His father, the son of this soldier the Larrabees had shown him, had been swarthy and tall, with upright military posture despite his lame leg, but had he looked like a man of color? Not to Andrew. To Andrew, he'd simply been a beloved father.

"I didn't wonder," he said. He handed her an envelope sealed with a length of waxed twine. "My father had so few keepsakes. We have his parents' marriage certificate. And the first actual photograph he had of himself is this one—with his draft registration card from 1917." He gave her the picture of his father, Julius, handsome and sober in the uniform of the U.S. Army Ambulance Service. "You can see what he selected in the Race category on the draft registration."

She studied the card. "The options are White, Negro, and Oriental. And he selected White. Maybe he didn't know. Maybe he opted to declare himself Caucasian to avoid dealing with prejudice. I wish we knew more about him."

"As you know, he was orphaned at the age of seven in the great earthquake and fire, so there are no photographs of him as a child, only the sketches of him made by his mother."

Natalie's eyes flew wide. "There are sketches? She made sketches?"

"We found them in the basement when the water heater was being replaced. It seems my grandmother was quite a fine artist. She kept illustrated journals as well, but I don't know what became of them. Blythe put them away to organize someday." Then doubts crept in. "Perhaps it was my mother who had the journals." The fright darted at him. Why couldn't he remember? *What* couldn't he remember? He felt it again, the yawning gap of memory, now filled with searing grief.

"I'll see if I can find them," Natalie said quietly.

She placed the card in the envelope with the marriage certificate. There were old newspapers and clippings as well. "Did you go through these other papers?"

"Blythe and I planned to do that together."

Natalie's eyes were as wet as the morning dew. "I have an idea. How about you and I read everything together?"

He smiled past the grief. What a blessing it was to have his granddaughter. "I'd like that, Natty-girl."

15

Natalie settled into the rhythm of the days, finding comfort in the routines of the shop. She came to love the hush in the morning before opening, turning on the espresso machine, and reveling in the heady aroma of the bakery delivery. When business was slow, she distracted herself from worry by looking after Grandy and keeping the shelves and tables tidy.

Peach was dealing with something in the basement. There was always something.

She still felt the little arrows of grief that darted into her at unexpected times, when she came across poignant reminders of her mother. A note of affirmation under the desk blotter: *Find a way or make a way.* A picture of herself in a drawer with Mom's writing on the back. *Gold stars for Natalie on Field Day.* She studied her tiny self, awkward and grinning, holding up a ribbon that had probably been awarded for participation. She'd never been much of an athlete.

The shop door opened and a guy with two kids came in. Natalie offered a nod of greeting. The kids scurried over to the children's section, and the guy went to browse the selection of cookbooks.

"Can I pick two, Dad?" the girl asked.

The little boy, her brother, was quickly decisive. "I'm getting this one. *Turn This Book Into a Beehive!* It's cool, see? A book you can turn into a beehive."

"Duh," said the sister.

"Hey," said the father.

"That's a good choice," Natalie said. "I used to live up in Sonoma County, and the people who kept mason bees in their gardens always had the best crops. Everything grows better with lots of bees to pollinate."

"I'm scared of bees," said the girl.

"Then you'll like mason bees. They don't sting."

She went over to the girl, who appeared to be agonizing over her choices. "I read this one last night," said Natalie, taking out a copy of *Lalani of the Distant Sea.* "It's about a girl who goes on a quest to save her mother." Natalie had read the story with her heart in her throat, wishing there had been a way for her to save her mom. "It's scary in places, but I think you'll like the ending."

"Hey, yeah!" Her face lit up. "Dad! I'm getting this one." She hugged the book to her chest.

Natalie had nearly forgotten how much she loved moments like this. A child, eager to dive into a book and get lost in the story. Their father selected a Mary Kay Andrews cookbook and set it down on the counter with the others. "Goals," he said, indicating the mouthwatering spread on the cover. He added another book to the stack—*Sex and the Single Dad*. "Also goals," he murmured. His gaze lingered on Natalie's mouth. He didn't look away as he produced his wallet.

He was cute, she allowed as she ran the charge and put the purchases in a bag. And single. Then she felt guilty for noticing he was cute. He was the second guy she'd noticed today and it wasn't even noon yet.

"Well," she said with a bright smile. "Good luck with that."

He smiled back, signing his charge slip. "Nice store," he said. "Just moved to the area. We'll come again soon."

"Great," she said. "We're open seven days a week."

His name was Dexter, she noted, putting the slip away. Dexter Shirley Smiley.

Peach emerged from the basement and sauntered over to the counter, a wicked-looking Sawzall in hand. "Just need to check on something," he said. "Okay if I go upstairs and take a look at the floor under the tub?"

"Sure," she said, then turned back to Dexter and his kids. "Thanks for coming in."

Peach headed upstairs with the big saw, tools clanking on his belt. For some reason, she had the impression he was watching over her. It was just a sense she had, maybe a false sense, but it helped her feel less alone. Working side by side day after day created a subtle, hard-to-define bond between them. She frequently reminded herself that he was not her friend. He was friendly. There was a difference. And the repair bills were adding up. She'd started writing book reviews for the *Examiner*, bringing in a small but steady stream of extra money.

At lunchtime, she went to check on Grandy. He looked cozy in his big reading chair, his feet close to the radiator and a pencil in hand as he read over the printed pages of the local history he and her mother had collected.

When she stepped into the apartment, he looked up, then took off his spectacles and wiped them on the tail of his shirt. "May I help you?" he asked.

Shoot. He'd seemed more lucid earlier today, but now his gaze was unfocused.

"I was about to ask you the same thing. What would you like for lunch? I was going to send out for Thai."

"We always get the soup special on rainy days," he said.

"That sounds good." They decided on tom yum soup from a place nearby that made deliveries.

"I'm ordering Thai for lunch," she told Peach and Cleo. "Do you want something?"

"My usual," Cleo said. "I always get the same thing from that place—pad thai, three stars."

"I'll have the same," Peach said affably. "Only make mine four stars."

"Brave man," Natalie said. "They like to go big on the spice."

"I can handle it," he said.

When the food arrived, she and Peach sat with Grandy in his apartment, enjoying the hot lunch while rain smeared the window, turning the view of the garden into a Monet painting. Her grandfather was in a talkative mood now, eager and energized by the family history project.

"People like to know where they came from," he said to Peach. "Gallagher is an Irish name. Your people came from Ireland, then?"

Peach nodded. "The first Gallagher we could trace settled in Atlanta and worked as a framing carpenter."

"An honorable trade," Grandy said. "Perhaps it's in your blood, then. I can tell you know your craft."

Peach had no idea how grateful she was that he treated her grandfather with such dignity and patience. As she returned to the shop so Cleo could have her lunch break, she found herself wondering—not for the first time—what Peach's wife was like. Did the two of them make dinner together after work, ask Dorothy about her school day? Would Peach talk about the old bookstore he was working on? Did he describe its crumbling walls and dotty old man tapping away at his typewriter? Would he mention the stressed-out woman who was probably going to lose everything while trying to save the shop?

In the final hour before closing time, no one came to the bookstore. Not one customer. Grandy had gone to a community dinner at the senior center with Charlie. Now they were playing canasta with their usual squad. Peach had finished the day's projects, and he was gone, too. Even Sylvia the cat had padded off somewhere, probably looking for a warm place to curl up as the autumn fog gathered and wandered through the streets. Bertie and Cleo were gone for the day,

Cleo to a table reading of one of her plays and Bertie to meet friends for a drink. He'd invited Natalie to join them, but she'd begged off.

Now she wished she'd accepted. So far, her social life in the city was a big fat zero.

The silence accentuated her solitude and despair. These were the moments that struck her like a blow sometimes. The reality of her mother's absence hung in the very air of the shop, redolent of the papery aroma of books and ink, spinning like dust motes stirred by the turn of a page. The ache of loss was almost physical as she yearned for more time with her mother. The two of them had had their differences, but at the core of their relationship was an indelible bond. She hoped with all her heart that Mom had felt the same way. It was utter torture to think about all the conversations she'd never have, all the moments she'd miss out on.

She rubbed her temples and closed her eyes, trying to swim up from the depths of loneliness. When she opened her eyes, she saw that a refuge lay right before her, as it had all her life. The books.

You're never alone when you're reading a book.

She had known the truism all her life. Not only that, she knew there was a book for everything. Her mother had taught her well.

From the publishers' preview collection under

the counter, she selected a novel with an intriguing premise—a woman discovers that she has the uncanny ability to know the outcome of every decision she makes.

Now, that, Natalie thought, opening to the first page, *is a superpower.* Within moments, she had sunk into the story and was happily lost in a different world, with people facing troubles that made her own seem like child's play.

A book was a powerful thing. It could take her away from all her incessant worries for whole minutes at a time.

Then she made the mistake of setting the novel aside to go through the latest mail. Bills and notices. On the spreadsheet under Daily Till, she wrote the word *pathetic.* If she was going to make this crazy enterprise work, she needed a small miracle. Maybe a big one.

On a corkboard above her desk, she looked at the checklist Dorothy and Grandy had made the day of the basement flood. Though written in a childish scrawl, the ideas for making the store more profitable showed a wisdom beyond Dorothy's years. Add yummy snacks to the café menu. Make an advertising poster. Have a book party for kids on read-aloud day. Go on the radio and tell people about the store. Give out punch cards to keep track of purchases. Host book signings. Send emails to customers and offer them a coupon.

Just looking at the list bolstered Natalie's determination. She knew she could make this work. Bookstores were important. People loved them. They added a special vibrancy to any community. The very idea had sustained her mother for decades, and now it was up to Natalie to carry on.

Glancing at the clock, she saw with some relief that it was closing time. She could finally pour herself a glass of wine and escape into the book she was reading, leaving the depressing spreadsheet for tomorrow. Then, as she went to turn the Closed sign around and lock up, a sleek Tesla sedan pulled up to the curb, insinuating itself into a prime parking spot that was almost never vacant.

A man got out and hurried to the door, his shadow blocking out the last light of the day. He let himself in before she could flip the sign.

"Oh, good," he said. "I was afraid I'd miss you."

"Um, I was just about to close for the day, and—" Natalie stopped in midsentence. The man looked familiar, though she didn't know him.

And then—dear Lord in heaven—she did.

He wiped his feet on the mat. "Yeah, sorry. Traffic, you know." He stuck out his hand. "You're Natalie Harper, right? My name is Trevor. Trevor—"

"Dashwood," she finished for him on a breathy rush of wonder. Her mouth went dry. Her mind emptied out. She scrambled to find something to say. She shook his hand, trying to remember how to speak. "I'm . . . Yes, that's me. Trevor Dashwood, oh my God. Wow, hi." *Holy shit*, she thought. *You sound like an idiot.* Because . . . *Trevor Dashwood.*

He was even more attractive than in his book jacket photo. This was quite a feat, because in general, jacket photos tended to be touched up or out of date. This guy, though. "And . . . wow, sorry. As you can probably tell, you caught me by surprise."

He let go of her hand and studied her with an unhurried perusal, his gaze warm and friendly. He had brown eyes and nicely shaped brows, and Mr. Darcy hair. "You don't like surprises?"

"I've never been surprised quite like this." She couldn't stop looking at him. How on earth was she standing here having a conversation with one of the most popular authors in the world? Somehow she kicked her brain into gear. "Please," she managed to say, blushing furiously. "Come in. Can I get you a coffee? Something else to drink?"

"I'm fine for now." He paused, glancing around at the dim shop. "Is this a good time, or—"

"It's a great time," she said, thinking about the lonely evening that had loomed ahead only a few moments before. They went over to a café table. She practically melted inside as he held a chair for her. "Sorry, I'm a bit starstruck. It's not every day an author wanders in . . ."

"I'm the one who should be starstruck," said Trevor. "Booksellers are a writer's best friend."

"What a nice thing to say."

"I'm not being nice."

"Yes, you are. And thank you. But I'm totally confused. What brings you here?"

"I came because of this." He took an envelope from his pocket and unfolded it on the table. "I get a lot of letters from readers, and most of them don't make their way past my assistant, but every once in a while, Emily spots a special letter like this one. I can't stop thinking about it. A little girl named Dorothy sent me a note about your shop."

"What?" Natalie scanned the note. It had been carefully written on lined schoolroom paper and illustrated with childish whimsy. The handwriting was familiar. *Dorothy.*

Dear Mr. Dashwood,

I'm worried about the bookstore in my neigh-borhood because it's very expensive to have a store around here. I'm worried because it might have to close and that would be a ~~Tradegy~~ Tragedy. I have an idea for you. I think you can save the Lost and Found Bookshop if you would do a book signing, because everybody loves your books and they would all come. Plus, I would like to meet you in person. The lady who owns the shop is named Natalie Harper. She is really nice!!! I know you're busy but please come. The librarian at my school said your Publisher would make sure you get this letter.

Sincerely, Dorothy Gallagher

On the back of the page, she had drawn a detailed picture of the shop with the display window and the cat napping on a shelf. The picture was labeled with the shop's slogan—*An Eye for Good Books.* There was an overly flattering portrait of Natalie, with flowing hair, curly eyelashes, and an hourglass figure, her red lips turned down in sadness. There was another page with a carefully rendered drawing of herself and Trevor, his bold eyebrows accentuated with slashes of black.

"Dorothy's one of my favorite customers. She's

adorable," said Natalie. "And a legit fan of your books."

"I can see why she likes this place," he said, scanning the shelves and bookcases. Then his gaze returned to Natalie. "And you."

Natalie's heart sped up. Was he flirting with her? How was that even possible? How could this guy—this American literary god—be flirting with her?

She decided to ignore the vibe. Surely it was her imagination. Women probably threw themselves at him all the time. She did not want to be reduced to a cliché, the lonely woman starstruck by an actual star. "Well then," she said. "Would you like to take a look around?"

She showed him the children's section, with its plentiful supply of his titles, which he gamely signed. Then he checked out the w.o.w. shelf by the coffee area.

"My mother curated this—some of her favorite words of wisdom," Natalie explained.

He opened a George R. R. Martin book. "'Mine is the blood of the dragon,'" he read, and looked over at Natalie. "Should I be scared?"

"Depends on how you feel about bloodthirsty women."

Sylvia padded over and checked him out with a disdainful sniff, then rubbed his leg and walked away with her tail in the air.

"I've had many first dates that went like that," Trevor observed.

"First dates are hard," Natalie agreed, feeling the flirting vibe again. Or maybe not. After what had happened with Rick, she didn't trust herself to read a situation anymore. "Too bad we can't just skip over them."

"Who says we can't?"

"The space-time continuum, for one thing."

"Oh, a smarty-pants, are you?" He smiled, exuding warmth.

It still felt surreal, having him here, as if he'd just walked out of a dream. "I don't mean to stare, but I can't believe you showed up out of the blue."

"I come to the city fairly often," he said. "I live in Carmel, but I've also got a place on Nob Hill."

"Well, I swear I didn't put Dorothy up to this. I had no idea . . . I did contact your reps to see about an event, but they weren't encouraging. You're a busy writer, scheduling events two years out, they said."

"They'd schedule my bowel movements if I let them." He grinned. "Sorry. I'm known for my potty humor."

"So are your readers."

"Do you mind if I ask . . . Is the shop really in trouble? Like Dorothy says?"

Natalie took a deep breath. "I don't mind. There are

challenges. That's no secret in bookselling these days. I believe in this place, though. I took over the shop under unexpected circumstances."

"Care to elaborate?" he asked. "You don't have to if—"

"I don't mind that, either. This was my mother's store. It's home to me, though. I grew up here—we lived in the apartment upstairs. She died in a plane crash, so now I'm in charge of this place."

He briefly touched her arm. "You've had a tough break. Worse than tough. I'm supposed to be good with words, but I don't know what to say. What happened is . . . damn. It sucks."

"Yes. Pretty much on every level. I mean, I do love bookselling, so it's not like I'm dragging myself to work every day. But the building's got major problems. Business is off. My grandfather lives in the downstairs apartment, and he . . . well, he's not in the best of health. My mom left behind a pile of debt she never told me about and . . ." She forced herself to stop the rush of words. "And I'm done complaining to you. I'm sure you didn't come here to listen to this litany. It's an honor to have you stop in."

"I don't mind hearing about your troubles. I want to help."

"My first thought when all this happened was that

I'd need to close the shop and sell the building. But it's complicated."

"I can do complicated."

He was so easy to talk to that the initial jolt of tongue-tied admiration was wearing off. "My grandfather and my mom opened the Lost and Found Bookshop the year I was born, and they've run it together ever since." She gestured around the room, shadowy now with the after-hours lighting. "I grew up between the stacks."

"Is there a story behind the name? Lost and Found?"

"There is, actually. They launched the bookstore with a collection of old books Grandy found in the basement."

"Grandy? You call him Grandy? That's really cute, and it makes me like him already."

"He's pretty great."

"I'm kind of nuts about rare books," Trevor said.

"Then you'll be really nuts about this." She got up from the table and went to the counter. "Legend has it that Mark Twain and Bret Harte used to drink here when this building was a saloon called the Ten-Foot Ladder. It's never been verified, but I like to think it's true." She showed him the glass-front barrister and under-counter display case of rare books.

He leaned close to her. "That's quite a collection." He indicated rare copies of *A Christmas Carol* and *Great Expectations* down near the floor. "You've relegated Charles Dickens to the bottom shelf."

"Great stories, but he's not my favorite," she said. "He was so awful to his wife."

"Ah. Well, then. Show me one of your favorites."

"There's a first edition *Prince and the Pauper*, but no other Twain in stock at the moment. My very favorite isn't Mark Twain, even though he had the most epic love story with his wife and treated her like a queen. I like Jack London because of his ties to the area," she said, opening the case. "This copy of *White Fang* has his verified signature and a letter in his own hand." She laid it carefully on the counter, a near-mint volume with a tooled leather cover and the author's signature on the title page.

"It's a beauty," Trevor said. "I started reading him when I was a kid and reread him a few years back. I'll never forget *Burning Daylight*, the one about the guy who throws away his entire fortune in exchange for true love."

"I still have my tearstained copy of *Call of the Wild*," she said. "I cried and cried. 'There is an ecstasy that marks the summit of life . . .'"

"'. . . and beyond which life cannot rise.'"

"You did not just finish that quote for me." She regarded him with cautious delight.

"Sorry, couldn't help showing off a bit."

"That's amazing. As Anne-with-an-*E* would say, we must be kindred spirits."

"You can have Anne and her green gables," he said. "Not a fan."

"Most guys aren't. Every girl is." Part of her stepped back as if she were having an out-of-body experience. She was actually here in her shop discussing literature with one of the most famous people in publishing.

"All right, then. I'll take this one." Trevor reached into his jacket.

"Wait. What? You . . . Are you sure?"

He laughed. "Is this some kind of test?"

She took a printed sheet from the back of the book. "It's valued at five thousand dollars." She was almost embarrassed to say the amount aloud. She couldn't read his expression as he regarded her for about three beats of her heart. Maybe he was getting a Lee Israel vibe from her, wondering if she was a fraud or forger. "Really, I—"

"Done, then." He took out a checkbook.

She stopped breathing for a moment. Then, somehow, she managed to shift into professional mode. "You're serious."

"Serious as a shushing librarian."

"Well. I'll wrap it up for you. And give you a certified receipt." Her hands shook a little as she took the check—from Flip Side LLC with a post office box address—and carefully wrapped the old volume and placed it in a bag—one of the nice bags, not the cheap ones. *Thanks, Jack,* she thought. *You're off to a good home.*

She tried to picture the book in Trevor's house. Did he have an elegant English gent's library? A bohemian book cave? A showy showroom?

"So about that book signing . . ." he said. "Remember, our mutual friend Dorothy says you'd like to schedule something soon."

"I'd love to host an event for you," she said. "But I understand how busy you must be. Your publisher and your rep were pretty firm about saying you're not available."

"They're just doing their job as gatekeepers. If you're game, I'll make time," he said.

"Really?"

"Really. Look, I get what you're going through. But bookstores are the lifeblood of this business. Let's make a plan."

Her heart skipped a beat. "Yes," she said. "Let's make a plan."

A **half** hour later, Natalie was convinced she had stepped into a dream. A pinch-myself-this-can't-be-happening dream.

Trevor Dashwood wanted to have a book signing. Given his high profile, it was going to be more complicated than simply setting up a table in the shop. The event was going to take a lot of planning. He insisted on making the plan over drinks at his favorite spot in the city—the Tower Library Bar.

The Tesla glided through the hills like a toboggan in winter, silent except for the silky electronic music of SwingLow drifting like a phantom caress through the speakers.

A valet stationed at the ground floor of the high-rise greeted him with discreet familiarity, and they crossed an opulent lobby to the rooftop elevator. As they waited, two young women approached, blushing but determined.

"Trevor Dashwood, right?" one of them said.

He smiled briefly and nodded.

There weren't many writers people could recognize by sight, but Trevor Dashwood was definitely a man of the moment.

The woman held up her phone. "I hate to intrude, but could I . . ."

"No problem." With an ease that likely came from long practice, he posed with her for a quick selfie and did the same for her friend. "Just do me a favor and don't tag the location for a few hours."

"Of course," she said. "I just want you to know I've loved your books ever since I discovered them at the age of ten, and I'm saving them for my own kids one day."

"That's really great. Thank you." When they were out of earshot, he added, sotto voce, "For making me feel older than rock itself."

Others nearby checked him out, but just then, the elevator arrived and they stepped inside the bullet-shaped glass car.

"I guess you get that a lot," said one of the passengers, a guy holding hands with another guy.

"A fair bit," said Trevor. "I don't mind." He gifted them with a grin and another selfie.

"Hey, thanks for being cool about it," the guy said.

As the elevator rose, Natalie studied the view, a magical panorama of glittering lights and flickering reflections off the water. The penthouse bar had an even more commanding view, and craft cocktails named after local or formerly local writers and their books—the Anne Rice blood orange martini, the Tsukiyama Samurai, the Christopher Moore Demon, the Joy Luck

Cocktail. The walls were lined with well-curated volumes from Ferlinghetti, the Bohemians, and a host of Bay Area bright lights.

"How's your drink?" he asked as they settled together at a cozy window table.

"The Lemony Snicket? Amazing," she said. "This whole night is amazing. I feel like Cinderella."

"Excellent. My plan is working," he said.

"That's your plan? This is your plan? You had a plan?"

"Guilty as charged. True story—I wrote the flip side of Cinderella when I was in fifth grade," he explained. "I illustrated the hell out of it, too. I named the stepsisters Grace Slick and Janis Joplin, and they kicked ass."

Natalie laughed. "So you've been at this for a while." She studied him across the table. He was so good-looking, she nearly drowned in him. "Why do you say guilty?"

"When I got Dorothy's letter, I looked up your shop online and read about your mom."

"Oh." The constant ache inside her flared up. "Yes, the story made the rounds."

"Unfortunately, human tragedy has a way of doing that," he said. "I'm really sorry, Natalie, sorry as hell."

She kind of wished he hadn't pretended earlier not

to know what had happened. Maybe he didn't want to scare her off by admitting he'd looked her up. "Thanks. It's been . . . I don't even know how to describe it. Like having the whole world pulled out from under me."

"That's pretty descriptive. I'm sorry," he said again, and he touched her arm. Briefly.

She liked his touch. It gave her a shiver.

"So before the cocktails take effect," he said, "let's get down to business. Can I add Emily and her assistant to your phone?"

She took it out and handed it over. "Of course."

Trevor started tapping the screen. "Emily is my assistant, and hers is Edison, and he is incredible. He'll work with the event planner and publicist to set everything up. How does sometime this month sound?"

"This month . . . ? You're kidding, right?"

"Not even. It's true that these things usually need a lot of lead time, but I have a break in my schedule, and a crack team. Edison can do it all—organize the online ticket sales, book the venue, coordinate with the publisher, everything. Each ticket sold is good for two seats at the event—an adult and a kid—and a copy of my latest book, so the sales should be pretty good."

Pretty good? Her head was spinning. *Pretty good.*

"What do you say, Cinderella?"

"You *are* Prince Charming," she said.

PART THREE

It was clear that the books owned the
shop rather than the other way about.
Everywhere they had run wild and taken
possession of their habitat, breeding and
multiplying and clearly lacking any strong
hand to keep them down.
—AGATHA CHRISTIE, *THE CLOCKS*

16

"We need to talk about your daughter," Natalie said to Peach the moment he showed up in the morning.

He grinned, always intrigued by her direct manner. "My favorite subject." He went around to the back of the truck and unloaded some of the gear he'd need for the day—including a saw for the attic beam he was replacing. The rotted one was downright scary, its insides powdered by termites. "What's up?"

"She wrote a letter to Trevor Dashwood, the author."

"Kid likes writing letters. She does that a lot, mostly to writers and musicians she likes. It's cool, right? I'd rather have her writing letters than getting addicted to a phone and forgetting the rest of the world exists." He paused, glanced over at her, then did a double take. She looked different today. Her eyes sparkled even brighter than usual, and her smile was quicker. She had shiny hair, polished makeup, a fitted turquoise dress, high heels. Could be his imagination, but she seemed to be upping her game.

He liked it when the sadness lifted, even briefly, no matter the reason. "So how'd you know Dorothy wrote to the guy?"

"He came to see me last night."

Peach frowned. "Came here? The writer who's so famous no one can talk to him?"

"Apparently he listens to Dorothy. He was really moved by her letter. She told him the store was in trouble and asked him to come for a book signing."

"No kidding." So that was why Natalie seemed different this morning. "What did the famous author say?"

"He's going to do it. A book signing like this will give us a huge boost. My head is still spinning. All because of that remarkable child of yours."

"My daughter is magic," he said, not even trying to suppress his fatherly pride. "And good for Trevor Dashwood for taking her seriously and showing up." *At night*, Peach thought. Was it weird that the writer had shown up at night? In person, rather than having his "people" call? Maybe writers were weird that way.

"No writer should be too famous to ignore a sincere letter from a fan," said Natalie. "Especially a fan like Dorothy. Not only did she tell him about the bookstore, she included a picture of herself and a drawing she had made of him."

"Wow. A triple threat. I don't blame him for wanting to help. Man, she's going to be so excited that her plan worked." He could hang around all day talking about his kid, but there was work to be done. Other clients and other jobs were stacking up like air traffic over a busy airport, so he needed to finish this project and move on. "It's going to be noisy in the back," he said. "Is your grandfather up?"

"Yes, he went to the senior center for breakfast."

"I'll get to work, then."

"Me too. I can't wait to tell Cleo and Bertie. Oh, and a heads-up—a reporter and photographer from the *Examiner* are coming to do a little feature on the shop. The publicity machine is already kicking in."

That probably explained the extra-pretty hair and makeup and clothes she was wearing.

"I'll stay out of the way, then," he said. "They won't want my ugly mug in their paper."

"You? Ugly?" She gave his arm a nudge. "Stop it."

"So you think I'm beautiful?" He batted his eyes at her.

She shooed him away. "Go. Get to work, Gallagher. I'd better let Cleo and Bertie know about the reporter, too."

Every once in a while he toyed with the idea of asking her out, but dismissed it. For one thing, he couldn't tell if she liked him. Sometimes he felt her watching him and thought maybe yes. But most of the time, she kept her distance and he figured she wasn't interested. Her boyfriend had died with her mom. The last thing she needed was another boyfriend. Which was for the best. Dating a client was a bad idea, something he'd learned from experience. Dating anyone was a bad idea, given his luck with women.

He was grateful for the autumn sunshine in the little back garden, a reprieve from a string of drizzly days. The attic beam had been custom fabricated, but now he had to put on a good finish and fit it with hardware. After that, he'd supervise the insanely treacherous task of hoisting the new section and seating it in place of the rotten one. He'd lined up a crane for that. Natalie had turned a bit green around the gills when he'd quoted her the cost, but one look at the crumbling wood had convinced her it had to be done.

Each time he accessed the attic to check on something, Peach had to pass through her apartment. When she'd first showed it to him, the place had been crammed with books and colorful clutter from her mother, who apparently was not super organized nor inclined to throw things away. He noticed that Natalie had been systematically conquering the clutter but managed to keep the color and charm of the place. The overstuffed love seat under the window had been excavated, and she'd turned it into a little reading retreat. There was an afghan and a couple of pillows, an antique side table with a nice stack of books, and a lamp with an old-fashioned painted shade depicting Yosemite Falls.

He tried not to snoop, but as he passed the bedroom, he got a waft of girly scent and lavender, and he noticed a Giants T-shirt hanging behind the door. He wondered sometimes if his own place—the big drafty house on Vandalia Street he shared with Suzzy and Milt—felt homey enough for Dorothy. God knew, the kid was adaptable, shuttling between Regina and Peach as the parenting plan dictated. Maybe one of these days he'd ask Natalie for advice on how to girly things up in Dorothy's room. The kid would probably love that.

Natalie had a lot on her plate, though. Maybe not the best time to ask for decorating advice.

Throughout the workday, Peach overheard Natalie with the reporter and photographer. They seemed to be capturing a day-in-the-life of the shop. She was so damn smart, helping people find the books they were looking for—and some they didn't know they needed. The customer of the moment was a middle-aged woman with a little white dog wearing a jacket. "Blythe's not here anymore?" the woman asked. "Did she retire, or . . ."

"Blythe was my mother," Natalie said quietly. Her gaze darted to the reporter, who occupied a stool behind the counter. "I'm sorry to say, she died in an accident. A plane crash."

Peach felt bad for her, having to explain the situation over and over. And then there was her grandfather, who kept confusing her with Blythe, needing to be told yet again that his daughter was gone.

"That's terrible," the woman said. "I'm very sorry. But also grateful that her shop lives on."

The reporter made some notes on a little pad.

"Blythe was always so clever about helping me find books," the woman continued. "There's one I heard described on NPR, but I didn't catch the name of it. Or the name of the author."

"What was it about?" asked Natalie. "Tell me a few details, and I'll give it a shot."

The customer launched into a rambling description of a book about a woman who was married and shared an illicit kiss with someone who was not her husband and had an email flirtation and got so freaked out about that it triggered a whole life reexamination.

"Okay, well." Natalie tapped her chin with her finger. "Doesn't sound familiar. Do you remember what program you heard it on?"

"Sorry, no. One of those podcasts, I guess. It just sounded like a good book, kind of funny and snarky but heartfelt at the same time."

Natalie was clearly at a loss, which sucked for her, since Peach knew she wanted to look professional. She was in luck, though. He knew exactly what book the woman was referring to. His ex-wife had read that book. He could picture it on her nightstand. Even after all this time, he could still picture her nightstand. Stepping over to the memoir section, he found the book and tipped it slightly outward. Then he pretended to tap at something with his hammer.

Natalie glanced over at him, slightly annoyed. He

pointed to the book, then headed back upstairs to work. "Do you think it could be this one?" he heard Natalie ask. "*Love and Trouble* by Claire Dederer?"

Peach whistled as he climbed the stairs for the dozenth time that day. He liked colluding with her.

At the end of the day, Peach took his time loading up. No rush to get home, since Dorothy was at her mom's tonight. He planned to grab a pizza and spend some time on the internet learning more about structural engineering. With a work crew lined up, he wanted to make sure the attic beam was going in the right way.

"Thanks for your help today," Natalie said, following him outside.

"No problem. I've got a crew coming tomorrow to hoist the beam into the attic."

"Oh! Good. I meant about the book. Keeping me from looking ignorant in front of the customer."

"You don't have to know every book," he pointed out.

"True. And yet you seem to."

He laughed. "Nah. That one happened to be familiar."

"Well, you're familiar with a lot of things I don't associate with a . . . is it insulting to call you a handyman?"

He grinned. "I've been called worse."

She tilted her head to one side, like she wanted to hear more. "Did you do a lot of reading when you were in the Marines?"

I did a lot of killing when I was in the Marines, he thought. "Always been a big reader," he said, "ever since I was a kid."

"In Georgia, right? Do you still have family there?"

"My folks are there." He supposed he could tell her about what had happened back in Atlanta, and what had set him on this path, but he hated that story. The only part he liked was that he now had Dorothy, the best kid in the world.

Natalie's phone pinged, and she glanced at it. "Hey, that vase we found? My friend Tess is coming in the morning to talk about it."

"Cool. Good news, I hope."

"We'll see."

When Tess arrived to talk about the old Chinese vase, Natalie was still floating from her meeting with Trevor. She told her friend about it over coffee and sweet rolls, which had become the most popular addition to the shop's inventory.

"I still can't believe it," she said to Tess. "He showed up out of the blue—out of a navy blue Tesla, actually—and introduced himself, and the next thing I knew, we were organizing a book event. This amazing opportunity just dropped in my lap. It's almost too easy."

"Too easy?" Tess cocked her head. "Since when do we complain about something being too easy?"

"I'm not complaining, just not used to it. The way my luck runs, I get suspicious when something seems too good to be true."

"The way your luck runs, you're due for something wonderful to happen. Maybe this is it."

"I hope you're right. Because this is pretty darn wonderful. *He's* wonderful."

"My kids love his books. I do, too, come to think of it. He's incredibly clever. Funny, but there's always a deeper message in the books. Let me know when you have all the details. I want to bring the kids down for the big book signing." Her gaze softened and turned out the window. "My mom is in Morocco, so we'll stay at her place in the Embarcadero."

"Your mom went to Morocco?"

Tess nodded. "Tangier. She's . . . this is going to sound ridiculous, but she went to reconnect with my father."

Natalie frowned. "Seriously?" From what Tess had told her about the situation, Erik Johansen was a scoundrel of the first order.

"That was what I said to my mom." Tess smoothed

her hand lightly over her stomach. "I'm trying not to judge. Could be he had his reasons for making himself disappear and leaving two pregnant women behind."

"Jesus. Go ahead and judge," said Natalie.

"Right?"

"Every family has its secrets, I suppose." Natalie showed Tess the picture of Julio Harper, the Buffalo Soldier in the Spanish-American War. "My grandfather's grandfather. We found out through the owner of that Dewey Medal. It wasn't really a secret—but definitely a surprise."

"That's amazing. Your granddad never knew?"

Natalie shook her head. "Not a clue."

"Well. Speaking of surprises . . ." Tess turned over the book Natalie had placed on the table. Her eyebrows lifted. "Hel*lo*. What's he like in person? Please say this picture isn't twenty years old."

"It's recent. And to be honest, it doesn't do him justice." Natalie couldn't suppress a blush.

"Well, look at you," Tess said with a grin. "You like him."

"Oh, come on. I don't want to be that awful," she said. "My boyfriend's only been gone a short while. I was so wrong about Rick . . . well, I've been questioning my own judgment. I've got no business thinking about another guy."

"You're not awful. You're human. You were about to break up with Rick. That doesn't make the crash any less tragic, but your heart had already changed."

Natalie sighed. "I've gone over and over that day in my mind. If he had proposed, what would I have said?" She shuddered, plagued by guilt. "I would've had to say no, and I would have felt horrible and so would he."

"And both of you would have muddled through and moved on," Tess said. "But because of what happened, you're stuck with an unfinished situation you'll never get to finish."

"Exactly," said Natalie.

"Listen, you have to let that shit go. Promise me."

"I'll work on that. It's hard, though. I want to believe happiness is going to be possible again one day. Then I think about my mom and I just can't."

"She would hate that."

"I know. Like I said, I'll work on it."

A cheery whistle and the jingle of the door alerted her that Peach had arrived for the day.

"Speaking of work," Natalie said, getting up. "My builder is here. He's been single-handedly patching up this poor old building." She briefly introduced Tess and Peach.

Tess fake-swooned behind his back, mouthing, *He's gorgeous.*

When he went upstairs to get to work, Natalie scolded her. "He's fixing my building, not my dating life."

"Okay." Tess sounded dubious. "About this building," she said. She picked up a large archival box and set it on the table. "Let's get down to business. I have information about that vase you found."

"Actually, Peach found it," Natalie said. "It was in the crawl space out back."

"Is your grandfather up?" Tess asked. "I think Andrew will want to hear this. And Peach, too, since he found it."

"I hope that means you have good news." Natalie went back to her grandfather's apartment and knocked. He was getting ready for the day, and he looked good. His shirt was buttoned correctly, and he was freshly shaved and combed. His eyes were clear and focused. "Morning, Natty-girl. I was just coming out for coffee."

"My friend Tess is here. She has news about that old vase. You two catch up and I'll go see if Peach wants to join us." Natalie went up to the attic. Bright morning light streamed through the windows at each end of the space. Peach was standing in the middle at full height, his metal tape measure spanning a section of the rotten beam. With the sunlight behind him, he looked like a living sculpture.

Focus, girl, Natalie told herself. "Hey, got a minute?" she asked.

He started, and the tape measure snaked back into its roll.

"Sorry," she said. "I didn't mean to sneak up on you. Tess thought you might like to hear what she found out about the vase."

"Sure," he said, clipping the tape measure onto his tool belt. "Let's go."

As they passed through her apartment, she wondered what he saw when he looked around. It still felt more like her mom's place than hers, although she'd done some tidying up and rearranging in the living room and tiny galley kitchen. The one area she hadn't tackled was behind the closet door in the bedroom. The thought of culling through her mother's clothes and shoes and personal items made her immeasurably sad. Sometimes she was tempted to simply hire a service to scoop everything up and carry it away. But then she feared she might miss something she didn't know she needed—a special memento or something that might spark a comforting memory for her or her grandfather.

In the back office, Tess set her box on the big library table, then used her phone to scan a code on the box. "Provenance tracking has gone high-tech," she said.

Natalie felt a flutter of excitement. If the object was worthy of high-tech tracking, that probably meant the vase was something special.

Tess opened the box and took out the vase, which had been carefully packed in layers of bubble wrap. Setting it on the table, she asked, "What do you see when you look at this?"

Grandy put on his glasses. "I've seen such things for sale in a hundred shops in Chinatown. It's quite pretty, isn't it? Were you able to trace this one?"

"It cleaned up so well," Natalie said. The figures were pearlescent, delicately formed and surrounded by swirling embellishments. The colors were intense and layered, with a depth that made the details stand out as if three-dimensional. She cringed, remembering how she'd nearly dropped the thing because of a spider.

"It's not from Chinatown," Tess said. "Any other guesses?"

"It's from the Qianlong period in the Qing dynasty," said Peach.

Natalie threw him a sharp look. He never failed to surprise her with the things he said, seeming to pull them out of his back pocket like a handy tool. "Tess, is that right?"

Her friend nodded.

"How would you even know that?" Natalie asked. "How would anyone know that?"

He grinned. "I read books and I know stuff."

"But— Never mind, smart aleck," she said. "You're just showing off."

He hooked his thumb into his jeans pocket and nodded toward the vase. "I took a picture of the porcelain mark on the bottom and looked it up. It's a Qianlong mark."

"Not bad," said Tess. Her gaze lingered on him for a moment with a gleam of admiration. "So the factors we consider are the market for a certain piece, its condition, and its provenance. And of course, its rarity. This one—super rare. The market for Asian ceramic antiquities is always vibrant. A piece with that mark is very hot right now."

"I wouldn't even know to look for a mark," Natalie admitted.

"A similar piece sold at auction in Paris for more than nineteen million dollars."

Peach gave a low whistle that expressed everything Natalie felt.

"Oh, come on. *No.*" She caught her breath. "Wow. Seriously?"

Tess nodded. "Antiquities can be serious business. This vase is in perfect condition—no cracks or chips, and it's well fired. That's the good news."

"Meaning there's bad news?" asked Natalie, her heart sinking.

"There's . . . other news," Tess said. "The value of a piece is affected by its provenance. If it's stolen or a forgery or otherwise compromised, its value will reflect that." She handed a document to Natalie. "I made you a printout of my research, and you can read it, but your eyes will probably glaze over."

"Can you sum it up for us?" asked Natalie. "Was it stolen?"

"Not quite. It belonged to the Tang family—a prosperous merchant clan affiliated with a guild in Hankou, which is called Wuhan City these days. The eldest son, Wen Tang, was born in Shanghai in the 1800s, and he was one of a handful of young boys sent to study in America. The vase and other treasures were sent with him as gifts. He was hugely successful in business, and when it was time to return to China, he elected to stay. To do that, he had to bribe immigration agents."

"So how did the vase end up in our building?" Natalie asked.

"Some of the immigration agents blackmailed the guy and took nearly everything from him. He managed to hide a few of his belongings away, and this is one of them. He died of bubonic plague before he could retrieve it."

"The plague? In San Francisco?"

"There was an outbreak in Chinatown in 1900," Grandy said. "Charlie's grandmother was taken by it, and he says this is why his father grew up to be a physician."

"Wen Tang's sons survived and started a finance and investment company. They're founding members of the Chinese American Heritage Society. It's a nonprofit, housed in an amazing Beaux-Arts building over in the Tenderloin District. It's kind of a big deal."

"So what I hear you saying is that it's possible to track down the rightful owners of the vase."

"With pretty high confidence, yeah," said Tess.

"Did you follow that?" Natalie asked her grandfather.

"It belongs to the Tang family, is that correct?" he asked. "In that case, we'll need to contact them."

"The decision is yours, Grandy." She looked at Tess,

who nodded. Her phone vibrated with an incoming text, but she ignored it.

"It's hard to anticipate how these things go," Tess explained. "You could make a claim of possession. With a piece of this value—"

Grandy held up a hand, palm out. "I wouldn't feel right keeping it, particularly since it belonged to an immigrant from China. We can only imagine the struggles of people emigrating to America in that period. The racism was objectively vicious. It would be wrong to claim something that was brought here at such a high human cost." He paused, eyeing the beautiful piece. "We should contact the Tang family and see what happens next," he concluded.

Natalie felt a surge of pride in her grandfather. Despite his confusion and moments of dementia, he was still the man she had always known. He possessed a shining humanity that demanded fairness and decency. Even though the found objects had taken up residence in his building for more than a hundred years, he never once considered them his.

Peach patted Grandy on the shoulder. "It's really cool of you to try finding the owners."

Watching him with her grandfather, Natalie got a warm feeling inside. A forbidden feeling. One she made herself shut down through force of will.

"I won't forget that you are the person who found the vase," Grandy said. "Without you, none of this would have come about."

"You led me right to it, Andrew. Anyway," Peach said with a nod at Tess, "I need to wrap it up early today. Plans tonight. It was great meeting you. Good luck with everything."

When he was gone, Tess picked up a file folder and fanned it at Natalie. "Down, girl."

Natalie flushed. "Knock it off."

"I don't blame you. He's hot in that ponytail-pirate, I-can-fix-anything kind of way."

"But not in that I-have-a-wife-and-a-kid kind of way."

"Oh, I didn't realize. I guess it's the old adage," Tess whispered. "The good ones are all taken. Judging by the way you looked at him, I'm guessing he's a good one."

"I'm not looking at him in any way," Natalie protested. "Or, if I am, it's just that there's more to him than meets the eye. He's read every book, and he's like a walking encyclopedia."

Tess shrugged. "Ah, well. On to the next big adventure."

"Yeah, about that." Natalie hesitated, then showed

her friend the text message from Trevor that had come in during their meeting.

Tess leaned back with a Cheshire Cat smile. "Well, well, well. I'm assuming this one is single?"

"Oh, yeah."

"Then the coast is clear. He wants to take you out on a date tonight. Imagine that, a date with a world-famous author who is single and even better looking than his book jacket photo."

"I'm tempted," Natalie admitted, feeling a thrum of excitement. He was almost too good to be true. "But I still feel weird about Rick— Hey!"

Before Natalie could snatch her phone back, Tess tapped a reply.

"Oh my God." Natalie grabbed her phone. "What did you do?"

She looked at the screen. Tess had answered Trevor's text with a smiling emoji and Sure. What did you have in mind?

The phone rang seconds after Tess sent the text. Natalie recoiled when Trevor's name appeared on the screen.

"Oh my gosh, I can't believe you did that!" She glared at her friend.

"Pick up," Tess said unapologetically. "Don't let it go to voice mail."

"I always let it go to voice mail."

"He knows you're by the phone, because you just sent him a text."

"*You* sent the text."

"He doesn't know that. Now, pick up, or I'll do it for you. Pick up. Pick up. Pick up."

Bursting with nervousness, she swiped the screen. "This is Natalie."

"What do you like?" asked Trevor.

"I . . . what do I like?" She glared again at Tess.

"On a date," he said. "Drinks? Dinner? Dancing? Theater? Opera? Live music?"

"Um, I . . . Thanks for asking. I like drinks. And snacks." She sounded like a total dork. Tess rolled her eyes.

"Then we have something in common." Trevor chuckled, his voice deep and smooth in her ear.

Tess carefully gathered her things, logging the movement of the vase on her phone app, and blew Natalie a kiss. "I'll be in touch," she whispered and stepped out.

"We could go to the French Laundry, or Auberge du Soleil. Or Rendez-Vous—they just got their second Michelin star."

It was almost impossible to get a table at the famous

wine-country restaurants. Maybe not for Trevor Dash-wood, though. "They're a long way from the city," she said. "What if we get halfway there and run out of things to talk about?"

"Good point," he said. "I like the way you think— or overthink."

"Sorry, I tend to do that."

"It's fine. Those places are a bit much for a first date. We both feel the same way about first dates. Tell you what—wear a pretty dress and I'll come up with something you'll like. Deal?"

He said "first date" as if a subsequent date was a foregone conclusion. She was quiet, and he added, "Anyway, let's not call it our first. Remember, those are awkward and we can't have awkward."

"How is it not a first date?"

"We went to the Library Bar."

"That wasn't a date."

"Why not? Because we didn't kiss good night?"

Natalie caught her breath. Had she wanted that? "Because you showed up out of the blue and bought a book from me. That's not a date. It's a transaction."

"I'm counting it as our first so this next one won't be awkward. I'm a fiction writer. I'm good at pretend-ing."

Natalie wasn't, though. The world she inhabited—

Grandy, the bookshop, the falling-apart building—was all too real. "I don't know," she said.

"Take a chance," he urged. "It'll be fine."

And maybe it would be. He was, after all, Prince Charming.

17

A half hour before closing time, Cleo shooed her upstairs. "Go get ready. Put on your lipstick and heels. I'll finish here."

Natalie sent her a grateful smile. "You're an enabler, like Tess."

"That's because I owe you one, for introducing me to Lyra."

"My one matchmaking success. I'll always be proud of you two," said Natalie. "It wasn't a stretch, though. An adorable playwright and an adorable opera librettist? A no-brainer."

"You know what might be a no-brainer? An adorable bookseller and a smokin' hot author."

"You say. This is just for fun," Natalie demurred. "I'm ambivalent, and I shouldn't be."

"I agree. He's perfect on paper and he's checking all the boxes and you're still skittish."

"I was so wrong about Rick," Natalie admitted. "I don't want to go down that road again. And come on. Trevor Dashwood? He's like that guy in high school you dream about dating but never do, the football captain type."

"Hey. *I* dated the football captain in high school," Cleo pointed out. "That's how I found out I like girls."

As she spoke, Peach passed through the shop, carrying a ladder out to his truck. "I'll just steer clear of this conversation," he said with a grin. "Have a good evening, girls."

"Go on." Cleo shooed Natalie again. "Make yourself pretty and have fun with Prince Charming."

Natalie went upstairs to get ready. It was right here in her mother's bedroom that she had dressed up for her first school dance. Eighth grade. She'd been yearning for Jordie Bates to ask her, but Jordie was way out of her league. So when Louis Melville asked her instead, she said yes and nearly threw up with nerves on the big day. "I look horrible," she'd said to her mother. "I have a zit. My hair's not right. I dance like a dork."

Her mother had waited patiently through the rant, as she usually did. "Are you finished?"

"Probably not, but I'll take a break."

"Remember *Forever* by Judy Blume? Everything you're thinking right now is the same thing every other girl thinks before a date."

"How do you know?" Natalie had been resentful. She wanted her pain and anxiety to be uniquely hers.

"You'll have to trust that I know. When I was your age, there was a Jordie Bates in my class, too. There's always a Jordie Bates. Mine was named Anders Gundrum. All the girls were in love with him but none of us was beautiful enough or funny or charming enough to be chosen by him. And that yearning—oh my God. I can still feel it to this day. It was all such a grand adventure."

Natalie had stared at her image in the old-fashioned oval mirror, which Mom called a cheval glass, which of course she'd learned about from one of those historical romance novels she read late at night. Staring back at her was a skinny, anxious girl with curly hair that went in the wrong direction and a prominent zit on her forehead. She was wearing a Betsey Johnson dress that all the girls at school craved. She prayed no one would know it came from a thrift store. Even though May Lin had expertly altered it to fit her perfectly, Natalie was paranoid that someone would figure out it was from a secondhand shop.

"I think I'd rather stay home and read," she said.

"Over here." Mom sat her down on the vanity stool. She placed a finger under Natalie's chin and went to work with a concealer sponge, then highlighter and a light dusting of powder, and finally strawberry lip gloss. She used a curling iron on Natalie's hair to smooth her frizz into soft waves.

"Now," Mom said as she worked, "I'm going to say all the things, and you won't believe me even though I'm right, but I'm going to say them anyway. Ready?"

"Ready," Natalie said glumly.

"Listen. You are everything you think you're not—smart, funny, pretty, polite, clever, and a joy to be with. And I'm not saying that because I'm your mother. I'm saying it because it's true and I wish you would believe it."

"You're really hard to argue with when you say all the stuff I was going to say back to you."

"I'll take that as a compliment." Her mother's eyes shone, the way they did when she was feeling emotional. "You're the most beautiful thing in the world to me, and I want you to have a wonderful time tonight." She swiveled the stool toward the mirror.

Natalie saw a pretty girl in the mirror. Not beautiful, like Mom said, but pretty enough. The zit was invisible, the hair was okay. A tiny smile pulled up the corners of her mouth. "Thanks, Mom."

The downstairs doorbell sounded, and Natalie ran to the window and looked down at the street. Parked at the curb was an old beige sedan that looked like a rejected police cruiser. "It's Louis," she said over her shoulder.

Mom came to look. "Right on time." Something must have shown in Natalie's expression, because she asked, "Now what?"

Natalie sighed. "That car."

"It's fine. We don't even have a car."

Natalie stared at the floor. "Kayla Cramer's parents hired a limo for tonight."

"Trust me, limos are overrated. Come on. Let's go meet Prince Charming."

As they went down the stairs, Natalie hissed, "Please don't embarrass me."

"I thought that was my job."

"Mom."

Blythe flung open the downstairs door, and there was Louis Melville. When he saw Natalie, the expression on his face exploded into a smile that made her feel warm inside. And with his crisply pressed white shirt and fresh haircut, he looked totally cute.

"Hiya," she said and introduced him to her mom.

"I brought you this," Louis said, holding out a plastic container. "It's a corsage."

"Oh!" Natalie opened it to find a fragrant starburst of a flower. "That's really nice. Thank you."

"I got the wrist kind. You don't have to wear it if you don't want to."

"Sure, I'll wear it," Natalie said, holding out her wrist so her mother could attach the corsage.

"You two have a great time tonight," Blythe said. She offered a wave to Louis's dad, who was behind the wheel of the hideous beige car.

When they got in the car, Natalie looked out the window and saw her mom alone in the doorway, brushing her cheek with one hand and waving with the other.

"Jesus Christ, Mom, I miss you so much right now," Natalie said to the empty room. She tried to stave off a wave of grief by staying busy. She took a shower, then did her hair and makeup with special care, and put on her favorite—her only—little black dress. Then as she stood in front of the cheval glass in the bedroom, she realized it was the same dress she'd worn to the memorial service for Rick. *Ah, Rick,* she thought.

She wished she hadn't noticed that, because it was a good dress. If she went with bare legs and heels and a flash of jewelry, it would look totally different, she told herself. Right? *Don't overthink.*

Briefly, Natalie considered culling through her mother's closet to find something to wear, but she wasn't ready for that.

She put her keys, cards, and phone into a small blingy bag. Added a twenty-dollar bill—something her mom would call mad money. In case you get mad at your date and need to get yourself home.

Get mad at Trevor Dashwood? *Highly doubtful, Mom.*

He showed up right on time, wearing casual but expensive-looking slacks and a Paul Smith sweater. She knew it was Paul Smith because the designer's bio, with the signature colorful pinstripes on the cover, was a steady seller at the bookstore.

"You look terrific," he said, holding the door for her. "Are you okay to walk a few blocks?"

She glanced down at her shoes. "No problem. They only *look* dangerous."

"Okay, then. I'm glad you said yes."

"I imagine you're used to hearing yes."

He didn't deny it. "Just so you know, I've heard plenty of nos in my life. Any writer who tells you getting published was easy is pulling your leg."

"I didn't mean about the writing," she said. "I mean women."

"I like women." He grinned.

She inhaled the city scents, so familiar from her growing-up years here—cable car brakes, ocean air, the occasional whiff of weed. "How is it that you're still single?"

"I'm complicated."

"How so?"

"I don't really know." He chuckled. "It just sounds like a good thing to say."

"Seems like a good way to tell me very little."

"Hey, I'm an open book. And I could ask you the same thing," he said. "You're lovely and smart and interesting . . ."

"Maybe I'm complicated, too," she said. "And not because it sounds good to say so."

"Because of the way you lost your mom so suddenly and found yourself running her bookstore," he said. "I swear, I'm not making light of that."

"I know you're not." She decided to tell him about Rick. All of it, including the fact that she had wanted to end the relationship at the precise moment he was planning a surprise proposal.

"Damn," said Trevor. "I'm sorry about that. It's a lot to handle. Are you . . . maybe getting help for all this stuff?"

"Therapy, you mean?" She shook her head. "Not

covered by my health plan. It's kind of you to ask, but please don't worry. Mom raised me on books, and I've been doing more reading than sleeping. There's no shortcut through grief and guilt."

"Bibliotherapy—I can relate. I hope you figure out a way to move on. When you do, I want to be the first to know."

"I'll keep that in mind." She steered the conversation to something safer, something that made her feel less vulnerable—books. Despite the stress of trying to get the business on track, Natalie loved talking shop. It was such a contrast to her former job, that steady, predictable safety net she'd inhabited until her final screw-you to wine inventory management.

"Sounds like you've found your calling," he commented.

"I don't know about that. The goal is to keep going. I hope I can. I've always believed there's something magical about a book. A bundle of paper and ink that can change your life. It must be so exciting for you to think about all the readers who love your books."

"I try not to think about that too much," Trevor said. "Messes with my head. I write stories for the kid I used to be—a misfit, looking for a way to be comfortable in my skin."

"You? A misfit?"

"I still feel that way," he said. "Insecurity doesn't go away just because my books are popular."

"Well. Your event is going to be a huge shot in the arm. I appreciate it so much, Trevor. We all do."

"Here we are." He stopped at a cozy-looking place called the Chalk Bar. "One of my favorite spots. And one of my favorite groups is playing tonight."

He casually placed his hand in the small of her back as he held the door for her. A few heads turned as they entered, but unlike the last time, they didn't encounter fans wanting a selfie. Still, Trevor had a presence. He exuded a sort of energy that captured people's attention. He was *noticed*. Not just by people who recognized him but by people in general. The hostess. A girl at the bar as they took a seat. The bartender. At his side, Natalie felt slightly exposed, though she knew it wasn't his fault.

The rustic interior of the bar was modeled after the vermouth bodegas in southern Spain, Trevor told her, where different spirits were stored in casks along the wall and served *de grifo* in slender tasting glasses. The bartender kept a chalk tally directly on the wooden plank bar itself.

"This is nice," she said. "I've always wanted to go to Spain."

"You haven't been?"

She shook her head. "Never had the time or the money. I spent a semester abroad in China when I was in college. Then it was right back here to finish my degree and get a job."

"Sounds like you were in a hurry."

"I had student debt," she corrected him. She still did, but she didn't want to appear even more lame. "Anyway. I never thought about sitting around and sipping vermouth. My knowledge of vermouth is of giant cases in the inventory I used to manage in my old job. Not these cool old barrels."

"It's different from the stuff gathering dust in the back of your parents' liquor cabinet."

"For the record, we didn't have a liquor cabinet," Natalie said. "I didn't have parents, either, just a single mom. And that sounds pathetic and really, it's not."

They sampled a vermut rojo—spiced fortified wine—which they drank neat with a slice of orange. The rich, botanical flavor was remarkably soothing. Trevor ordered a selection of simple, insanely fresh plates of tapas—local olives, nuts, and cheese, all served on tiny platters.

"This is wonderful," she said.

"Glad you like it."

"I have a confession," she said, relaxing over her second sample of vermut. "I'm intrigued by your 'About the Author' page."

"You like it?"

"It's intriguing."

"And that's bad?"

"No, but there are ambiguities. You grew up in the Desolation Wilderness?" She had seen it once on a scenic plane ride with Rick, swooping across the south end of Lake Tahoe over what looked like impenetrable woodlands. "I didn't think anyone lived there. Is that even allowed?"

"Right near the boundary. My folks were early advocates of living off the grid. The house had a full solar power array, battery storage, propane generator, everything needed to survive miles from nowhere."

"And you were homeschooled and wrote a novel at age seventeen and attended Oxford. Your folks must have been so proud of you."

"Let's drink to that," he said, lifting the small glass. "Better yet, let's listen to the opening set. Looks like they're just warming up."

Okay, so he didn't want to discuss his bio. He had probably been asked the same questions a million times. Natalie turned her attention to the corner area of the bar. The band had been busily setting up mixers, speakers, mics, and amplifiers in a darkened alcove.

Sound checks and tuning mingled with the house music. Then the piped-in music went silent. A guy in a kitchen apron stepped up to the mic and made a few introductory announcements about upcoming events. Then he said, "Please welcome one of our local favorites, from right here in the heart of the city—Trial and Error."

Track lights came on over the dais, illuminating the four-person ensemble—a woman with long blond hair and a fiddle, a bass player, a guy on acoustic guitar, a drummer.

"Hey there, thanks for joining us tonight. My name's Suzzy Bailey, and we're Trial and Error. Welcome to the Chalk Bar." The blonde adjusted the mic, the way performers tended to do. "We're glad we get to spend a little time with you, here at one of the best spots in the city. Let's start with a tune I wrote last summer about the weather. And some other things."

The piece started out with a waterfall of guitar riffs, played by a tall guy in a tight black T-shirt with long hair and—

"Holy crap, I know that guy," whispered Natalie, nudging Trevor's arm.

He leaned over and put his lips close to her ear. "Yeah?"

She nodded, feeling the strangest leap of her heart.

"He's . . . his name is Peach. He's working on repairs at the bookstore."

"Small world."

"It gets smaller. Remember our mutual friend, Dorothy?" she asked.

"My pen pal. Indeed I do."

"That's her dad."

She had to adjust to seeing Peach in a wildly different context. His hands delicately teasing the strings of the guitar were the same hands that had been ripping plaster and lath from the walls of her building.

"This next one's something new from my buddy Peach," Suzzy said. It was a duet, and his voice was utterly surprising—perfectly on key, with a slightly gritty texture that somehow made the lyrics ring with sincerity. It was a romantic song, and he and Suzzy seemed connected as they traded lyrics back and forth.

What about your heart?

It's the last thing on my list.

Natalie tried to figure out if Peach's wife was in the room, watching and listening. Probably not. She was probably home with Dorothy.

The music fell like warm rain, and Natalie stopped speculating. For a few moments, she forgot entirely that she was sitting with Trevor Dashwood. She forgot that her grandfather was losing himself and the shop was failing and the building was falling down. Those several minutes took her somewhere else, and when the song ended, she was in a better place—just for a couple of seconds more.

Trevor nudged her shoulder during the applause. "See what I mean? They're good."

"They're good," she agreed.

"And your drink?"

"It's . . . oops. I finished it."

"I'll get you another." He left the table and went over to the bar. Natalie looked over at Peach, trying to readjust her thoughts. So many things were surprising about him, but his artistry on the guitar and his soulful voice were probably the biggest surprises of all.

Trevor set a fresh drink in front of her. "This one is con sifón—with a little carbonated water."

"Thank you." She smiled across the table at him. "It's all so delicious. I'd better pace myself."

After several more numbers, mellow and sincere like the first, the group took a break. Natalie said, "Let's go say hi."

Peach had set his guitar in a holder and was guzzling a glass of water.

"Hey," she said.

He put down his glass, and his eyebrows shot up. "Hey, yourself."

"You didn't tell me you were Eddie Vedder."

He checked out the dress with a sweep of his eyes. "You didn't tell me you were Audrey Hepburn."

She flushed, stepping aside and gesturing at Trevor. "This is Trevor Dashwood, Dorothy's favorite writer."

"Good to meet you." Peach stuck out his hand. "Peach Gallagher. My kid is crazy about your books, man."

"I hope I get to meet her," said Trevor. "She's coming to the book signing, right?"

"Wouldn't miss it for the world. She's going to go nuts when I tell her I saw you tonight." The drummer motioned to him. "Gotta go," he said.

Trevor steered her away for a final tasting of vermut, this one a sweet, herbal concoction from white grapes. The next set was so good, featuring another duet with the earthy, bohemian, beautiful Suzzy. Then Peach sang a solo he'd written about a guy delivering a package. *He didn't see it coming, but things like that escaped him* . . . She didn't quite get the metaphor, but the melody and emotion of the piece were unexpectedly moving.

By the time the set wound down, Natalie was feeling the pleasant effects of herbal vermouth and good live music. She smiled at Trevor, and it felt good to smile. "I should get home," she said. "Saturday's a big day at the shop."

He went over to the end of the bar and paid the tab, and the guy with the chalk wiped out the markings on the wooden surface. "Every transaction should be that simple, right?" he said, holding out his hand as she got up from the table.

"I wish." She glanced over her shoulder to see if Peach was still around, but he was busy helping break down the set. She wondered if his wife liked his performances, or if they were old hat to her. Did he sing to Mrs. Peach?

Lost in thought, she didn't realize Trevor was speaking to her. "Sorry, what?"

"Walk slowly," he said, his lips close to her ear. "I want to make the evening last." The night was chilly, and with natural ease he slipped his arm around her and held it there for a long moment.

Coming from someone less polished, his line would have sounded impossibly cheesy. Yet Trevor said it with humor and sincerity, and she was charmed. They took the stairs down the side of Lombard Street, which was decently quiet and smelled of dry leaves and eucalyptus. The amber streetlights created a dreamy atmosphere, adding to Natalie's sense of wonder about the whole evening. They encountered the occasional dog walker or jogger, and on one landing, a musician scratched a tune on the fiddle while his feet played percussion on a digital foot drum. Trevor slipped a bill into his violin case as they passed.

"I used to run down these stairs when I was a kid," Natalie told him. "Trying to get home in time for curfew. My mom was strict about that."

"Sounds like she was being protective."

"I suppose. I wasn't the kind of kid who got in trouble. My biggest infraction was losing a library book a time or two."

"Come on. You never skipped school? Drank a bottle of cheap wine and puked everywhere? Shoplifted?"

"Nah. Too timid to try that stuff." Her mother had issued a stern warning—if she stepped out of line, her scholarship to St. Dymphna's would be in jeopardy. Then she'd have to ride the bus to the scary, overcrowded school down the hill. Now that she knew Dean had been behind her tuition payments, she felt a stab of resentment. Why hadn't her mother told her?

"How about you?" she asked Trevor. "Were you a rebel?"

He chuckled. "I was lost in a world of books. Still am, most of the time."

They stopped at the residential entry door beside the

bookstore. Natalie briefly flirted with the idea of inviting him up, but shut herself down with a vengeance. The last thing she needed was to complicate things with a man who was going to do the biggest event the shop had ever seen.

"This was fun," she said. "Thanks, Trevor."

He smiled down at her, his gaze lingering on her lips.

No, don't do that, she thought. *Not yet, anyway.*

He seemed to read her well, stepping back toward his parked car. "Let's hang out again soon," he said, keeping hold of her hand as he stepped back.

"I'd like that. But I'm going to be busy getting ready for this event. It's so incredible, Trevor. Thanks again."

"Got it," he said easily. "One thing at a time."

18

Peach trolled the block, looking for a place to park near the bookstore. It was raining—the wet, slick, chilly kind of rain that slapped like an insult—and the nearest spot was half a block away. The walk through the pissing weather made him wonder why he had bothered with a morning shower.

By the time he reached the store and set down his gear with a metallic clank, he acknowledged that he was in a foul mood. This happened sometimes, particularly when Dorothy was with her mom and Regis. He missed his kid. Last night, he'd stayed up too late, and—it had to be said—Natalie Harper had shown up at the Chalk Bar with a date.

Not just any date, but Bachelor Number One. That

literary darling *auteur* who sold all the books to adoring fans and made all the women swoon.

Well. It wouldn't be the first time Peach had ended a relationship before it began.

It might, however, be the first time he regretted it.

Whatever.

He used the entry code Natalie had given him, then let himself in. As he wiped his feet on the mat, the cat slipped past, giving him a disdainful glare. "Good morning to you, too," he muttered, shaking the rain from his jacket. The dry, papery aroma of the books mingled with the scent of fresh coffee and something from the bakery.

Natalie came bustling out of the back office, her face lit with eagerness. She looked as fresh as springtime this morning, and he had to wonder if she and that guy— *No. Don't even go there.*

"Oh, hey," she said. "I was hoping you would get here early today."

"Cool," he said. "You got your wish." When Dorothy was away, he treated Saturdays like any other workday.

She didn't seem to notice his foul mood. "That was a surprise, running into you last night."

Ditto, he thought.

"Your group is fantastic. I'm really impressed, Peach."

"Yeah? Glad you liked it." He'd been planning to roll out a new song at the Chalk Bar, a duet with Suzzy about a woman who lived in an attic garret and read romance novels late into the night, but he'd changed his mind about that.

"Your whole group," she said. "So good. Now I know where Dorothy gets her musical talent. Have you been making music all your life?"

"Yep. Mom's a music teacher. Still teaching piano back in Georgia."

"You sound great. She must be really proud of you."

He nodded, not necessarily in agreement. He and his parents had a complicated past. He and his younger sister, Junebug, had grown up in a grand house on Peachtree Road that came with all the trappings—private schools, tennis lessons, trips to Europe, a household staff. His first guitar and composition teacher had played with R.E.M., and on his twelfth Christmas, he'd received a genuine Rickenbacker guitar.

Everyone who was anyone would have agreed that the Atlanta Gallaghers had it all—until everything had come crashing down in twin disasters. Peach and Junebug had been seventeen and sixteen at the time. His father, who'd built an empire in finance, was arrested for defrauding his investors and was sentenced to three years in federal prison. Almost overnight, the family fortune had vanished. At the same time, Junebug had fallen into the vortex of addiction, lured by painkillers she'd been taking for a field hockey injury. To pay for her treatment and rehab, Peach had liquidated his entire college savings plan, the only family money that hadn't been confiscated in the raid on his parents. Instead of going to college, he'd enlisted in the Marine Corps and never looked back.

Years later, his parents lived in a tiny home he'd built for them outside the city. His mother gave music lessons. His dad built patio furniture out of old whiskey barrels and reminisced about the old days, as if he hadn't destroyed anyone's future. Junebug worked as a tennis pro at a country club, hanging on to sobriety by a thread. They weren't close anymore. They were like disaster survivors who made one another uncomfortable because their very existence was a reminder of the trauma.

His mom hadn't heard him play music in a long time.

"Grandy will be out in a minute," Natalie said. She paused, casting a hesitant look at him. "I have news about that vase. Turns out it's even more awesome than Tess predicted. We contacted the Tang family, and they were blown away by the find. They're going to donate it to the Chinese American Heritage Society, and it'll be featured in a collection of rare Chinese antiquities. There's an annual gala coming up, and they're holding a special reception to announce the acquisition. The governor and mayor will be there, along with big donors, *Smithsonian* magazine . . . And probably lots of other stuff. Anyway, it's a big deal."

"Sounds great. Hope your grandfather is happy."

"He is, sure." Another pause. He wondered what was on her mind. "You're part of the story," she added. "You know that, right?"

"I didn't run away screaming when a spider crawled out of it."

She flushed. "I'm glad you were there to catch the vase. It could have been a disaster."

"Glad to be of service."

Another beat of hesitation. "So there's an invitation." She went to the back office and returned with a letterpressed card on thick, fancy paper. "They invited Grandy and me and the bookstore staff. Would you like to come?" Her gaze darted to and fro, and her words came out in a nervous rush. "I thought since you found it, you might want to join us."

"A gala, huh?" Was that what was making her nervous?

"It's, um, kind of formal. Like, really formal. A

dressy thing. So if you'd rather not, I understand completely."

And so did he, finally. There was no humor in his grin when he said, "Love to. When is it?"

"Oh! It's . . ." She showed him the invitation. "Sorry, it all came together so fast. The vase unveiling is a last-minute addition to their annual event. We were given tickets as the guests of the Tang family. Again, I'm sorry about the short notice. They just let me know."

He flipped through the schedule in his head, the one that managed Dorothy, his work projects, the band, and his nonexistent personal life. He and Regina tried to be flexible with their parenting schedule. "Sure, I can make it."

"Great! It's being held in the most amazing space— the Moon Lee Mansion. Do you know it?"

"Over by the Palace of Fine Arts. I worked on a restoration job on the roof a few years back. Never been to a function there, though." Of course he hadn't. In the world of exclusive clubs, it was one of the most exclusive, according to the contractor he'd worked with on the project. From what he'd heard, you practically had to give blood to enter its rarefied halls. And now a nobody in a tool belt had been invited. All because of that vase. It must be some vase. "So I'll see you there," he stated.

354 · SUSAN WIGGS

She swallowed, turning the card over in her nervous hands. "Well, there's, um, a dress code. It's a black-tie reception. That means—"

"I bet I have a black tie left over from my days of waiting tables." He couldn't help laughing at her expression. "Natalie. I won't show up in a denim tux."

"I didn't mean—"

"'You can never be overdressed or overeducated'; isn't that what Oscar Wilde said?"

Her cheeks turned pink. "He probably did. You'd know, wouldn't you? I swear, Peach, the stuff you come up with . . ." She handed him the thick letterpressed card. "I wish we'd had more advance notice, but they really wanted to present the vase at the gala. And if—"

"Am I late?" Her grandfather made an appearance, his gait uneven as he emerged from the apartment in back.

"Come sit." Natalie gestured Andrew over to the café seating area. "We were just talking about the reception where the vase is going to be unveiled."

Peach detected a glimmer of concern in her eyes. Old Andrew had his shirt buttoned wrong, and he was still in his bedroom slippers. He smelled funky, too. *Damn, that's hard*, he thought, *watching a beloved grandparent struggling with the simplest of things.* The old guy was smart and had led a long and interesting life, but he was fraying at the edges. Maybe even unraveling. "Hey, man." Peach stood up. "Let me help you with your shirt, okay?"

"My . . . Oh. Hello. Are you here about the radiator?"

"It's me, Peach," he said, quickly fixing the buttons. "The radiator is on my list." The old iron hulk was a hundred years old and needed to be removed. "Is that shower bar working out for you?"

He nodded vaguely, giving no indication that he understood. Peach held out a chair for Andrew.

Natalie sent him a grateful look. "Here's the *Examiner*. Save the crossword for me."

"Very good. It's a print day. There used to be a print edition every day," Andrew said. "Now it's only three times a week. The other days, Blythe prints off the pages from her computer. Have the morning glory muffins been delivered yet? I should like one with my coffee."

Natalie got up and opened the bakery box. "Here you go. So, Grandy—"

Her phone went off, and Peach saw a name and a picture flash on the screen—Trevor Dashwood.

"Excuse me," she said, grabbing the phone and stepping away from the table. "I need to take this." She ducked into the back office, but the phone was on speaker and he could hear their conversation. He pretended not to.

"About Friday night," Trevor said. "Do you like boating?"

"Depends on the boat," she said. "And the weather."

"Well, I can assure you the boat is seaworthy, and the forecast is good for sunset. Can you get away?"

The boat is seaworthy, Peach grumbled inwardly. *Tell me more, pretty boy.* There was something phony about this guy. Just a hunch Peach had. He'd been raised by a pair of fraudsters. He was tuned in to the signs. Maybe. On the other hand, could be he just envied the guy for asking Natalie Harper out on a date.

"When I was a young man, I married the wrong woman," Andrew said out of the blue, distracting Peach from his eavesdropping.

"Sorry, how's that?"

"I had a terrible heartbreak. My one true love was forbidden to see me. Her parents were very strict Chinese immigrants, and they wouldn't hear of her associating with a *gweilo*. In my disappointment, I had an impulsive love affair with a woman I scarcely knew, and in almost no time at all, she was pregnant. The marriage was my greatest mistake, yet it resulted in my greatest achievement—my daughter, Blythe."

"I like your way of looking at it," Peach said. "I

THE LOST AND FOUND BOOKSHOP · 357

wouldn't trade Dorothy for the world. Hell, she *is* my world."

"Of course she is. But it's the nature—no, the duty—of a child to grow up and leave you. Doesn't seem fair, does it? The person you love most in the world is destined to leave you and break your heart."

"Well, when you put it that way, it's even more depressing." Peach finished his coffee and rinsed the mug. "And on that note, I'd best get to work." He hung his mug on a hook and briefly gripped Andrew's shoulder. "I'm sure sorry about your daughter, man. I wish I'd had a chance to meet her."

"You will," Andrew said vaguely, staring down at the crossword puzzle as if it were in Mandarin. "Perhaps you will."

Natalie had grown up watching the ferryboats and sightseeing catamarans coming and going from the docks of the Marina District. As a girl, she'd attended a couple of parties at the St. Francis Yacht Club, hosted by her school friends whose parents seemed to be drowning in money. She'd been on the high school sailing team, and she and her best friend, Millicent Casey, had become experts at maneuvering their double-handed Vanguard-15 around the bay. However, Natalie had never been aboard any of the luxury yachts with their shiny hulls and helipads and incognito celebrities lounging on the decks. She was always speculating about them from the outside, looking in. Her mother had given her an annotated copy of *The Great Gatsby* to read, in case there was any question about the toxic effects of idle wealth.

Thanks, Mom.

The autumn weather was changeable, but tonight, Indian summer paid a visit, rendering the sky a hard, clear blue. Following the directions Trevor had sent to her phone, Natalie arrived at the yacht club and made her way to a gated entrance. As soon as she gave her name at the guardhouse, the pampering began. The offer of a cold beverage, a cocktail, perhaps? A hot towel? Directions to the ladies' lounge? Wi-Fi password?

Although the red clay tiles of the race deck looked familiar, she felt like an imposter here. Women with Birkin bags and Hermès scarves and sunglasses strolled around in chatty groups, taking in the scenery. Empty-nester couples shared drinks at bar tables on one of the decks, looking like a layout for an idealized travel article. Watching them, Natalie remembered that as a kid, she'd tried to put her mother in a picture like this, certain her beautiful mom belonged here among the polished couples.

As Natalie had gotten older, she came to understand that most people found a lasting love. This realization made her wonder about her mother's heart. She would see handsome, youthful couples together enjoying the good life, and it made her wish her mother could find—and keep—a great guy. When she was in junior high, she'd asked her mom if she was gay.

"Nope," she had said simply. "Why do you ask?"

"Because you go out with guys, but nothing ever lasts. So I thought maybe you might be gay but trying to be straight." Her frenemy at school, Kayla Cramer, had posited this theory.

"Please," Mom said with a laugh. "This is San Francisco. If I was gay and I wanted a relationship, I'd have a girlfriend."

Through the years, Natalie had brought up the subject from time to time. "You've met some wonderful men," she'd said one summer when she was home from college and working in the bookstore. "You're really pretty, Mom, and you're a total catch—an independent woman with her own business? Guys love that."

Blythe had laughed. "Hey, *I* love that. I love my life."

"What about falling in love with a *guy*?" That year, Natalie had been dating a foreign student named Diesel, and she was completely smitten by his clean-cut, chiseled-jaw looks and his mad skills in the bedroom. She'd been convinced that they would marry and have kids and live some undefined fantasy life abroad. Being in love was so heady and addictive that she couldn't believe her mother managed to do without it.

"Like in a chick lit novel?" Mom grinned. "Been there. Done that. Read the book. And then moved on." She must have noticed something in Natalie's expression, because she said, "Listen, I'm in love with my life, my business, my father and May, and my daughter. I have everything I need right here."

Natalie remembered thinking about that feeling of being in a man's arms, the intimacy, the orgasms . . . "People always ask me why you're single," she'd said. "'Your mom's so gorgeous. Why hasn't some guy swept her away?' I hear it all the time."

"And what do you tell them?"

"That you don't want to be swept anywhere."

"Ha. I trained you well."

"Seriously, Mom. Were you so snakebit by Dean that you never want another relationship?"

Blythe had waved away the question. "Honestly, I didn't even like him that much. I was too young to know my own heart—about the same age as you are now."

"You're not too young now," Natalie had pointed

out. "And you're always pushing me to fall in love. Why me and not you?"

"We're very different, you and I," her mom had said. "Your heart was made for love."

"And yours wasn't?"

The frustrating conversation had repeated itself in many forms through the years. When Rick had come along, Blythe had been thrilled for Natalie.

Natalie had brought him home to meet her mother, showing him off like a prize tuna from the fishing docks.

"He's wonderful," Blythe had declared. "A total keeper."

Natalie had tugged her aside and confessed her doubts about Rick. "He *is* wonderful, Mom. But I'm just not sure . . ."

"That's because your father has been totally unavailable to you all your life. Now you've found a man who *is* available, and it probably feels weird to you. I hope you can learn to trust that he'll be there for you."

Dean must have done a number on you, Natalie thought now, scanning the marina as she waited for Trevor. Maybe her mother was onto something. Maybe Dean had conditioned them both to be suspicious of men who made themselves available.

She shivered now, pulling her light sweater more

snugly around her. *Aw, Mom. I hope you were as happy and fulfilled as you said you were,* she thought. *And why didn't you level with me about Dean?*

Trevor showed up, panting. "Hey there," he said. "Sorry to make you wait. I was getting the boat ready." He looked wonderful in chinos turned back at the ankle, flip-flops, and a striped shirt open at the collar, the sleeves rolled up.

"I was enjoying the views," she said. "You were right about the weather. What a brilliant evening."

He led the way to the security gate and entered a code. They went down a ramp to the moorage docks, laid out like the teeth of a comb. Most were lined by slips with sleek sailboats and schooners and power yachts. "I'm so intrigued by boats," she said.

"Yeah?"

"Uh-huh. Their names and where they're registered—like that one. *Andante.* Is the owner musical? Or Italian? And that one over there—from Fiji. How did it get here all the way from Fiji?"

"I could give you answers, but I'm an unreliable narrator."

"I'll keep that in mind." A light breeze sang through the masts, and the colors of the sky deepened by the minute into a dramatic swath of amber and pink. They came to the end of a dock, and he stopped at a gleaming boat with a picnic deck and portals aglow from the inside.

"Oh boy," she said.

"That's what I said when I saw it. Come on aboard, and I'll show you around."

She walked the impressive length of it and checked the stern. *Flip Side*—Carmel-by-the-Sea. "I don't know what to say," she told him. "It's fantastic."

"When I moved to Carmel, I decided to get a boat that I could bring to San Francisco."

"So cool." Natalie held the polished rail and stepped aboard, and instantly felt as if she'd been swallowed up in luxury. Every surface gleamed, reflecting the water and sky. Soft music thrummed from hidden speakers. There was a lounge area and a bar, and steps leading down to a galley and what she assumed was a stateroom. "Do you run this thing yourself?"

"Sometimes. We'll just take a short cruise tonight. Sound good?"

"Sounds magical," she said. "What can I do?"

"Drink this." He gave her a glass of champagne. "I'll be right back."

Trevor started the engine, then brought in the lines. They sat together at the bridge and motored slowly away from the marina. The sun seemed to balance on the horizon, gilding the scenery as it dipped almost imperceptibly. As they headed toward Alcatraz Island, the city slipped past in a glitter of winking lights. Natalie couldn't resist taking pictures of the gold-tinged scenery. She was tempted to photograph the boat to show Cleo and Bertie, but she didn't want to be an obnoxious fangirl.

The world looked so different from the water. She found herself thinking about Grandy's old stories of Julius Harper, shoved out to sea on a barge to escape the burning city. When he'd looked back, what had he seen? The whole world lit by fire, his mother lost in a surge of people. Now the city bristled with skyscrapers, dominated by the bullet-shaped Salesforce Tower.

Trevor switched directions, and they went under the Golden Gate Bridge. She took more phone pictures, capturing the massive towers and web of cables against the twilight.

"It's really beautiful," she said. "Thanks for bringing me."

"Glad you like it."

She nodded, savoring the last of her champagne. For the first time since the day of the reception at Pinnacle Fine Wines, Natalie had a moment of uncomplicated pleasure. *Is this what you wanted for me, Mom? How about you send me a sign?*

They glided back across the smooth water to the

marina, where he moored the boat and cut the engines. "Make yourself at home," he said, stepping down into the galley. "I've got a snack for us."

She poked around the main salon, drawn to the bookshelf. "I've always believed you can tell a lot about a person based on the books they keep."

"Yeah? What can you tell about me?"

"Judging by this collection, you're very practical— all these books on piloting and navigation and boating guides."

"Shoot, I don't want to be seen as practical. I want you to think I'm exciting. Romantic. Irresistible."

She pulled out a thick copy of *Chapman Piloting*. "I once dated a guy who hid porn behind his collection of classic novels. We didn't work out so well." Diesel from college. Recently she'd seen him on an online alumni group. He was paunchy now, with a wife and two kids.

"Not a fan of porn?" He emerged from the galley with a tray and set it on a table. "What about food porn?"

She surveyed the array of small bites—artisan cheese and fruit. And something that looked like caviar and crème fraîche. "That's incredible. Did you do this?"

"Please," he said. "I'm awesome, but not that awesome."

She laughed and sampled a ripe raspberry. Trevor

poured two glasses of sauvignon blanc, and they had a seat on the sofa.

"Cheers." He tapped the rim of his glass against hers.

"Cheers," she said. "I recognize this bottle."

"From your former job up in Sonoma? Do you miss it?"

He'd listened. And remembered. What a concept. She tasted the wine with an indulgent sip. "That job used to be my life. Now it feels like a lifetime ago. And no, I don't miss it." Maybe she missed the steadiness and predictability, but nothing else. It was amazing how quickly her world had been turned on its head, from plodding and predictable to uncertain and chaotic. "What about you? What was your former job?"

"Staying ahead of the bill collectors," he said with a chuckle. "I don't miss that, either."

"Well, congratulations on all your books. What an extraordinary achievement, Trevor. Really."

He crossed one leg over the other and leaned back. "I like you, Natalie Harper," he said.

"Thanks. To be honest, I'm a bit tongue-tied around you."

He threw back his head and laughed. "Okay, now I more than like you."

"What a nice thing to say." She turned toward him on the sofa, tucking one leg under her.

"Remember what I said—guys don't want to be thought of as nice." He feigned a wounded look.

"Well, you should. Nice guys are my favorite kind. Every woman I know would agree with me."

"What's your least favorite kind?" he asked.

"Married guys." It just popped out of her.

He set down his wineglass. "Something tells me there's a bit of background to that. Is there a married guy who did you wrong?"

"No. Not that I know of, anyway. I sure hope not." She helped herself to more wine. "The guy who fathered me was married. Mom didn't know until she was pregnant."

"Damn. Some guys are too shitty to live." He put his hand on her leg. "I hope your mom found somebody good enough for her."

"I think about that a lot," Natalie said. "She had boyfriends. Good guys, as far as I knew. But nothing that lasted."

Tilting her head to one side, she studied him. He was put together. Handsome and charming. Too good to be true? She hoped not. "How about you? Mom and dad . . . ?"

He grinned and looked away, shifting the wine bottle in the ice bucket. "Still together."

"And are they still living off the grid?"

"You could say that, if a gated community in Palm Springs is considered off the grid."

"They must be incredibly proud of what you've achieved in your career," she said.

The way he was watching her mouth left no doubt as to what was on his mind.

She skirted the thought. "So . . . what about you? Unattached? Dating? Heartbreak?"

"All of the above. But not currently."

"Okay, then . . ." She shifted on the sofa. They talked about things—the books they both liked. Films they wanted to see. How the fall weather in the Bay Area always ended in gloom. He was nice to talk to, despite not wanting to be thought of as nice. He listened. He didn't challenge her or pressure her. And he had good taste in wine and snacks.

Before she got too comfortable, she finished her wine and turned to him. "I should probably go. I need to open in the morning."

He paused, studying her for a moment. Then he took out his phone. "I'll call for a car."

"Oh, thanks." She'd taken the cable car and bus over

and walked the rest of the way, but in the dark, a car would be great.

As they walked to the exit of the marina, he took her hand. "I like hanging out with you," he said. "I hope we can do it some more."

"Yes," she said. "I . . . so do I."

It turned out the ride he'd called wasn't Uber or Lyft, but a sleek black car with a driver in a suit. Trevor existed in such a different world from hers.

At the curb, he drew her against him and kissed her good night. It was new. It was a little bit awkward, a little bit exciting. A feeling of warmth flickered and then settled. She pulled back and smiled up at him. "Thank you. See you around, Trevor."

19

"What are you wearing to the gala?" Natalie asked Cleo. She had been reading the society pages, combing them for insights. It was one of the most celebrated social events of the year, the kind people like her only read about in breathless, aspirational gossip columns. The attendees came from the city's elite old guard Chinese American community, with roots that went back more than a hundred years and fortunes that made her do a double take.

Cleo beamed. "Valentino," she said. "I found this amazing vintage couture cocktail dress at a thrift shop, and my aunt did the alterations. It's yellow chiffon with a woven bodice, open at the sides. I'll look like a character from *Crazy Rich Asians*."

"Sounds perfect. I can't wait to see it," Natalie said.

"What about you?" asked Cleo.

"I doubt you'll mistake me for a crazy rich anything," Natalie said. "Actually, I could use your help."

Cleo turned to Bertie. "Fashion consult. It's an emergency."

He scanned the shop. Browsing customers, a pair of women having coffee and chatting. "Go," he said. "Find her something to wear that doesn't make her look like a schoolmarm."

"Is that what I look like?" Natalie glanced down at her gray slacks and comfortable flats. "A marm?"

He peered at her over the rims of his reading glasses. "If the sensible crepe-soled shoe fits . . ."

Natalie stuck out her tongue. As they went upstairs, she asked, "What's a marm, anyway? Does anyone even know?"

"It's the opposite of how hot you're going to look once we find something for you to wear."

Natalie took out her go-to cocktail dress, the fitted black sheath with a boat neck and a slit in the hem, holding it up for Cleo's approval.

"Boring, sorry. The only way that would work is with Manolos or Jimmy Choos. And a major statement bracelet or arm cuff."

"Not in my budget, unfortunately. I do have a hair and nail appointment."

"Come on, this is going to be a once-in-a-lifetime evening. You found a lost treasure and you should look the part. Get in touch with your inner Lara Croft."

Natalie laughed briefly. "It's black tie. Not black leather."

Cleo went through Natalie's collection of dresses, neatly hung on the back of the bathroom door. Everything was muted and subdued, Natalie observed. Safe choices, not designed to draw attention.

"My clothes are boring," she admitted. "Shoot. Maybe *I'm* boring."

"Bullshit. I forbid you to think that way. Let's have a look in your mom's closet," Cleo suggested.

Natalie winced. "Do we have to?"

"It's time. You've been putting it off, and believe me, I totally get that. I won't force you, but I do think it would be good for you to get started on . . . you know."

"Going through her stuff. Throwing things away. Because God knows, I need to feel my heart break again."

"I'm sorry," Cleo said.

"I know. And you're right." Natalie sucked in a breath, held it around her heart to cushion the blow. "Mom would've been so excited by all this."

"She would have," said Cleo. "Suppose you find something of hers to wear? That'd be cool, right?"

Natalie hesitated, picturing her mother putting together an outfit for going out. "She did have really good taste."

"It'll be okay, Natalie. Let's clear out her closet."

"What?" Natalie felt a thrum of panic in her chest.

"I'll help. We can remember things about your mom."

"I've been avoiding this."

"I know. One of these days, the memories will make you happy."

"How'd you get so smart?" Natalie asked softly.

"I'm not smart. I just sound that way. And I read that new book on grief recovery that's been selling so well for us. Feel your feelings, and let shit go. That's the message."

"It took a whole book to say that?"

"We'll make three piles—keep, trash, and donate. Sound good?"

Natalie nodded. "This place is so small. I could definitely use the closet space."

"I bet we'll come up with just the thing. Your mom had a gift for finding treasures in vintage shops."

"She did. I used to go along with her sometimes, but all I got was a headache from the old-clothes smell. I'd end up with somebody's used Gap sweatshirt, and Mom would find a couture sweater or Gucci sunglasses."

Natalie braced herself as she opened the clunky bifold doors of the closet. Confronted with the rack of clothes and shoes and bags, she was hit with a wave of nostalgia. A person's clothes held their very essence. The garments exuded the unique scent of her mother and reflected the colors and textures that had most pleased her eye.

Her mother had been drawn to rich jewel tones—cobalt blue, turquoise, fuchsia, emerald, marigold. She liked to dress for her customers, her outfits changing with the seasons. Natalie pictured her mom choosing what to wear and putting things together, her mouth quirked in that thoughtful way she had as she paired tops and bottoms, shoes and scarves and accessories.

Her hands shook a little as she handled her mother's dresses and blouses, passing them to Cleo for the sorting piles—keep, donate, discard.

She came across a wispy butterfly-sleeve blouse in a bright silk print. She shuddered, remembering one particular trip with her mother to a thrift shop.

"You're growing like an avocado seed in a compost heap," Mom had declared. "Let's find you some new threads."

"Clothes," Natalie had said. "Not threads."

"I like the Children's Hospital Shop because it's a

nonprofit," Mom said, unfazed. "Makes for higher-end donations."

While her mom checked out shirts from Esprit and Ralph Lauren, Natalie had made a glum search through a rack of denim. Why couldn't they just shop at I. Magnin all the time, like everybody else?

"Ooh, this is really cute." Mom held a butterfly-sleeve top against Natalie. "Looks *very* expensive."

"Hey, Natalie!" Kayla Cramer came into the shop with her mother. They each carried a cardboard box labeled DONATE TO CHARITY.

Natalie wanted to shrivel into nothingness. She quickly stepped away from the butterfly blouse and her mom. "Hey, Kayla."

"We're just dropping stuff off," Kayla said, her sharp gaze darting to Natalie's mother.

With her best customer-greeting smile, Mom said, "It's nice to see you, Kayla." She introduced herself to Kayla's mother, a rail-thin woman wearing Belgian shoes, a camel coat, and tortoiseshell glasses.

"Hey, maybe some of my hand-me-downs would fit you," Kayla suggested. "Want to have a look?"

Natalie would rather have a root canal. She was fumbling for an answer when Mom came to the rescue. "We're in a bit of a hurry," she said, putting the silk blouse on the counter. "Just this," she told the clerk.

Natalie tried to dismiss the recollection in favor of better memories. All the years of her girlhood seemed to surface as she absorbed her mother's essence. Sometimes when a favorite book was featured at the shop, they'd try to dress like the characters. Natalie had been obsessed with her mother's high heels, parading in front of the tall oval mirror like Belle in *Beauty and the Beast*. Somewhere in her head, her mother's laughter floated briefly, vivid as yesterday, and then abruptly faded, a warning that the memory might disappear for good one day.

You were my best friend, Mom. Did you know that? she thought for the millionth time. *I lost you too soon.*

Let go. She repeated the phrase like a mantra.

"Giving away her stuff means she's well and truly gone," said Natalie, regarding the garments piled on the bed. "Oh God. It's like carrying her out with the trash."

"Hon, she's gone whether or not you hang on to her things. Come on. Let's keep going. Take pictures of stuff you want to remember but don't need to keep. That will preserve the memories without the clutter."

Though her stomach was in knots, Natalie knew what she had to do. One by one, she removed things from the closet, feeling the memories burn through her. The clothing bore her mom's scent, her sweat, her stray hairs, the shape of her body. A gum wrapper and a grocery list folded in a pocket. Spare change and a hair tie in the bottom of a bag. She could picture her mom in that jacket or that skirt, that sweater and slacks, smiling as she greeted people in the bookstore.

It all had to go. These things were weighing her down, keeping her from moving away from her grief.

In an empty suitcase, she found some papers—an unfinished passport application. "I used to get so mad at her for never going anywhere," Natalie confessed to Cleo, studying the printout. The place for the photograph was an empty oval demarcated by a dotted line. "I'd ask her why she confined herself to the bookstore. Why didn't she ever sink her teeth into life? Why didn't she fall in love? Or go traveling, see the world?"

Cleo shrugged. "She was content doing what she did. We both saw how happy she was with the life she had. It's not such a bad thing, is it? To be content with your lot?"

"We should all be so lucky." Natalie accelerated the pace, filling the suitcase with handfuls of garments, not bothering to fold them. There was something savage and decisive in her movements, a sharpness that poked through her grief.

She surprised herself with how little she really wanted to keep. The pile on the bed was small and manageable. But there were treasures, to be sure—a classic cherry-red cashmere dress coat from the now-defunct I. Magnin. A lovely vintage watch that didn't run, some glittery bangle earrings, a pair of gold-heeled sandals still in the box, as though her mother had been saving them for a special occasion. A Coach belt her mom had splurged on and wore often. A few things Natalie had given to Blythe as gifts, some of them never worn. *Let go*, she reminded herself. *Just let go.*

"Jackpot," said Cleo, producing a jade silk shift with intricate hand embroidery in metallic thread around the Nehru-type collar and cap sleeves outlined in marigold piping. "This would be perfect for the event. Try it on."

"It's not really my style," Natalie said, eyeing the bright colors.

"Neither is attending swanky museum galas," Cleo pointed out. "This is gorgeous. Pure silk. Try it on."

Putting on the dress felt, just for a moment, like a reunion with her mother. Cleo zipped it up the back. Natalie smoothed her hands over the rich fabric and looked in the mirror. It was beautiful but slightly large on her and needed to be hemmed. Yet the color complemented her hair and skin, she had to admit. And the ornamentation would spare her from needing any jewelry other than the beautiful broken watch they'd found.

"It needs alterations, and then it will be totally perfect," Cleo said.

"Where am I going to have it altered on such short notice?" asked Natalie.

"Please. It's the family business." Cleo found some bulldog clips to cinch the dress where it needed to be taken in, and marked the hem. Then she whisked it off Natalie. "I'll take it to my aunt right away. Are you okay finishing on your own here?" She gestured at the piles on the bed.

"Sure." Natalie gave her a hug. "Thank you," she said. "I literally could not have done this without you."

She put on some music to keep her company and worked until the closet was empty, finding a rhythm and decisiveness that got her through the ordeal. The sadness flowed through her, but it was a cleansing sadness, as though her grief had finally burst through a dam.

She took stock of the discarded items—*Don't overthink*—making her peace with them. Then she stood in front of the closet and regarded the empty space. There was one long, deep shelf up high, and a rod that sagged in the middle like a sow's belly, hangers swinging like bird bones.

Natalie selected her mom's favorite dance party song—"Yertle the Turtle" by the Red Hot Chili Peppers. When she was little, they'd play the song on Blythe's boom box and dance themselves silly. Even now Natalie could feel her mother's hands on hers as they whirled around, laughing. Closing her eyes, she danced alone, imagining her mother dancing along with her.

"That is one funky song," Peach said, standing in the doorway.

Natalie jumped, then turned off the music. She swiped her sleeve across her face. "It was our song. Mom's and mine. One of them, anyway."

"Glad you had a mom who liked to dance with you. She sounds cool. I wish I'd known her."

Natalie nodded, grabbing a tissue. "We had our moments. But damn. I miss her." She dabbed at her eyes. For some reason, she didn't feel self-conscious around Peach. Maybe because he'd already seen some of her worst moments. She thought about the morning he'd shown up, expecting to start on a job and finding out the person who'd hired him had gone down in flames. "She was really something," Natalie said.

"I can fix this closet for you," Peach said.

"It's not broken," she said.

He paused, his gaze soft as he studied her face. "You

could use a better design—open shelves, double racks, maybe a light fixture. Sliding doors instead of these flimsy bifold things."

She could instantly picture it, neat shelves and cubbies, the space perfectly organized. "That's tempting, but it's not in the budget."

"On the house, Natalie."

"You don't have to—"

"I know. And you don't have to let me, but I'm doing it anyway. And trust me, you *want* this closet."

"I trust," she said quietly.

He unclipped a tape measure from his belt and quickly made some measurements and calculations, jotting notes with his flat carpenter's pencil. "You missed something here," he said, reaching deep into the back of the shelf.

He pulled out a flat portfolio box made of marbled paper stock and tied with twine. She grabbed a rag to wipe away the dust. There was a sticky note in her mother's handwriting that read *Colleen/Hearst letters— for scanning.*

"Colleen from the Ten-Foot Ladder days. And Hearst?" Natalie untied the twine. "There's only one Hearst I've ever heard of. But letters?"

"More pieces of your puzzle."

She opened the box, causing the dried paper to

crumble. "Looks like some journals in here as well. I thought maybe Grandy had imagined this. He said they were going through old papers and letters, but I never dreamed he was talking about something like this." She opened the top journal to the first page. There, in ink that had faded to brown, was a carefully lettered phrase in a girlish hand. *My Book of Days.*

My name is Colleen O'Rourke. I am fifteen years old, and all alone in this world. This is a record of my days, as I live them.

"Amazing," said Natalie. "And look at her drawings. She was talented. I can't wait to dive in."

"That's really cool, Natalie. You'll get to know your great-grandmother."

"Great-great-grandmother," she said, counting off the generations on her fingers. "Colleen O'Rourke. It's nice to finally meet you."

The Heritage Society sent a car. It was the second time in less than a week someone had ordered a car for Natalie. She leaned out the window of her apartment and saw the liveried driver and Bertie loading her grandfather's wheelchair into the trunk.

"He's early," Natalie said to Cleo, who had come up to help her put the final touches on her outfit.

"I'm sure he's used to waiting." Cleo came to the window to have a look. "My whole family is super impressed that I get to go to this shindig. It's like getting an audience with royalty. Everybody knows who the Tangs are. Just everybody." She drew Natalie over to the mirror. "Now, let's check you out."

Cleo was like those little bluebirds of happiness in Cinderella, flitting around until Natalie had been transformed into a princess. A fraudulent one, to be sure, but a princess nonetheless.

The silk dress from her mother's closet had been transformed into a couture masterpiece by the sartorial skills of Cleo's talented aunt. The sheath now fit like an extremely flattering glove. Its color, and the bright handwork accents, echoed the colors of the precious vase—jade green, turquoise, marigold, and fuchsia with veins of cobalt blue. She paired it with the gold-heeled sandals, the vintage watch, and a gold snake belt borrowed from Cleo. Earlier in the day, Natalie had splurged on a salon that had groomed her like a show poodle, coordinating her makeup and polish with the colors of the dress.

Cleo was radiant in the yellow chiffon Valentino,

and she sported a glorious fresh streak of hot pink in her hair. "Look at us," she said. "We look incredible."

Natalie opened the closet to find her one bag that would pass as an evening bag, a small clutch with paste jewels. As she slid the new doors apart, she heard a gasp from Chloe. "I know, right?" she said. "That was my reaction when I saw it."

"Were you up all night working on it?"

"It's all Peach. He took away the donations and discards, and rebuilt this closet, just to be nice." He had worked late, whistling and humming. The interior of the closet glowed with lights that came on automatically when the door opened, illuminating the new custom shelving, racks, and drawers. Even with Natalie's fairly ordinary things, the display resembled a high-end vintage boutique.

"That is a glory to behold," said Cleo, testing a clever pullout shelf. "He's really something."

"Peach is like my mom's last gift to me. She contacted him right before she died."

"He's really good. I wish we could keep him."

"I can't afford to keep him. I'm just hoping he'll be able to stop the place from falling down." She put her keys, invitation, lipstick, credit card, and phone in the small bag. "Let's go see if Bertie and Grandy are ready."

They headed down to the foyer. Bertie was there, checking the shine on his dress shoes.

"Oh my God, you look fantastic," Natalie said to him.

"Yeah?" He straightened up and tweaked his bow tie. "Not too Pee-wee Herman?"

"Hardly. That's a wonderful suit. And those shoes." Natalie stepped back, beaming at both Bertie and Cleo. "I swear, if there were an award for best-looking book-store staff, we would win it."

"True," Bertie said. "You're beyond gorgeous."

"Really?"

"Absolutely."

"Well, two hours of hair and makeup will make anyone a natural beauty."

"Stop it. You're always beautiful. I'm getting misty looking at you, because you're channeling Blythe. In the best possible way."

The door to the downstairs apartment opened and Grandy stepped out, leaning on his cane. He was dressed in his best suit, and there was a boutonniere in his lapel. Bertie had taken him to the barbershop for a luxury shave and a haircut, and he looked like an elder statesman—white-haired and distinguished.

When he spotted Cleo by the door, he stood stock-still. For a moment, Natalie thought he was having a stroke or something. "Grandy?"

He took Cleo's hand and gave her the happiest smile Natalie had seen on his face since the plane crash. "My darling May," he said. "I wish I could say something profound about your beauty, but I am rendered speechless."

Natalie cringed. Cleo, bless her, simply smiled and said, "Sorry, dude. That's not the way I roll."

"Grandy, it's Cleo," Natalie said. "Not May Lin."

He paused, then dropped Cleo's hand and shuffled toward the door. "Is she coming, then? I haven't seen her yet today."

Natalie held the door for him, her heart wrenched by his confusion. "May is gone, Grandy. Tonight, we're guests of honor at the Chinese American Heritage Society. It's about the vase, remember?"

He nodded vaguely, then walked out to the curb, waiting patiently as the driver opened the door. "Where's Mr. Gallagher?" he asked.

Natalie breathed a sigh of relief, hoping her grandfather's mind was coming back into focus. "Peach will meet us there. And you're the one who's being honored tonight, since you opted to restore it to the Tang family. Not everyone would have done that. You did a good thing." She'd made sure Grandy understood the value of the piece he'd given away. He had assured her that he had no interest in profiting off someone else's possessions.

She scooted into the back seat of the limo and patted his knee. "Here we go."

Cleo and Bertie sat across from them. There was a tiny bar with a crystal decanter and matching glasses, a bucket of ice, and a selection of beverages. "Let's have a toast," said Cleo. "Sparkling water only, so if we spill, it won't stain." She poured and they clinked glasses.

"To Andrew and the magnificent vase," Bertie said with exaggerated dramatic flair. "May its long, strange journey end well."

Their arrival was heralded by white-gloved doormen at the grand entrance of the huge neo-Gothic mansion. A special attendant brought Grandy in his wheelchair up a side ramp. When they stepped into the main ballroom, Aisin Tang met them at the door. The president of the society was dazzling and distinguished, effusively thanking Andrew, then turning his refined charm on Natalie and the others. A couple of photographers moved in to take pictures.

"He's fabulous," Cleo whispered in her ear. "Check and see if he's single."

"Stop it," Natalie hissed.

"I've heard he's loaded, too," Cleo went on. "He should give you a reward or a finder's fee, right?"

"I brought that up with Grandy," Natalie told her. "He's not having it. He says it's enough to restore the lost treasure to the family."

"The *loaded* family."

"Stop it," she said again. "And just so you know, they *aren't* loaded. I checked. Besides, I'm not here to—oh my gosh." She spotted the governor, surrounded by a well-dressed cadre of admirers. She'd heard his daughter's wedding had gone off without a hitch. Her days at Pinnacle seemed like another life, when a make-or-break business deal had meant so much to her.

Along with the politicians, there were Hollywood types and Silicon Valley millionaires—possibly billionaires, Cleo pointed out. All gorgeously coiffed and expensively dressed, chatting and mingling with familiar ease. More photographers trolled the room, discreetly capturing shots of people who seemed to be having a conspicuously good time. The tables were festooned with tasseled jewel-toned silks, gold-painted porcelain china, and crystal stemware.

"I am way out of my element," Natalie said. "I feel like a total fraud, an interloper."

"Bullshit," Cleo said. "You have every right to be here."

"These are not my people." Natalie watched a woman walk by wearing a necklace that was probably worth more than the vase. "I'm a working girl. A bookseller. I have nothing in common with them."

"Too late to turn back now, Cinderella," said Cleo. "Quit looking so panicked."

"I wish I had your confidence." She eyed Cleo's feather tattoo, her swath of pink hair, and the way she carried herself, as though strutting in a couture runway show.

Surveying the polished crowd, she saw Bertie and Grandy sampling canapés of caviar and truffles and tried to relax a little. Then she thought about Peach and tensed up again. This was not his crowd, either.

"Now what are you worrying about?" asked Cleo.

"He is going to be so out of place here," said Natalie.

"Who? Peach?" Cleo grinned. "Think he'll wear his tool belt?"

"Maybe I shouldn't have encouraged him to come. I mean, he deserves to be included, but is he going to feel totally awkward?"

"He's a big boy. He'll deal." Cleo fanned herself as a gorgeous woman walked by, shadowed by a glittering entourage and stalked by a photographer with a big black camera.

"I don't see him." Natalie craned her neck toward

the door. "Maybe he changed his mind. Does he even have something to wear?" When told to dress up, most guys—even grown men—defaulted to pleated chinos and a clip-on tie.

"Don't worry until I say it's time to worry."

Natalie tried to follow Cleo's advice. But now that she was here, everything seemed so stiff and formal and awkward. She pictured Peach in his workman's garb, and then in his house band outfit of ripped jeans and tight T-shirt. That was his comfort zone. Not this. Maybe he wouldn't show at all, she thought. Maybe—

"Oh boy." Cleo looked over Natalie's shoulder at the ballroom entrance.

Natalie turned to see. In walked a vision of elegance that might have just stepped off the pages of a Jane Austen novel. She didn't even bother trying not to stare. Peach Gallagher had arrived. And all her expectations exploded.

Not only did he appear to understand the meaning of black tie, he walked into the reception room as if he had invented the look—a perfectly fitted tuxedo jacket and matching trousers, a shirt with studs and cuff links, an expertly tied bow tie, and black laced oxfords. His long hair managed to make the attire seem more formal.

He was every crush she'd ever had from junior high

onward. Every album cover she'd stared at, listening to torch songs until she cried. Every mooned-over heartthrob she could never have. Which made her a horrible person, burning with envy over his wife, the aptly named Regina.

Two waiters with trays nearly collided, hurrying over to serve him. He politely smiled and shook his head, declining the proffered champagne and dim sum, then scanned the room. She could tell the moment he spotted her and Cleo. His eyes lit and he quickened his stride as he came over to join them.

"Hello, ladies," he said. "You both look beautiful."

"Mr. Gallagher, I presume," Natalie said, trying to believe she *wasn't* flirting.

"You're looking rather toothsome yourself," said Cleo. "I like saying 'toothsome.' It doesn't mean what people think it means." She tipped her glass to them, and a photographer stepped forward, asking for their names.

"Who are you with?" asked Cleo.

"*Prestige Hong Kong*." He handed her a card.

"Cleo Chan," Cleo said. "I'm a San Francisco playwright, and I'm wearing Valentino. This is Natalie Harper, owner of the Lost and Found Bookshop, and Peter Gallagher, the building designer who found the vase that's on display over there." She gestured with a flutter of her hand. The photographer made some notes, then moved off.

"Building designer," Peach said with a chuckle. "I like it."

"I figured 'hammer for hire' would require too much of an explanation." Cleo gave them a wink and went to mingle with the glittering crowd.

"Think we'll show up in *Prestige Hong Kong*?" asked Natalie.

"They'd be crazy not to feature us. We're lookin' fly."

"The vase is the star of the show tonight." She gestured at the lighted museum glass case; the piece was surrounded by more admirers than the governor himself.

Peach helped himself to a glass of champagne from a passing server. "It's really cool, seeing all the interest."

"You should have seen my grandfather's face when they brought him in." She gestured toward him, now thronged with people.

"Sorry I missed that," Peach said. "I didn't mean to be late, but Dorothy's mother couldn't take her tonight. I had to get a last-minute sitter." His tone was edged with annoyance.

Couldn't take her seemed an odd choice of words, Natalie thought. Take her where? "Oh, I . . . well, I'm glad you and your wife worked it out, anyway."

He frowned slightly; then his lips quirked into a smile. "She's not my wife."

Natalie returned the frown. "Sorry, what?"

"Dorothy's mom. Not my wife."

"You're not married?" Well, that was a common enough situation, she supposed.

"We were. We're divorced now."

And just like that, the world shifted. This was new. This was unexpected. This was welcome news. She pretended to be chill about the information. Like it was incidental, no big deal, no surprise.

Deep down, however, a dance party was starting up. Peach Gallagher was single. *Single.* There was no Mrs. Peach. That meant Natalie wasn't horrible after all for feeling drawn to him. For wanting to tell him everything, wanting to stay up all night talking to him. "Oh, I see," she said. "I'm sorry to hear that."

"It's okay. Tough on Dorothy sometimes, but you probably noticed—she's pretty adaptable."

"She's pretty great," Natalie agreed. "So you and your ex share custody."

"Fifty-fifty," he said. "I had to fight like a bearcat to

get it that way. Sometimes it's a juggling act, but I love every minute with my kid."

"How long has it been? I mean, if you don't mind my asking."

"Couple of years." He finished his champagne, and they moved closer to the display.

"And it's, um, you're okay?" Most of her friends who had gone through a divorce ended up all right— but getting there was often a long and painful process. It was one reason, Natalie supposed, that she'd never been in a hurry to marry. The potential for heartache seemed enormous. So was the potential for happiness, but she'd never been tempted to take the risk.

"I'm good. My ex lives with her boyfriend now. They're investment bankers—Regina and Regis. Cute, huh? They have a place on Nob Hill, close to Dorothy's school. It was disconcerting as hell at first, finding out the person you love has checked out of the relationship and didn't bother telling you."

"I'm sorry," she said again. "That must have been hard."

"I'm over the hard part. Don't worry about me." He put his hand on the small of her back and gently pressed her toward the display. "Let's check this out."

It was just his hand, she thought. But it was thrilling. And ridiculously liberating to find out at last that the undercurrents she'd sensed between them were not actually forbidden. But there was much she didn't know about this man. Much she hadn't let herself know. Realizing he was single might be a game changer. Then again, it might be nothing. She had no idea what he thought of her, or if he thought of her at all, other than as a client.

They joined the group around the vase. The display case and dramatic lighting brought out the intense colors of the porcelain. "It looks so important now," Natalie said. "It's hard to imagine it in some context, in someone's home, before it ended up in our crawl space." She studied the detailed storyboard outlining the journey of the vase from its merchant family beginnings in China, to San Francisco, to its discovery in the Sunrose Building.

"I'm famous," Peach said with a chuckle, bending low to whisper in her ear. "See, it says 'found by a workman during renovation.'"

Natalie tried not to shiver at the feel of his breath on her neck. "They should have mentioned you by name. If not for you, the vase would still be forgotten."

"Nah, I'm good with being 'a workman.'"

"You don't look like one tonight."

"I'm not working." Again with the low, intimate whisper. "Although I'm feeling partial to 'building designer' these days." He finished his champagne and helped himself to another glass.

She took a half step away from him, trying to figure out if he was flirting. Trying to figure out if she *wanted* that from him.

The last panel of the display featured a wonderful photograph of her grandfather and Aisin Tang together at the bookstore, sharing a warm greeting.

"I'm really proud of him. He could have tried to claim ownership of the piece. Could have wiped out the debt and back taxes, then retired in luxury to Ibiza. But he didn't. He gave it back. I like to think I'd have done the same thing."

"You would have done the same thing," Peach told her.

"How do you know?"

"You seem like the type of person who wouldn't keep something meant for somebody else."

She looked up at him. His eyes were very, very blue. "I hope you're right."

He held her gaze for an extra-long moment. "I'm right. And—"

Another photographer took their picture and asked for their names.

"Flair MacKenzie and Dirk Digler," Peach said without missing a beat.

Natalie managed to hold her laughter until the photographer moved on. "You've already had too much champagne," she chided him.

"It's a gala. We're supposed to be drinking. Come on, let's find our table."

They were seated with Cleo, Bertie, and Grandy at their designated table. The others in their group were friends of the Tang family. Natalie guessed, judging by their clothes and jewelry, and the attention they were getting, that they were VIPs. She found it awkward to make small talk with them, but Peach and Bertie took over, keeping up a lively patter.

A parade of servers came through with domed platters of incredible food—handmade Chinese dumplings and dim sum shaped like tiny pomegranates and tangerines, gorgeously presented noodles in every color of the rainbow, and dishes with ingredients Natalie could only guess at. A red tea called Da Hong Pao was served, and one of the people at the table said it was so rare that it couldn't be bought for any price but had to be received as a gift. Natalie found it earthy and bitter, but the whole meal delighted her, because Grandy was clearly savoring every bite.

The featured speaker was a historian who had been a protégé of Li Xueqin. His talk was mercifully short and surprisingly witty, concluding along with the elaborate dessert service. As the mingling and socializing started up again, Peach leaned over to Natalie and whispered, "Let's go have a look at the night garden."

She eagerly agreed. The moon garden of the mansion was famous, having been designed with night-blooming flowers lining the pathways and hillocks of the landscape. They stepped through the open doors, went down the wide stone steps, and were greeted by the heady perfume of late-blooming autumn flowers. The pale blossoms were lit from below, setting a mood of mystery. A fountain of natural stone rose up out of a pond surrounded by terra-cotta sculptures.

"It smells so nice out here," Natalie said. "What an incredible garden. I could get used to hanging out with the *haute monde*."

"You like the good life, then."

"Do you blame me? Don't you?"

He shrugged. "I like life. It's all good."

"That's a very healthy attitude. Your parents must have raised you right."

"I reckon they'd be pleased to hear that," he said.

A few other visitors strolled the grounds, their murmurs of conversation drifting as they passed. Natalie felt an urge to take his arm but thought better of it. She sensed something new between them, but it could be just her imagination—or wishful thinking. Despite the tux and black tie, he was still Peach, the guy who had installed a new low-flow toilet in her apartment and was keeping the roof from falling in.

They passed a special display—marked by warning signs—of poisonous plants. Natalie had always been intrigued by the pendulous white angel's trumpets and the small, deceptively innocent-looking berries of deadly nightshade. "That one's a favorite in murder mysteries," she said. "Supposedly ten berries will kill a person. The poison's called atropine."

"The name comes from Atropos, one of the three Fates," Peach said.

"Oh, now you're showing off again."

"What good is knowing stuff if you can't use it? Atropos was a bitch of a Fate. She could take you out by cutting the last thread of your life's tapestry." He made a snipping motion with his hand.

"I'll steer clear of her."

The path ended at a wrought-iron railing at the edge of the hill. Natalie's breath caught as she surveyed the view. In the distance below, the lights along the shore and bridges reflected off the bay. "I love this city," she said. "After college, I couldn't wait to move somewhere else, but now that I'm back, I appreciate it so much." She glanced up at him. His face was in shadow but a glint of light showed the curve of his smile.

"I like it here, too. I like the crazy charm of this city. Maybe I even love it here, and so does Dorothy."

"How long have you lived in the city?"

"Let's see . . . we moved from Atlanta the year Dorothy was born. Regina landed a job in investment banking right out of grad school. I was just out of the military. The plan was to swap baby duties. I'd be with Dorothy during the workweek, and her mom took over while I did renovations after hours and on the weekends. It seemed like a good system, but it wasn't so great for the marriage."

"Sounds hard," she said, trying to imagine the struggles of a young family. She felt like asking him a million questions but didn't want to inundate him. Realizing he was single had caused such a swift realignment of her impression of him that she wanted to dig down a layer. Questions that would be inappropriate to ask a married man were suddenly possible.

"You're looking at me funny," he said.

They were unbalanced. After all the hours he'd spent in the bookstore, he knew everything about her. Yet he'd never leveled with her about his own life. It made her wonder what else he hadn't told her.

"I feel like I'm just getting to know you," she said.

"What? I'm an open book. Ask me anything."

"How is it you're so smooth at a black-tie event? Did you have some kind of fancy life back in Atlanta?"

"Ha. You could say that. Or you could say a *phony* life."

"What was phony about it?"

"Damn, where do I start? My dad was in finance. The kind you're picturing—big house in an old neighborhood, a staff, private schools, plenty of black-tie action. It was all great until Dad went to prison for fraud."

"What? No."

"Yep. My sister and I were teenagers. We didn't know what hit us. Everything went away, practically overnight. The only money we had was in our college savings plans. So instead of college, Junebug went into treatment, and I joined the Marines. The only things left had no value, like how to wear a tux. Which fork to use. How to saber the top off a bottle of champagne."

Natalie absorbed the information. It made her head spin. "Junebug's your sister?"

"Yeah. June Barbara. She had some trouble with prescription drugs. Seems to be okay now."

"I don't know what to say." What most fascinated Natalie about Peach was the way he seemed to take life in stride. Clearly he'd had his share of ups and downs—a massive family drama, a stint in the military he didn't talk about, a divorce—yet nothing seemed to faze him. She wished she could be more like that.

A breeze lifted her hair, and she shivered slightly.

"Cold?" he asked. "You want my coat?"

"I'm fine."

"You're cold." He quickly took off his tux jacket and draped it around her shoulders, keeping hold of the lapels.

She savored the delicious warmth of his body heat enveloping her. "Well, thank you."

"It's a shame to cover up that pretty dress," he said. "It looks really nice on you."

"It was my mother's," she said, smoothing her hands down the silk. "Cleo and I picked it out when we emptied her closet."

"That makes it even nicer," he said.

She nodded, snuggling into the jacket. "I keep thinking I'll stop missing her. And then I realize I don't want to stop missing her. What I want," she said, letting the raw admission slip out, "is to stop it from hurting so much."

"Ah, Natalie." Very gently, he slid one arm around her back. "I'm sorry. Wish I could help."

She paused, sending herself a stern reminder to be

here now, not back in the morass of grief that sucked her in with brutal regularity. "You *are* helping," she blurted out. "I don't think you realize that, Peach. You've been around through this whole mess, and you've been steady, and good to my grandfather, and you're fixing my house and you made me a closet, and whether you know it or not, that's helping. I honestly don't know how to thank you."

He gazed down at her. The intent look in his eyes stopped her breath. "So this Trevor guy," he said. "Is he your boyfriend?"

"My . . . No," she said quickly, almost urgently. "Why do— I mean, we went out a couple of times, that's all."

"Hm," he said.

"What's that supposed to mean?"

"Just, hm." He lifted a stray curl from her face, and then kept his hand there, cupping her cheek.

"You never told me you were single," she said.

"You never told me it mattered," he said.

And then he pressed her up against the wrought-iron fence and kissed her.

It was *that* kind of kiss. She recognized it instantly— the soft lips, the champagne-sweet taste of him, the melding of their breath for the first time. She leaned in, her lips parting slightly, and willingly lost herself. She let everything fall away—grief, worry, confusion, loneliness. When he pulled back, she felt dazed.

He looked utterly pleased, his mouth curved in a beguiling half smile, his gaze studying her.

She felt the need to say something. "That was . . ." She took a breath, started again. "I'm flustered."

"In a good way," he said.

"I don't like being flustered," she said.

"Do you like being kissed?"

"Depends on the guy." She took a step back, trying to regain her balance.

He grinned, then took her hand and started walking back to the ballroom. "Good to know," he said.

PART FOUR

A book, too, can be a star . . . a living fire
to lighten the darkness, leading out into
the expanding universe.
                    —MADELEINE L'ENGLE

20

Each morning, Natalie awakened with her heart racing. It was ridiculous. She was like a revved-up teenager in the first flush of infatuation. She'd made out with her share of guys. The awkward teenage make-out sessions. Beer-fueled sloppy kisses in college. Grown-up kisses with men she liked, or maybe even loved. There had never been a kiss like this, though. Not in her life. Maybe not ever, for anyone. In the history of the world. When thoughts like that greeted her each morning, she knew she was in trouble.

And quite possibly delusional. Because the morning after—she thought of it as the morning after, as if they'd shared a night of raucous sex instead of a mere experimental kiss—he had shown up on the job as usual, in his workman's garb, an oh-so-casual smile on his face. "That was nice, last night," he'd said. "Thanks for inviting me."

"I'm glad you were there," she said.

"I came on to you in the moon garden," he said, direct as always.

"You did. Maybe it has a romantic effect on people."

"Maybe *you* have a romantic effect on me. Hope you didn't think it was rude."

Rude? *Rude?* "Nonsense, you were a perfect gentleman."

"Good to know," he'd concluded, echoing his words from the night before. "I should tell you, though, that I have a policy about getting involved with a client."

Her heart sank. And her guard went up. She felt too vulnerable with him. Retreat seemed the safest course. "Very professional of you."

"Anyway, maybe one day you won't be a client."

After that, he had gone about his business, leaving her alone with her angsty, adolescent thoughts. Since that kiss, every word they exchanged seemed to have a different meaning. To her, anyway.

She'd never been comfortable with powerful feelings. In her experience, they couldn't be trusted. She was her mother's daughter, after all, shielding her heart from a deep and dangerous attachment. When it came to men, her judgment was flawed. Rick was the perfect example, a man she'd thought she could love, yet her heart had failed her.

Maybe this was different.

Then again, maybe not.

She was determined not to let that moment in the garden become a big deal, dominating her thoughts when she was supposed to be focused on work. It was perhaps serendipitous that Peach had another historical restoration job going over in the Russian Hill District. There was still plenty to be done on the Sunrose Building, but she couldn't afford to do it all at once. Despite the bonanza created by the Trevor Dashwood event, she'd had to order all the books in advance and cover all the other expenses involved in putting on a major book signing.

She missed having Peach around, whistling through his teeth, humming under his breath. She missed hearing his easy conversation with Grandy, but she didn't miss him enough to tell him so.

Tess came to the city to have dinner with her father, who was visiting from Tangier. After learning the stunning news that he'd been living overseas her entire life, Tess was moving cautiously to get to know him. She stopped in at the bookstore on a blustery November day. "It's a boy," she said, outlining the baby bump with her hand. "I wanted to be surprised, but the last ultrasound gave it away, even to my untrained eye. Takes after his brothers and father."

"That's wonderful," Natalie said. "Need a baby name book?"

"We still have those from our first two. I do need a book, though. It's my father's birthday," she explained. "So I thought I'd pick out some books."

"What kind of books?" Natalie asked, gesturing at the display tables.

"Good question. I barely know the man. I mean, what do you do with a guy who faked his own death and disappeared for decades, and then returned wanting to 'reconnect' with the daughters he never knew?" She grinned at Natalie's expression. "Complicated, right?"

"Like a telenovela. And I thought *I* had daddy issues."

"After all the drama, I do want to get to know him. He was lost to us since before we were born, and I'm struggling to make peace with that. Now that I understand everything that happened, I get it. And even though it's hard, I do like having him in my life. He reads all the time, so I can't go wrong with a few books."

"What about a novel?" She handed Tess a copy of *The Extraordinary Life of Sam Hell*. "About a guy who travels halfway around the world. Or is that too on-the-nose?"

"I'm not sure." She set it on the counter and picked out a couple of can't-miss nonfiction bestsellers—one by Erik Larson and another by Timothy Egan. "And this one, because it's my favorite," she added, grabbing *The Art of Racing in the Rain*.

"I've always thought you can get to know someone by the books they love."

"Can't hurt." She chose a Clairefontaine notebook and pen.

"You're going to need a bigger gift bag," said Natalie, getting one from under the counter.

While she wrapped them up, Tess asked, "So how are things with Mr. Wonderful?"

"He has another renovation going over on Russian H—" Natalie stopped herself. "Oh, you mean Trevor Dashwood."

"Do I?" Tess raised an eyebrow. "What's going on?"

"He's not married," Natalie blurted out.

"Slow down. Which Mr. Wonderful are we talking about?"

"Peach," she said.

Tess paused. "Oh. The hammer for hire."

"All this time I assumed he was married—because

of the kid. At the gala, I found out he's been divorced for a couple of years."

"And this makes a difference because . . . ?" Tess's eyebrow went up again.

"Because there was a vibe," Natalie admitted.

"And of course you had been ignoring it because you thought he was married."

Natalie nodded. "It's different now, but . . . I don't know, Tess. We had a moment at the Heritage Society gala. I guess it was a moment." Actually, it had felt much bigger than a moment—more like an earthquake. "I have no idea what he's thinking." She was pretty sure he hadn't tossed and turned half the night and awakened with his heart racing.

"Ask him," Tess suggested. "Ask him what he's thinking."

"That would be weird." Now that his marital status was clear to her, she had a million questions for him, things that would not have been appropriate to ask a married man.

She glanced at the computer screen. "It's been taking all my willpower to keep myself from stalking him online. It seems sketchy to pry into his life by looking him up on social media or googling the name of his band or his ex or any other little detail he might have dropped."

"Probably a good policy," Tess agreed. "When a person wants you to know things about him, he'll tell you."

"Exactly." Natalie realized Peach had told her only a little about himself. Lack of interest? Ambivalence about his family? Or did he consider her just a client? He had a policy.

"Or you could ask," Tess repeated.

"Stop it. We're not a match, anyway. He's divorced with a kid, and he was really honest with me about how hard that makes things for him."

"Dominic was divorced with *two* kids when I met him," Tess pointed out. "And hell yes, it was hard. Still is. His older kids' mom isn't the easiest person to get along with—and I'm being generous here."

"You're proving my point. Why would I get into a relationship that's probably going to fail?" She shuddered, shying away from a feeling of terrible vulnerability. Was that what had kept her mother alone all her life? Fear? Doubt? Lack of trust that hurt was not just around the corner?

She now understood Blythe's devotion to the store. Unlike men, books were easy. They filled you with all the emotions in the world—joy, dread, fear, hurt, gratification—and then they came to an end. People were different. Unpredictable. Impossible to manage.

"Because it might *not* fail," Tess pointed out. "And trust me, the right relationship makes everything better."

"I'll keep that in mind."

Tess studied the poster announcing the Trevor Dashwood event. "Maybe keep *him* in mind, too."

There was no denying that Trevor was the full package—talent, looks, charm. Natalie didn't wake up in the morning still dreaming about the kiss they'd shared. But it was just one kiss, and they were new, and maybe she shouldn't jump to conclusions. About either guy.

"He's keeping me very busy. The event is out of control. Sold out, as a matter of fact."

"Glad I got tickets early. The kids are totally excited. And is *he* still Mr. Wonderful?"

"Are you kidding? Of course." She told Tess about the sunset cruise, and their upcoming dinner at Rendez-Vous in Napa. He was taking her there after the book signing.

"Okay, now *I* want to date him."

"Very funny." Natalie handed her the wrapped books. "Listen, I'm happy for you and your sister, getting to know your father. Good luck, okay?"

After Tess left, Natalie was swept into the whirlwind that was Trevor Dashwood. The phone started ringing, Bertie and Cleo showed up, and she had to attend to the myriad little details of the upcoming event. Even with Trevor's expert planner, they had to roll up their sleeves and work together. "The Flip Side with Trevor Dashwood" was spinning into madness. The Unitarian church on the corner was the chosen venue, and Natalie, Cleo, and Bertie were happily inundated with preorders and special requests.

Through it all, Trevor truly *was* Mr. Wonderful, enlisting an army of help from his publisher. His publicist set up an interview with *Bay Area Life Magazine*. There would be a print article and a video companion piece. A reporter, photographer, and videographer would be coming to the bookstore that evening.

Natalie kept checking the clock, obsessively tidying up the store, wondering what they would ask her and hoping she wouldn't come off sounding weird or phony. Trevor showed up early with a gift that made her nearly faint with gratitude—a wardrobe, hair, and makeup stylist.

"How did you know?" she said, unable to keep from smiling.

"A little Bertie told me." Trevor acknowledged him with a nod.

"Bertie and Cleo are amazing," she said, and for a moment, emotion overtook her. "I love you guys," she said. "When I was working at the wine place, I never had coworkers I could say that to."

The stylist was named Shelly, and she was ultra-cool, with an asymmetric pixie haircut and a tattoo on her clavicle. Even better, she had a great eye and skills honed, she said, by working behind the scenes at Disneyland as a stylist for the princess attraction. She picked out a fitted navy top, dark wash jeans, and wedge sandals—nothing too busy for the camera, she explained. Spotting Blythe's jewelry box, she rummaged around and found a lime-green bangle and a pair of gold hoop earrings.

Natalie hadn't yet tackled the jewelry box. Its contents, though not valuable, evoked all sorts of memories. Through the years, her mom's admirers had gifted her with any number of baubles. She even remembered the guy who had given Blythe the hoops. Langdon somebody, a poet who had a beard and smelled of French cigarettes. Mom had met him when his publisher set up a poetry reading in the bookstore. Natalie had been in middle school and was helping at the cash register during the event. She remembered thinking it was her lucky night, because a group of students from Greenhill Prep showed up. Natalie had just begun thinking about boys as something other than an alien life-form. Every Sunday, she studied the Pink Pages in the paper and dreamed about going to a concert with a boy, maybe having her first kiss while Counting Crows were playing at Slim's.

The clean-cut, straight-arrow guys and blond-ponytailed girls from Greenhill had intrigued her. She even caught the attention of one of the boys, a kid with perfect teeth and a twinkle in his eye. He sat in one of the metal folding chairs in the back and patted the empty seat beside him.

She had practically floated as she went to sit next to the boy. "I'm Natalie," she said. "I work here."

"Prescott," he'd said, and she wasn't sure if that was his first or last name. Rich kids tended to have first names that sounded like last names.

"You like poetry?" she asked.

"Nah. Our English Nine teacher said we'd get extra credit if we came."

Natalie's mom introduced the poet, supposedly one of the most gifted protégés of Lawrence Ferlinghetti, the pride of the Bay Area. He sure seemed to be channeling Ferlinghetti with that beard and bowler hat.

The boy named Prescott took notes in a theme book with a marbled cover. Tucked between the pages was a brochure from Mr. Lee's Driving School—that was *the* place where everyone learned to drive. Everyone except probably Natalie. Even though driving was a few years away, her mom was already warning her that there was no point in taking driving lessons because number one, they didn't have a car, and number two, driving in the city was impossible anyway.

Prescott noticed her looking and drew a little thumbs-up next to the brochure. Then in the margin of the page, he wrote, *What's your number?*

Natalie nearly fainted, but she grabbed his pencil and wrote it on the page next to her name. When the author started reading, the poem seemed kind of low-key, a collection of images about trains and tunnels. Then she heard one too many references to grinding gears and thrusting pistons and a woman outlining her moist mouth with a lipsicle . . . and that was when the elbow jabs and snickers started. Most of the subsequent poems were filled with further obvious references. Natalie's cheeks and ears caught fire, and she slumped in her chair, feeling trapped in a vortex of the poet's loud, gruff voice and the hisses of suppressed amusement from the high school kids. When the guy recited a piece about going to the zoo and seeing a gorilla eating a raw hot dog, she nearly melted into a pool of mortification.

During a pause in the presentation, the earnest adults sitting in the front of the room started a discussion, and Prescott asked her what school she went to.

"St. Dymphna's," she whispered. It wasn't as prestigious as Greenhill. "Maybe I'll go to Greenhill for high school," she added. Yeah, right. If she asked to go to Greenhill, her mom would say they Couldn't Afford It, which was her answer to pretty much everything.

"You're not in high school?" Prescott asked. He looked down at the number she had neatly penciled in his notebook. "Maybe I'll call you in a few years, then."

Natalie tried to force herself to die right then and there. When that failed, she slunk away, exiting through the stockroom and up the back steps to the apartment. Grandy and May were watching *Northern Exposure*. When Mom came up later, Natalie pounced. "That guy was totally weird, Mom. Those poems about churning and burning . . . geez."

Her mother had laughed, her big blustery laugh that everybody loved. Instead of kicking off her shoes and shrugging out of her work clothes, she took a coat from the closet. Her good cherry-red one from I. Magnin. "Those are my favorite parts. He's not weird. I think he's nice."

Natalie recognized her mom's tone. She tended to get fluttery when a new guy came around. "What? You're going out with him?"

"Sure." Mom leaned toward the hall mirror and fluffed her hair. "As soon as I put on my lipsicle." She winked and took out a tube and turned her mouth into a red oval.

"*Mo-o-om.*" Natalie turned the word into an elongated complaint.

"Don't worry. I probably won't keep him long."

"Close your eyes and hold still," said Shelly the stylist, tilting Natalie's face up to the light. "I'm going to give you a tiny bit of eyeliner, just for definition."

Natalie shut her eyes. As her mother had predicted, the poet hadn't lasted long, but she had kept the hoops. When Shelly finished her primping, Natalie couldn't help grinning at the image in the mirror. "Wow, you're good," she said.

"I'm just gilding the lily here," said Shelly. "Let's go downstairs. They're probably ready for you."

The camera crew had arranged a cozy seating area in front of the floor-to-ceiling shelves. The dramatic lighting highlighted the rolling library ladder and fretwork on the antique oak. Even Sylvia the cat made an appearance, padding around and sniffing things.

"My heart just skipped a beat," Trevor said when Natalie stepped into the light. "I mean, you're always gorgeous, but—"

There was a knock at the door. She looked over and

saw Peach. What was he doing here after hours? She hurried to let him in. "Hey," she said. "Come on in."

"Forgot my stud finder," he said.

She stepped aside. "Find away. We're doing a spot for the book signing this weekend."

He gave her a long look, his gaze warm as he took in her fancy hair and makeup. "Yeah?" he said. "You look—"

"Hey, man, good to see you again." Trevor Dashwood stuck out his hand.

Peach shook it. "My daughter is looking forward to your book signing."

"Can't wait to meet her. Dorothy, right?"

The tension between the two guys was palpable. Natalie couldn't see it, but she sensed it, two bucks circling, about to lock horns. Then Peach took a step back. "Okay, then. I'll just grab my stuff and be out of your way. Good luck with your . . ." He gestured at the lighted seating area. "See you around."

Everyone said the article and companion webcast came out great. Natalie took their word for it because she was too bashful to actually watch herself on video. Besides, there was no time. The day of the event was a whirlwind as she shuttled between the shop and the auditorium, attending to last-minute details. She was a ball of nervous excitement.

The one dim spot was that her grandfather was feeling ill—again—and he was going to miss the festivities. The doctors still couldn't figure out why he kept losing weight and had trouble breathing.

As the hour approached, Natalie worked with Bertie and Cleo, setting up the cash register in the vestibule. They could see people gathering outside. It was a rare, glorious afternoon, the sun turning everything a rich golden hue. "It's happening," she said. "I feel as though I'm in a dream."

"And I hear you've got a date with Mr. Darcy afterward," said Cleo. "Rendez-Vous?" She fanned herself.

"It's not . . . I don't know what it is," Natalie said. "I barely know the guy."

"That's why it's a date," Cleo said. "So you can get to know him."

"Just be safe," Bertie said. "Promise."

"Safe?" Natalie rounded on him. "Have you heard something?"

Bertie shook his head. "Not a thing. He's a celebrity, so . . ." He shrugged. "There's almost no information other than the material in his bio. And that stuff looks so . . . curated."

"He grew up off the grid," Natalie said. "I bet his

parents are freaks about privacy. He's fine, Bertie. You worry too much. But he's not—I just don't see us together. I mean, the guy's one of the bestselling writers in the world."

"And you're the best bookseller in the world, and you should totally date him," Cleo said.

"I'm not the best bookseller in the world," Natalie said. "I'm the luckiest, though."

Bertie went to open the doors. Kids streamed in with their parents and grandparents, eager to see their favorite author. Tess and Dominic arrived with their crew, large and small. "You look fantastic," Tess told her. "Those jeans—perfect. God, I can't wait to not be pregnant anymore."

"Go grab a seat. I—" Natalie spotted a familiar face and did a double take. What was *he* doing here? With two kids in tow. "Excuse me."

Dean Fogarty came over to her. "Hey," he said. "I heard about this event, so I thought I'd bring the twins to see their favorite author." He gestured at a girl and a boy, who looked to be about ten.

"Pop-pop, can we go get seats at the front?" the boy asked. He wore a soccer shirt and had a skinned knee. Natalie flashed on her first—and last—soccer practice. The one that had been ruined for her when she'd encountered Dean with his "real" kid.

"Go ahead, Hunter," Dean said. "Save me a seat."

"'Pop-pop'?" Natalie frowned.

"'Grandpa' made me sound too old," he said.

"They're your grandchildren."

"Look, if it's weird for you, my being here—"

"It's not weird." It was totally weird. "They're going to love Trevor Dashwood."

"They already do." He lingered a moment longer. "Hey, I read about that rare vase you found in the bookstore. Pretty remarkable, Natalie."

He seemed about to say something else. Natalie's stomach was in knots. Did he want to connect with her? Did she need to tell him she knew about the tuition?

"Dean, listen," she said. "I wanted to let you know that Mom never told me you paid my tuition. St. Dymphna's and the college savings plan. I found out about it after she was gone."

"I left it up to Blythe," he said.

"That was . . . a surprise. And it was good of you. I appreciate it a lot, Dean." She held out her hand.

He took it. His was warm, enclosing hers. "Thanks for telling me. You know, there was a time when I was out of my mind with love for Blythe. When she told me she was pregnant, I wanted to leave my wife and kids for her. She wouldn't let me, though."

Every single aspect of Natalie's life would have been changed by that. Her perception of men had been shaped by Dean's absence. Now she realized he had kept his distance out of respect for her mother.

"Mom made a difficult choice," she told Dean, remembering her conversation with Frieda. Her mother fell in love—but didn't stay that way.

"She did." Dean let go of her hand. "I'll always regret that I put her in that position."

Natalie stepped back. All she could think about was that he had broken her mother's heart all those years ago and left her alone. He'd raised a house full of kids with the wife he'd cheated on, and now he had grandkids.

Mom should have had grandkids, Natalie thought. That, of course, would have required her daughter to untangle her reluctance to get married. God, what a mess. No wonder Natalie had no idea how to have a family she could trust. She'd never had a role model for a relationship, so she ended up with guys like Rick and Trevor. Perfectly good guys with whom she couldn't connect. Did her trust issues stem from Dean? Did he have that much power over her?

"Well, I need to get busy," she said, edging away. "Hope those kids enjoy the show."

"Hiya, Natalie!" A bright, high-pitched voice broke into her thoughts. Dorothy hurried toward her, pulling Peach along by the hand.

"Dorothy! Welcome to Trevor Dashwood. Your seats are in the VIP section. Front row, kiddo." Natalie gestured toward the auditorium doors.

"Yay! I can't wait." Dorothy looked adorable with her hair in braids, rainbow-colored leggings under a flared skirt, and a shirt with a Janus head on it—an illustration from one of Trevor's book covers.

Natalie met Peach's gaze, then quickly looked away, feeling a flush of color in her cheeks. That kiss. She'd lived for days on that damn kiss. That moment in the moon garden had transformed him from an impossibility to a tenuous option. One she wasn't prepared for.

"Hey," he said, looking at her over Dorothy's head.

"Hey," she said back.

"Pretty impressive event, Natalie."

"Thanks."

"Is your granddad here? I miss seeing him."

She shook her head. "He hasn't been feeling well lately."

"Sorry to hear that. Think he'd be up for a visit one of these days?"

"Of course. He'd love to see you."

"Come on, Dad." Dorothy tugged at his sleeve.

"We're VIPs. That means very important people. Let's go!" She towed him toward the rapidly filling auditorium.

Natalie went backstage, where Shelly freshened her makeup and hair. It was surreal that she had a hair-and-makeup person. Shelly had put together her outfit—jeans and white sneakers, a white T-shirt, and a rainbow-colored silk scarf. A kid-friendly look, Shelly had explained. Fun and approachable. It was something Natalie's mother might have chosen to wear, and she felt like an imposter in it, but she trusted Shelly.

The stage was set with three stools and a small table furnished with water bottles. The backdrop was a folding screen decked with the titles and cover art of Trevor's books.

As she prepared to go onstage, Natalie's mouth went dry and her throat tightened. Glancing at the red numbers on a digital countdown clock, she saw that she had exactly one minute to pull herself together. The buzz in the huge room crescendoed. Trevor came up behind her and rested his hands on her shoulders. "I used to get nervous, too."

"I'm ridiculous, I know."

"You're not. And here's something else. I used to tell myself it was just a room full of kids. Why would any thinking adult be intimidated by a bunch of kids? That didn't help, though. An audience of kids is just as tough as an audience of adults. With more squirming."

"This isn't helping," she whispered.

"I know. Nothing helps." He squeezed her shoulders. "We're just going to power through it. And by the way, you're beautiful and I'm excited about dinner tonight."

"And you," she said, "are too good to be true."

He let go of her and gave her a gentle nudge toward the stage. "I'll remember you said that."

The stage lights came on and the house lights dimmed, creating a surge of noise from the audience, followed by a collective hush. Natalie flashed on memories of her mother through the years, confidently striding out to the bookstore podium to introduce an honored guest. She'd been so polished, fluid and witty, warming up the crowd. *Be like Mom*, she told herself, smoothing her hands over the bright scarf.

She thought about the time she'd stood at a podium facing the people at Pinnacle, her chest clammy with the wine her coworker had spilled on her conservative, buttoned-down blouse and blazer. A disaster had happened that day. She was bracing herself for a disaster now.

She took a step forward, and it felt a bit like stepping off a cliff, but somehow her legs carried her to the center of the stage.

"My name is Natalie Harper, and I'm excited about the Flip Side books," she said. "Who's with me?"

Applause and hollering. Stomping of feet. She waited for a lull, then said, "I thought so. Thanks for supporting San Francisco's own homegrown bookstore, the Lost and Found Bookshop."

Light applause, mostly from adults being polite.

"You're not here for that," Natalie acknowledged. "You're here for America's favorite author, Trevor Dashwood."

Heavy applause now.

"Here's what I know about Trevor. He showed the world that there's a flip side to everything. Another side to every story. No matter what the situation, Trevor can find the flip side and turn it into a story. His books have won awards. They've been published all over the world. But the reason we love him is for the stories he tells. So please welcome Mr. Trevor Dashwood."

The applause and cheers drowned out everything, even her stage fright. Cameras pointed at her, and bloggers and members of the local press clustered near the front, taking notes. She would probably collapse from relief later, but at the moment, she stood smiling as Trevor strode to the middle of the stage. He was a natural showman, wonderfully at ease, and dressed like the coolest kid on the block, including a baseball cap with a caterpillar logo.

She reached out to shake hands with him. He took her hand, but instead of shaking, he bowed, and then twirled her like a ballroom dancer as the applause continued.

He kept hold of her hand and waited for a break in the noise. "Not so fast," he said to Natalie. "I want everybody here today to know who this nice lady is. She's a bookseller. A purveyor of dreams. A writer's best friend. You see, a bookseller is the link between the stories we tell and the readers we tell them to. Without that, a story has no life outside the writer's imagination."

Like a seasoned showman, he doffed his cap and put it on backward. A butterfly on a nylon filament popped out and fluttered around his head. Murmurs of delight rippled through the audience.

"I don't know about you," Trevor said, "but when I see someone reading a book I love, I automatically count them as a friend. So if you're here for my books, you're among friends. I didn't have a lot of friends growing up. That was what books were for. Do you know what homeschooling is?" he asked. As lots of hands went up, he said, "I was homeschooled, so for me, going to the bookstore was more than just a shopping trip. It was a safe place to learn, and to do what I love more than anything else—reading." He gestured at the audience. "You're doing something good by being here. Not just for me, but for this bookstore that's been a neighborhood treasure for decades."

"Thank you," she said, smiling up at him. "That was beautiful."

He offered a formal bow with a flourish and set aside the trick hat. "Okay, kids. Boring sentimental part's over. Let's have some fun!"

Natalie was grateful to leave the stage. She went down a side stairway and slid into the end seat on the front row. "Nice work," Bertie whispered, leaning toward her.

She swiveled around to check out the packed auditorium. "I keep wishing my mom were here to see this."

He patted her hand. "Who knows? Maybe she is."

"Taking over the shop is the hardest thing I've ever done, and I'm loving it anyway." Natalie bit her lip and focused on the stage. She would never get over her mother not being here. Maybe the point was not to get over it but to live with it. *It's so hard*, she said to her mother. *And that means you mattered.*

Trevor told a funny anecdote about himself, using

the flip side theme. *The flip side of school is home-schooling. The flip side of being an only child is having a sibling. The flip side of living in the city is living in the wilderness.* He painted a charming picture of himself, a boy who grew up apart from the rest of the world, with books as his companions and imagination fueling his speculation about how other kids lived.

"He's acting," Bertie whispered after a well-received laugh line.

Natalie frowned. "What's that?"

"He's acting. I can tell."

"The guy performs all the time. Of course he's acting."

"Yeah, but there's something else . . . it's a subtle thing. Like he's not telling his own story."

"Well, judging by the reactions of these kids, it's working just fine."

Then Trevor switched gears, bringing two kids—preselected by his handlers—from the audience on-stage with him, each representing an opposing view. Brother and sister. Dog and cat. Fat and skinny. To the delight of the audience, Trevor would suggest a setup and let the kids dramatize the story. Natalie leaned forward and looked at Dorothy and Peach, who sat several seats down in the middle of the row. The little girl watched Trevor with rapt attention, completely absorbed by the performance. Peach was covertly checking his phone.

When Trevor called Dorothy's name, she was beaming as she hopped up to the stage and perched on one of the stools. Natalie leaned forward and caught Peach's eye, giving him a thumbs-up sign. He put away his phone, then turned his attention to the stage. The expression of pride on his face made her smile.

The other girl, named Mara, was already there but was so bashful she literally couldn't speak.

"That's okay," Trevor said easily. "I'll come back to you, maybe find a way to flip your silence into noise." Then he turned to Dorothy. "What's your story?" he asked. "Toss me an idea, anything that's on your mind. It can be anything at all."

"It's kinda hard," Dorothy said, her voice high-pitched with nerves.

"It is," Trevor agreed. "But you want to know something? The best ideas are big ideas that come straight from your gut, not your head. Ideas that give you big feelings."

"Oh! Um . . ." She glanced from side to side.

"Something big. Don't think, just toss," he exclaimed. "Think big."

"I hate my parents' divorce!"

There was a pause, a sudden vacuum weighted by

uncertain silence. Feet shuffled. People coughed. Then Trevor said, "All righty, then. That's exactly what I'm talking about, Dorothy. A big idea and big feelings. So. You hate your parents' divorce."

She stared down at her knees and barely nodded her head.

"I bet plenty of kids feel the same way," Trevor added.

Natalie looked over at Peach. He sat motionless, as if his daughter's raw admission had turned him to stone. Then she noticed one of his hands was twitching.

"Sounds like a bummer. Major bummer," Trevor said. "Now, here's how the story works. What's the flip side of hating that divorce?"

She kicked at the rungs of her stool, her cheeks turning red. "I'm sorry. I shouldn't—"

"You *should.* You absolutely should. Because listen. Your feelings are your feelings, and there's no right or wrong when it comes to feelings. They just are. So *is* there a flip side?"

She shrugged her shoulders, lifting them helplessly up to her ears.

"There's always a flip side. See, if I was writing the story, I'd list the things I like about the divorce. Like . . . having two different places to live. Two rooms to mess up! Am I right?"

Dorothy lifted her gaze to him and gave the slightest of nods.

"Have you ever had two birthday parties? One with Mom and one with Dad?"

"Yes," she said. "And two Christmases."

"Good work," Trevor said. "You're finding things to not hate about that divorce. Let's think of another word for divorce. Because it's one of those words nobody likes. We can do that, you know. Think up a new word for a word we don't like." He turned to the audience. "How about it? Any ideas?"

With gathering force, nonsense words rolled up toward the stage. *Divnado. Pre-Nope. Bilgation. Madliness. Foligeddish.* In minutes, laughter overtook the audience, and finally Dorothy succumbed to a fit of the giggles.

"My really smart mom used to say there'd be things in life I don't like, but that's no reason to stop liking life," Trevor concluded. "Do me a favor, Dorothy. When you get home, write down ten things you really, really like. Can you do that?"

She nodded, now with her usual bright eagerness. Natalie sneaked a glance at Peach. His hand had stopped twitching.

"How about you, Mara?" Trevor turned his attention to the bashful girl. She'd been watching the exchange between him and Dorothy with an expression of horror, which had gradually turned to fascination. "Ready to talk story? Tell me what's on your mind, and we'll make a story."

The girl mumbled something. Trevor held the microphone closer to her. "One more time, because that's a good one."

"I can't swim," she said, her voice thin and a little shaky.

Within moments, he was leading the audience through a zany story, seeming to revel in their raucous participation. He held his listeners captive, and then there was a rush for pictures with him.

Dorothy was beaming as she posed for a photo with Trevor and held up her book. It was a kindness, what he had done, but was there also a hint of opportunism? There was no disputing the delight in Dorothy's eyes, though. Trevor was a pro. He knew what he was doing.

As they said goodbye for the evening, Trevor and Peach shook hands. "Thanks for smoothing out that thing onstage," Peach said.

"No problem. Kids have a way of keeping things real."

21

"You're very quiet." Trevor's comment broke in on Natalie's thoughts.

She turned to him from the passenger seat of his sleek electric car. After the signing, she'd changed into a dress with leggings and a cashmere shawl her mother had worn for years. It was fitting to be wrapped up in her mother's shawl after the shop's most successful event.

"I'm taking in the scenery," she answered him. The sun was setting over the hills of Napa, creating a landscape so beautiful it almost didn't seem real, more like an artist's idealized conception of a flawless scene. The rounded crests and shadowy valleys formed a cradle for the cotton-candy clouds riding high above the undulating horizon.

"I love the wine country," Trevor said. "I'm glad we get to share it tonight."

"It's so gorgeous," she agreed, relaxing in the luxurious leather seat. Each winery they passed had its own peculiar character. Some were ultramodern architectural pieces. Others were rustic and fiercely individualistic, and a few were as grand as the châteaux of Europe. Her mother had designated a section of the bookstore to wine-country books. Far preferable, Mom had often said, to fighting the traffic to visit in person.

"But you don't love it," Trevor said, resting his wrist on the top of the steering wheel. They glided up and over a hill, its dun-colored grass swathed in evening shadows, mist gathering in the valleys.

"I . . ." Natalie paused. "Back when I worked in Sonoma, I never really connected with the area. It's beautiful, but it never felt like home to me, not the way the city does."

"So the city feels like home," he concluded.

She gave him a quick smile. "The traffic sucks and it's unaffordable, but it's still my world. All my memories of my mother are tied up with the city, and when I'm there, I feel closer to her."

"Tell me about her," Trevor said. "A favorite memory."

So many moments, she thought, vivid as yesterday. The scenery out the window melded into memories, and she described them for Trevor. Before school started each year, she and her mother used to make an annual trip to I. Magnin in Union Square. Its soaring main hall, the glass murals and gold ceilings, the glittering cases and Lalique crystal light fixtures ruined her for all other department stores. The dazzling marble ladies' room had been a destination itself, and if it had been a good year, they might go to the café for a crab Louis. In leaner times it would be french fries at Kerry's and a trip to the creepy Musée Mécanique with its clockwork toys. They always had something in their pockets for the street musicians and buskers they passed. Though her mom didn't have a car, she sometimes borrowed one when the Blue Angels were practicing. Traffic would be stopped on Highway 101 when the perfect formation of jets came in for a landing over Moffett Field.

Natalie shook herself, realizing she'd drifted off into the past. She hated the reminder that memories were all she had now. "Sorry for all the reminiscing," she said to Trevor.

"I like hearing you talk about your mother," he said.

"Cherish your mom while you have her," Natalie advised.

"Trust me, she's a big part of my life. I think we've

arrived." He turned at a low-lit sign marking the vine-covered building. "I can't wait for you to see this place."

A valet whisked the car away, and they were led through the beautiful dining room to a shell-ceilinged nook overlooking an abundant kitchen garden.

"This is lovely," Natalie said, scooting into the velvet-upholstered half-round banquette. "Amazing." Everything about the place exuded discreet, tasteful luxury.

"Good," he said. "You deserve to be amazed."

"I've always wanted to come here," she confessed. "Unfortunately I'd have to sell a kidney just to be able to afford it."

He laughed. "In that case, I'm happy to keep you from self-mutilating."

A sommelier appeared with pink champagne in crystal flutes, which she served with a flourish.

"To the Lost and Found Bookshop," Trevor said. "Thank you for hosting me today."

"Thank *you* for breathing new life into the shop," she said.

They touched glasses and sipped. Heaven, with bubbles.

"The pleasure was mine," he told her. "And thanks to little Dorothy Gallagher for getting us together. She made it all happen."

"She did." The mention of Dorothy made Natalie think of Peach, and thinking of Peach while drinking champagne with Trevor made her feel guilty. And feeling guilty was irrational. What on earth did she have to feel guilty about?

"That was quite a moment when she blurted out that she hates her parents' divorce. You handled it really well." She pictured Peach's face, his clenched hand on the arm of his seat—that quiet, helpless agony.

"You think?"

"Totally. You're a quick thinker."

"Thanks for saying so. No matter how many kids I meet, someone always manages to catch me off guard. When you hang out with kids, you never know what you're going to hear."

"You had just the right touch. You took her seriously but brought the smiles, too."

"I doubt I made her like her parents' divorce any better. So damn hard on kids. I was tempted to say the flip side would have been her folks staying together and fighting it out for a few more decades, but I didn't want to go there."

A server came forward with an amuse-bouche. The tiny bite of house-smoked abalone with nettle pesto on a rustic waffle chip took far longer for the server to describe than it did to eat. It was delicious, though.

"So," Trevor said, savoring the next wine pairing. "Do you think the patient will live?"

She frowned. "Oh. The bookstore, you mean." Now that she understood the state of her mother's finances, she would need to gloss over a few things. One successful book signing with a hugely popular author had been an incredible shot in the arm, but even that wasn't enough to dig the shop out of the hole she'd found it in. She summoned a smile, bright with hope. The success of today's event was something worth smiling about, for sure. "You were a godsend," she told him.

His face lit with pleasure. *He really is dazzling*, she thought. It was a singular feeling, being with someone who was so completely *everything*—kind and smart, handsome and funny. He seemed focused on not just helping her, but spoiling her rotten.

"Are you always this nice?" she blurted out.

He laughed, and his laughter was as charming as everything else about him. "Trust me, I can be a dick sometimes. Not now, though. The fact is, I'm way into you, Natalie Harper. Way."

She laughed, too. "What's that supposed to mean? Into me."

"That's me just trying to tell you, in my super-immature way, that I have a crush on you. It feels really good. I haven't been with anybody special in a while, and when you came along, my heart just about exploded."

She was too flabbergasted to reply. And then she found her voice. "I have no idea what to say to that."

"Just say you're excited about this amazing food."

"Trust me, I am," she said. Trevor was perfect. Rick had been perfect. *She* was the one who was flawed. She was still processing this when the dinner started in earnest. The impeccably trained waitstaff made the meal a seamless experience. One by one, nine tasting courses with wine pairings appeared in a parade of indulgence. There were wildly exotic mushrooms and herbs she'd never heard of as well as luxurious bits of creamy cheese and local produce, sips of wine, even an entire array of exotic salts of the world in a formal presentation box.

"This," she said, "is the meal of a lifetime. Seriously."

"Glad you like it. I wanted to impress you."

"It's been a two-hour extravaganza," she said.

He leaned back and patted his stomach. "Thank God for grappa," he said, taking a small sip of the clear liquid.

The sommelier had given them a lesson about the stomach-settling qualities of grappa, a humble liqueur made from something called pomace. "A fancy word for what's left after the juice is squeezed out of the grapes," Natalie explained. "It was never a bestseller at my former company, but it has its place."

"*Cin cin,* as they say in Italy," he said.

"Well, thank you a million times over," she told him, relaxing into a comfortable state of tipsiness. "For the event today, for a glorious drive into the countryside—for just everything."

He took her hand and brought the back of it to his lips. "I have good news, and I have bad news."

"Oh?" She studied the back of her hand, where he'd kissed her.

"The bad news is, I just tasted nine kinds of wine and I'm not fit to drive. The good news is I have a room for the night."

"Oh," she said again. It wasn't a question.

He smiled and reached forward to touch her shoulder, very gently. "Don't go all Sabine on me. It's a two-room suite."

She flushed and laughed softly. "I'm impressed by the Sabine reference."

"It's something I remember from an art history book. When I was twelve years old, art history books were my *Playboy* magazine. *The Rape of the Sabines* was a two-page spread in *The Ultimate Encyclopedia of Roman History.* I couldn't stop staring at all those boobs."

"So what were you like as a twelve-year-old?"

"You mean besides obsessed with boobs?" He chuckled. "Like Huckleberry Finn, without the pipe smoking. No TV or video games. No internet. I probably didn't appreciate it at the time, but I really did have a magical childhood, surrounded by books and nature."

"Your folks ought to write a manual on parenting. How to unplug your kid. It'd be a bestseller."

"Spoken like a true bookseller." He polished off his grappa. "Shall we retire, madam?"

She felt a dart of panic.

He held her hand and drew her to her feet. "You're channeling the Sabines again."

"I'm not." She kept hold of his hand as they strolled through the torchlit gardens toward the inn adjacent to the restaurant. The night air chilled her skin, and she flashed on a memory of the moon garden with Peach. *Go away,* she told him.

The inn was called L'Auberge Magnifique, a Victorian mansion with a wraparound porch that spanned the front like a white-toothed smile. Inside was a wilderness of chintz and flounces, cabbage rose wallpaper and ornately carved wood.

"They haven't embraced the minimalist aesthetic," Trevor whispered. They were shown to a suite designated "The Parlour."

Natalie couldn't help saying "'Step into my parlor,'" and Trevor finished, "'said the spider to the fly.'"

She got the giggles as he put his arm around her and caught her against his chest.

Still giggling, she looked up at him, and they kissed. "Listen," he said, whispering into her ear, "I'd like to do more than kiss you. I'd like to make out with you all night long. But not unless you say. I promise I'll be a gentleman. I want to get this right, Natalie."

"You don't strike me as a person who makes many mistakes."

"I love that you just said that, and I hate that you're dead wrong."

She took a step back. "You're too good to be true. You know that, right?"

"I know that—wrong," he said.

"Bertie thinks you're acting."

"Acting like what?"

"Like . . . an actor."

"I'm not too good to be true. And I'm sure as hell not an actor. I've made my share of mistakes, and I've had more than my share of luck. And right now, I'm just a guy. A guy who likes you a lot. Hope you're okay with that."

"We flipped a coin for the big bed," Natalie told Cleo the next day. On Sundays, the bookshop opened at eleven in the morning, and the two of them were getting set up. Trevor had dropped her off early so she could look in on her grandfather. She'd kissed Trevor goodbye, a lingering kiss, filled with yearning—and confusion. As in, why was she holding back from going all in with this amazing man?

The moment Cleo had arrived, she'd pounced, wanting details.

"What? Flipped a coin?" Cleo gave her shoulder a little shove. "Oh no you didn't."

Natalie laughed, setting up a stack of books Trevor had autographed the day before. "Yes, I did. It was a high four-poster bed with way too many pillows. Very pink. Very fluffy. The bed in the other room was more like a daybed. Not as fussy and a lot smaller. That's where he slept, because I won the toss."

"But . . . Trevor Dashwood."

"I *know.* The whole evening was incredible. Last night . . . we weren't there yet, you know? We were both pretty tipsy and way too full from dinner. It's early days, Cleo. We're new to each other."

"That's the best time to sleep together," Cleo pointed out. "To see if it's a thing."

"I'll keep that in mind," said Natalie. She ducked into the back office to get some inventory and book-keeping done. Thanks to Trevor's signing, this would be the best month in the history of the shop. It was, she hoped, the start of better times. She studied the loan consolidation documents, wondering if her mother had understood what she had signed. Natalie had appoint-ments with the bank and with a tax counselor to set up a plan to resolve what she could. She didn't want to press Grandy about selling everything and moving, but unless a miracle fell from the sky, that was where she was headed. Now there was a tiny glimmer of hope, and she studied that glimmer until her head ached.

A package arrived, and she welcomed the diversion. Colleen's journals had been professionally archived, and the historical society was cataloguing the originals. The parcel contained facsimile copies, put in order, for Natalie and her grandfather to read.

Finding the war medals had been intriguing. Discov-ering the ancient vase was ridiculously exciting. But the cache of Colleen's letters and drawings—that could be life-changing, a window into the history of their family.

Natalie would probably never know whether or not her mother had realized their significance or how they had come to be hidden away, apparently unread and undisturbed, for generations.

Needing a break from the twenty-first century, she went to find her grandfather. He was outside in the tiny rear garden in his wicker lounge chair, a Mackinaw blanket tucked around him, his hands in fingerless gloves turning the pages of his book. He couldn't seem to shake the symptoms that had his care team so puzzled, especially the fatigue and poor appetite.

Seeing him amid the yellow leaves and berry-colored hips of the spent roses, and the fading hollyhocks gone to seed along the garden wall, filled her heart. In that moment, she understood why her mother had made so many seemingly reckless financial decisions, all with the goal of taking care of this beloved old man.

"What are you reading?" she asked him.

"A lovely book." He held it up so she could see— *Being Mortal* by Atul Gawande.

The book was a perennial bestseller in the shop, a meditation on living with joy even at the end of life. Even when medical interventions had run their course. "And you're finding it lovely? How so?"

"Because it's honest. I do know—sometimes, most of the time—what has been happening to me."

She sat at the end of the chaise and rested her hands on the blanket. "Oh, Grandy. Is it . . . are you afraid?"

He hesitated. "I am sometimes, when the confusion is so very intense and I don't know what is real and what isn't."

"I'm sorry. How can I help?"

"Being here, in my place in the world—that is the help I need." He gestured around the garden. "This is where I played as a little boy. Where I lived with Blythe and made a swing for you when you were a little girl. Where I used to sit and hold hands with May Lin. And now it's where I spend time with a book, enjoying the autumn sunshine." He covered her hand with his. "Help me remember the important things," he said. "I don't want to forget all the love in my life."

"If you do, I'll remember for you." She tried to speak lightly, forcing the words past the ache in her throat. "And now, there is this." She picked up the shipping box and opened the lid. "The scanned copies are back. I thought we could read Colleen's story together."

"I'd like that," he said. "You'll have to do the reading, though. I find the handwriting hard to decipher."

"So do I," she said. "But I'll give it a shot. The archivist put things in what he thought was chronological order."

He put up his feet and settled back on the wicker chaise. "Let's begin, then."

PART FIVE

Try to be conspicuously accurate in everything, pictures as well as text. Truth is not only stranger than fiction, it is more interesting.

—WILLIAM RANDOLPH HEARST

22

My name is Colleen O'Rourke. I am fifteen years old, and all alone in this world. This is a record of my days, as I live them. In the year of our Lord 1887, Mam lost another babe after Michaelmas, and Declan took his vows, and Da came home from the ropeworks with ill news. There was no more work for him. The great starvation was upon us. It was determined that we would go to America—Da and Mam, and the two little ones, Tristan and Liam. Da's brotherhood, Clan na Gael, had a group in San Francisco called the Knights of the Red Branch. That was our destination.

Such tales we heard, this land of milk and honey, much of it nonsense as I am fast discovering.

Thanks to Da's skill as a deckhand, he traded

work for passage to New York City on the <u>Mary Dare</u>, and we made the crossing, a treacherous business to be sure.

We were under way when the ship's fever took them all. Mam breathed her last on a Sunday. Because of the contagion, the fallen were laid to rest at sea, a harsh business that repeated itself day in and day out amongst the passengers. In a shroud of fog, she was shipped overboard like a sack of ballast, sinking into the gray-green hillocks of waves that undulated like the wind through a field of barley.

When the boys fell ill and succumbed, I was too broken inside to rage against the fates that took them. Da drifted in and out of fever dreams and at the last, he looked at me and called me by name, and said I was a treasure and may the world treat me with kindness. As the roaring ocean swallowed him up, I was not merely broken inside but utterly hollow, as if everything had been scooped out of me, leaving me an empty vessel.

Indeed there was a thought as I stood at the ship's rail that I might follow them into the next world, the paradise promised in our catechism. A slide into the icy depths, a brief and brutal second baptism, followed by blessed oblivion.

In that moment, a vast nothingness offered more comfort and solace than existence alone in a strange new world. I cannot write of the sadness that tore into my very marrow, my own dear family forever gone. Never again will I feel the brush of Mam's hand on my cheek, or hear Da whistling through his teeth as he sharpens his cutter for the day's work. Never to hear the boys squabbling and laughing.

In the city of New York, a Good Samaritan guided me to the railroad station, and I used the tickets provided by the Red Branch. The journey across this vast and frightening land lasted for days. While on board, I had the good fortune to meet Miss Josie Mendoza, who has a boardinghouse in the city of San Francisco. As she cannot read or write well, she asked for help with her papers and with reading the news of the day.

People wonder why I, born in a dirt-floored bothy with nary a prayer of coming up in the world, came to know my reading and letters and fine drawing. That I owe to the Wentworth family. Their daughter Annabelle was sickly and craved my companionship, and they indulged her every whim. At Annabelle's side I learned to read and write, to draw and play the piano. I was afforded every advantage—except, of course, the privileges of her family's wealth.

Mam was suspicious of allowing me to learn matters above my station, but the squire's lady assured her that it was the Lord's work I was doing, befriending a sick girl who was desperate for companionship. I considered it a blessing from on high when Mam allowed it.

The tutor was a miracle, nothing less in my eyes. The housemaids whispered that M. Hugo had been expelled from a post with the Belgian royal family, because he was guilty of something referred to as "the French vice" and sent to the west of Ireland to be exiled.

He had an extraordinary gift, and I learned to read the great books of the ages, and to write with a fine hand. But the greatest gift of all was the drawing. He had been trained at the Académie Royale des Beaux-Arts and shared those lessons with me.

I absorbed the principles of drawing and composition, but any skill I might have, I owe to the natural world around me. In every spare moment I practiced. I drew the things of nature, leaves and berries, shore grasses and nuts and long fronds of fern. I drew a curlew perched at the end of a pier, *and a cormorant with wings outstretched to catch the breeze.*

Drawing is a way to make sense of the world in my heart and mind. I speak through my drawing and sometimes I discover my own feelings that were hidden from me.

Eventually I told Miss Josie of my plan to find my way to a church and beg for help.

She burst out with a big brassy laugh and said as how the church might save my eternal soul, but what I needed was food in my belly and a place to lay my head.

Natalie paused in her reading so she and her grandfather could look through the young girl's work. "Colleen was remarkable," Natalie said. "Her writing and her drawing. This is amazing."

Several pages were filled with sketches, presumably of the voyage that had been a time of staggering grief for Colleen. The most sophisticated drawings showed birds in flight or hovering over the ship's rigging, and flying fish skimming across the surface of the ocean.

Another page depicted a row of somber faces—swift-stroked line drawings of a woman in a shawl, two young boys, a man hunkered over a coil of rope.

"Her parents and brothers," said Grandy. "Our family history seems written in loss."

"And survival," said Natalie, returning to the narrative.

Never have I seen the likes of this strange new place. It is both frightening and fascinating. There are people from the Orient—Celestials, they are called—in a world of their own known as Chinatown. There are people speaking Spanish and playing music in the streets. Soldiers at a military station roam the neighborhood at night, drinking and looking for women. I have taken to wearing trousers and boots, my hair clubbed like a boy's.

Miss Josie's saloon is a raucous place, as wild and confusing as the portside bustle. It is in fact a fancy-house, which is what they call a brothel in these parts. Miss Josie pays me nothing. For my tiny cave in the cellar and scraps to eat, I work from dawn until dark. I undertake all manner of chores. The laundry and mending. The chamber pots. I sometimes work in the kitchen, but the cook is from China and I cannot understand what he's saying and he scolds all the time, clucking and shooing like a wet hen.

In between the scrubbing and the laundry, I am

THE LOST AND FOUND BOOKSHOP · 459

charged with taking the rubbish to the bins at the bottom of Fenton Hill, where the refuse is barged out to sea. An execrable task, yet in the wake of sending my entire dead family into eternity one by one, the harshness of all else is muted. In fact, I discovered a nearby field and shore teeming with birds and wild-growing plant life. The renewal of springtime renewed my soul. From the depths of winter, the world is made all over again. With my drawing, I capture these moments to remind myself that I must go on.

For half a day on Sunday, I'm given leave to attend Mass. And though I may burn in the fires of eternity for my sin—I never go. Instead I take myself out to the wild fresh air and I draw. In my mean circumstances, I make do with discarded paper and charcoal pencil, losing myself as I create images of the world around me.

Most passersby pay me little notice, but one day I met a man named Billy who lingered to watch me draw. I had tired of reading the <u>Examiner</u>, a tedious compilation of the news of the day. I had spied an interesting pair of mallard ducks and was making sketches directly on the newsprint. The bold strokes of my charcoal obscured the columns of print as I created the scene. The stranger asked me why I covered the printed news with my sketch, and, blunt as a paddle, I admitted as how the facts and statistics struck me as tiresome. The newspaper was better suited to drawing than to reading.

He guffawed and slapped his knee, declaring my review more honest than his entire editorial board. "Oh no," he said, "I am the owner of this paper and I aim to make it thrive. What would keep your interest, then?"

I had never met a person of such import. I confessed that I am more drawn to stories of dramatic human struggles, humorous poems, or the sharp and brilliant writings that bring the world to life in the mind's eye.

"I must cater to the reader," he declared. "Not to sophisticates and historians."

After this unusual exchange, our Sunday meetings have become a regular occurrence. He is exceedingly generous, giving me all manner of books to read, and supplies for making art. He proudly tells me of the talented writers he now publishes—Mr. Ambrose Bierce and Mark Twain.

And then one day, a surprise. Billy is leaving San Francisco for good. He came to the saloon to say farewell. The presence of this fancy gentleman created a stir, and he brought with him a magnificent gift—a set of books so large that a servant or foot-man carried them to my humble room in Miss Josie's basement. The large parcel contained a complete set of engravings of America's birds by Mr. John James Audubon. The volumes stand an arm's length high! The sheer beauty of the work took my breath away—herons and swans and egrets with graciously curving necks, songbirds in flight, shore fowl in their habitat.

I was overwhelmed by such a grand treasure, but he assured me that he had little interest in pictures of birds, and he would rather see them in the possession of someone who would appreciate them.

Tucked behind the page was a letter in different handwriting.

To my treasured friend Colleen, in appreciation of our friendship, please accept the gift of these volumes, which contain the complete set of hand-colored engravings by Mr. John James Audubon. I know they will find a home with you, whose accomplishments might one day rival his own.

In appreciation and respect,
William Randolph Hearst

Natalie looked up from her reading. "I don't know what to say. It's a wonderful story. Do you think it's true? Could this letter be authentic?"

"I wish I knew," he said. "My father was so very young when he lost her. He did recall her beautiful pictures, and he spoke of 'Mam's birds,' but assumed they were actual birds, or perhaps her own drawings. He was too young to know what she was about."

"If this is true, she was acquainted with William Randolph Hearst. Could he truly have given her a set of *The Birds of America*?"

Grandy focused on the journal drawings. "Her renderings of birds look exactly like the Audubon versions."

Shadows gathered in the gardens, bringing the evening chill with them. "Let's go inside," Natalie said. "We can finish reading later."

Cleo had closed up shop for the evening. Natalie made a pot of tea and sent out for dinner—Moroccan lentil soup and sourdough—and they sat at Grandy's table. She found a couple of replica editions of Audubon's works on the shelf and showed them to her grandfather. Some of Colleen's drawings were direct copies, as if she had been learning from the master himself.

Natalie sent a message to Tess, asking if it was possible to find out if the Hearst family had ever owned a copy of the seminal work.

Grandy added honey to his tea. "I hope your friend can enlighten us. Let's finish reading, shall we?"

Natalie cleared away the dishes while he tucked himself into his reading chair. The amber glow of the reading lamp illumined his timeworn features, now set in an expression of contentment. Though his hands trembled over the pages and his body was thin and fragile, his eyes were bright with interest. There were things that had not yet been stolen from his memory. This, she realized, feeling a wave of love, was probably why her mother had been adamant about keeping him here in the home he'd always known.

———————

May 1897. I went to watch the football matches at the Presidio, and there I met the most extraordinary man. He is a soldier encamped at Astor Battery, and he did not take part in the games that drew a crowd this fine day. I heard someone strumming and singing and was drawn to the sweetness of his song. His name is Julio Harper, and he belongs to a regiment of colored soldiers. His mother, he said, was a Spanish camp follower, cooking for a regiment of infantry soldiers, and his father was a freed slave from the state of Texas. He is ever so gentle, and he sings the old Spanish songs of his mother. We are shy with each other, yet filled with the most tender and magnificent love anyone could imagine.

August 1897. Julio and I were married by a sympathetic chaplain. Before we can live as man and wife, Julio must complete his military service. But oh, such dreams we have. A farm where apples grow and the grass is sweet, somewhere in the hills north of the city. After so many years alone with my books and sketches, I am awash with bliss.

"Soldiers go to war," Julio tells me. "It is what we do." He tries to soothe my distress at the prospect of his leaving. Here in San Francisco, there are no pirate raids or attacks by Indians. He must keep his fighting skills sharp. He is trained to operate a large wheeled gun called the Hotchkiss revolving cannon, but his targets are imaginary enemies out on the misty bay, inciting the sea lions to bark. The drills and duties at the Presidio are all for show.

May 1898. It is the height of irony that the one man who nurtured my dream is the same man who stole it away. Mr. William Hearst will likely have forgotten that he once fostered my art and fed my craving for learning. And he will never know that he is in part responsible for separating me from the man I love.

Since that time he has created a sensation across the land. The Examiner was only the first. Now his many newspapers have incited the populace to call for war with Spain. I cannot even look at the banners screaming across the front of the paper. He has separated me from the person I love. From my husband. From my husband. Julio was selected to embark with the first expedition on account of his facility with the Spanish language and his knowledge of the cannon.

I nearly fainted from unseasonable heat as the troops passed through the Lombard Gate of the Presidio on their march to the waiting ships. I rushed along with the crowd to Market Street and then to the docks. All was shouting and chaos as men, supplies, and livestock boarded the steamships. The destination was the port of Manila in the Philippine Islands, a place I'd never heard of. I cannot even imagine a place so far away.

When we said goodbye, I didn't know about the baby.

"That's so sad," Natalie said to her grandfather. "That was the last time she ever saw her husband."

"And she blamed Hearst. His papers exaggerated and even manufactured events to incite the war that took her husband from her. I believe that's where we get the term 'yellow journalism.'"

"Why would he do that?"

"To sell papers. Hearst and Joseph Pulitzer. The papers whipped everyone into a frenzy about Spain and didn't let up until war was declared."

"Are we doing any better now?" She thought about the current online shouting matches and misinformation campaigns, and it made her wonder. "The world is still a mess, but journalism—real journalism—is a lot better. I like to think so, anyway."

Colleen's later entries were briefer and less frequent, likely a consequence of looking after a baby.

By the time my beautiful son was born, Julio was gone, missing and presumed dead. Killed by native rebels.

Only the existence of my baby boy keeps me from following Julio into death, the way I yearned to follow my departed family. My son, Julius, is my only anchor to this world.

See how he thrives at just six months. Sunny and

happy, the very picture of health, though he was born with a bad foot. My sweet cherub. He will never know his da.

"Look at the sketches," Natalie said. "These are pictures of your father."

They went through the drawings, one by one. There was Julius as a baby and then a toddler. And then a small boy, slender and doe-eyed, dressed in knickers.

"Could this be the old apple tree you remember?" Natalie showed her grandfather a sketch of the boy, barefoot and shirtless, sitting on a low branch. Under the drawing was the name *Julius Harper* in childish lettering.

My boy shows such promise, Colleen wrote in 1906. *The good brothers at Saint Swithin's concur, and it is with bittersweet pride that I send him off each day to their care.*

"He was going to school," Natalie said. "Oh, Jesus. Look at the day."

The last entry they found was the sixteenth of April, 1906.

Two days before the earthquake struck.

PART SIX

Voici mon secret. Il est très simple: on ne voit bien qu'avec le cœur. L'essentiel est invisible pour les yeux.

—ANTOINE DE SAINT-EXUPÉRY,
LE PETIT PRINCE

And now here is my secret, a very simple secret: It is only with the heart that one can see rightly; what is essential is invisible to the eye.

—ANTOINE DE SAINT-EXUPÉRY,
THE LITTLE PRINCE

23

Trevor came to pick up Natalie and her grandfather for a theater performance. Bertie had a role in a Noël Coward play, and Trevor was taking them to see it and to a light supper after. It was a rainy evening, and she had just finished closing for the night.

"He's courting you," Grandy said, bending down to fill Sylvia's water bowl. His tremor was bad today, and the water sloshed.

"He's doing a good job," Natalie admitted, grabbing a paper towel and wiping up the spill. Despite a ridiculous schedule, Trevor found time for Natalie, and she appreciated his patience. He was like his series of books—two-sided, embodying opposite concepts. A wildly popular loner. Successful and insecure. An open book of secrets.

She turned to her grandfather, studying his face. "Are you feeling all right?"

He waved a hand. "I'm feeling old. I'll be out in the shop, chatting with your suitor."

She sent a message to the doctor, mentioning Grandy's tremors and his wheezing. *Please don't let me lose him now.*

Jude Lockhart, the associate from Sheffield Auction House, came by the shop, shaking the rain from his shoulders. "Sorry I didn't call first," he said. "I have news."

Natalie briefly introduced him to Trevor. As the two men took each other's measure, she felt a twinge of exasperation. "What's up?" she asked.

Jude handed her a folder of printed documents. "George Hearst owned a copy of *Birds of America*."

"No kidding. Did you hear that, Grandy?" Natalie turned to Trevor. "His grandmother's journals make mention of the Audubon books. We had this crazy notion that she might have been given a rare original edition." She looked back at Jude. "George Hearst was the father of William Randolph Hearst?"

"Right. He was a politician, made his fortune in mining. He had one of the original hand-colored editions, four huge volumes. There were only two hundred copies produced, most of them lost and the rest in private collections or institutions."

Jude turned to a page in the folder. "Our handwriting analyst at the firm has high confidence that the letter you found is authentic."

"Good Lord." Trevor studied the provenance report.

"Right? I suppose we'll never know what became of them. Forever lost, like Colleen." Natalie patted her grandfather's hand. It was ice cold.

"It's sad, losing pieces of ourselves," he said. A bright bead of blood slipped from his nostril.

"Oh, Grandy—" Natalie gasped as her grandfather slipped to the floor as if his bones had turned to liquid. She looked up at Jude and Trevor. "Call 911."

They kept her grandfather overnight for tests and observation. The physical symptoms, Natalie was told, were secondary to the dementia, and the tests failed to pinpoint the cause. They treated him with steroids and antibiotics, and by morning, he was ready to be discharged.

While waiting for the paperwork, Grandy dozed. Natalie sat by his bed, reading yet another guide to dealing with dementia. The books and brochures offered plenty of information and strategies, but little in the way of hope.

She studied the process of applying for guardianship. It was a likely next step, but she shied from it. Had Mom considered such a move? Sometimes when Natalie came across her mother's wild expenditures, she would feel frustrated. The amounts Blythe had spent on alternative treatments, shamans, so-called healers whose only credential was a fancy website, often sent Natalie's frustration spinning into anger.

She understood now. When a loved one was in distress, you would try anything.

"You miss Peach," said Grandy suddenly, blinking awake.

"What?" The observation startled her. "Why would you say that?"

"Because I'm old, and I have no filters."

"Oh, Grandy." She set aside the guide. "I wish I could help. I wish I knew what to do for you."

"I was thinking of you, not myself. You've kept me well and you've given me joy. And joy will keep you well, but you have to let it. If it's any consolation," Grandy said, "I miss him, too. Not the way you do, of course, but I did enjoy our conversations."

"What do you mean, the way I do?" She felt oddly chastened and defensive.

"He lights you up."

"I don't know about that." She did, though. Too often, her thoughts lingered on that evening stroll in the moon garden. That kiss. "It's great that he was able to take care of so many repairs. But that was . . . it wasn't a relationship. It was just work." She had to admit, though, that she did miss him. She had become accustomed to having him around. Now that he'd moved on, she caught herself wishing she could hear his tuneful humming, his wry observations, his easy laughter.

Grandy waved a hand as if to dismiss her comment. "Stop it, Blythe. You get more than one shot. Do you understand that?"

"Grandy—"

"Dean Fogarty was not your one and only chance at love. Heartbreak is a terrible thing, but it's not a permanent condition. If you allow it, your heart will renew itself and find joy once again."

Rather than argue with him about her mother, Natalie smiled at him. "Is that what happened for you?" she asked. "Was May Lin your second shot?"

"She was everything I needed," he said. "Loving her was the crowning achievement of my life. Your mother was so preoccupied with other things that she never found the one thing I wanted for her."

Natalie studied his lined, beloved face, seeing the

wisdom and compassion that had guided her in ways she was only now discovering. "Was it hard for you," she asked, "wishing your daughter would find a love like that?"

"As a parent, wanting so much for your child isn't the hard part," he said. "The hard part is convincing you to believe it. You need to believe in that possibility."

She wasn't clear on whether he thought he was speaking to her or to her mother.

The discharge nurse and social worker came in with prescription slips and final instructions, and at last it was time to go. Her grandfather didn't speak as they took a taxi home. Despite the chilly day, he wanted to sit in the garden while the sun was out. Natalie brought the Mackinaw blanket and tucked it around him in the chaise.

"Do you think she was lonely?" she asked him, still thinking about her mother.

His eyes misted with memories as he seemed to drift through time. "She lived for the books that filled her days. And of course, she had the most delightful of daughters. It's quite impossible to feel lonely when you're in the presence of a delightful child."

"Was I?" asked Natalie. "A delightful child? I don't think I'd ever describe myself as delightful."

"Well, of course no child is entirely, but yes. You certainly were. You were also an anxious child," he said. "A worrier. You worried about matters beyond your years, many matters. Money. Air pollution. Stray cats. Your grades. And you worried about the people in the books you read. We thought it was charming, but you did lose sleep over the Boxcar Children."

She smiled. "I still don't know how they made it through Violet's illness in that first book." Then she looked around the fading garden, which was in a state of semineglect, the flowers spent and gone to seed. There were a few loose boards on the shed, and a broken windowpane, and her first thought was to call Peach. She knew she wouldn't, though.

"May Lin always kept it so beautiful out here," she said to her grandfather. "I'm going to make time to fix things up. Does that sound good?"

"I'll ask her tonight," said Grandy. "I'm sure she'd like to help."

Natalie felt a pulse of concern. "May Lin is—"

"I see her in my dreams," he said. "Every night."

She bit her lip, then reached over and covered his hand with hers. "Let me know what she says."

"Where's Prince Charming taking you tonight?" Bertie asked Natalie.

She was wearing her mother's good red coat and heeled boots. "Not sure." After the fiasco with her grandfather, Trevor had promised to cheer her up. A comedy club, maybe. She checked her phone to make sure Charlie was on his way. Lately, she worried about leaving her grandfather unattended.

"To bed, I hope," said Cleo. "It's time, if you ask me."

"No one asked you," said Natalie. "Don't you have a book club to get ready for?"

She gestured at the snack table and the stack of mystery novels waiting for the club members to arrive. "I'm ready. Really, I don't know what you're waiting for. He's great, and you're great, and he treats you like a queen."

"He's wonderful," Natalie agreed.

"I hear a 'but,'" said Bertie.

She sighed. "I'm an idiot. He seems perfect for me." She wanted Trevor to be the one. He was the easy choice, the no-brainer. Life with him would flow by with no effort. But she'd failed so badly with Rick. She questioned her own judgment now. And with everything going on with Grandy, she was in no shape to start something. Yet Trevor kept coming back, and she kept—

"Oh boy," said Bertie. "We've got company."

A woman in an army surplus jacket and scuffed

boots came in, bringing along the ripe scent of alcohol and recently smoked cigarettes. Her face bore the crags of harsh living, and her eyes gleamed in a restless assessment of the displays. Given the shop's location, they got their share of homeless visitors and panhandlers. Sometimes, though, people just wanted to talk.

This one made a beeline for the counter. "You Natalie?" she asked.

Startled, Natalie glanced at Bertie, then back at the woman. "Can I help you?"

"There are some things you might wanna know about your boyfriend." The woman picked up a Trevor Dashwood book that was displayed on an easel. *Real and Make-Believe.*

Natalie's gaze skated around the shop. There were a few browsing customers, though they didn't seem to take notice of the woman. "Sorry, what?" she asked softly.

She turned the book around to the photo of Trevor on the back. "You think you know him? You don't know him."

"Ma'am," Bertie said. "Is there something we can help you with?"

"Help me." She curled her lip. "How 'bout I help you. For one thing, that ain't his name. This is Tyrell Denton. I reckon I'd know, being as I'm his mother."

Natalie looked at the woman through a blur of utter confusion. "Sorry, I don't understand—"

"'Course you don't," the woman said. "I'm Doreen Denton, his dirty little secret."

Now a few customers looked over. Natalie had no idea what to do. "Ma'am—"

"Hey, Doreen." A young woman with a cell phone came into the shop. She looked vaguely familiar.

At first Natalie couldn't place her. Then she realized it was Emily, one of Trevor's assistants.

"Glad I found you," Emily said to the woman. "We need to get going, okay?"

"I ain't going nowhere with you, missy." Doreen gave a disdainful sniff. "I got a few things to say about that boy o' mine."

Emily pressed her lips together. Natalie murmured, "I think she's talking about Trevor."

"I know. It's complicated . . ."

"You mean . . ."

Emily nodded, then turned again to Doreen. "Can we go now?"

"That's right, sweep me under the rug."

The tension strained the very air in the room. A moment later, Trevor strode into the bookstore, phone in hand.

"Oh, look, everybody, Mr. Big Shot has arrived." Doreen waved her hand at him.

A couple of the customers edged closer.

Trevor's face was stiff and pale. "There's a car waiting outside," he said. "Come on, I'll help you out."

Doreen sneered at him, but somehow, he and Emily managed to escort her to the street. Doreen kept up a strange rant, laced with profanity, as she got into a shiny town car.

Natalie looked at Bertie and Cleo. "Oh boy." She grabbed her bag. "I'll fill you in later."

"Mandatory," Cleo said, shooing her toward the door.

Outside, Natalie joined Trevor on the sidewalk. He was watching the black car drive away, his shoulders rigid, his face impassive.

"Hey." She touched his arm, and his muscles felt like stone. "What's going on?"

"She told you," Trevor said. It wasn't a question.

"I imagine there's another side to the story." *A flip side.*

He took a deep breath. "Let's walk."

They fell in step together through the bone-chilling fog. "I'm sorry you had to see that," he said.

"I'm not sure what I saw."

He turned up the collar of his charcoal-gray overcoat. "You saw my childhood," he said. In the next block, he ducked into the foyer of a boutique hotel with a quiet lobby bar. He ordered two old-fashioneds and told the bartender to make his a double.

"We need to talk," said Natalie.

Trevor gripped the edge of the table and looked across at her. She had never seen him unguarded before. She did now. He looked utterly bleak and defeated. "My mom's a lot of things. But weirdly enough, she's not a liar." He took a deep swig of his drink.

"I'm listening," Natalie said. "It's okay, Trevor. Her name's Doreen Denton?"

He nodded. "The two of us lived in a Carson City trailer park. My father was some drifter I never met. She drank and worked in a casino. Sometimes she remembered to toss me a loaf of bread and a jar of peanut butter. Maybe a box of cereal. I managed to drag myself through school, and every chance I got, I holed up in the library. That was my sanctuary."

"So it's all—your background, your bio—it's all made-up."

"As fictional as one of my novels. A total hoax."

Natalie sipped her drink while her mind reeled. She was shocked—but also sad. Despite all his success, his wealth, his homes in San Francisco and Carmel, his jet-setting lifestyle . . . the nonprofit he'd founded for children of addicts, he had been living with this secret. "So your mother—Doreen . . ."

"She doesn't live in Palm Springs. I got her a place in private care, and she's been to rehab more times than I can count. I'm so fucking sorry, Natalie."

"*I'm* sorry you had to grow up like that, and that you felt you had to hide it."

"You know how hard publishing is. When I was trying to market myself, I created this persona, and when the books took off, I just went with it. It's shitty, I know."

"The world loves you."

"The world doesn't know me."

"You are who you are." She reached across the table and touched his hand. "You know what I wish? I wish I could go back in time and find you as a little kid and give you a hug and tell you you're going to be just fine."

He took his hand away. "You wouldn't have wanted to hug me. I was covered in lice and bruises."

"Even more reason to hug you," she insisted. "Ah, Trevor."

He took a drink. "You know what they say—it's never too late to have a happy childhood. I'm happy now, babe. You make me happy."

Yet there was a sadness inside him, and Natalie knew she couldn't fill that void. She wondered if his attraction to her, while seemingly romantic on the surface, actually stemmed from his wanting to be with someone who was steady and dependable and predictable, everything the awful mother was not.

Natalie finally understood why she hadn't been able to be all in with Trevor. It wasn't her bad judgment about guys. It was her instincts, telling her—shouting at her—to pay attention. She should have listened to herself. She'd been right to hold back from Trevor, even if she didn't understand why.

"Were you ever going to level with me?" she asked, not bothering to soften the edge of anger in her voice.

He shrugged his shoulders. "I like to think I would have, eventually."

She thought about him as a little boy, and the deplorable mother, and the anger subsided. "For what it's worth, it wouldn't have mattered."

"You're sweet." His smile was fleeting. "And I kind of love you."

That brought her up short. Was he Trevor Dashwood or Tyrell Denton? A practiced liar. A man damaged by a terrible mother. Natalie vacillated between compassion and irritation. "I love what you've done with your life. You turned it into something really beautiful."

"But . . ." Over the rim of his glass, he sent her a knowing look.

"But I'm not what you're looking for." Her throat felt raw as she scraped the truth from deep inside. "I guess you could say I've been acting, too. Acting like someone who knows how to have a relationship, who knows what she wants. And the fact is, I don't. And that sucks for me, because you're pretty wonderful," she said. "I'll never forget what you did for me and Grandy."

"Shit," he said.

"I'm sorry."

"I know." He rattled the ice cubes in his glass.

"Everybody in the world thinks I'm an idiot, because you're fantastic."

"I'm a fraud," he said.

No wonder he flipped everything in his books. "What would America's favorite author do? Come up with the flip side, right? Write down ten things you really, really like. Can you do that?"

"One way or other, I've been rewriting my own story in every book I write."

"You did something incredible with your life, and

I'm sure you're doing the best you can for your mother, and you deserve everything and more."

"You know," he said, "as breakup talks go, this one is pretty damn kind."

"A kind breakup? That sounds like a flip side story."

"You're a good person, Natalie." He offered a sweet, sad smile. "Promise me one thing."

"What's that?"

"When that rare first edition of the bird book magically appears, make sure I'm the first one you call."

24

Natalie returned from a meeting with the private lending firm in a state of utter defeat. Even the sight of customers milling around the shop didn't boost her spirits. Bertie was doing a dramatic reading of *The Book with No Pictures* to a group of delighted toddlers. Cleo was at the counter, working on her latest play. She took one look at Natalie's face and motioned her into the office.

"Tell me," she said.

Natalie took a long breath. "It's bad. The principal on the loan is huge, and Mom was in arrears for more than three years. The amount they want on the payment plan is way out of our reach, even now that our revenues are up a bit. And then there's the tax situation . . ."

"Aw, shoot. I'm sorry."

"I'm out of options. Grandy got lost yesterday on the way to the senior center, and he panicked. It could have been bad. He could have walked in front of a car, or . . . He needs a higher level of care, and that's my number one priority. Oh God. He's going to freak out when I tell him we have to sell."

"He's going to tell you no. Then what?"

She blinked back tears. "I'd have to take him to court. Assume guardianship. I don't know if I can do that, Cleo. I don't know if I have it in me to take that from him."

"Man. This is really hard, Natalie. I wish there was something I could do."

Natalie looked at Cleo, the friend she'd known all her life. "You're doing it." She offered a tremulous smile. "Guess I picked the wrong time to dump my bazillionaire boyfriend." She'd filled Cleo and Bertie in on the Trevor/Tyrell situation, and the drama gave them something to talk about for days.

"I bet he'd love a second chance," Cleo suggested.

"I would never. Do you hear yourself right now?"

"I'm grasping at straws."

Through the open door, Natalie saw a customer approaching the counter, two cranky-looking kids tugging at her coat and whining. "I'll go," she said. "I could use the distraction." She eased into bookselling mode, which now felt as natural to her as breathing. Despite her troubles, she managed to summon a smile as she greeted the customer. "Can I help you find . . ." She paused, studying the woman's face. "Kayla?" She was sure it was Kayla Cramer, her girlhood nemesis.

"Hi, Natalie. It's good to see you. We just moved back to the area, so I thought—"

"Mo-om," said the little boy. "I'm hungry."

"Me too," the little girl chimed in. "I want cock-porn."

"We'll get popcorn on the way home," Kayla said, her cheeks turning red. She looked haggard and heavy, her lips thin with exasperation.

"Have a bookmark, you two," Natalie said, handing them out. "There's a maze you can do on the back. Now, let me finish helping your mom. She picked out some totally amazing books for you."

The kids stopped whining and regarded her bashfully.

"How've you been?" Kayla asked Natalie. "Gosh, it's been a million years. Are you married now? Kids? We'll have to catch up."

"Single, no kids, one cat, one grandfather," Natalie said.

"Mom, I need a pen to do my maze," said the boy.

"I need a pen, too, Mom," said his sister.

"And this one's for me," Kayla said, impulsively adding a novel to the stack.

"Good choice," said Natalie. "*Mrs. Everything* was one of my favorites last year. I hope you like it."

"I'm going to dive right in as soon as I get these monsters to bed. A book and a glass of wine are the perfect antidote for a nasty winter night." She looked around the shop. "I always envied you, living here," she said. "Surrounded by all these books."

The kids started whining again and tugging her toward the door. "Stay single," she admonished. "Trust me, you'll live longer."

Years ago, Natalie had pictured Kayla Cramer living some kind of fabulous, carefree life. And apparently Kayla had envied *her*. Natalie remembered one of her mother's favorite quotes from Anaïs Nin's memoir, which had a permanent spot on the W.O.W. shelf: "We don't see things as they are, we see them as *we* are."

A few minutes later, Dorothy Gallagher came in on a swirl of cold wind. Her cheeks were bright red, and she smiled as she pushed back her hood.

Natalie's pulse raced with anticipation. If Dorothy was here, that meant Peach wasn't far behind. Maybe he'd stop in to pick her up. *Down, girl.*

"Hi there, kiddo," she said to the little girl. "Nice to see you."

"Hiya." Dorothy unzipped her jacket. "I need a birthday present. Whitney Gaines from my class invited me to her party."

"What sort of book do you think she would like?"

Dorothy gave a dainty sniff. "Probably no book at all, unless it's about trying on clothes and having a boyfriend. That's all she and her friends care about. The only reason she invited me is that the teacher has a rule that you have to invite the whole class or you can't pass out your invitations at school." Dorothy attended an ultraexclusive private school called The Enclave— her mother's choice, according to Peach. It was known for its sky-high tuition, its STEM program for girls— and its veiled but undeniable snobbery.

Suddenly the picture came into focus for Natalie. "I see," she said. "So do you *want* to go to your friend's party?"

Dorothy shrugged. "My mom thinks I should go on account of she expects me to get along with all my classmates and not be the odd one out."

"Probably a good idea," Natalie said. "But it's hard to make yourself do something you don't want to do." Like taking over a failing bookstore. Like ignoring your feelings for a guy. Like having your grandfather declared incompetent.

Dorothy nodded glumly.

"When I was your age I felt like the odd one out a lot of the time," said Natalie.

"You did?" Dorothy's eyes widened.

"Totally. I had kind of an unusual family. It was just me and my mom, and we lived upstairs with my grandfather and his girlfriend, who was Chinese. Most of my friends had both parents and they lived in big houses with yards and garages, not apartments above a shop."

"Really? But living above the bookstore is the best thing ever."

"Other kids thought it was weird."

Dorothy tugged at her braid. "Kids at school think I'm weird, too, because I live in two places and Dad's house is with his bandmates."

"That's not weird. That's cool. Way cooler than a bookstore."

"Did your friends say stuff about you?" asked Dorothy.

"Sure. Questions like 'Where's your dad?' And 'Why don't you have a car?' And even though I should have ignored them, I had a hard time doing that. Now I kind of wish I hadn't let their opinions matter so much." She wondered if it had bothered her mother to see her so concerned about what other people thought. "Do your friends say things?"

"Not really. It isn't PC anymore. At our school, we embrace diversity. But I get those looks, you know?"

Natalie did know. Those condescending, too-bad-you're-not-like-me looks. "When I was your age and kids said stuff, my mom would tell me something from her favorite book—'It's never an insult to be called what somebody thinks is a bad name. It just shows you how poor that person is, it doesn't hurt you.' That's from *To Kill a Mockingbird*." She showed Dorothy a copy of the book. *And I'm turning into my mother,* she thought.

"Let's see if we can figure out a book your friend might actually like." She went to the shelf of middle-grade readers and briefly studied the selection. Then she plucked a copy of *Wish Upon a Sleepover* from the shelf. "This is about a sleepover party that gets all mixed up. The girl in the book makes a list of all the people she *doesn't* want at her party, but they accidentally get invited instead of the ones she wanted."

Dorothy perked up. "Oh, and then what happens?"

"Your friend will have to read the story to find out, but I promise it's a good one. Even for kids who don't like to read."

"Okay. I'll give it a try."

"Great! How about I gift wrap it for you?"

"Good idea. Thanks, Natalie." Dorothy's worried

expression softened with relief. She cast a look around. "Where's Mr. Harper?"

"He's in bed, probably reading. He's been really tired lately. Would you like to say hi?"

Dorothy nodded. "Sure."

They went and knocked on his door.

"Come in." Grandy's voice was thin, like the creak of a rusty hinge. When he saw Dorothy, his wizened face lit with a smile. "Hello, my dear. What are you about today?"

In exhaustive detail, Dorothy related the saga of Whitney Gaines. Grandy listened with his usual patient attention. "Fetch me that box from the table," he said.

Dorothy brought him the box. "Your typewriter keys?"

"Perhaps you could share a favorite letter or two with your friend."

"She might like that," Dorothy mused, and picked out the girl's initials. "Thanks, Mr. Harper." She moved closer to the bed. "Natalie said you've been sick. What's the matter?"

"I have symptoms," he said. "The doctors say it's idiopathic. I think that means the doctor's an idiot and the patient's pathetic."

Dorothy leaned down and gave him a quick hug. "I'm sorry you don't feel well."

"That hug just made me feel a hundred times better," said Grandy.

Natalie was putting the finishing touches on the gift wrap when a supermodel walked through the door. Maybe she wasn't a supermodel, but she looked like one and even carried herself like one—confidence edged with hauteur. She was tall and slender, with pin-straight golden hair and enormous eyes, professionally lashed; flawless makeup and manicure; heeled boots and a luxurious coat that looked as though it had stepped off the runway.

Dorothy waved at the woman. "Hi, Mom," she said.

Natalie had to regroup at lightning speed. This glorious unicorn woman was Dorothy's mother? Peach's ex? What the—

She pushed the brightly wrapped parcel across the counter. "I think Dorothy picked just the right thing for her friend's birthday."

"That's great. Good work, you two," said the woman, handing over her platinum card.

Regina. Peach had mentioned that name.

"Thanks for your help." Regina looked around the shop, taking in the cozy seating areas, the cat curled up in front of the electric fire. "I can see why Dorothy likes this place."

"Thanks," said Natalie. Her mind raced over the idea that Peach had been married to this gorgeous creature.

And now he wasn't.

None of which had anything to do with her.

With a careful smile, she handed over the card and the gift. "Have fun at the party," she said to Dorothy.

"I'll try."

"'Overrated' is a perfectly good rhyme with 'complicated,'" Suzzy said to Peach. She sat at the studio piano, their songwriting notes propped on a music stand.

"Yeah, but *complicated*? Everybody writes that song."

"Because everybody likes songs about complicated relationships. Because everybody loves them— including you."

He'd thought about calling Natalie, but never got around to it. She was probably busy with her sick grandfather. Could be a certain famous writer was keeping her busy, too.

"Speak for yourself," he said to Suzzy. "I don't do so hot with complicated women."

"Or as most people call them, *women*," Suzzy answered, scowling at the pages. The writing session was dragging today. Nothing seemed to work as they struggled through a song about a rain check. Some days, writing flowed like butter. Other days it was like passing a kidney stone.

"Yeah, why is that?"

"Seriously," said Suzzy, "if you're looking for an uncomplicated relationship, get a dog."

"Dorothy would love that." His daughter was yet another complicated female, one he adored with every bit of his heart. Her blurted admission—*I hate my parents' divorce*—still haunted Peach like a lingering echo. His chief goal in life had always been to give Dorothy a life that she loved, all day every day. He could put a roof over her head, teach her to sing, take her to the doctor for vaccines and checkups, buy her shoes and books, listen to every word she spoke. But he could not give her the thing she missed most—her family of origin.

Despite the care he'd taken to live close by and to share in every aspect of parenting, his little girl knew her world would never be the same. She carried a sadness around, an unspoken yearning for the three of them to be together in a way they could never be, in a house full of love.

He and Regina had set out to create exactly that, the

way people did every day, every time they said *I do*. But life was a pathway of twists and turns, and cracks appeared. They started out as invisible fissures deep in the foundation, unexamined until the damage was too great to repair.

Regina's discontent had hidden behind a mask of ambition—crave more, strive more, achieve more— and his behind long days at work followed by writing and recording and practice sessions. By the time either of them glanced up from their preoccupations, they were looking across a gulf too wide and deep to cross. Eventually, they both agreed that the marriage was over.

But Dorothy. The kid had zero say in the matter. Her world had been rocked by an earthquake and the pieces would never again be put back in place.

The one thing she wanted was the one thing Peach couldn't give her. And the one thing *he* wanted was . . . complicated.

"What kind?" Suzzy asked.

"Sorry, what?" He had lost track of the conversation.

"What kind of dog?"

"A rescue, I suppose," he said. "Not too big. No emotional baggage."

She laughed. "So, a puppy, you mean."

"A puppy is a blank slate."

"Puppies are a lot of work. Ever raise a puppy from scratch?"

"I have, actually. When I was a kid, just a bit older than Dorothy, somebody had a litter of pups in a Publix parking lot, and I brought one home. I caught hell from my parents, but my sister and I convinced them to let us keep him—Buster was his name." His mother had engaged a professional trainer, and his father had hired a contractor to construct a doghouse and dog run on their Buckhead estate.

The memory reminded him that, before everything had collapsed, his childhood had been a magic carpet ride through blissful ignorance. He'd been raised with no idea that his father was a thief and his mother a maven of Junior League artifice. Neither he nor Junebug had known that their entire life as a family was built on fraud and deception. He had gone to bed each night with his dog curled next to him in a house that felt like a fortress against the world.

Maybe that was the childhood he wanted for Dorothy—a sense of carefree adventure, a secure feeling of knowing what you'd wake up to each morning. He and Regina had not resorted to fraud, of course. But subterfuge? Probably. Not on purpose, but probably.

"Buster was awesome," Peach said. "Do you think

if we got a dog, Dorothy wouldn't mind the divorce so much?"

"Did you ever consider that maybe Dorothy wouldn't worry so much about the divorce if her dad was happy?" Suzzy suggested.

"I'm happy and she knows it," he snapped, annoyed.

"Uh-huh."

"Shut up and write, Suz."

"I will. Instead of this dumb rain check idea, I'll write a song about a guy who likes a girl who works in a bookstore but he won't tell her."

"And the clichés keep coming," he grumbled.

"Quit being one, then," she said.

Peach was on a new project in Russian Hill, a restoration job on a 1920s town house that hadn't been touched, probably since the 1920s. The client and his wife were both physicians—highly successful ones, judging by the budget for the reno.

He was surveying a defunct radiator, trying to figure out the best way to remove the old iron hulk. It was stamped *Honeywell Heat Generator*, and as he circled it with his Sawzall, he noticed a mushroom-shaped pot was connected to a container on the bottom of the device. Fitting a cast-iron blade into the saw, he was about to get to work when something tweaked a memory. Working on old buildings meant watching for hazardous materials. The little contraption behind the heater might be a big problem.

Setting aside the saw, he did some quick research on his phone. A few minutes later, he realized he was looking at a mercury pot, and it probably contained several fluid ounces of mercury.

"That's some bad shit," he muttered. He knew he needed to be careful with the removal so nothing would be released from the unit. Even a tiny pinhole could be a hazard. He kept the thing intact, holding it in a vertical position, and placed it into a thick plastic contractor bag, then put the bag into a five-gallon bucket and surrounded it with sawdust to hold it in place. He labeled it *Mercury—do not open.* Then he set the thing in a box in an empty shed and called the transfer station to pick it up. The client wasn't going to be happy with the disposal charge, but it was better than getting mercury poisoning.

He sent a message to his client and stayed late at the job site. Dorothy was at her mother's, and Peach had nothing going on. He took a break to sit on the front steps and chow down on a burrito. The porch was a shipwreck of peeling paint and broken fretwork, but it was going to be a beauty once he finished. For the moment, it was a fine place to survey the neighborhood despite the winter chill. From his vantage point, he could look down Lombard Street, sloped like a ski jump toward the waterfront.

Natalie had told him that the journals she'd found described a parade of soldiers heading to the docks on their way to the war in the Philippines. Had they been like him when he joined the Marines, vacillating between adrenaline-fueled excitement and gut-deep dread, wondering what they'd gotten themselves into? He'd been barely eighteen when he plunged into twelve weeks of boot camp followed by combat training—and then deployment. He'd been in a daze, having to pivot from his plan to study architecture at Emory to cashing in his college plan so his sister could go to rehab. Natalie had been incredibly gracious when he'd told her about the situation. She was a damn good listener.

Natalie again. His thoughts always seemed to circle back to her. She was the first person since the divorce he actually thought he could love. He actually *wanted* to love.

His phone buzzed, and his client's number came up. "Hey, Dr. Jantzen," he said.

"I got your message about the radiator. Good thing you caught that," Jantzen said. "Even a little bit of mercury is toxic as hell."

Peach exhaled a sigh of relief. He'd come way too

close to chopping up the unit with his Sawzall. "I followed the guidelines to the letter, except I used sawdust instead of kitty litter when I packed it up."

"That's good. If you catch yourself having an epic stomachache or slurring your speech, go see your doctor. There's a whole host of symptoms associated with mercury, and even just inhaling the vapors can cause organ or neurological damage, anything from mood swings to respiratory and abdominal ailments to tremors."

"Tremors—like hands that shake?"

"Hands, head, sometimes."

"Okay. The pickup's scheduled for first thing in the morning." Peach put away his tools and locked up, toying with song lyrics in his head. *You're the cause of my tremors and mood swings, baby* would never make it onto anyone's playlist.

When he got in the truck, a slip of paper fluttered down from the visor—a receipt with a logo of the winking sun and the slogan *An Eye for Good Books*.

Damn.

He wadded up the receipt and tossed it aside. He was just about to head home when something, another tweaked memory, stopped him. He picked up the receipt and smoothed it over his knee.

During his stint in the military, his daily work had

been juggling cause and effect. Paying attention to the sequence of things. Andrew Harper—a man with no obvious health issues—suffered a fall. Afterward, he'd moved to a different part of the building—a tiny downstairs apartment. And then his health started to fail. *Why?*

For decades, the apartment had been used as a storeroom. Andrew's father had been a compounding pharmacist. Who knew what kind of concoctions and amalgams had been stored there? And later, Andrew had stored things for his typewriter business—acetone and lubricants. But most recently, according to Natalie, the room had been crammed with books, which had been hastily moved out so Andrew could live on the ground floor.

Peach impulsively turned up Perdita Street and drove to the bookstore. Parking in the loading zone, he went inside, causing the bell to jangle. "Hey," he said to Cleo, who was at the counter. He didn't see anyone else in the shop.

"Hey, Peach." She glanced at the clock over the door. "I was just about to close. What's up?"

"Is Andrew around?"

Cleo shook her head. "Natalie took him for a doctor's appointment and then they went to dinner. He's been sick lately. I'm worried about him."

"Would it be okay if I checked something in his apartment? It'll just take a minute."

She shrugged her shoulders. "You have the door code, right?"

Peach nodded and hurried to the back of the building. He hadn't been here in a while. The place looked good, probably thanks to Natalie's pinpoint organization. Andrew's apartment held the smells of old paper, old ink, old man. A lamp on the nightstand cast a glow. The soft groans and hissing sounds of the radiator filled the room.

Peach switched his phone to flashlight mode and hunkered down, putting his cheek against the floor to see behind the apparatus. "I'll be goddamned," he said, eyeing a small iron vial with a slender neck and a bulb at the bottom.

The radiator. The goddamned radiator.

25

Andrew's thoughts fluttered like curtains in a breeze through the window. The wind would part them momentarily and he'd see a flash of crystal clarity. Then the next eddy of air would obscure the view, and the haze would come up again.

Although there was no standard cure for mercury poisoning, the chelation therapy was helping in every organ except the brain. That much he knew, based on the frequent blood and urine tests.

Within hours of Peach sounding the alarm about the mercury, Andrew had been admitted to the hospital. He'd come home to find that the apartment—indeed, the entire building from basement to attic—had been decontaminated and tested. The metallic taste in his mouth was gone at last. His appetite had returned and he could walk a straight line. Feed the cat without spilling. He might never regain the lost pieces of himself, but after the sudden drama of removing the toxic radiator part, he felt more hope than he had in a long time.

He also saw things with intermittent clarity.

And he knew what he had to do. He took out the threadbare green ribbon that had lived in his billfold since his father had given it to him. His tie to Colleen, who had never found her way back.

"Come and sit," he said to Natalie when she appeared at his door. "We can look out at the rain. It's a restful sight, isn't it?"

She squeezed his shoulder, leaned down, and kissed his cheek. Natalie. His Natty-girl. She of the butterfly kisses and worried forehead and huge heart everyone trusted but herself. Then she had a seat, placing a folder of printed pages on the table between them. It was the story of the Sunrose Building, the one Blythe had started—was it only a year ago? It seemed like much longer. Natalie was determined to complete the narrative, bringing in the trove of information from Colleen's writings and drawings.

"I'm so very grateful," he said. "I don't tell you that enough, and I want to make certain you know."

"I do know. How are you feeling today?"

"Good," he said. "I checked the calendar, and for once there's no doctor or lab on the agenda. I have a notary coming to help us this morning."

She frowned. That pucker of worry endearing. "What for?"

He took out the forms from Ms. Hart, the lawyer. "I'm giving you my general durable power of attorney and guardianship. It's long overdue."

"Oh, Grandy. Are you sure?"

"I've had a good long time to think about it. Yes, I'm sure."

"Then I'll do my best to take care of things, I promise. You've taken care of me all my life, and I'll do the same for you."

"You've kept me well because you give me joy. And joy will keep you well, but you have to let it."

Her heart ached. "I'll try," she said. "I'll try to let it."

"Your first task is to find a buyer for this old place."

"What? You want to sell?"

"It's time, Natalie. You've known it all along, and you're absolutely right. I've also reserved a spot"—he held up a brochure—"at this assisted-living residence." He'd stayed up late, studying the booklet Natalie had given him in October, a glossy compendium of silver-haired people playing golf, sitting on porch swings, watching the sunset over the Sonoma hills.

"You want to live *there*?"

Of course he didn't. But it was the most sensible choice for them both. "You can return to Archangel. I'm sure your firm would love to have you back."

Her cheeks lost their color. She started to speak, but he held up a hand. "I've made my decision. We're selling the building, and also the shop and all its inventory. We need to act quickly before it's foreclosed and we lose all control."

She brushed at her eyes. "I'm not going to do a thing until we make sure this is what you want."

"It is, I assure you. I've been a foolish old man. I can blame the mercury, but it's likely my own stubborn nature. I tried to hold on to this place because it guards my entire life within its walls."

"Grandy—"

"Let me finish. This place is an empty shell without May Lin and Blythe. Without my long-gone parents. They will be just as absent from my life whether I stay and wait for the inevitable, or whether we move far away." He covered her hands with his. "I want to be near you in a place where we don't worry that something else will fall apart each day. Can we make that happen? Please?"

"Are you absolutely certain?" she asked. Her worried eyes probed like Dr. Yang's scope. "Absolutely one hundred percent?"

The uncertainty ached in his bones. But this was Natalie, his heart, and he could not be a burden any longer. "I know what's happening to me. And I know how it ends," he said. "I don't intend to leave you with a mess on your hands."

"You're not a mess," she said. "I'll do whatever it takes to keep you here."

He held up a hand. "My mind is made up. No more twelve-hour days. No more threatening notices. I want to enjoy the time I have left without those constant worries."

"But—"

"Enough, now. It's time to move forward, Natalie."

She took a deep breath, and for the first time in a long time, the worry eased from her face. "There's a woman who left me her card—Vicki Visconsi. I looked into her firm, and it turns out she's a broker for high-end real estate. Mom was talking to her, before . . ."

"She would probably welcome your call." He set the paperwork aside. "This can wait until we meet with the notary."

"Oh, Grandy." Natalie's eyes were filled with tenderness. "We're going to miss this old place, aren't we?"

His smile was a twist of irony. "My forgetfulness might be a blessing." Then his smile disappeared. "I'm not worried about forgetting the building. But you, Natty-girl. You."

"Listen. If you forget, I'll remind you. I will love you with all my heart, and you're going to feel that love, because even if you forget here"—she touched his head—"you'll remember here." She gently laid her hand on his heart. "I promise."

He took her hand and pressed a kiss on it. "You make me remember what a lucky man I am." To stave off a wave of emotion that threatened to carry him away, he changed the subject. "So, about your mother's project. It appears we now know the ending." He smiled, and it felt good to smile. He was giving his granddaughter the best gift he could—freedom from worry and want. "Let's finish Blythe's story, shall we?"

Natalie's smile was tremulous. "I've been putting it off—as if finishing it would mean I'd forget her. I'm trying to lose the grief but hold on to the love."

"You're very wise," he said.

"A sign of good parenting," she told him. "I didn't always appreciate that. And I think I've figured out the reason. I grew up resentful about the things we didn't have, but thinking back through the years and reading over Mom's notes, I can see what I overlooked. We had an amazing family after all—just an unconventional one. You and Mom, and then May Lin. We had all the things that matter, didn't we?"

The fog was moving in again, but he fought it, keeping hold of the bright colors of his granddaughter's face. "We did," he said. "Perhaps that's how the story ends."

She opened the file to the top page. "'The Lost and Found Bookshop: A _____.' Mom left it blank. What did she mean to say?"

The silence yielded no answer. Andrew gazed at her lovely face, and he saw his daughter looking back at him.

She took a deep breath and wrote something in the blank, then turned the page, showing it to him.

"A Grand Adventure," he said with a nod. "Blythe would have liked that just fine."

Natalie dropped her grandfather off at the Silver Beaver Lodge in Archangel, the residence she'd found for him. She'd never dreamed he would acquiesce to moving, but here they were. The director of the place greeted him warmly, and Grandy gave Natalie a grin and a thumbs-up sign as he got into the golf cart to begin his introductory tour.

Please let him like it here, she thought.

"I'll be back in an hour," Natalie said, tucking his scarf into his collar. It was a windy day. "Are you going to be warm enough?"

"He's in good hands," said the director. Round-faced and smiling, she had kind-looking eyes.

Natalie drove to Pinnacle Fine Wines and did the thing that she dreaded. She'd never turned in her employee access card, and it still worked at the reception scanner. As she made her way to Rupert's office, she passed the cube farm of her old department. Like a couple of prairie dogs, Mandy and Cheryl popped up to watch her over the dividers.

She used to worry so much about office gossip. *What a waste of headspace*, she thought now.

"Natalie, what brings you here?" asked Mandy, checking out her jeans and sneakers. It was quite a contrast from the way Natalie used to dress—A-line skirt, blazer, too-tight shoes.

Natalie smoothed her hands down the front of her jeans. This was who she was, who she'd always been. Comfortable clothes, no pretenses. "Looking for Rupert," she said, and took the stairs to his corner office.

She'd called ahead, and he was waiting for her. "Welcome back," he said, greeting her with a politician's smile. "Or should I say, welcome home."

"Thank you," she said.

"I was glad to hear from you," he said. "I think we can mend that little rift."

"Of course," she said, all business. "Do you have the contract from HR?"

"Right here. You can take a bit of time to go over it, but don't take too long. The inventory department hasn't been the same without you."

No surprise, she thought. "Thanks again, Rupert," she said. "I'll get back to you soon."

As she left the building, a gust of wind snatched the pages from her, and she had to chase them down. Mandy, who had stepped out for a smoke at the side of the building, stopped them with her foot. "Whoa there," she said, eyeing the HR letterhead.

Natalie picked up the form, now stamped with Mandy's boot print. "Thanks," she said.

"Guess I'll see you soon." Mandy blew a plume of smoke into the wind.

Natalie didn't want to acknowledge the knot of anxiety in her stomach as she drove away. She knew she'd be welcomed back to Pinnacle. The job was waiting for her. But she hated the idea. She used to think it was the perfect job. Now she knew her time was too precious to spend on a pursuit that didn't mean anything but a paycheck.

She needed something else, then. Something that

felt better, like the comfy sweater and lived-in jeans she had on at the moment. It wasn't an outfit her mother would have worn to work, but it suited Natalie. Maybe the bookstore in Archangel would hire her.

It's just a job, she reminded herself. A steady, predictable job so she could provide her grandfather with a worry-free life.

Telling Cleo and Bertie about her decision was harder than Natalie had anticipated. It was the end of the day, and they'd been busy hauling out the Christmas displays.

Every year, she and her mom and Grandy went to the Guardsmen Tree Lot up at Fort Mason to pick out a tree for the shop. The volunteers in their green jumpsuits and cheery smiles were the heralds of the season as they delivered the perfect tree, and Mom always donated books to their program for at-risk youth.

This year without her mother was going to be brutal, a deep, unbearable ache. *I miss your voice,* she thought, *the way you sang carols off-key when we decorated, and the inside stories we knew about each ornament we hung. So much of me went with you, Mom.*

"It's going to be our last Christmas," she said quietly, holding up a slightly battered angel whose arms formed a book display stand.

Bertie and Cleo both turned to her. "What?" Cleo asked in a whisper.

"Grandy agreed to close. We've got a buyer, and Grandy and I are moving up to Archangel."

"Oh, sweetie." Bertie's expression crumpled and he drew them both in for a group hug. "I'm sorry. I can't say it comes as a shock, but I'm sorry."

"Me too," Cleo said. "Natalie, you worked really hard and we're proud to know you."

She gave them a squeeze. "The target date is the first of February, but you should feel free to go anytime after the holidays."

Cleo sighed. "Working here was my favorite excuse for not writing. Now I guess I'll have to knuckle down and finish my play."

Bertie nodded. "And I'll have to get a role in a bigger production. Take down my walls and go deep. That'll make my acting coach happy."

"Oh, you guys. You're the best friends I've ever had and I'll love you forever." She shooed them toward the door. "Go, before this gets too maudlin."

After they left, she looked around the quiet shop. Sylvia came over and slipped in a figure eight between her ankles. Natalie bent to pet her, and for once the cat didn't lash out. "What are we going to do with you?" she asked. "Are you going to like it out in the country?"

She sighed, feeling an ache in her heart. She'd been so frustrated and angry with her mother for the sloppy bookkeeping, the past-due bills, the money pit she'd been saddled with. Yet she had rediscovered her mother's magic with stories. She'd fallen in love with the bookstore, finding the joy that had sustained Blythe Harper all her life. And now it was over.

She did a few chores to fill the time while she waited for Peach Gallagher. He was coming by to collect some tools and a final check for his services, and the prospect of seeing him again made her nervous. Catching a glimpse of her reflection in the dark shop window, she smoothed her hands down her sides and wondered if she should change. Instead of her usual conservative skirt and blouse, she wore lived-in jeans and an oversize cardigan. She decided not to dress up for him. This was who she was now, finally at ease with herself, surrendering to the decision she'd made. She wondered if Peach would notice the difference.

Her feelings for him were unlike anything in her experience. She'd never gotten it right with a man, but with Peach, the potential was there. That's all it would ever be, because she was leaving.

She wanted to see him again, though. She needed to tell him that what he'd done for Grandy was beyond price. She'd never be able to thank him for that.

When she saw him in the foyer, she jumped up to let him in. He arrived on a gust of damp winter wind.

"You were right," she said to him in a rush.

He grinned. "I like where this is going," he said.

Dear God, she loved his smile. "About the mercury," she said. "They started treatments right away. It's helping a lot. The dementia is a separate issue, but the other symptoms have improved. He feels much better." *Now that he isn't breathing mercury vapor every night*, she thought with a wave of guilt. "I don't know how to thank you, Peach." What she really wanted to tell him was *I miss you. Please come back.* But she didn't because she was dealing with so many changes, not the least of which was the fact that she was moving away.

"Is he around? I'd like to say hi."

"He's probably in bed already. The treatments are exhausting. Maybe tomorrow, if you have time. In other news . . ." Her hand shook as she showed him a business card. "I have a buyer for the shop. Apparently my mom had been discussing it with a big commercial outfit, but Grandy wouldn't budge. I was on the verge of taking him to court. And now I don't have to, because he finally decided to sell and settle all the outstanding debt. I just need to figure out a way to say goodbye to this place." She felt a wave of nausea as she regarded Sylvia curled in her spot by the reading chair. "We're moving to Archangel, up in Sonoma. I can get my old job back if I want."

"I thought you hated that job," said Peach.

"Not as much as I love my grandfather."

"He's one lucky guy. And I bet he knows that. I'm really glad he's feeling better. Sad about the shop, though."

"We both have too many memories tied up in this space. My mom . . . God, this whole place is a shrine to her. I can't figure out if being here makes me miss her more, or if it's a comfort to me." Natalie looked around the familiar space. Her mom had been her first real friend. She could hear Blythe's laughter every time the bell over the door rang. She could feel her touch when she brushed her hair or wiped away her tears. Even now, she still reached for the phone before realizing her mom wasn't there. A part of Natalie would always dwell on the one moment that had stolen her mother from the world. But another part had come to realize that Mom would never leave her, because Natalie had known her all along. She saw Blythe Harper every time she looked in the mirror.

"I hope it's been a comfort to you," Peach said quietly.

She sighed. "It has been, and it's going to be hard

to leave. I never thought bookselling was for me, but it turns out I really love it."

"Your—uh, Trevor. He's not interested in helping you out?"

"Trevor?" She realized Peach wasn't aware of what had happened. "He's not . . . we're not . . . whatever it is you're thinking. Not like that."

"He's not your boyfriend."

"He's not my boyfriend." Since the day his mother had come to the bookstore, Trevor and Natalie had talked a few times. She'd assured him there were no hard feelings, that his past was his past and no one would think ill of him for it. "Even if he were, I sure as hell would never lean on him to bail me out."

"You might have told me, Natalie."

"And why *might* I have done that?" She heard the tightness of irritation in her voice.

"Because I might have told you that it matters to me. *You* matter to me. Which you would already know if you'd talk to me."

"If *I* talk to you? Like that's my job?"

"I didn't say that. But this would go a lot easier if you'd tell me what you're thinking."

"This? *This?* You're going to have to be more specific, Gallagher." She felt flooded with everything. Relief about her grandfather, apprehension about what lay ahead. Confusion about Peach, standing in front of her with his heart in his eyes.

"Look, I'm sorry you're sad," he said. "I'm sorry your mom died along with your boyfriend. I'm sorry you have to sell a place that you love. I can't fix those things. Hell, I can't fix anything but your old building." He took hold of her hands. His were damp and chilled from the rain, rough and calloused from work. "What I can do is love you, Natalie Jean Harper. That's what I can do. But only if you let me."

She stared at him in amazement. She didn't even know where to start. "How did you know my middle name?"

"I guessed. Was I right?"

"No." She looked down at their joined hands, and then up at his face, and in that moment, she knew. Something was going to happen between them—something big. Bigger than her doubts and fears. Bigger than her bookstore woes. Bigger even than the road ahead for her and Grandy. It was going to be the biggest thing that had ever happened to her.

"You okay?" he asked. "You look a little pale."

"I'm okay. Just so we're clear. You said you can love me."

"Yeah. If you'll let me."

"That's what I thought you said."

"What'll it be, Natalie? Will you?"

She started to speak, but there was a lump in her throat. She looked down at their hands again. Held on for dear life. Swallowed hard. She had almost missed this. Her instincts had been right all along, but she'd kept questioning them when she shouldn't have. In a small part of her heart, she resented her mother, because Blythe had taught her that men couldn't be trusted. This was different, she thought. *I'm different.*

She'd almost failed to let Peach in, and that would have been devastating. Somehow in all the turmoil since the plane crash, she had found something she hadn't even known was missing. That it was happening at all was kind of a miracle. She wanted to remember every moment. But remembering was not enough. The first time she saw him, had she known? She wished she could have those moments back, make them better, brighter, shinier. More memorable.

Instead, it had been an inauspicious beginning. He'd come upon her miserable on the sidewalk, crying, confused. Maybe that was what she should have noticed, right off the bat. He'd seen her at her worst, and he'd taken it all in stride. No judgment, just acceptance.

"Would you like to spend the night?" she asked him.

It was their first time, and there were some first-timey things that were to be expected. Awkward moments. Waves of bashfulness. But most of all, what broke through all the newness was an undeniable sense of wonder. That she could feel this way about someone. That someone could feel this way about her.

In the big bed, in the cozy apartment she'd slowly transformed into her own, she surrendered with a sigh that was part excitement, part relief. Something deep inside her was coming to life, something she'd thought was out of her reach. She was going to love someone at last.

His big, work-roughened hands were gentle, and he was generous, kissing and touching, looking at her, smiling when she gave a short, earnest gasp of pleasure, and then shattered. It was that quick, perhaps because it had been building forever. He gave a long, luxurious thrust and joined her, and they sank back to earth together, entwined, not speaking for long moments as their heartbeats settled and the world came back into focus.

She lit a candle, one of the scented ones they sold in the shop, the fragrance labeled "Old Library." Then they smoked some weed from her small supply in the drawer of the nightstand, and she wished the feeling of bliss would last forever. "I dreamed of this," she whispered, blurting out the admission on a wave of honesty before she could stifle herself. "But I never believed my own dream. I didn't think it was possible. I thought it was . . . I don't know, maybe like a story in a book somewhere, hidden within the pages."

She lightly traced her finger over the tattoo on his upper arm. "A shamrock?"

He shrugged. "Cheesy, I know. Proof I was young once." He tuned up her old guitar and played her a song—"What About Your Heart?"—and she melted. "I wrote that right after we met," he said.

"What? No."

"Yes. You were looking after everyone but yourself. I saw it every day. You kept putting yourself last on the list. Don't do that, Natalie."

"I just wanted to make a nice home for my grandfather."

"You did a good job. I liked this place the minute I saw it," Peach said. "The furniture, the girly smells. I got a boner every time I walked past this bed," he told her.

"How romantic."

"I'm not being romantic. I'm being real. This is not our first rodeo," he said. "The first time I saw you, you were crying and I saw these sweet abs . . ." He traced them with his finger, light as a feather. "And I felt like a jerk because I didn't know you but I still wanted to . . ." He bent his head and lightly brushed kisses across her skin until she gasped. He looked up at her. "The way I feel about you is . . ." He took hold of her wrists and pressed them down above her head, and he moved on top of her and they were at it again, more slowly this time, urgency giving way to tender exploration.

Endless minutes later, she felt a gentle bump, and the candle flame flickered wildly. She froze, looking up at Peach. He was frowning.

"Earthquake," she whispered.

"Yeah? Damn, I've never felt one before."

"Pretty sure I'm right." She reached over and turned on a light.

A second later, the rumble was followed by shaking and rolling. The light blinked. The pictures on the walls swayed. Books jumped from the shelves. Somewhere in the distance, several alarms sounded.

Peach rolled off her and sat up. "What do we do?"

She pulled him to a doorway and grabbed on to the frame for maybe thirty seconds, which felt like a lifetime. Peach held her with one arm. "Damn, girl. We made the earth move. Cool."

"Ha, ha." She couldn't help smiling, but as soon

as the shaking stopped, she said, "Let's go check on Grandy, make sure he's okay."

"We'd better get dressed first," he said, grinning at her.

They threw on clothes and raced downstairs together. Grandy was sitting up in bed, putting in his hearing aids. The lights flickered again, then stayed on.

"Everything okay?" Natalie asked him.

He put on his spectacles and gazed at her, then at Peach, taking in her hastily donned Giants T-shirt and Peach's bare chest, his jeans with the top button undone. "Everything is fine," he said. "I'm going to turn on the news."

"Oh God. He knows," Natalie said as they went down and entered the bookstore.

"He's always known." Peach took hold of her shoulders from behind and nuzzled her neck.

"What's that supposed to mean?"

"He said something almost as soon as I got to work on his place. Sometimes I wasn't sure if he was talking about you or your mom."

"What did he say?"

Peach turned her in his arms. "That you've been disappointed in love. But you've never disappointed anyone." He placed his lips on her forehead and held still, gently pressing. "I won't disappoint you, Natalie. You picked a good one."

She shut her eyes and leaned into him. *At last*, she thought.

"Hey," Peach whispered, brushing his thumb across her cheek. "What's wrong?"

"You're my glimmer." She blotted her tears with her shirtsleeve.

"I'm a glimmer?"

"A short time ago, the shop was going into receivership. I was about to take my grandfather to court to have him declared incompetent so I could make the decision to sell it. I needed a glimmer. Just one little glimmer of hope." She looked up at him, put the flat of her hand on his bare chest, over his heart. "That's what you are."

"Oh, baby—"

"But I'm moving, and you have to stay here for Dorothy, and I don't see how—" The lights blinked yet again. This time they went out. "Oh, no. Now what?"

Peach went to the front door and looked out. "The rest of the neighborhood's still on. Let's check the breakers." He turned on his phone flashlight and moved the beam around the room.

528 · SUSAN WIGGS

"Oh, man." It seemed half the books had leaped off the shelves and tables. A few stoneware mugs had shattered in the coffee area.

"I'll go check the breaker box."

She followed him to the basement. He opened the box and flipped the main switch. "I wonder why it tripped," he murmured, pulling the string of the overhead light. "Oh, shit," he said, surveying a crack that went from the floor to the back wall. "Looks like some damage here."

Natalie's heart sank as she assessed the crumbled brick and earth. "Great. Just when the buyer was about to make an offer." She stepped closer and spotted a large gap behind the broken wall.

Peach shone his light at it. "There's something down here."

"Fortunato," she whispered.

"Who?"

"You know, from the Poe story—'The Cask of Amontillado.' Guy bricks his friend up in the basement wall."

"Some friend. Never read it, though."

"Finally, I schooled you in something."

He grabbed her and gave her a long, deep kiss. "You schooled me in everything, Natalie Jean Harper."

"Inga," she said.

"What?"

"My middle name is Inga, same as my mom's. We're named after her grandmother Inga."

"I'll keep that in mind."

"Is the building safe?" she asked, looking down at the cracked floor.

He thumped his fist on the wall. "You'll need an inspection." He removed a few loose bricks and peered into the gap. "There's some kind of locker or tool chest."

"More war medals?" asked Natalie.

"Too big for that." He grabbed a shovel from the rack of tools.

Working together, they moved the fallen bricks and debris and eased the box out through the gap. The thing was the size of a table, and it weighed a ton. They slid it along the broken floor and brought it to the workbench under the window, where the light streamed in from the just-risen sun. The locker was covered in dust and scratches, and the latches and hinges were corroded. And it was locked.

"Should I force it?" asked Peach.

Natalie remembered the old key they'd found lodged in the sump pump. "I have an idea," she said. "Wait here."

She dashed upstairs and grabbed the key from the

jar on her desk. "This is the one you found when the basement flooded."

Peach gave it a try. After some jimmying, the key went in and he was able to turn it. "I'll be damned," he murmured. He gave the hinges a spray of lubricant and pried the big box open. Inside lay four large, flat parcels wrapped in what appeared to be waxed canvas. Each parcel contained a leather case like a portfolio.

"Maybe these are more drawings," Peach said.

Natalie could barely hear him through the pounding in her ears. She didn't dare speak as she unbuckled the first cover.

Then she stopped breathing. The book was huge, bound in red Morocco leather with gilt borders. "These are not Colleen's drawings."

She had to remind herself to breathe as she lifted the heavy cover to reveal an elaborate frontispiece with copperplate lettering. "I think maybe we found . . . my God, Peach. I need to sit down." She lowered herself to a stool. "What if we found *The Birds of America*?"

"An Audubon book, you mean. Cool."

"No. I mean, yes. I always thought it was a family legend, for sure. But then we found Colleen's journals, and now this . . ."

"Looks vintage," said Peach. "And it's in good condition. Think it's collectible?"

"That would be an understatement. It's not *an* Audubon book. I think this might be *the* Audubon book."

"That's a damn big book," Peach said, nuzzling her neck.

The nuzzling sent a frisson of warmth through her, but she stayed focused on the large volume on the bench. "It's printed on double elephant folio paper. That was the largest available at the time of printing. Audubon wanted the drawings to be life-size."

She opened to the middle of the book. The hand-colored print of a pair of sage hens bore the artist's signature precision and delicacy, the caption printed in ornate style. "It took him something like ten years to publish this in the 1830s. If this is what I think it is, it's . . . God, I'm scared to say. The two most recent sales were for about ten million." She nearly choked on the amount. "I need to call Tess."

"There's something we need to do first." He started nuzzling again.

"Now? Seriously?" she said, wavering between desire, amusement, and urgency. She stood up and turned in his arms and he kissed her, deeply and tenderly.

"Seriously." He sank to one knee, and she grabbed him, thinking he'd fallen. Then he looked up at her, and *she* nearly fell.

"Peach—"

"It would probably be smarter to wait, but when it comes to you, Natalie Inga Harper, I'm not smart." He pressed his lips to her hand. "Listen. You might have just won the lottery—or not. Maybe it's El Dorado. Or maybe it's fool's gold. So I'm asking you before we know the answer. That way you'll know I'm asking because I love you and I want forever with you, no matter what."

Again she said, "Peach—"

He stood up. "I want to marry you. I'm asking you to marry me."

The ridiculous words shook her. Tears blurred her vision, and yet she laughed. He always made her laugh. And something inside her knew that he always, always would. "You're crazy," she said.

"Maybe. Yeah," he agreed. "And you're going to love that about me, I swear."

She already did love that about him. "But, Peach—"

Reaching up, he touched a finger to her lips. "Pretty sure I started falling for you the first day I saw you crying on the sidewalk in front of the bookstore."

Natalie would always remember that he had been kind and patient that day. She wanted to forget what a mess she'd been at that moment. She took his hand away. "You thought I was a homeless woman."

"I thought you were sad and beautiful and someone I wanted to know. Every moment I spent with you made me feel alive again. I wrote songs about you . . ." He paused, and she was shocked to hear a quaver in his voice. "Say yes, Natalie. It's not hard."

It wouldn't be easy, either. She was not so naïve as to think this would be a walk in the park. Peach would challenge her. He would also love her with his whole big giant soft heart. Last night, she'd told him she was about to lose everything, and it hadn't mattered at all to him. Instead, he'd made it clear that *she* mattered.

She laughed with the madness of it all. He had already changed her heart, made her feel braver, bolder. "If this is what I think it is," she said, gesturing at the folio, "can we honeymoon in Spain?"

"We can honeymoon on the moon if you want. But honestly, I'd go anywhere with you. A beach motel. A cave. Seriously, anywhere."

Her laughter fluttered into wonder. And even though it was the biggest leap of faith she'd ever taken, she trusted that. Trusted him. Trusted whatever the future held.

Epilogue

RARE AUDUBON MASTERPIECE SELLS AT AUCTION FOR RECORD $11 MILLION

SAN FRANCISCO—John James Audubon's four-volume masterwork, *The Birds of America*, sold in a fiercely competitive bidding war at Sheffield Auction House, to a bidder who requested anonymity. The buyer, a philanthropist and connoisseur of rare books, will gift it to the California Museum of History, Arts and Sciences. The work is the artist's crowning achievement—a four-tome folio of 435 hand-colored prints depicting life-size birds in their natural habitats.

According to provenance expert Theresa Delaney Rossi, the recently found treasure was originally the property of William Randolph Hearst, who acquired it from his father, Senator George Hearst. During his post-Harvard years in San Francisco, Hearst gifted the set to a woman of his acquaintance, an Irish immigrant named Colleen O'Rourke, who was presumed killed in the earthquake and fire of 1906. Her son, Julius Harper, was one of hundreds of orphans who survived the disaster and was raised in the San Francisco Orphan Asylum.

As a young man and veteran of World War I, Julius Harper discovered that his childhood home, the Sunrose Building on Perdita Street, was still standing, but in a derelict state. He acquired the property and lived there for the rest of his life, always convinced that his mother had left a treasure behind, but it was never found.

The building now belongs to Andrew Harper, 79, owner of the Lost and Found Bookshop. The December earthquake caused significant damage to the building, and in the aftermath, the books were found behind a basement wall that had collapsed in the quake.

[Caption: *Pictured above: Andrew Harper and his granddaughter, bookstore owner Natalie Harper, in front of the Sunrose Building.*]

Mr. Harper was inundated with offers from private collectors and institutions. "It's a treasure in my possession, but it doesn't belong to me," he said in a statement. "It belongs to the world. Once I look after my own obligations and settle my debts, the proceeds will fund conservation."

True to his word, Andrew Harper created a non-profit sustaining fund to benefit the National Bird Conservation Society. He also founded the Perdita Street Memory Center, a residence providing compassionate care for patients living with dementia.

LOCAL PLAYWRIGHT WINS MAJOR AWARD

SAN FRANCISCO—Playwright Cleo Chan has won the Bay Area Critics' Circle Prize for her drama, "The Lost and Found Bookshop: A Grand Adventure," a beguiling play based on a speculative relationship between a scullery-maid-turned-artist in old San Francisco and William Randolph Hearst. Inspired by true events, the story traces the journey of a rare book and its impact on one local family.

The production opened at the Sutter Theatre and quickly gained acclaim for its imaginative historical content. The performance of dramatic actor Bertrand "Bertie" Loftis, whose compelling and unexpectedly vulnerable young Hearst has been lauded as his breakthrough role, earned him a citation for Best Actor in a Dramatic Role.

[Caption: *Pictured above: Playwright Cleo Chan, actor Bertie Loftis, with real-life owner of the Lost and Found Bookshop, Natalie Harper Gallagher, at Sutter Theatre.*]

The ceremony was held at the Hilltop Marquis. Both Chan and Loftis dedicated their awards in memory of the late Andrew Harper, Bay Area philanthropist.

BIRTHS DEATHS MARRIAGES

MERCY HEIGHTS HOSPITAL—Peter "Peach" Gallagher and Natalie Gallagher announce the birth of their son, Andrew Julius Gallagher.

Andrew Julius arrived on Monday, March 23, at 4:47 A.M., weighing in at 6 pounds, 6 ounces, 20 3/4 inches in length.

His sister, Dorothy Gale Gallagher, is twelve and an honor student at Greenhill Academy.

Acknowledgments

T his book started as a conversation with two of the best writers I know—John Saul and his partner, Michael Sack. Thank you, gentlemen, for the uproarious brainstorming that launched an idea. The story was further refined with advice from the brilliant story analyst and friend Michael Hauge.

My mother, Lou Klist, was my first writing mentor and first reader, and she inspired the character of Andrew Harper in this story. Love you, Mom.

Every book I write is enriched and informed by my literary agent, Meg Ruley, and her associate, Annelise Robey, and brought to life by the amazing publishing team at William Morrow Books—Rachel Kahan, Jennifer Hart, Liate Stehlik, Tavia Kowalchuk, Bianca

Flores, and their many creative associates who make publishing such a grand adventure.

Special thanks to Laura Cherkas and Laurie McGee for smart and insightful copyediting, and to Marilyn Rowe for proofreading help.

I'm grateful to Cindy Peters and Ashley Hayes for keeping everything fresh online.

Like all writers, I'm grateful to the many book-sellers who have enriched their communities—Jane and Victoria of Eagle Harbor Book Co., Suzanne and Suzanne of Liberty Bay Books, and so many others. Thanks to Donna Paz Kaufman and Laura Hayden for research help.

Most of the books and authors cited in this story are real. They are writers whose work I love, and I highly recommend them.

About the Author

SUSAN WIGGS's life is all about family, friends . . . and fiction. She lives at the water's edge on an island in Puget Sound, and in good weather, she commutes to her writers' group in a twenty-one-foot motorboat. She's been featured in the national media, including NPR, PRI, and *USA Today*; has given programs for the U.S. Embassies in Buenos Aires and Montevideo; and is a popular speaker locally, nationally, internationally, and on the high seas.

From the very start, her writings have illuminated the everyday dramas of ordinary people facing extraordinary circumstances. Her books celebrate the power of love, the timeless bonds of family, and the fascinating nuances of human nature. Today, she is an international bestselling, award-winning author, with millions of copies of her books in print in numerous countries and languages. According to *Publishers Weekly*, Wiggs writes with "refreshingly honest emotion," and the *Salem Statesman Journal* adds that she is "one of our best observers of stories of the heart [who] knows how to capture emotion on virtually every page of every book." *Booklist* characterizes her books as "real and true and unforgettable."

Her novels have appeared in the #1 spot on the *New York Times* bestseller list and have captured readers' hearts around the globe with translations into more than twenty languages available in thirty countries.

The author is a former teacher, a Harvard graduate, an avid hiker, an amateur photographer, a good skier, and a terrible golfer, yet her favorite form of exercise is curling up with a good book. She divides her time between sleeping and waking.